Sassafras

By Jack Matthews:

Novels

Hanger Stout, Awake!
Beyond the Bridge
The Tale of Asa Bean
The Charisma Campaigns
Pictures of the Journey Back
Sassafras

Short Story Collections

Bitter Knowledge
Tales of the Ohio Land
Dubious Persuasions

Poetry

An Almanac for Twilight

Nonfiction

*Collecting Rare Books
for Pleasure and Profit*

SASSAFRAS

Jack Matthews

Houghton Mifflin Company
Boston
1983

Library of Congress Cataloging in Publication Data

Matthews, Jack.
Sassafras.

I. Title.
PS3563.A85S2   1983   813'.54   83-12623
ISBN 0-395-34640-1

Printed in the United States of America

S   10 9 8 7 6 5 4 3 2 1

For Barbara . . . again, and still.

Those Enquiries will necessarily produce Principles and Hypotheses, though for want of sufficient Light, they may be precarious and groundless, yea, sometimes possibly Absurd and Phantastical, yet will evidently shew, that the Philosophers who devised them, were Men of Search and Reasoning, of Knowledge and Experience.

—William Wotton, *Reflections upon Ancient and Modern Learning,* 1697

I am grateful to the Ohio Arts Council for an Individual Artist Grant, which was of great help to me during the writing of *Sassafras*.

Sassafras

1

Man is composed physically of three great classes of organs, the predominance or deficiency of each of which is called a predominant or deficient temperament, both giving a particular form to the body — shape being its index — and likewise a particular set of phrenological developments, and consequent traits of character.

— Fowler's *Phrenology*

KNOW YOURSELF is the old rule that people talk about, and who in his right mind would ever argue that it's not important?

Still, it's easier said than done, as a lot of human critters have found out, often to their dismay. Tricky business. For one thing, you never know how other people take the things you do. Ask a deaf man why he talks so loud and he'll tell you he didn't know he was talking loud at all.

It's this way with more than deafness. Some things you'll never know, like how you look when you're asleep or how strong your grip is when you shake hands.

Still, a man's a fool if he doesn't learn a few things about himself. Even if there's no real understanding behind it, he ought to have an idea of how he strikes other people as different or maybe wrong in some way. It may not make sense to him, but he ought to be able to figure out when something isn't working just right. He ought to know if something isn't coming across the way he thinks he's sending it out.

You take a prognathic man, for example. He may think he's generally admired because of his strong and manly chin, and he might get in the habit of assuming a posture, lifting his profile in a pose that would embarrass Caesar. He might do this all his life, and never catch on that to nine people out of ten he's nothing but a damned fool and the only wonder he excites is how he can carry a four-pound jaw around and not get tired enough to let his mouth hang open. I know I've made the critter in this example sound like a considerable fool, but it's my conviction that such is not necessarily the case. In spite of his foolishness in this regard, the specimen I'm talking about might be an astute merchant, or a benign father, or be able to compose music that would make a covey of Quakers start in dancing.

Nevertheless, a man is a bogwit if he doesn't figure out *something* about himself, and there are three things I have learned in the way of self-knowledge. First, I've always had an eccentric memory. In some ways, it's considerable tenacious; in others, it would embarrass a sieve. Sometimes it's wax to impress and marble to retain, as they say; and other times it's just the opposite. When he was a schoolboy, Gall noticed that all of his classmates who had good memories were exophthalmic. I figure if this was true, I'd have one pop eye and the other sunk in like a cave, which I'm happy to say isn't the way I'm formed.

The second trait I am unnaturally strong in is Hope, which is located beside the coronal sutures on both sides of the head. Gall didn't figure this was primary, but I'm convinced it is. Gall said it was part of the various faculties of desire, and didn't bother to try to locate it in the skull. However, I don't see it this way. I am convinced it is primary and critical. It is right up there exactly where it should be, at the zenith of the skull when a human being is standing upright, the posture he alone of all critters is meant to assume. Hope is an uppermost quality, physically as well as spiritually. It's the highest reach of yearning, and without it you can't have faith or vision.

I'm proud to admit I have full Prominence of Hope, even though it's not an unmixed blessing. Too much hope can make you arrogant or sassy. Also, it's often connected with innocence, which is a kind of ignorance. Never mind all that. There are worse human qualities. Sometimes I figure Gall was himself deficient in this respect, and that's why he gave it short notice and didn't bother to isolate Hope on the skull. But that's no doubt hard on the man, for he was a true scientist, which fact even his enemies would admit.

The third trait or disposition I can lay claim to having beyond the normal allotment is going to sound odd. In fact, most people wouldn't consider it a trait at all. I've never known it to be isolated and studied — not even by Spurzheim or Gall or Combe, or any of the other great students of anatomy. And it's certainly not mentioned by any of the old ones, such as Aristotle, Pliny, or Vesalius.

Since this trait doesn't have a name, I'll name it myself. I'll call it the Tendency toward Coincidence. There was a time I would have agreed with the majority, that it wasn't a trait at all. But it eventually came to me that there was something inside my character that made me *susceptible* to coincidence. I attract coincidence as the lofty oak attracts lightning. I am sensitive to it, the way some people are sensitive to poison ivy or eating strawberries. Coincidences just naturally happen to me more than to other folks. Mathematics tells us there are a billion people in the world, so there's probably about a thousand of those people who have improbable things happen to them at a rate far beyond the average.

I figure I'm right up there near the top of those thousand people who suffer from exaggerated coincidence. It's a phrenological principle that if something is in your character it will be signified on your face or skull. The tricky part is knowing how to see what's there, or to feel it. It's here you reveal your understanding or ignorance of form.

Comparison (*Sagacité comparative*) is located at the top of the bare region of the forehead. Its location connects with Benevolence on top and Causality on both sides. If you can picture the area where these three regions interconnect, you can see where I figure there may be a trace of what you might call a person's secret sympathy with events outside, in the world of nature, which I call a flair for Coincidence.

I don't think anybody could ever get used to the kind of coincidences I have experienced, much less ignore them. There's no way to explain some of the things that have happened to me. There's no way to explain how one man could ever run into the likes of Henry Buck, William Bone, Half Face, Lily de Wilde, Stillingfleet, and a dozen others, except by acknowledging the fact that he has a way with coincidence. Or maybe it's more a *gift*. Or maybe something even deeper than that. It could be part of a critter's fate. This is what the configurations of the skull signify, as well.

Most people live their whole lives without having authentic coincidences; they may think they do, but that's just because they've learned the word and have got it in their heads, and they have to make it fit some experience or other, so they just think of something that's happened as a coincidence, and let it go at that. It's like a pretense with them, only they don't really know they're pretending.

But compared to somebody with a true gift for coincidence, theirs are nothing. They might as well be color blind or tone deaf and yet go around thinking they understand painting or music. One of the most relentless tenors I ever ran into was a man who hardly ever hit a note right. But did that stop him? Not for a minute. He always had a tune more or less in his mouth. And he lived his whole life thinking he was a good singer. He didn't know any better, and since he was otherwise a mean son of a bitch, I figure there weren't many who ever wanted to tell him.

But if you're born to coincidence, you know better. Some are marked in this way. It's an instinct for adventure, or a flair for surprises of the striking sort. It's a little like having perfect pitch when you sing, which that damned tenor would never have figured out if he'd lived a hundred years. Also, it's considerable like having premonitions.

There's no area of the brain or skull either one that is associated with a gift for coincidence. But I figure it's there, just waiting to be discovered, probably right up in front, where I mentioned. Wherever it is, I figure it has to be manifest in some way, because what I'm talking about is an expression of something inside that is secretly managing things behind the scenes, you might say, and bringing off tricks that make the sleight of hand in a magician's show look like mere dilly-dallying in contrast.

These are some of the things you should know before you read the story of my life so far, as I've written it all down.

I was born on August 12, 1825, in a small village near the Ohio River. My folks belonged to an offshoot of Quakers that sang hymns like the Methodists and Baptists. My Pa had once been a gunsmith, and sometimes people would point out the incongruity in a Quaker making firearms. What sort of work was this for a Quaker? they'd say. Was he a hypocrite, or just ignorant? He didn't lose his temper but tried to make the point that the beasts of the field were made to feed Mankind, and it was his calling to help things along. He also argued that, while he'd never take up arms against another man himself, if one of his guns happened to be used to kill somebody, that was just too bad, and he couldn't help it.

But that was before I came along. Pa gave up gunsmithing and bought 160 acres in Gallia County, on Big Raccoon Creek, about fourteen miles up from the Ohio River. I figure those questions had finally proved too much for him, and he got so he didn't believe the answers he gave. Whatever the reason, by the time I came along, Pa had taken up farming and was leaning toward the Methodists, who had the only church thereabouts.

Prayers, stern sobriety, and silent hard labor were the meat and potatoes of my childhood. It was a pretty gray time. They said that early in life I showed an awesome amount of sass, along with a talent for asking questions, not to mention other kinds of cussedness, like having an awful temper. All of this wasn't much help in the business of growing up.

One time Pa took me to Gallipolis, where I had a raspberry ice and met an old Frenchman who'd been one of the original five hundred emigrés who'd founded the city. I saw some flatboats gliding as silent as clouds down the Ohio River. That was a scene I'll never forget. I got so excited I all but started to spin like a cobbler's wheel. I almost departed from this earth for joy. I jumped up and down at the sight, and whirled around like a puppy on a rope. That was the first time I realized how big and breezy the world is and how many great things there are that a body can do.

A steamboat had passed a few minutes before, but we'd just missed seeing it and couldn't wait for the next one. If I'd seen one of *them*, it might have been too much for me. Pa saw me looking at the flatboats and maybe guessed what was going on in my mind, because he grabbed my head in his big fist and said, "Do you suppose they know where they're headed, Thad?"

I said, "Yep, they're headed downriver," which gave Pa a considerable laugh. He didn't laugh very much, so I remember it well.

But that question has stayed with me all these years, even though it had been aimed a great deal higher than a boy's intelligence. I forget what I said to Pa afterwards, but I reckon I said something, knowing me. That question is still clear in my mind, and I can still hear it now and then when I contemplate the variety of human enterprise.

One reason I remember that time so well was that Pa was in a kindly mood, which didn't happen very often, because he was a troubled man. I was the youngest of seven children, and Pa had to stay busy just to keep us stocked with corn mush and pork gravy. These were bad times, and Pa was religious, which made things harder for all concerned. He said I had more sassafras than a bucket of puppies or any two boys he'd ever seen, but Momma told him I couldn't help myself.

One day when I was twelve years old we were out cutting wood about two miles from our house, clearing some land for a township road. Pa owed some back taxes, and it was agreed he could work the debt off by helping clear this road. Money was short and shaky in those days. There was a bank near Chillicothe that listed a walnut table for its capital assets. Sum total.

My sisters were visiting their cousins downriver near Portsmouth, and both of my brothers were working for a man named Grubacher, where they lived in, so my mother was all alone in the cabin. She'd been what you'd call sickly ever since I was born, but there shouldn't have been any danger in her being home alone, Pa figured. There weren't many Indians left in Ohio, and the few that remained didn't give much trouble.

But it wasn't Indians we should have been worried about. When we got back to the cabin that evening, Momma was lying in bed all covered with blood. Her eye was swollen up like a plum, and her nose was broken. She was hardly conscious. She said hello to us and said she'd tried to wash the blood off, but she wasn't strong enough. She kept apologizing about the blood and the mess in the house — everything turned over and smashed and scattered; and all this time Pa kept yelling at her to tell him what had happened.

She finally got it out. Some man had come up to the door, asking for food. She said he was drunk and wouldn't even raise up his eyes to look at her. She invited him in, the way you do beyond the mountains, and turned to the hearth to get some mush for him in a bowl. It was right then he knocked her down and beat her up and what they called attacked her.

When she finished telling this, she started in again apologizing about how bad the place looked, and it was right about then I realized that something was wrong with her head, and it scared me something awful. She talked like she was half asleep, and wasn't sure who we were. She kept on apologizing about the mess everything was in, like we were distant relatives who'd dropped by for an unexpected visit. She didn't even look at us right. She seemed to be curious about who we might be. The only thing she could talk about was the awful state things had been in and how she'd tried to wash the blood off herself, but didn't have the strength and had to lie down.

She went on like this, over and over, while Pa kept asking her what the man had looked like and which way he'd gone. Finally, he just told me to stay there and watch over her. He told me not to let her get up, even if she felt better, and not to leave her for a minute. He said he was going to get some help from the neighbors. He'd ask one of the Hamner girls to come and stay with her. The Hamners lived about half a mile down the road. They were Germans, but they were good people. Maybe they'd know something about this drifter, whoever he was.

When Pa left, he took his rifle with him, and I don't think he intended to use it to knock a squirrel out of a tree if he saw one. I think that right then Pa stopped being a Quaker, and would have killed the man who'd hurt Momma.

It was then I changed, too. It was then I stopped being a Quaker pretty much forever.

Well, he never did find that God damned scoundrel. Nobody could tell him much except there had been a mean-looking critter come on the stage at Chester that evening. He was headed north, for Chillicothe. He said he was looking for work in town, somewhere, because he was near crazy from herding hogs. They said he acted like it.

Pa figured this was the man, so he took the stage to Chillicothe, sending word back with Eli Cameron that he'd return as soon as he could. Mother received the news like she couldn't remember exactly who Pa was. Eli sent word to my sisters to come home at once, because Momma was in a bad way.

She let her work go. Sometimes she'd just sit in a chair with her hands over her face and not say a word. Then she'd start in talking and all she could talk about was the house and the way she looked. One time she told me never to hurt a woman. She went on and on, and it got so it was all I could do to keep from yelling out. I didn't understand what she was talking about. At first, I figured she was talking about what bulls do to cows and boars to sows and men to women, and that sort of thing. But then it came to me this wasn't what was bothering her at all. It was something else, and it was worse. Even though it was connected with that other business in ways that even Momma didn't understand. Along about this time, she practically stopped eating and wasted away something awful.

When Pa came back, he told us he hadn't accomplished anything at all. He had lost track of the stranger. He hung the rifle back up above the fireplace and just sat there and looked at Momma sitting in her rocker. Auntie May Roebuck, who was a Presbyterian and wasn't an aunt at all, but everybody called her that, stayed with us to take care of Momma and help out. Momma had to eat or die, Auntie May told us; and my sisters told her we knew that was the case and were sure worried. Pa didn't say a word, though. He didn't seem to be listening to Auntie May Roebuck or any other voice in this world.

We all prayed and sang hymns and cried, including Auntie May Roebuck who was an alto. We asked for God's blessing upon us. Pa was worried about the land he'd promised to clear for the township, but he didn't step outside the house once, until we found Momma dead one morning and Auntie May Roebuck sent my sisters off to tell all the neighbors.

That was a thing I'll never forget. Our prayers hadn't helped, and being pious and hard-working hadn't done any good. We might as well have been a family of muskrats, for all the good we could do. Momma died, and that was that.

Her death was a turning point in my life. It was a turning point for Pa, too. I'll never forget the time he took his rifle down and went after that scoundrel who'd caused Momma's death. I didn't discuss it with him, because it wasn't the sort of thing I figured I could ever talk about. But deep down inside, I made a decision. If

I ever found the critter who'd hurt Momma, I'd blow his damned brains out.

Then maybe I'd become a Baptist.

We buried her on a cold, sunny March morning. All the neighbors were there, singing hymns loud and pretty enough to make your heart ache. There was also considerable crying. Everybody had liked my mother and they said so. They told us she'd been a good Christian woman, and they'd always miss her.

Something was wrong with Pa, though. Something had busted inside, you could tell. One time there at the funeral I looked at him, and he turned his head away, like he was sorry he'd seen me. Later, I saw him point at me when people spoke to him, and that's when they came over and told me how much they were going to miss Momma.

The preacher was a Methodist named Moses Gowdy, who wore a frock coat. He talked about what a good woman she was, and my sisters started in wailing again. You could hear them over the sniffling of the neighbors, like cats on a windy night. Then all of a sudden Pa interrupted Brother Gowdy and started yelling at some hound dog that had come trotting in among the gravestones.

"Get that dog out of here!" he yelled. I don't think I ever heard him yell that loud. Everybody was quiet, but Pa went crazy and took off running after that poor dumb critter and chased him off.

Brother Gowdy was patient and waited until he came back, and then everybody got quiet. Even my sisters shut their mouths and stopped crying.

But before Brother Gowdy could get on with the funeral, Pa started talking in a loud voice. He said, "Dogs don't have any place in a graveyard." It didn't even sound like Pa, but you could have heard him clear up on the hills that overlooked the cemetery.

"Not that I don't like a good dog," he went on after a bit, conversationally, shaking his head. "A good dog has his place in the realm of creation. Nobody can deny that. I figure the good Lord has a place for good dogs in the scheme of things. Yessir! Dogs are all right! I always did like a good hunting dog. I knew a man once name of Tucker who could feel a dog's nose and tell how good a dry tracker he was. I figured the wetter a dog's nose was, the better a dry tracker he was, but old Tucker said it was more than that. He said it was the *feel* of the nose more than anything. The way you can feel cloth and tell wool from linen."

Nobody said a word while Pa was going on like this. Right then it began to sink into everybody's head that he'd gone crazy, and nobody would look at him. Most were embarrassed and sorry. However, an old woman named Click whispered that it was disgraceful the way he was acting, but one of her daughters shushed her.

Finally, Brother Gowdy managed to get his sermon over with, even though Pa kept on mumbling somewhere in back of the crowd and wouldn't stop. He wouldn't come near the grave, either.

When it was all over, I heard him say that Momma had never been quite right since she'd given birth to me. He said she'd been sickly ever since. And when he said this, he pointed at me with his thumb. He didn't call me Thad, either, but just said "Him," like he didn't even want to say my name, or had maybe forgotten it.

Brother Gowdy came up to me and said, "Don't feel too filled with sorrow, Thaddeus. You must know that your Momma is in Heaven if ever a mortal got there! You know she's in Heaven, don't you?"

I said, "Yep, but I'd rather she was down here."

Pa heard this and said in his loud voice, "She was sick from the day she gave birth to that critter. He was too lively and took all the vital power from her loins. That's why he's tuned too high, like a fiddle string. She had nought but stillborns from the day she give birth to that critter standing over there." Then Pa kind of shook his head back and forth and looked puzzled, like he'd heard somebody else speaking the words he'd just said.

"Don't you listen to your Pa," Mrs. Hamner whispered. "He's gone crazy with grief and don't know what he's saying!"

Pa must have overheard that, too, because he just stared at the poor woman until she blushed and turned away. When it comes to true madness, there is no handle you can grab.

Then Pa rubbed his hand over his face like he was all of a sudden weary and ready for sleep, and he said, "Why ain't all these folks out working the way they should be? Tilling the field and felling the giant oak? What's happened to folks all of a sudden?"

"It's all right," Brother Gowdy said, coming up and clapping Pa on the shoulder.

But Pa acted like he didn't know him. And then he said something that almost scared my sisters out of their wits. He asked where Momma was, and for a minute there wasn't a sound in that little graveyard, except for the cool breeze blowing through the limbs of the little cedars that had been planted along the south edge.

I heard somebody say in a low voice, "Come on, it's time we should all be going."

Brother Gowdy prayed again, and after the Amen, Pa nodded and said, "Yep, tilling the field and felling the giant oak!"

Mrs. Hamner came up to my sisters and said, "You take care of your Pa, and if you need any help, you know you can depend on us. Any time, day or night."

They decided I should go and live with my Uncle Henry near Cincinnati. Pa recovered his wits pretty much and stated a number of times that I couldn't help it about Momma. He pointed out that it wasn't my fault she'd been poorly ever since I was born. He said this several times a day, and always ended up saying he was sorry for me.

My sisters kept quiet, and my brothers were back at the Grubachers', working their way in the world. Everybody figured that's what a boy should do as soon as he could — fly the coop. One of my sisters was keeping company with a boy named Chase, and she'd probably be married soon.

When they told me I'd be going to live with Uncle Henry, I asked why I couldn't go and live with my Great-uncle Thaddeus, the one I'd been named for. He was a Quaker missionary among the wild Indians west of the Mississippi somewhere. We never heard from him.

But Pa wouldn't consider it. He said it was just one more of my sassy, bull-headed, unexpected ideas, and he didn't even know if his Uncle Thaddeus was still among the living, and anyway, that was no life for a boy, out yonder. He pointed out that there was a crazy streak in the family. As a matter of fact, I showed a good sample of it myself, he said, the way I was so strong-headed and couldn't see the right side of things, no matter how hard they were explained. He said I was argumentative and irreverent. He said he'd never seen a boy one-half as full of sassafras. He asked me if I wasn't aware of this fact, and I told him, "Nope, it never occurred to me," and one of my sisters went into a laughing fit. She almost got hysterical, and even Pa kind of grinned and nodded his head.

Then he pointed out it would be best for all concerned if I went away. He said I didn't fit into life in the hills. He said I didn't understand religion and had a cussed streak that was too much for him. He said maybe Uncle Henry could do something with me, although he doubted it. Still, it was possible I'd get a step-up in the world. There were opportunities in a place like Cincinnati that Big Raccoon Creek couldn't match.

He talked on like this for a considerable while, but I didn't listen much because I was scared. I have never known fear like that since, because back then, when I was so young and ignorant, it was undiluted by experience. It was fear in a pure state, and it was worse because I knew that from then on, I would never have Momma with me. Maybe in Heaven, but never in the world I knew about and could recognize. Except for that trip to Gallipolis, I'd never been away from home in my whole life.

When he finished talking to me, Pa asked if I understood everything. I lied to him and said, "Yep, but I'd rather stay home," and Pa told me it wasn't going to be home to me anymore.

I didn't have any choice in the matter, it looked like, so I was sent to live with my aunt and uncle and their nine children and my aunt's mother. They didn't actually live in Cincinnati, but out in the country a considerable way, near Zeller's Bridge on the state turnpike.

It wasn't such a bad life there. I got along. I minded my business and kept my eyes open. I went to school and did chores. They had milk cows and hogs, which means plenty of work. But I managed to have a high old time, now and then, in spite of Uncle Henry. It was in those days that I learned to gamble and chew tobacco and smoke segars and ride a horse like a Comanche, which are four of the most important things I've ever learned in life.

When I was fifteen I was apprenticed to an atheist printer named Samuel Chadwick, who worked me ten hard hours a day. I soon began to get a feel for words, which was a pretty good education in itself, as a lot of other printer's devils have found out. And I read a great deal, since there were books, and pamphlets, almanacs, and newspapers always around.

Samuel Chadwick was a fat, lopsided old man with a snuff-smeared vest and ill-fitting eyeglasses. He smelled of one part printer's ink and sweat and two parts spittoon. One of the books I read in those days was Franklin's *Autobiography*, and it right away came to me that Samuel Chadwick looked a lot like Franklin's picture. I figured he tried to imitate Benjamin Franklin in several respects.

Along with his religious skepticism, Samuel Chadwick had other fixed prejudices and convictions, some of which were peculiar. He had a morbid fear of pregnant women, and would cross the street if he saw one coming toward him. Many a time I saw him do this. He knew it was odd, but he couldn't help himself. He said he figured this whole business had been caused by the death of his wife thirty years before from childbed fever. That had been an awful tragedy and he'd never live it down. The mere idea of pregnancy bothered him. I told him this reminded me of my mother, and told him the whole story, but he didn't seem to hear what I said.

One fine June day I remember we'd stepped out in front to take a breath of fresh air and rest a moment from our labors, when we saw a pregnant woman climb down out of a carriage. Samuel grabbed my shoulder and hissed, "There comes another one." I figured by the way he said it that it wasn't the woman he was talking about but the unborn baby. He was considerable agitated over the experience.

Sometimes when he talked about the horrors of a woman giving birth, he reminded me of Pa. It's considerable strange, when you think about it. We are vomited into the world accompanied by pain and moaning and uncertainty as our Birthright. It's no wonder that some men are afflicted by the idea. I can see their point, although it doesn't bear too much brooding over. Most things are problematic, if you think about it.

Samuel Chadwick kept a notebook filled with accounts of his dreams. The first thing he did when he woke up each morning was to write down every dream he could remember in careful detail and then close the big folio volume with a thump. After doing this, he figured it was all right for the day to begin. That thump was like the crowing of Chanticleer.

He'd often hold forth on the subject of his dreaming. He was what you'd call a loquacious man, given to considerable repetition in his conversations, which were filled near to capsizing with philosophy and strange historical facts. He was a relentless talker, with the busiest mouth I'd ever heard, and recited various wholesome and edifying maxims for my benefit.

When he walked, he would double up his fists and hold them waist high, like a man who had to push his way through an airy throng. He read a great deal among the older authors, professing a contempt for all modern books. It didn't make any difference if they were political or literary. One of his peculiarities connected with this habit was his loyalty to the style of the eighteenth century, so that he always told me to begin words of substantive worth with a capital letter. He said, "Some words require emphasis, Thad, and I say start them off with a capital!"

Life didn't always run smooth, working with Samuel Chadwick. He was a great man in his way, but awful absent-minded. The trouble was, I was considerable absent-minded myself, especially when it came to practical matters having to do with business.

"You must perfect your memory," Samuel Chadwick told me, after we'd just spent an hour looking for some misplaced quires of blotting paper. He packed snuff in his cheek and sat there in his rocking chair talking around his thick fingers. He'd told me this same thing a hundred times, only he'd forgotten it. He only talked to me about my poor memory when he was packing snuff. I figured there might be some mysterious connection between the two.

"Do you want to hear what I advise?" he asked.

"Yep," I said. "Fire away."

"I'll lend you some books to study," he said, "and I recommend that you memorize large portions of them. You'll be surprised at how easy it is to do, once you get the swing of it. There's a rhythm to memorizing, you know. Would you like to give it a try?"

"Yep," I told him, "I'm game for it."

The books he picked out were from dusty stacks of odd copies that had been left in his shop. One was a Latin-English dictionary. The man he'd printed it for was named Alonzo Cheefer and he'd left over a hundred copies when he'd died in the cholera epidemic.

"Take this and read it at odd moments," Samuel told me, giving me a misbound copy. "You'll pick up a few spoonfuls of Latin, which is the attainment of a gentleman. I know you don't look upon yourself as a gentleman, Thad, but why shouldn't you? What's the point of living in a free country unless you attempt worthwhile things, like becoming a gentleman? You must perfect your memory."

He also gave me a reading book for advanced students. About thirty of the sonnets of Shakespeare were included, and Samuel told me to memorize them, too. It would help me perfect my memory, he said.

So I memorized all the sonnets and hundreds of Latin words, but it didn't make things any better around the shop. I still misplaced binder's samples or a jar of camphor when we had to clean the rollers. I still neglected to lock the door at night and feed the cat, which was named Rochester.

In short, Samuel and I were both just about as absent-minded as ever, even though Samuel couldn't see it this way. He fancied I'd improved miraculously. He was convinced that I had cured just about all of my memory problems, and he often said so. He was proud of me, and told everybody of the fact.

I know he meant it, too. He would praise my memory to people who came into the shop. He would tell them what he'd recommended and how well I'd done the job. Sometimes he'd ask me to recite a sonnet by Shakespeare, and I'd recite it with meaningful gestures, which Samuel Chadwick greatly enjoyed and encouraged. He liked grand oratory and often used it, when the opportunity arose. When I finished reciting, he'd point out how easy it was to perfect your memory if you really put your mind to it.

He also urged me to adopt a grander style. "Write with eloquence, too," he said. "Just as you speak. Even if you are only leaving a brief note or writing a letter to a friend, use rhetorical figures. Embellish your letters with felicities. There is no reason our casual and ephemeral communications should not be distinguished. Why should they be without the touch of beauty? And if you are writing a letter to a friend, don't just refer to the setting sun, but allude to the day's orb reclining in the west. If it is raining, say that the earth is imbibing her fill. If you are feeling sadness, write that despondency is faintly troubling your mind. There are myriad ways to be eloquent, and you must explore them for the effects they provide."

This must have been an important issue, to his way of thinking, because he repeated it so often. But he repeated himself in just about everything. I figured one reason for this was that he'd forgotten when he'd said something already, and gave it another shot.

He'd go on and on. He'd amplify and elaborate, and by the time he got through, he'd forgotten the beginning, and would start all over again. One bit of advice he gave me was that I should learn prudence. "You are too blunt, Thad," he'd say. "Too blunt by far. Learn to mitigate your harsher observations. Folks don't want to hear the truth. They don't want the trouble. And you have a way of arguing that puts people off. Relax about the truth and let falsehoods be. Truth is only truth, after all, and its value is often exaggerated."

He repeated this sermon to me a hundred times, until I would have learned it by heart, even with a faulty memory.

Sometimes this business could be mighty irritating. If Samuel Chadwick had been put up before a firing squad and was asked if he had any last words, I figure he'd start repeating himself and pretty soon the firing squad would have gotten befuddled and forgotten what they were all supposed to be doing there, but after a while they'd shoot him anyway, just to shut him up.

My salary was two dollars a week in addition to bed and board, which was not bad for an apprentice. I lived in the back room with old Samuel Chadwick for five years and worked hard for him. He was like another father to me. I figured I learned a great deal from him, even though he was considerable odd, so that part of what I learned he hadn't meant to teach.

One day we printed some handbills for a lecture by a visiting phrenologist named Dr. Felix Carstairs, and I got so curious I decided to go myself and hear what he had to say about Destiny and the Human Head, which was his topic. I remember the date, November 7.

Dr. Carstairs was tall and stooped, and bent to the side, like a man who's trying to hear what a small child might have to say.

He was what you'd call very genteel and had long silver hair that curled over his collar and glistened in the lights. I found out later that his high-bridged nose, large and intelligent eyes, and monumental forehead, signified a man of intellect and sensibility. His dignified elocution and manner didn't lose any time in winning over the audience. He trilled his r's like a man gargling. He was a master of the English language. He could have talked a mouse out of a cheese cupboard.

Not only that, people were startled when they witnessed his cranial analyses of various subjects completely unknown to him. He looked into the human head like it was a crystal ball. The demonstration was a cause for wonder. Everybody said so. I was impressed, too, by what I witnessed there in the Lyceum that first evening. In fact, it was like he was talking to me alone and it was up to me to receive the message.

When I went back to our room at the back of the shop, I kept Samuel Chadwick awake for most of an hour talking about what I'd seen and heard. My old Master was tolerant and polite, but after a while it was obvious he wanted to go to sleep. Samuel had long ago renounced his faith in any kind of belief and didn't see any reason to take a stand on the findings of phrenology. The fact that it was of current interest, and part of the modern world, was enough to make it seem trivial in his eyes. His incidental fears and superstitions provided enough foundation for him, and I figure they gave him all the interest and security he needed for happiness and peace of mind.

But I couldn't get the business out of my thoughts. Here was a science that wasn't based on airy metaphysical suppositions, but on the hard-headed fact that our natures are waiting to be discovered through the unmistakable evidence planted right there in the shapes of our skulls.

Men and women differ from one another in thousands of ways, just as their heads differ from one another. And there's a correspondence. Function follows form — phrenology says so. The skull isn't just a kind of soup bowl made for carrying facts, ideas, and dreams, but a seed-pod of possibility, and the projection and imprint of what we are. The head is a domain whose geography we are only beginning to explore and understand, but it's one that has already revealed a landscape of significant fissures, mounds, valleys, swales, and plateaus. The wild, unexplored regions of the western continent are practically nothing compared to the human head.

Dr. Carstairs' ideas blew through my mind like leaves in a storm. I couldn't settle down for two whole days. Then I made up my mind and went straight to the great man and told him I wanted to join up with him and learn everything there was to know about the human head.

He must have been impressed by my energy and determination, because after he asked me a few questions he agreed to take me on. In fact, he acted like he'd practically been waiting for somebody like me to come along.

When I went back to Samuel Chadwick and told him about my decision, he acted pretty much the same way. It was like he'd been expecting it, too. I figured this was something of a coincidence, but the old printer explained it in a slightly different way.

He told me he'd been expecting something like this for days. He said he knew I wasn't going to stay around much longer. He gave a couple of proverbs by way of warming up to his subject, then he got into a discussion of my character. My mind was about to drift off when he took this sudden turn, which snagged my interest right away.

For a while, Samuel Chadwick talked about how odd I was, in spite of my appearance of being just like other people. He told me I was headstrong and had ideas of my own. He said people didn't like that sort, it made them uneasy. But he admitted I had some redeeming qualities, such as having a natural affection for other people.

But that wasn't enough. There was something in me that was out of reach. The old man shook his head and carved off a plug of tobacco, which he commenced stuffing behind his lip. He told me I had too much sassafras in my spirit. He said I was full of sass. He went on and elaborated on this theme, until I figured I knew it by heart, but then he took off in a different direction. Only a minute later, it turned out it wasn't a different direction at all but the one he'd started in, only entered from a different path. He'd started in telling me about his dreams, but then he made the connection that it was because of his dreams that he'd known I was about to leave. He said he wasn't taken by surprise at all. He mentioned this four or five times, trying it out in different keys and with different instruments. Finally, he wound up and said, "Yessir, Thad, I'm not a bit surprised to hear you're leaving! I half expected it, did you know that?"

"Yep," I said, "I half expected it."

Samuel Chadwick thought about that and nodded.

I couldn't figure out what it was he'd really been trying to tell me, but it was obvious that the old man was trying to give me advice. The only problem was, he didn't seem to be too sure of what was wrong with me, exactly, and so he couldn't be clear in his recommendations.

It was all considerable murky, and I figured I wouldn't worry about it. Even if it appeared that Samuel Chadwick judged it something deserving of worry, I wouldn't take it on myself. There were too many other things to occupy my mind.

2

For it was with seriousness and consideration that I took these journeys, from conviction of duty, that God required it at my hands.

— Lorenzo Dow's *Journal*

THOUGH I WAS only twenty years old, I figured I was pretty much a man and ready to take my place in Dr. Carstairs' troupe. Everywhere he went, he was accompanied by his pretty young wife, a dwarfish German maid, and an assistant named Henry Williams, who had wavy hair. Now, I would join them and become a part of this group.

For a couple of years we traveled up and down the eastern seaboard, following the good weather as well as we could. I used considerable midnight oil studying phrenological science. And one hot summer day when Dr. Carstairs' assistant ran off with his young wife, even taking the dwarfish maid with them, I was prepared to jump into that damned perfidious young scoundrel's place. I figured I was already more conversant with the principles and techniques of the science than Henry Williams had ever been. He had just been biding his time, combing his wavy hair and waiting for his chance. And when it came, he by God took it.

The hightailing of Williams gave me my opportunity, but the fact that he'd taken Dr. Carstairs' wife with him brought misery and despair to the old man. He took to the liquor jug, often the solace of weaklings and desperate men. And one night in western Pennsylvania, in the town of Washington, about a month after my promotion, I had to conduct the lecture all alone, while the critter who was supposed to be the center of attraction — the cynosure of all eyes, so to speak — snored away drunkenly on some piles of dirty canvas in the stage wings. There was a dribble of saliva hanging out of his mouth, and the posture he was sleeping in made me wonder if his neck was broken, but it turned out it wasn't.

After this, our relationship changed considerable. The more he drank and lost control, the more he acted irresponsible and petulant, like a child, so that before long I was taking care of him in a way that would have seemed more natural if our ages had been reversed.

I was curious about why he'd sold his soul for whiskey. I wondered what he got out of it, so I drank an occasional glass myself, by way of experiment, and was considerable exhilarated by the effect it had. After a few sips, I could look out upon a world that appeared to have more promise of adventure and excitement in it than the other world we get used to. After a glass of whiskey, I would feel the way I'd felt that day when I'd first looked upon the mighty Ohio River — *La Belle Rivière*, as La Salle named it — with flatboats floating downstream, grand and shadowy and bound for distant places, like Louisville and Memphis. After a glass of punch or whiskey, it was almost like Momma was still alive, and Pa was rational and kindly again, and everybody was all right and happy back in our log house on Big Raccoon Creek. But you can't bring back the past or build a faith on such visions, no matter how hard you try.

One time when I ran into the phrenologist lying drunk in his room, I stood by his bed and studied him. What pitiable critter was this, lying there all snarled up like a great big pale catfish caught in a net of stinking bed clothing, gazing drunkenly back at me? How could I have ever looked upon this wretched sot as wise and genteel, not to mention eloquent, and figured he might teach me something useful about life?

Our finances were low at the time, which was a fact he didn't have much grasp of, because all he could think of now was the dark bottle and the jug that plays a siren's tune. I tried to explain the situation to him, but he kept losing sight of the subject, until I finally lost my temper and stood there yelling and cussing at him until I'll be damned if he didn't all of a sudden look away from me — start to grin, like I'd just said something funny. I couldn't figure it out.

Such dismal scenes got to be frequent. The old man was drifting toward his end and acted like he was in a hurry to get it over with. He could hardly wait. He grew steadily worse. He sank into the reeking pits of excess, as they say. He fumbled around like a sleepwalker in a strange tavern, and exuded fumes of rum punch and whiskey like a week-old stewing pot.

One morning early in September, I went to him and put our cards on the table. I put it to him straight. I told him we had to move on, because we'd used up all the local curiosity about our science. I told him we'd out-stayed our welcome.

But it turned out that the old fool didn't figure he *wanted* to leave. He listened to me until I finished, and then he half closed his eyes and gazed off at some point behind my ear.

"Well," I said, "what do you have to say?"

"Say?" he cried, focusing his eyes on me with an effort and breathing hard through his nose. "Why, damn you, I'll tell you what I have to say! I'll say more than you want to hear, Thaddeus Burke — damned if I won't!"

This took me back considerable, especially when the old man fell abruptly silent and just sat there picking at a loose thread on his coat sleeve.

Finally, when he didn't give me any idea of what was eating at him, I said, "Well, what do you think? Do we get up and move on, or don't we?"

Once again he fixed a hard look on me, only this time his mouth curled up in a sneer. "By God," he whispered, "you just can't wait, can you!"

"Nope," I said, "I want to move on."

"That isn't what I mean, and you know it!"

When he said that, I told him I didn't have a tinker's fool's notion of what he was talking about.

He laughed scornfully. "Oh, you *know* all right! A young man as busy as you are gets to know everything that's useful to him. And nobody can say you haven't been *busy*! Why, you're the busiest critter I ever laid eyes on! You're busy with this, and busy with that. You've been busy ever since you joined up with me. Always in a stir, you are! You're busy with your good spirits and humor, always waiting in the wings with the right word. Full of epigrams and repartee, you are, eager to spout 'em forth!"

He paused right about here, and I figured he was finished, but it looked like he was just getting his second wind.

"*Busy, that's* what! Busy learning the science and busy listening to everything I say, just waiting like a panther to pounce upon the least little error and humble me. Always in a stir, you are, and full of attentiveness! Always eager to pick up on things. Saucy with a hundred answers, every time I turn around. And the *questions!* Why, the answers ain't *nothing* compared to the *questions!*"

Along about here I started to interrupt, but he out-yelled me: "Looky here, I'll tell you something, you damned scoundrel: it was *you* that drove Williams and my dear wife off together! Before you came, Williams was like a son to me, but you and your busy ways put him on edge like you was filing a knife on a grindstone and wouldn't stop, no matter how many teeth you set to chattering and no matter how many chills you sent shooting up the backbone like a school of icicles!"

I was considerable surprised by this attack, and for once I didn't know what to answer. I just stood there and took it like a preacher and didn't say a word. Only it looked like the poor old wretch took this behavior as a sign of guilt. So he went on and told me I didn't know friendship from a sack of dead squirrels. He told me I was too busy to ever show that I needed the good will of another, let alone the help. He called me a rabid wolf and said I was too breezy to live in a suffering world. He said he hoped I'd live long enough to be old and helpless. He said that was the greatest curse he could lay on a sassy critter like me.

I didn't quite get the connections he was making in all this summing up for the prosecution, but I figured it would be best to ignore it. The old fool was out of his mind, you could tell.

"You think I'm just raving drunk, don't you?" he finally asked, smiling with his mouth puckered up in a tight little seam.

"Yep," I said. "That's about the size of it."

He snorted with contempt. "You and your breezy ways! Why, you're the type that would joke to the hangman! You're too blithe and *busy* to repent or say a kind word or shed a tear."

Then he told me once more that he hoped I lived to be an old man, and then maybe I might understand a thing or two.

But I didn't stay around to listen to the next warrant he was waiting to serve. I figured that rum and whiskey had transformed him into a slobbering lunatic, because before that time he'd never once acted like he was anything but a true guide and friend.

His misery came to an end as sudden and unexpected as a clap of thunder out of a clear sky.

Along about six o'clock the next evening, he meandered out of Jonathan Wright's Tavern right into the path of a speeding collier's wagon trundling down a steep hill in the road. He was knocked down and run over and killed.

They say there wasn't a moan or squeak out of him. Not a prayer, grunt, or a cuss. Nothing. He just died, as quiet as you stamp out a segar. Sometimes I've thought that maybe he saw that wagon coming out of the corner of his eye and just didn't have the heart to stay drunk any longer.

A couple of men carried his bloody corpse inside, wrapped up in his own coat. One of the horses had stepped on his skull, and the features were considerable smashed, so that his best friend could hardly have recognized him. The face was lopsided, with the left portion fixed in a winking smirk, what you'd call a rictus, which was incongruous when you compared it to the unworldly expression of the half-opened eye, on the other side. The Mound of Causality (*Esprit Métaphysique*) was indented, showing where the skull had been crushed, killing him.

Not much of this was lost on me, you can be sure. I thought about what a tragic and ironic last act this was for the man he'd once been. Nature mocks us, often by way of coincidence. How else would we ever learn one kind of lesson?

I sat there in the dark, away from the fireplace that evening, brooding over the whole sad business. A couple of circuit lawyers were arguing county politics. And when I finally went to bed, my sleep was interrupted a couple of times by a dream of that smashed head floating around in the air. Samuel Chadwick would have been impressed. Once I yelled out, and a Methodist preacher who was three or four bodies away asked if I was saved, and I told him I didn't know for sure. But I guess he was too tired to trouble himself over my soul that night and went back to sleep.

Later on, I dreamed about my mother and that eased me a little, because she seemed all right in the dream. She was holding a broom.

I stayed beside the old man's body, all next day, and then saw to his burial on the day after that. I hired a preacher for five dollars. He was the kind that would have cried for ten, so I'm glad I couldn't afford that much. Five dollars is enough for a funeral, anyway, as any sensible critter would agree.

Since I didn't know about any relatives, I couldn't figure out what to do with the old man's worldly possessions. There wasn't much money in his purse, because he'd squandered most of it in those last months when he'd pursued his profession so indifferently and had hardly earned enough to keep a cat.

So I sold some of his equipment, together with all his clothes and personal belongings, and paid the hotel and tavern bills out of the profits. I didn't have much money left, but I kept some of his books and phrenological charts, which I figured I'd need in my new profession. The probate judge had bigger fish to fry and didn't see much worth bothering with in the present case and declared the old man's death intestate and told me to skedaddle.

I had gotten up early the morning after the funeral, which wouldn't have been much for a pet terrier, if you take attendance into account, and after a breakfast of ham, fried catfish, biscuits, and gravy, all washed down with a water glass filled with cold pale Catawba wine, I took off in the morning sunshine, headed in an eastern direction, back across the mountains toward Philadelphia, where I figured there'd be considerable more heads than here in the western part of the state.

3

The sympathy and kindness of woman are also proverbial. She will go much farther than man (with reverence, and to her ever lasting honour, be it recorded) in her assiduities and unremitting attentions to the sick, the needy, and the afflicted; she will do, she will suffer, she will sacrifice any thing and every thing to relieve distress, to bind up the broken-hearted, and to pour the oil of consolation into the wounds of a troubled soul; and all from pure motives of kindness, affection, love, and duty. The phrenologist alone, is capable of developing and explaining this interesting mystery. He can place his finger upon her superior organs of benevolence, conscientiousness, adhesiveness, and philoprogenitiveness.

— Fowler's *Practical Phrenology*

I WORKED pretty hard in those days, traveling and lecturing in schoolhouses, churches, lyceums, and opera houses in a hundred towns and selling pamphlets I'd had printed on good laid paper tinted a robin's-egg blue, along with big elephant folio cranial charts. And whenever I got the chance, I used my time profitably, studying books as well as the print of human nature. I heard most of the arguments raised against phrenology, and learned the arguments to counter them. I learned the strategies of argumentation and the tactics of rebuttal. I had to think on my feet in those days. You never knew what would come up next.

People were curious and wanted to hear what I had to tell them. It was profitable, I'll have to say that. I was taking in knowledge and dollars both. This gave me more self-confidence, which most people figured I had several pounds too much of to begin with. By the time I was twenty-three years old, I couldn't hardly find a group of men I wasn't at ease with. And I wouldn't have turned down a chance to argue with any critter alive. I was convinced that I knew the world pretty well, which turned out not to be the case.

Even though I'd learned to drink my glass of whiskey as occasion presented itself, I couldn't forget the sorry fate of Felix Carstairs, my mentor, so I tried to be careful and not get drunk too often. My temper took off galloping every now and then, and I'd cuss and let my mind gallop just about anywhere it wanted. By this time I'd drifted off a considerable distance from my Quaker beginnings, as you can no doubt imagine.

I also made use of venery, as Benjamin Franklin recommended, for the sake of my body's health. Although you'd be telling a lie if you said there wasn't any pleasure in it. And the fact is, I had always been attracted to the bodies of women, above and beyond the administration of prudence or moral choice. Even as a little boy I liked them. I liked to be picked up and fondled by women. You might have thought I was getting in practice already. And women seemed to know the way I felt, and they liked to pull me up into their laps and tickle me and tease me. When I got older, of course, I put all this off, as if it were nonsense and I was a little man of war, all bristling with cannon. Women saw this, too, and left me alone, even though you could tell they were amused by the whole business and they never stopped smiling at me.

Many a time, as a phrenologist I'd get amorously excited when I had to analyze a female head. I couldn't help it. Sometimes touching female heads and feeling their warm bodies next to mine could get embarrassing. Don't tell me that Nature doesn't have a sense of humor.

But when it came to getting serious and settling down, I judged that most of the maidens I examined were deficient in promise. I had gotten so critical of the structures I studied that I met very few marriageable girls whose heads I figured qualified them for the role of wife. Everybody knows that physicians who've developed excessive skill in diagnosis are likely to be jumpy and a mite dubious about people. I was the same way. I figured that if Dr. Carstairs had been more analytical and less passionate about that woman he'd married, he wouldn't have brought himself to such a miserable end, because right after I'd learned the bare rudiments of the science, I could see that his wife didn't have a talent for marriage. Some things in the skull you just can't doubt. In her, this was revealed by the undeveloped Mound of Conjugality low on the occiput. I could see this right away. It was all as clear as crossed eyes or a broken nose to other people.

I was considerable surprised the first time I noticed this one day when her dwarfish German maid was brushing her wheat-colored hair and lifted it up in back. How could Dr. Carstairs have ignored such evidence? One glance and you could tell she'd be the type to run off with some wavy-haired apprentice. But love had made him blind.

Speaking of the German maid, I might as well admit that I'd taken possession of her body a number of times. She was mighty passionate and practically attacked me the first time we were alone. Aside from her affliction, she was a pleasant-looking young woman.

She's the only dwarf I've ever diddled.

The Romans said that you could drive out Nature with a pitchfork, but she would return on both sides, and I have found that the same thing can be said of human error. Also, ignorance of the world and self, whichever may be deemed prior.

I mention this because I now have to tell about something that changed my life. I was traveling in the East when I got an invitation to a genteel gathering in Baltimore. I remember it was a fine cold winter day, only the ground was free of snow. As soon as I got there, somebody promptly let it out that I was a professor of phrenology. It was like a bugle call. Everybody got quiet. Then there was a big stir among those present, the way it usually happens. They wanted me to probe and fathom their skulls so they could find out what they were. They wanted to be formally introduced to themselves, and I was the man who could officiate at the ceremonies.

I did the heads of a couple of matrons and gentlemen and told everybody what I'd found out. And then I saw a young woman of spectacular beauty. I asked about her and was told she was "the Coloratura Soprano, Miss Lily de Wilde."

If my eyes hadn't told me about this young woman's excellence, I knew my fingers would have. Her cranium was a compendium of virtue, warmth, and sensitivity. I could tell all this just by looking. Also I couldn't help noticing that her speaking voice was melodious, which isn't always the case with operatic-type singers. Not only that, her speech was deliberate and perfectly styled, like sentences being read aloud from a book on etiquette.

I invited her to sit for me, and when I palpated the lobes and spheres of her skull, my mouth got as dry and hot as if I'd just taken a bite of unbuttered toast.

I had trouble keeping my voice from shaking when I referred to the pronounced but gentle swell below the inion, which is the Mound of Amativeness. Here, for the first time, I actually felt heat in the region. I had read about this. Gall said he'd first noticed it in a hysterical widow. But this was the first time I'd actually felt it.

The most remarkable thing was the balance of the various features. In all my experience, I've come across only one other head with this harmoniousness in the regions of Inhabitiveness, Benevolence, Veneration, and Conjugality.

She seemed to like me, too, and said she found me most interesting. Those were her exact words — "Most interesting." We talked together for a long time, and then I saw her the next day and the day after that. In fact, we started keeping company. Her parents were dead, but she was living with her uncle.

Our discussions were a marvel. She had the most formal diction I've ever witnessed. She talked like a living elocution book. If you'd never heard her, you could hardly believe that so much correctness could exist inside one head.

I told her about my ideals and philosophy of life, and one night the two of us discussed elective affinities until the moon had almost turned over.

I put her on a high pedestal, and if she'd tried to step off, I would have pushed her back. Her ideality was important to me, and I wasn't going to touch her body until it was proper. I vowed I'd hold her above carnal desire until we got married.

What you've got to remember is that I was still pretty young. In fact, I was younger than I had a right to be. Also, I was three parts a fool and one part goat, as the following events will show.

I figured Lily was the toast of Baltimore. I don't know how I got that idea, exactly, but I got it somehow; and I just naturally assumed that she was the Belle of the City. She certainly acted that way, and as far as I could tell, nobody doubted it. People liked her, you could tell. They smiled when her name was mentioned. And she sang angelically, as everybody agreed, and knew by heart all the recent Italian arias.

One afternoon at a recital in a mansion on Calvert Street, I was smoking a segar and drinking a glass of Madeira wine with a neurasthenic type of man that was about twice my age. After Lily had sung "Una Voce Poco Fa" and was chatting with some women, I sipped from my glass and watched him. He kept clearing his throat when he wasn't guzzling wine, and his expression was as bilious as a dyspeptic toad. He had the most melancholy countenance and physiognomy I've ever seen. His forehead bulged like a melon. He had a sallow complexion, and morbidly dark eyes. Wisps of damp-looking black hair rested upon the domed brow. Intellect glowed from that face and sadness rested in those eyes.

This specimen was standing there aloof from the crowd, looking like a general who's considerable disgusted with his troops. His right hand held a glass of wine. His other hand was sort of fumbling at his vest. It looked like he might be trying to raise a belch. His shirt was soiled by wine stains and miscellaneous accumulated grime, and yet he gave an impression of nobility of birth and distinction of mind. That head looked like it might be stuffed as full as a lyceum, and I couldn't help but be interested in him, so I walked up and greeted him.

"This is what I'd call a lively gathering," I said. "Popping like corks, all around."

"Lively," he agreed, nodding.

"And Miss de Wilde sure does have a lovely voice."

"Lovely," he echoed. Then he sort of dipped his head into a fresh glass of wine he'd just picked up.

"And what a beautiful figure," I went on, taking care to speak in the politest tones at my command. "Such arms, such a throat, such a tiny waist . . ."

"Who, Lily?" the stranger asked, jerking his head up out of his glass. He acted as if he'd just now figured out who I was talking about.

"Yep," I said. "You sound like you know her."

Before he answered my question, he gave me a real close look, as if he'd just noticed I had three eyes or a missing nose.

"Well, I certainly know *of* her. Beyond that, deponent sayeth nought. Before she changed it, her name was just plain Lily Chubb. That was when she hadn't yet discovered she had what they call a singing voice. Good God Almighty, what I know about that critter would fill a book! Are you a stranger in town?"

"Yep," I said. Then I thought a second and said: "I guess maybe I'm more of a stranger than I figured."

"Well, let me tell you something, stranger, before you decide to become too infatuated with her. She's known by just about every philanderer east of the Mississippi as one of the most gifted nymphomaniacs in Christendom. Yessir, a luminary of the bed; a genius of the couch, if there ever was one. And there *have* been. Many. Many."

I was what you'd have to call staggered. I asked him if he was sure we were talking about the same woman. I asked if it was the same Lily de Wilde we were talking about, just as if there might have been a whole regiment of nymphs with the same name.

"To me," he answered frowning as he gazed into his glass, "as well as to two thirds of the male population of the city of Baltimore, and God knows how many up and down the Atlantic seaboard, she is plain, simple Lily, sometimes known as 'Lay-Me-Again Lily,' sometimes as 'Lily-the-Lips,' sometimes as 'Lascivious Lil,' some- times as the 'Baltimore Whore-iole,' or 'the Warbling Streetwalker.' Surely, you can't be *that* new in town!"

"Yep, I think maybe I am," I said. Then I started to say something else, but I don't remember what it was. The fact is, I could hardly get my breath. My head felt like it was inside a feather mattress. And it was right then I realized how drunk I was. Not to mention deceived.

"Oh, my God," the stranger said melodramatically, pretending to stagger. "Let me have a breath of air! You can't have *fallen* for that venereal old bag, can you?"

I mumbled a little and just sort of ambled off. Somebody asked if I was well. I shook my head and somehow got out of that room, and wandered numbly along the street for a while.

Love is blind, like they say, but like a lot of platitudes and truisms, you have to find this out for yourself, everybody in his own way, in his own time.

Right then, drunk as I was, I could see her in a new light. What

I'd figured were her charming ways began to look like something a whole lot different. Her coquetries all of a sudden looked like tactics. Her shy smiles were all of a sudden converted into leers that would offend a possum. Her coyness all of a sudden began to look like the tired expertise of a jaded, immoral, and world-weary woman.

I forgot all about the tragic end of that old sot Carstairs and abandoned myself to the perfidious solace of drink. I drank up two storms and a flood. And the next morning, boozy as I was, and full of shakes like an old ice skater with palsy, I got a set of handbills ready and sent them off by stage for Washington, D.C.; and then I promptly began to drink some more whiskey. A hair of the dog. I remember I even had a toothache.

But that was secondary. I drank to erase from my mind the thought of what a total God damned fool that bitch Lily de Wilde had made of me.

4

If one is not an anatomist, he's not a Surgeon.
— Vesalius

MANY TIMES in my travels I came upon maidens I'd think of in the role of wife, but then I'd start to brood over some defect or other in their cranial structures. There were a lot of them: Delilah Warner, with her snub nose and underdeveloped regions of Concentration, below the obelion and over the lambda; Anastasia Cunningham, acquisitive and alimentive, according to the enlarged configurations above the temporal muscle and before the ear; Zelda Doans, sweet as a puppy, but with hypertrophied Mounds of Secretiveness and Adhesiveness swelling the back of her head. I could have loved them all, but I'll be damned if any one of them was exactly right for that lasting relationship that marriage is supposed to be. I have always been an idealist. I told myself to tread carefully, and that's what I did.

Those were busy years. I traveled up and down the country and began to get a reputation for analysis that I figure you could say was bordering on Fame. For six months in Cincinnati I studied medicine, but gave it up when my funds ran dry. By this time Samuel Chadwick was dead, and so was Pa. Ten years to the day of Momma's death, he marched out into the cemetery with a gun and blew his brains out over her grave. My sister Agnes was married to a lawyer, and I visited her at her home in Lexington, Kentucky.

But in all this time, I didn't give up the search for the perfect woman I'd vowed I'd get for my own someday. I figured she'd be worth waiting for, whoever she was.

I didn't give much thought to the world of affairs. Like Samuel Chadwick, I had a flair for missing out on the issues of the time. I hardly ever read a newspaper or joined in a political argument, even though they were going off like pistols all around me. I kind of hoped that my anachronistic weakness wasn't exactly the same as the simple antiquarian whimsy of Samuel Chadwick, however. I hoped that when you came right down to it, my ways would prove to have some enduring seed of truth that would outlast the political and social fireworks of my contemporaries.

Then I started to get restless. I was getting tired of the same old academy halls and meeting houses and lecture rooms. I had begun to tire of the same old cities and the familiar roads that I'd once traveled with Dr. Carstairs.

I took a long look all around and could not help but notice that the country was drifting westward. I'd seen many a wagon filled with gold seekers, Zionists, farmers, and just plain adventurers headed for the Great Plains, the Rocky Mountains, and points west. The frenzy of the westward movement was beginning to get to me. It was like a contagion. So one day I decided to fall into the stream that rushed with such prodigious violence, you might say, toward the setting sun.

However, I figured I'd go there by gradual stages, lecturing as I went. There was no law that said I couldn't make a dollar or two on the way. So I bought a Conestoga wagon and had the body painted a bright and shiny blue. On the white canvas top I had red and blue lettering, along with a cross-section of the human skull. I was considerable impressed with the result. It was colorful. It also featured the good old red, white, and blue, dear to the heart of the patriot.

When the wagon was all fixed and ready to go, I filled it up with technical paraphernalia and other necessaries. It was pulled by two mules, which I named Romulus and Remus. So with no ties of any sort, I set out westward, crossing the Ohio River at Martin's Ferry on a soggy, rainy April morning, and arrived once again in my native state.

I traveled all about the countryside that summer, visiting hamlets and villages, schoolhouses and churches, and cities that were cropping up on the rolling farmlands, wooded hills, and prairies of Ohio, Indiana, and Illinois.

I had my share of adventures, because phrenology was bringing out more and more skepticism. Mockers and clowns often interrupted my lectures and demonstrations. Almost every audience had a percentage of these scoffers and twitmongers, intent upon bringing down the edifice of phrenology in ruins upon my head.

But these troublemakers had their antagonists, too, for there were probably as many stout defenders of phrenology as there were briny critics. The contest was usually divided pretty equal, about like controversies on the subjects of Universalism and Infant Damnation, I'd say. In those days I participated in more than my share of heated debates, conversations, discussions, and arguments. And I took to it like a fox takes to chickens. I always loved a good argument, and still do.

I figure that people know there are few things more important than finding a guide to measure human nature. Know yourself. The old principle again. We've got to study ourselves and find out what we are, because it's our natures that bring about what happens to us, nine times out of ten, and this includes accidents. Even coincidences, as I've found out.

One of the worst predicaments I ever got myself into took place in Illinois. It was late autumn and I'd driven my wagon into town after setting things up by sending a bushelful of notices to the local newspaper and giving some handbills and cardboard signs to a schoolmaster traveling in that direction. He'd agreed to hang them in conspicuous places.

I'd rented the local schoolhouse for Friday evening and then again the next morning. As usual, I checked the audience out, to see what sort of critters they were. And then I told them a few jokes and humorous stories, trying to sort of loosen them up, because people get nervous in a situation like that, where they figure they're going to have to listen to the truth.

I told them the one about the Angel and the Mule Driver, and then the one about the 'Possum and the Cat. I told them what the banker's widow had said to me in Buffalo, New York, one time, and was going to tell them about the Shipwreck and the Little Babe but decided not to, because it began to look like they had too much gravity for my levity. They just didn't respond the way an audience should. Normally, I can infect people with my particular dose of sassafras, but it looked like these folks had been vaccinated. No, something just wasn't quite right, somehow. I could sense it, the way an old veteran of the lecture circuit learns to sense things. It was like a symphony conductor can hear somebody hitting the wrong notes somewhere in the brasses, but he's not sure whether it's a trombone or a tuba.

But there was nothing to do but go ahead with the music, so I started in with my usual introduction. I'd hardly got a head of steam on when there was a sudden clamorous ringing of bells nearby. Everybody figured there was a fire someplace, so they all jumped to their feet, but before they could get out, a man stopped them and said it was only another phrenologist who had started in ringing the bell to announce his lecture. It turned out that he'd made arrangements pretty much like mine, only he'd reserved the church instead of the schoolhouse.

I'd noticed that the turnout wasn't much, and I'd been disappointed. Now I knew the situation. I had competition, and he was ringing the church bell so lustily that it was hard for me to make myself heard, but I kept on as well as I could, raising my voice to a quarter-mile yell when the ringing got too loud.

But after a while he managed to get stopped, and I was able to go ahead with my lecture. Then about half an hour later, I started giving some cranial analyses, and when I was occupied with a fat young mother, there was a sudden interruption at the back of the room. A great big husky yokel came through the door, followed by a small herd of ruffians, and they all started walking down the center aisle between the school desks. They walked heavy, like their boots owned the floor. Right away, I saw they all had a steaming drunk on.

I paused and gave a boiled-egg stare at the leader for a second or two, and then I asked him what in the hell he wanted.

"Are you one of them head readers, like the sign says?" he asked.

"Yep," I said.

"Well," he said, "the professor who calls himself Dr. Stillingfleet over there in the church has just finished reading my head, and I wanted to see what *you* had to say about it. I wanted to see if you two professors *agreed* about what my skull is trying to say."

A couple of his cohorts kind of laughed, but I hung on to my dignity pretty hard and told that son of a bitch he'd have to wait until I'd finished with this fat young mother sitting there in the chair before me.

I was surprised when the leader agreed. I'd figured he'd come after me right then and there, with a knife or without, but he didn't. He just stood and waited, with his arms crossed. They looked about as thick as the thighs of a good runner.

I took my time, and when I was ready for him, he came up and sat in the chair, and I started to probe and palpate and comment on my findings, which were of considerable less than average interest, except for the fact that he had a pointed nose, which Aristotle claimed was a sign of irascibility. I mentioned this fact, only I doubt if anybody knew what irascibility was.

They all sat there quiet as a congregation of turnips while I spoke. When I finished, the young fellow stood up and pointed his finger at me and said, "God damnit, that is *exactly the opposite* of what that Stillingfleet said. Sure as hell, one of you two professors is lying!"

Then he turned around and began to give it to the audience. He harangued them. There is nothing like the passionate indignation of a drunk. He fried them like so many strips of bacon in a skillet. He was a gifted troublemaker, you could tell, fated to become a politician or some other kind of leader. He asked them if they were hayseeds and asses to be taken in by any mountebank that passed. He appealed to their civic pride. "Are the people of this town going to be duped?" he shouted, shaking his fist like he had dice in it.

Just about everybody there shouted no. They said they were not, and they were getting mad, you could tell. They were halfway to being mesmerized, and they responded to this Sorehead like their mouths and throats were nothing but so many valves of a trumpet, and his powerful ignorant lungs were busy pumping air through them.

The events following this are still considerable unclear to me. I remember that all of a sudden about a dozen torches were flaring outside the windows of the schoolhouse. And then there was a whole mob of them that came up and tied my hands with the rope from a hayfork. I was marched and prodded outside, where I faced a fresh mob, angry as the first. You could tell their tempers had just about reached a galloping boil. All bore on their faces an expression of savage ecstasy, as if I personally had been sent just to entertain them in a way I sure as hell wouldn't have picked out for myself.

I'll never forget the look of one of them. He was a crippled boy with a fat face and puffy, slanted green eyes. About ten years old,

I'd say. He leaned on his little hickory crutch and just kept on spitting on my trousers. Then I was jostled and jeered. I was shoved and calumniated. They seemed to hate me with a passion that was what you might say akin to love. It was almost religious.

Down a little hill about two hundred yards away, another group came toward us, thick as hiving bees as they clustered about somebody I couldn't see. They danced around like lunatics, and their torches wavered and flickered in the darkness.

Right then somebody yelled "Here they come!" and everybody in my group turned around, quiet and attentive, in one motion, like a field of ripe wheat with a sudden breeze passing over it. When this other mob came close enough, the crowd all around me separated, so that three or four men could bring in a stranger wearing a top hat to face me. This critter had a hatchet face and a sickly, sallow complexion.

The mob lapped it up. They loved it. I saw everything. Some of them were drinking from jugs. They were drinking whiskey and cider both, I figured. And there was even a little outbreak of singing. The blood-faced bully who'd first come into the schoolroom and interrupted me was named Boggs, and in spite of his youth, he was a leader of sorts, you could tell. He mounted the three steps leading into the schoolroom and began to talk to the crowd, explaining how at least *one* of us had to be a liar, but probably *both* of us were.

"Tar and feather them!" an oxycephalic woman with a big wart on her cheek shouted, and everybody took up the cry with fervor. They jumped back and forth, from one foot to the other, like Indians getting warmed up for a minuet.

But I held up my hand, which surprised them and stopped them like a rifle shot.

"He wants to speak his piece," somebody said, and somebody else seconded the notion by saying "Well, let him!"

I cleared my throat and said, "You're not figuring on tarring and feathering us just because we *disagree* with each other, are you?"

"Can you think of a better reason?" a big wrinkle-faced critter said. "Sounds like fraud to me."

"Fraud it is," somebody seconded. It sounded like the same voice that had done the seconding before. It was probably somebody created just for the purpose of seconding motions made by various and sundry.

"Why, if you do that," I told them, "you'll have to tar and feather every lawyer who comes to court, let alone the politicians hereabouts."

"You leave lawyers and politicians out of this," the big fellow said, and the seconder said, "That's right, they got enough trouble already," which made everybody laugh.

Then I told them I was surprised to see them act this way. I told them the heads I'd analyzed didn't show any tarring and feathering tendencies that I'd perceived. I kind of elaborated upon this for a while, but it wasn't too long before their attention wandered, and where it wandered was toward the tar kettle and the gunny sacks filled with chicken feathers.

So I shut my mouth and let them yell awhile, but then Boggs quieted them down and said he had a better idea, which would prolong the entertainment and milk it dry. He said they ought to simmer us in jail that night, and then the next day, the two of us would have it out on the courthouse steps. His idea was that this Stillingfleet and I would be put on trial. We would be confronted with three people we'd never seen before and we'd have to analyze their skulls. Our conclusions would be written down on paper, so they'd have to be honest. Then the results would be read aloud, and put to a vote from all the assembled spectators. The winner would be set free, but the loser would be given a ride to the tar buckets, where he'd be tarred and feathered and run out of town, and his equipment would be burned or confiscated.

All the time Boggs talked, there were gusts of cheering from the crowd. The torches flickered in the night air and cast roving lights over the pale face of Stillingfleet. I've never seen a mixture of fear and desperate cunning like that on a man's face.

All the time this was happening, that crippled fat boy kept spitting on my trouser leg. He spat slowly and methodically, like he was being paid a substantial sum for doing it, and he was honest enough that he didn't have any thought in his head other than earning his salary this way.

5

Who shall decide when doctors disagree,
And sound casuists doubt like you and me?
— Pope

IN MY TIME I've had to suffer through many a miserable night, but there are few that can match in wretchedness the dark hours passed with that son of a bitch Stillingfleet in the little cell we were confined to that evening.

The jail wasn't anything more than an empty shed made out of fresh whipboard lumber. There were two little windows no bigger than a lady's hand mirror right under the eaves. A cat might have crawled through one, but a man could hardly have gotten his arm through, even if he could have reached that high. Inside, there wasn't even a bed or chair. The stump of a tallow candle burning on a narrow shelf near one of the windows revealed a crude bench, made out of eight-inch boards nailed together. A damp and filthy gray horse blanket lay wadded on the ground. It reminded me of a dog's corpse. There wasn't any floor at all, just packed mud. I've never known a place that smelled more of plain, dull misery than that place. And on top of everything else, I had a toothache. It was an upper premolar on the right side that had been giving me considerable trouble lately.

I guess we were lucky it wasn't dead winter, but there was a cold rain that began to fall in the middle of the night, and it kept on dripping until dawn, when it got tired and stopped. But Stillingfleet and I had gotten to be deadly enemies long before this. We sat as far apart as we could on that bench and folded our arms. We didn't say a word to each other for a while. One of us was going to be thrown into the tar pit, according to the terms set forth, and we weren't likely to forget this fact.

I bit off a plug of Virginia tobacco and just sat there chewing and contemplating the fix I was in. But after half a dozen spits, I calmed down a little and gave myself a talking to. I told myself that it is not right to prejudge a man, even if he does have the head of a catfish and is the cause of considerable trouble to yourself. I grew mellow in my thoughts, and actually began to contemplate the possibility of offering a chew to the poor wretch who was sitting there beside me in the dark. Maybe I was wrong about him.

But before I could come to a decision about offering him a plug, Stillingfleet ruined everything. He capsized the boat of charity. His timing couldn't have been more perfect if he'd known exactly where I'd gotten in my decision making.

"What I'd like to know," he said, making me jump a little because of the suddenness of his voice, "is how you always figure out ahead of time where I'm going to be."

"What in tarnation are you talking about?" I asked him.

"I'm talking about Terre Haute, Indiana, and Lima, Ohio. I'm talking about Sharpsburg, Mifflin, and Cairo. I come on your traces everywhere, and don't think I don't hear how you vilify me and seek to defame and denigrate my reputation. Don't think I'm in the dark any longer, because I know it was you all those times, even though you used different names — which is the way with critters like you who have set your sights on destroying an honest man!

"Crafty, that's what you are. Why else would you use different names if you wasn't crafty? Answer me that enigma, and I'll explain the ways of the Almighty! Insinuating your course hither and yon, just so's it'll crisscross my own plotted journeys, trying to educate the people and earn an honest dollar by means of my science!

"And don't talk Christianity to me, neighbor! I've heard all the arguments you people use, and they ain't worth a fart in a whirlwind! Why, don't you think I have spent many a lonely night trying to figure out your cussed ways and trying to understand the wherefore of all these infernal connivings? Don't you?

"But it didn't take. I worked at it and sweated like two mules and a nigger, but it just plain by God didn't take. Many's the time I tried to bygone you, but it wasn't no use. Many a time I . . ."

"What the hell are you raving about?" I shouted, interrupting him.

"Just exactly what I'm saying: no more nor no less. Work at my calling, I'm talking about. And how you come along everyplace I go and start up some kind of whispering campaign, saying I am a fool and a knave. I've tried to bygone you, but it never worked. 'Let bygones be bygones, Horace,' I told myself, but do you think that'll work in a world like this? God-and-double-damned *no*, it won't! You may have pulled the wool over my eyes before this, but the rag has been stripped away, and now I can see it all. I ain't in the dark no longer, and don't never intend to step forth into darkness again, because now I know who you are, you smooth-talking fiend from hell. The minute I looked at you I knew what you were because of them Bumps of Destructiveness above the ears. I'd be a blind fool not to see them, even if I wasn't a cranial scientist!"

The shock of all this fire and fuming was considerable, and for a few seconds I just sat there thinking about what he'd said. It was a lie in every syllable, including his statement that he wasn't in the dark, because there wasn't a spark of light in that pathetic little hut of a jail. The tallow candle had burned out in about the time it would take to play two hands of poker, maybe three, leaving us as much in the dark as a human being can get, which is considerable.

"Well," I said after a couple of breaths, "I don't know who you are, Mr. Stillingfleet, but I figure you are afflicted with lunacy if you believe what you just said."

"Don't deny it," he cried. "You've sown my furrow with salt, you damned villain! I've come on your spoor everywhere, and it's no wonder I can't give my lectures in peace. Every time they break out in laughter or hiss or boo, I hear the echoes of what you've been telling them. What I can't figure out is why you ever arranged for a showdown in *this* damned place!"

"I've never even *heard* of you!" I shouted.

With this, Stillingfleet started to snicker or cry, I couldn't tell which. Then something occurred to me that just about froze my blood, as the saying goes. I was suddenly aware of the fact that the bench felt different underneath me, the way a bench feels when somebody you're sitting with stands up. You can feel the difference.

The instant this came to me, I felt considerable fright and eased off the bench into a crouch, wondering what the lunatic was planning. What I figured was, he probably had a knife and was trying to measure where I was sitting by the sound of where my voice had been. So I moved, and about two seconds afterwards, the bastard lunged at me.

In the first scuffle, I felt his top hat pop off his head as I swung out with my fists as fast as I could. Mostly I was hitting air. He was flailing away at me, as well, only I was pretty sure he had a knife in one of his hands, and I didn't have one. I did some kicking, too, figuring that if he did have a knife he'd be cutting up from underneath, trying to split my brisket or maybe slice my throat open.

Then I kneed him a good one, right in the belly, making him grunt; and quick as a wink I swung out to where I figured his head ought to be and felt my fist hit solid skin and bone with a jolt that I could feel all the way up to my shoulder. Then I heard his body hit the ground with a whump and knew I'd put him out of action.

I dropped on him then like a hawk and grabbed along the arms until I found the hands, only they were both empty. But then I felt a little seam of pain on my forearm, after which I could feel warm blood seeping down my wrist.

I stayed on my hands and knees, patting the ground with the palms of my hands, searching for the knife, but I'll be damned if I could find it. Stillingfleet groaned and stirred, and I reached out and fumbled my left hand up his shirt front until I found his throat, which I squeezed good and hard, and then popped him another good one on the jaw, which dropped him promptly.

But where was the damned knife? I fumbled around and around, going at it so furiously that I even started talking to the knife, asking where it was. And then finally when I grabbed at the blackness, I felt the blade slice into my fingers, and as much as it hurt, I was what you'd have to call thankful.

I hissed from the pain, but got the knife by its handle and stood there holding it. Stillingfleet was laid out like a corpse, it sounded like, and I could even feel my knuckles hurting from the blows I'd laid on his bony phiz. I've seldom popped a man any better than that, and even though both of my hands were filling with blood, I knew that it was nothing too serious, because there was no arterial spurting, just the welling of venous bleeding.

I stuck the knife between my knees, jerked off my coat, and then tore strips from my shirt, with which I bandaged my left forearm and then my right hand. Everything seemed under control, so I thought about going over and slicing Stillingfleet's throat. I'll have to admit it was a temptation.

But after considering the matter, I figured it would be unwise to kill the son of a bitch, since I would then have to face a murder charge the next morning, and the local populace would have no way of knowing whether I'd had due cause or not.

So I went back to the bench and sat down, keeping the knife in my left hand. My right hand felt like a fistful of paste after a while, but that was all right. I'd likely endure a lot worse than that before my piece had been spoken here on earth.

About half an hour later, I heard a stirring and felt the bench jar a little from a weight being carefully deposited on it. I figured Stillingfleet had been lying there a long time after he'd regained consciousness, trying to figure out some other way to do me in. If he'd had a second knife, he probably would have sneaked up and given it another try, so I kept pretty alert, with his knife in my left hand.

Along about dawn, I saw something strange happen. I didn't turn my head away from the other side of the bench for a second, and looking in that direction, I saw the form of Stillingfleet gradually appear as the inside of the hut grew lighter. He grew more and more palpable as I watched.

It was a curious experience, and a little uncanny. Stillingfleet was staring straight ahead, with his top hat in his lap. He wouldn't look at me, so all I could see was his profile. But this was enough to let me know that overnight I had changed his features considerable.

It was a depressing time, but at least I'd forgotten about my toothache. That is until it was pretty well daylight, when it started in aching again, joining the cuts on my forearm and hands in a sort of stew of misery.

But everything has an end, and a sausage has three — as the saying goes; and about an hour after the light of dawn had begun to glow through the holes near the roof, I heard the thud of a military drum. It sounded water-soaked and funereal. And after a while we heard voices, signifying the approach of men. The oak door was given a couple of solid shakes, and then unlatched, and we were taken out into the light of a cold and gloomy day.

All around us stood those of the night before, pretty much the same cast of players, bearing upon their drink-swollen faces the expectant look of bilious and angry sportsmen. They looked like they were determined in spite of all obstacles to have some fun, even if it killed us. Stillingfleet groaned and with trembling fingers adjusted his top hat on his head.

"Well," a big hefty man with straw-colored hair and a freckled and wrinkled face said, "it looks like you two fellers had yourself an interesting time last night." I remembered him from the previous night. He'd been the only talker, as distinguished from yeller, in the crowd. Excepting maybe Boggs. He glanced at Stillingfleet's face and then at my bloody hands. "Fists and knife, was it? And looks to me like fists got the better of it."

"He attacked me," Stillingfleet muttered, "and since he was bigger and stronger, I didn't have any alternative but to do what I could to save my life."

"That's a lie!" I yelled.

The big fellow closed one eye and thought. "I doubt if there's an ounce of truth in either one of you, but that's not the issue this morning."

Right then, I knew him for a lawyer, so I said, "If what he says is true, ask him where his knife is."

The big fellow raised his eyebrows and looked at Stillingfleet, who said lamely, "He stole it from me."

With my good left hand, I reached into my pocket where I'd put the knife and dropped it on the ground. "There it is," I said, "and if I'd wanted to, I could have cut this miserable scoundrel's throat like it was a cheese."

"Defendant presents a good argument," the big fellow said, closing his eye again and sighting at a distant tree. Right then I figured he might be a judge, as well as a lawyer. This could be an advantage, although it was hard to tell, since I'd met a fellow in Indiana who ran for clerk of courts on the sole platform that he'd been tried on every charge in the books, and therefore knew the law.

But this straw-haired feller was a judge all right, because somebody in the crowd yelled out: "Let's get on with it, Judge. This here ain't the trial we was looking for."

The judge nodded. "Point well taken," he said.

But you could tell he didn't want to leave any part of the law hanging. He stood there between us for a minute and then said, "Of course, if the plaintiff had proper counsel, said counsel would no doubt put forth that even if defendant had attacked plaintiff with his fists, such would not of necessity point to an intent to kill, but perhaps merely maim or do other bodily harm. But of course, plaintiff could not have been aware of intent in the heat of, ah, battle, so that he might naturally avail himself of whatever weapon was available — to wit, the knife lying there on the ground." The judge leaned over and picked it up. "Keeps it sharp, don't he?" he said to me, and I agreed with him 100 percent.

Then he winked his eye at me and said, "Ain't so high and mighty this morning as you were last night, are you?"

I told him there were ups and downs in life, but that was all the satisfaction I'd give on that topic.

"Well," he said thoughtfully, "I studied you pretty hard back there in the schoolroom, and it come to me then."

He wanted me to ask what had come to him, but I'd be damned if I'd do it. So we just waited there, with that motley crowd breathing in and out all around us.

"I suppose you want to know what come to me," the judge finally said. "That'd be only natural, wouldn't it? For you to wonder such a thing?"

"Maybe," I said.

The judge nodded. "What come to me was, that Head Reader is doing something I can't quite figure out. There's something at work there that don't exactly figure. He's got an airy manner. Do you know what I was? I was perplexed."

"Phrenology has its abstruse dimensions," I told him. "Like poker and marriage. Maybe even horseshoes."

But he shook his head. "Nope, a joke won't help. That won't do it. That's not what I'm talking about. I'm talking about something else you were doing up there, which ain't got a name for it, so far as I know. It was the way you acted, mister. *That's* what it was!"

By now, he'd gotten my curiosity up, not to mention the crowd's. They were listening like he was speaking of hell fire, first hand. He was some orator, you could tell, and good at arithmetic.

"What was it?" one of them finally asked. He was a milk-eyed feller with cheeks pouched like a squirrel's.

The judge nodded. "Well, the longer I watched and *listened*, the nearer I got to figuring it out. And what it was, was: Here is a man who ain't never had to face up to life. Here is a man who acts like a little boy on a Sunday School picnic. There is something missing in this man, otherwise he wouldn't be so lighthearted and cocksure and smart up there on the platform. This critter hasn't learned his lesson of fear, yet! *That's* what I thought."

"Is that all?" the milk-eyed man asked.

"That's enough," the judge said.

The crowd thought about that a minute, but seemed generally to come to a different conclusion, because a few of them called out for the judge to get things started. They wanted a showdown, and even the drummer seemed to agree, because he started in drumming again.

So the judge didn't have any alternative except to give the command for everybody to go on over to the new courthouse, which was an unpainted frame structure considerable larger but not much more to brag about than the jail. We marched there, with the drummer who was practically a dwarf, beating time to our steps, and the bystanders cheering us like we were a whole company of militia passing by with flags flying.

There were more folks waiting for us, and they began to cheer, too. We might as well have been a traveling circus or the carriage of a prince. On the wooden porch of the courthouse there were two prim little chairs sitting about six feet apart, facing out toward the crowd. Stillingfleet and I were each led up to a chair and introduced to it, and then two men and a woman were brought forth. The men were introduced as "Caesar" and "Michael," and the woman as "Rebecca." You could tell that a lot of overnight planning had gone into this business. I studied the three of them, looking for signs of the harlot, the village idiot, or a local preacher. I figured they'd be up to some such trickery.

I figured Stillingfleet was doing the same thing. Damned if you couldn't feel the excitement of the crowd. It was like the change in the air before a thunderstorm. It looked like there was no way out: either Stillingfleet or I would suffer this day, because the mob was bent upon it, unanimous as a regiment of grenadiers. And the loser might be facing more than simple, everyday, down-home discomfort, because it's a well-known fact that tarring and feathering can bring about suffocation of the pores, and every now and then the star of the performance dies.

As a matter of fact, I could tell at a glance that the heads we were supposed to analyze weren't much, one way or the other. There wasn't anything exceptional about them. But the hush of the hundreds who crowded in front of the porch made the whole business seem pretty dramatic.

And don't think I didn't work at it. I concentrated harder than I ever had in my life, trying to ignore my toothache and feeling around with my good hand for subtler signs of Judiciousness or Imbecility, Compassion or the configurations of Moral Turpitude, that I might not have been able to detect at a glance.

When we got through with each analysis, we were given sheets of paper and pencils, and told to write down our findings. I found that I could stick a pencil up through the stiffened bloody rags of my hand and write pretty well. There wasn't a noise out of that crowd of people. They were stretched as tight as a rope on a house pulley. They were transfixed. In spite of themselves, they were fascinated.

I was studying the last head, that of Rebecca, and for some reason the thought of Lily de Wilde came to me. Then I looked up into the sky, and I saw two crows flying overhead. Right then and there I'd have sold my soul to the Baptists to be as free and uncomplicated as those crows, paddling their wings in the sweet clear air of Heaven. For a second I could visualize how things must look from the air: all the structures of mankind gliding like the sunken ruins of Nineveh and Tyre underneath those breezy trails.

But such was not to be, and before I could waste any more time thinking about the freedom of birds, our written findings were being read aloud to the mob by a dark-eyed old sinner who was wearing a mossy-green top hat that looked a little like Stillingfleet's.

To the average, untrained, home-grown ignoramus, our reports probably sounded pretty much alike, but I knew in a second that Stillingfleet's grasp of phrenology was practically nonexistent. He was a sham and a counterfeit. What he said about the head of the man named Caesar might have seemed pretty close to what I'd reported, but this wasn't the case. That charlatan's ignorance of the regions of Imitation, Marvelousness, and Hope was profound. In fact, I figured the frontal major region was pretty much an undifferentiated blur to his hands.

But the mob didn't waste time on what they probably figured were tiresome subtleties. They wouldn't have understood them, anyway, and they were by God going to have some fun at our expense, and nothing this side of the U.S. Army would stop them. A change of wind brought the stink of hot tar. They were concocting it over a big bonfire that had been built and stoked to roaring beside the blacksmith forge across the road.

We were given a chance to make a statement before the vote. This wasn't much of a surprise, because everybody likes a little argumentation and debate, and I figure this opportunity was given to us just to prolong the entertainment.

They told me to go first, and when I kind of hung back, one of them prodded me forward with a heavy, freshly carved ashwood cane I'd admired earlier. I said a few things, most of which I can't remember. I don't figure my talk was very well organized, though. I got in a couple of things about Albertus Magnus being one of the first to associate phantasia with the posterior regions of the brain, but I can't figure out why I brought this particular business up. I must have been rattled. But everybody listened hard, I'll say that for them. They even acted like they understood what I was talking about, which I considered a good sign.

Then I took off in another direction. I tried to get the idea across that I hadn't been trying to gull or milk them. I said that phrenology still had plenty of rough spots in it, no doubt, but it was an important part of the human critter's struggle to understand himself. Then I mentioned Stillingfleet and said I didn't know him or anything about him, so I wouldn't comment on his abilities as a man or phrenologist, but I could vouch for the fact that he had no more human decency than a garfish. I figured this was being magnanimous.

Then I wound up with what I figured was a pretty mild statement disapproving of what they were doing, and told them I hoped they'd soon learn better and get some sense into their damned thick heads. Along about here a note of anger and exasperation crept in.

After I sat down, Stillingfleet had his chance, and I could tell right from the start that things weren't going to go right. He got a preacher sound in his voice and told the following story: he said that during the night in our cell I'd come to him scared half to death about what was before us. He said I'd admitted I didn't know a human head from a hedge apple, and that I threw myself on his mercy, begging him to save me from the mob. So he'd agreed to take pity on me because of my obvious youth and teach me a few basic phrenological principles. We'd agreed beforehand to memorize certain things to say about the first, second, and third subjects we were given to analyze. Then he said he'd taught me a few key terms and agreed to say roughly the same things, so that we'd both come out looking like we knew our business and might therefore be vindicated and released without harm.

Then he said that after I'd milked enough phrenological information out of him, I'd grabbed him and started to beat on him, until he'd been forced to protect himself by any means possible, including the little knife he carried in his pocket. He said he could tell from the way his face felt that it bore evidence that I'd beaten him within an inch of his life. However, if *my* story was true, he said, would I be here to tell it? Could any of those present believe that a man with a knife could not kill an unarmed man if he chose to?

What he told that mob stunned me. I couldn't say anything and I couldn't move. I couldn't even think for a minute. Stillingfleet ended his talk by giving a plea for Christian forgiveness on my behalf, because of my youth and ignorance, and it was all I could do to keep from knocking him down and kicking him in the face. I wanted to grab him by the throat and wring it and twist his damned head off like a chicken's. I was so stupefied by his mendacity and cowardice that I finally went off like a bomb. I gave way and lurched in his direction, only a group of men grabbed me and pulled back. One of them tried to twist my right arm behind me, another hugged my left leg, and one of them had his arm around my neck. We twisted there like a family of acrobats for a minute, and all you could hear was our heavy breathing as we tussled. Before long, a considerable portion of my blood was on them as well, and the crowd watched with what you'd have to call fascination.

But they didn't shut my mouth, so I started in yelling and ranting.

I raved, cussed, and fumed. The crowd stayed as quiet as parishioners in the presence of a good sermon. I knew this, even back there behind all the noise. I don't think they'd ever seen a temper tantrum like this, and they were impressed.

Finally, I had to give up. I was out of breath and had to give up the struggle. They pushed me back down in my chair. There still wasn't a sound from that mob. Stillingfleet was looking off away from me somewhere in the direction of Canada and didn't move a muscle. The same two crows were drifting high up in the air. And seeing those two crows moving lofty and slow, it all of a sudden came to me that nobody was moving at all. Everybody acted like they were frozen for a minute right where they were.

Well, no doubt I'd made a fool of myself, the way I usually do when such fits come over me. But they always leave me feeling peaceful, like a mystic after a vision, and for a little while there, I wasn't any more anxious or scared than if I was about to mount a sweet-natured old mare and trot for a mile in the autumn sunshine.

Then I noticed something odd and completely off the point. A lot of white smoke was coming out of a chimney across the road. It wasn't just coming out of the top of the chimney, but out of the caulking, between the stones. That chimney was smoking like a steamboat pushing upstream, and it was leaking smoke all over like a big sieve.

Now it's true that chimneys catch fire pretty often, and usually it's not much in the way of a crisis, because a few pans of water thrown up against the smoldering bricks or stones will take care of it. But this fire looked to me like a more ambitious undertaking. It looked to me like this fire meant business, the way it was pouring thick clouds of smoke out of four or five different places, and nobody was attending to it. A fire like that might resent being ignored by a crowd absorbed in humiliating a couple of head readers.

While I was studying the matter, I saw one of the logs start to smoulder, and I took hope. I also got an idea. If I could just keep their attention long enough for that fire to get a good start, they would soon have their hands so full they'd forget all about Stillingfleet and me.

So I stood up once again and picked up where I'd left off in the yelling. I don't know what I yelled, exactly, but I do remember reciting one of Shakespeare's sonnets along with several Latin words that came to me in the fit of inspiration.

That mob paid me the courtesy of full attention, and by the time somebody discovered the fire, even the roof was beginning to smoulder. You could tell it was going to be a good one, in spite of last night's rain. There were also a number of buildings close by, so I knew the folks hereabouts were going to have their hands full if they wanted to save this town.

And such was the case. That mob went off like a charge of gunpowder when somebody yelled fire and they all spun around and looked where he was pointing. Never in my life have I seen pandemonium like that. They ran every which way but up and down, and they would have done that, too, if there'd been ladders handy.

I guess there were people with enough sense to run for water, but I didn't stay around to watch. In fact, a man next to me asked me sort of conversationally why I didn't take off. For a second or two, I didn't catch on, so he lost patience and said, "Now's your chance. Git!"

And that's exactly what I did. I said, "Yep," and took off. I don't figure I ran any faster than a lot of people there in the street; the only difference was, I knew pretty much what I wanted and went in only one direction.

My wagon was still standing there next to the schoolhouse, and Romulus and Remus were tethered nearby. I figured somebody had watered them. I figured people might be vicious and unfair to a couple of phrenologists, but they weren't going to mistreat a team of mules.

I harnessed them, and then remembered that I'd left two cranial charts in the schoolhouse. I hoped they'd still be there, so I tied the mules to a tree and took off like a scared buck, right on up to the door, which was open, even though this was a Saturday. I ran inside and saw a lot of books and papers on the teacher's desk, along with a considerable amount of the same scattered on the pupils' desks. But I couldn't find my cranial charts anywhere.

I stopped looking for a second and tried to figure out whether they'd been stolen or destroyed. This equipment is expensive and hard to get, so it was going to be a considerable inconvenience if I had to go off without it. I went back to the teacher's desk and shuffled through the drawers. I figured the mob would have plenty to occupy itself in fighting the fire. Maybe the whole town would go up. They'd probably forgotten about Stillingfleet and me by now.

Maybe I was in there five minutes looking. It's hard to judge. I took out my plug of tobacco and bit off a good chew. I got control of myself and slowed down, so that in a minute I was pretty calm, convinced that the mob had forgotten all about me.

Then I happened to look out the window and saw a Conestoga wagon banging on down the mud road, pulled by two cantering mules that lurched in the slippery tracks and splattered mud as they were whipped forward. A sectioned diagram of the human head, the sign of the phrenologist, was brightly painted on the side of the canvas.

It wasn't my wagon, but Stillingfleet's. And right then I figured out who'd stolen my cranial charts. How the bastard had gotten to the schoolhouse before I had, I'll never know. He must have shot off the instant the fire was discovered, whereas I had held back a minute to enjoy the spectacle. Although he might have been a fast runner. There's nothing in the skull to indicate fleetness of foot.

Right then I whirled about and raced to the front of the schoolhouse, vaulted over the wooden railing off of the steps, and ran to my wagon. I untied the mules, jumped up into the driver's seat, and whipped the beasts into a hard gallop.

In a couple of seconds, we were speeding across the bumpy grass, and then we settled into the deep tracks Stillingfleet had left in the road. We were on our way. The chase had begun.

Any time you meet somebody like Stillingfleet you have to stop and realize that you've been honored in a way. There aren't very many people in this world who are so pure in any way as Stillingfleet was in lunacy, cowardice, and villainy. A man like that is a little like a weasel or a pike — they're not admirable in themselves, because they're ugly and vicious; and yet they're admirable because, *for what they are*, they are pretty near perfect and considerable impressive.

6

But, to his native centre fast,
Shall into Future fuse the Past,
And the world's flowing fates in his own soul recast.
— Emerson

THAT ROAD was bad. It was clotted and syrupy with mud from the hard rain of the previous night. I was running my mules so hard in pursuit of Stillingfleet that it looked like I might go off the road or the mules might founder or the wagon get stuck. But I figured that Stillingfleet was hindered equally and I'd sure as hell catch him if determination played any part in the outcome.

He was about a quarter of a mile ahead of me at the time I'd sped away from the edge of town. The road here was bordered by an unbroken wall of sumac, elm, and yellow poplars. You don't often see roads this near town lined with unbroken timber.

There were times when I couldn't see Stillingfleet's wagon at all, because of the curves in the road. But I knew he had to be ahead of me somewhere, because there wasn't any place to turn off, neither trail nor path big enough for a wagon.

One time, right before his wagon disappeared behind a wall of trees, I saw him turn and look at me. I saw the top hat, and the pale blur of his face, and I fancied that even from that distance I could see the lineaments of Fear and Outrage etched upon it.

Gradually I began to close in on him. I could tell I was getting closer. I think he must have known it, too.

Then, rounding another bend in the road, I saw that his wagon had gone clear off and was tilted to the side. The right rear wheel was half sunk in the mud, and over the canvas top of the wagon, I could see Stillingfleet's top hat jerking back and forth as he stood up in front and whipped his mules.

But his frenzy was wasted, because that wagon was stuck for

good, and mine was coming up fast. When I got up to about forty
feet of him, I pulled on my reins and yelled "Whoa." Right then,
everything got still. All you could hear was Romulus and Remus
panting and the crack of Stillingfleet's whip.

I couldn't see Stillingfleet, and he didn't show himself until I'd
gone around to the rear of his wagon. My heart was beating fast,
because I figured he was a dangerous and unpredictable man, seeing
as how he was easily scared. All of a sudden he peered around the
edge of his wagon, and damned if he wasn't quivering a Deringer
at my face. "Do not step any closer," Stillingfleet commanded. His
voice didn't shake the way I figured it should have.

I stopped in my tracks and stared at that bruised and battered face
of his, which was pretty hard to believe. I don't mind admitting that
I was considerable uneasy, because it was obvious he had it in him
to pull the trigger. He didn't have any more morals than a fox.

"All I want is my charts and notes," I said.

"Raise your hands and step forward," Stillingfleet told me.

"Just give me what you took and cut out the sassafras," I told
him.

He shook his pistol at me and grinned. "You do what I say or
I'll blow your head off. Raise your hands and step forward. Now
don't you think that's a good idea?"

I took a good look at his pistol and said, "Yep, sounds good
enough," and did as he'd told me.

"Now," he said, "turn around and keep your hands raised."

I did, and then I heard the wagon creak as he climbed down.

"Now, go unhitch your mules and I'll get me a rope and you
can tie them to my wagon tongue and by God we'll pull her right
out. Yessir, pull her right out, like a spoon out of butter. She'll
come out easy as a charm. Yessir, two birds with one stone." He
talked like a man who talked to himself a lot. I know the type,
being one of them myself. You get so you talk to yourself in an
encouraging, cheery sort of way.

He got a rope from his own wagon, while I just stood there
holding my mules. Without them or the wagon, I could have taken
off, but that would have been to abandon everything I owned. I
didn't have a firearm of any kind in my wagon, my only weapons
being a long knife and a hatchet strapped under the seat.

So, even though I was considerable clumsy because of my hands, I managed to tie my mules to Stillingfleet's wagon tongue, just like he said, and then I commanded them forward, so that with both teams pulling, we finally got his wagon up out on the road.

"Now, untie them mules of yours and whip 'em away," he said.

That sounded like too damned much, so I told him he couldn't really expect me to do a thing like that.

"Oh, but I fully intend it," he said. And then when I didn't move right away, he just sort of shook his pistol up and down, still pointing it at me.

Well, there wasn't anything else I could do, so I walked up and untied Romulus and Remus and coiled the rope and put it over my shoulder. But by then I'd figured out a plan: I pretended to lead the mules out to a place where I could shout and yell at them, and scare them off, and then I moved around to the opposite side of Remus, and all of a sudden dropped the lead rein and coil of rope and took off on a run directly away from Stillingfleet.

I heard him yell out, but he didn't dare risk a shot because he knew he might miss, and then I could come back before he could reload and even with only one good hand grab him by his damned throat and choke the living breath out of him.

About a hundred yards away, I turned off into the woods. My legs ached considerable from running with all that mud clinging to my feet, and I was panting fit to die. Back in the woods, I stopped long enough to catch my breath, and pluck some of those big scabs of mud from my boots. But I didn't want to tarry, so I right away circled back toward the wagons, being careful to keep hidden in the underbrush.

I heard Stillingfleet yell as he chased one of my mules away, and then he did the same with another. All of a sudden I could hear the sound of hoofs splashing in the mud, and then Remus came crashing through the underbrush, right toward me, as loud as a herd of horses in the leaves. It stamped its hoof once, like it was saying hello, and then it just stood there and waited. I could hear Romulus crashing through the underbrush somewhere beyond.

I didn't go up and take hold of Remus. What I did was creep up as close as I could to Stillingfleet's wagon, where I saw him standing there by his own gee mule, holding on to its halter. He was looking back at my wagon. He probably figured I'd taken off for good, which is what he'd have done under the circumstances.

I didn't have any trouble figuring out what was going through his crafty mind. He stepped back from the mule and for a minute just stood there and looked carefully all around, to see if I was somewhere near. When he didn't see me, he took off slogging back to my wagon and climbed in. Then he started stacking my books and charts and other possessions on the seat, where he could throw them into his own wagon and make his escape.

I figured this was all the diversion I needed. I hunched down and moved as quietly as I could up to Stillingfleet's wagon and scrambled up onto the seat, quick as a terrier. Then I unwrapped the reins, lashed the mules, and yelled "Giddap!"

Those mules were considerable surprised, because my voice was different, and the gee mule skittered sideways. For a second there I figured it might pull us back into the deep ruts at the edge of the road. But the haw mule hunched forward, so I kept on yelling and cracked them good and hard with Stillingfleet's whip, and in a couple of seconds I had them plunging down the middle of the road, splashing mud in all directions.

I heard a little pop sound, which I figured was Stillingfleet's pistol being discharged. But the ball didn't even come close enough for me to hear it, so I gave out a big whoop that echoed in the woods and the mules relaxed into a fast canter, taking me at a good clip away from that vile son of a bitch.

That night when I made camp, I looked through my new possessions, and found out that old Stillingfleet had traveled in what you might call high style. One thing that caught my fancy was a wax bust of Daniel Webster, which I figured Stillingfleet had used in his demonstrations. It was lifelike, you could tell, and it was considerable inspiring to pass my hand over the noble physiognomy and cranium of the great Orator. If that bust was true to life, Daniel Webster was everything they said he was.

I felt good as I was lying in my bedroll that night. I figured I'd have a doctor look at my wounds and maybe have my tooth pulled. I figured things were looking up. I'd just gone through an ordeal pretty well, with flags flying, and by God I'd come out of it with more and better material possessions than I'd gone into it. I was pleased at the thought.

Then I made plans. I figured I'd buy a good dependable firearm and head westward and cross the Mississippi River. Then I'd proceed still farther west, lecturing and demonstrating here and there in the regions of western Missouri, and on into the Missouri Territory. Eventually I'd come out on the Great Plains, which I'd often read and heard about.

Yep, that's where I'd head. It was a good idea from every angle. I always was an optimist, as a lot of people had tried to tell me, and right then I didn't have any doubt that I'd made a decision I'd never be sorry for.

7

A great number of Indian heads and skulls, from many of the different American tribes, has fallen under the author's observation and inspection; and he had found, as a general feature common to them all, an extreme development of destructiveness, secretiveness, and cautiousness, together with a large endowment of individuality, eventuality, tune, conscientiousness, and veneration, and, sometimes, firmness . . .
— Fowler's *Practical Phrenology*

ONE LATE afternoon the next summer I was banging along down a barely visible trail toward Wellston's Ferry on the Missouri River. That trail wasn't much more than the part in a man's hair. It was a quiet, hot, early August day. The flow of wagon traffic on the main roads had dwindled to a trickle at this time of year, because most of the grass on the plains had died or been eaten by the oxen of the wagon trains the past spring and summer.

I was driving my mules at a good pace, and the Conestoga was rocking and groaning, and its contents were clanking and banging from the rocky shallow descent. The terrain was what you'd call pretty rough. I have always liked to travel off the main roads, pretty much the way I like to go alone, for reasons I've never quite figured out.

I'd planned to cross the river that evening, but the mules were tired, and I was thinking I might just as well make camp on the near side. I'd heard about 260 sermons on the subject of the dangers in traveling alone, but the message didn't take. Like now, for instance. This was a secondary, little-traveled route, and it was a general rule in those days that the farther west you traveled, the greater percentage of what you might call the criminal element you came across. It was a good thing that the area was no longer occupied by whole tribes of hostile Indians, even though there were a lot of renegades and half-breeds who'd steal your horses or cut your throat, if you gave them half a chance. But somehow, even though I knew all this for a fact, it just didn't seem to speak to me, personal.

I nodded along, half-asleep, toward the river, and then stopped for a brief rest. I got out and stretched my legs and then climbed back in my wagon. I just sat there a while, thinking, and then I cut a plug of tobacco and packed it in my jaw. I was about to ease over and spit, when all of a sudden I caught a glimpse of some quick movement up ahead and to the right of my wagon. It was only a big jackass rabbit, but it had been startled by something, so I twisted halfway around and grabbed my carbine.

It could have been a coyote that had jumped that rabbit from cover, but I had a notion it wasn't. And I was 100 percent right. It wasn't another animal at all. And it didn't look like a brigand, either. At least not the common sort. What came into sight at that moment was considerable hard to believe: it was an Indian of average size and proportion, walking along *backwards*. Right through the dense waist-high brush of the bottom land.

I reined in my mules and pulled up so I could take a good look at this funny business. For about half a minute I watched that Indian. He just kept on walking backwards through the bushes. He had to pause about every third step and edge this way and that through the scrub. But by God, he kept on going.

I didn't hardly move a muscle, except to lift my carbine onto my lap and give a quick scan of the area. I figured the Indian might be followed by enemies, and this might explain his actions.

The direction he was headed in was pretty much the same as mine, so our paths would cross at an acute angle about two hundred yards ahead. I decided to stay right there in my wagon with my rifle at ready, and see what was up. In a minute the Indian would be in a position where he couldn't help but see me. Of course, he might be walking with his eyes closed, which didn't seem too farfetched, when you considered that here was a man who'd walk backwards out in the middle of nowhere.

His eyes were open, though. When he'd gone about eighty yards to the front and right of my wagon, he stopped in his tracks and just stood there and looked at me.

Holding the reins in one hand and my carbine in the other, I yelled Giddap, and launched my wagon down the trail toward the Indian.

When I'd gotten about twenty yards away from him, I stopped my mules again and said, "Would you tell me just what in the hell you are up to?"

At first, he didn't answer. Maybe he didn't understand English. It looked to me like he might be an Osage. The top hat he wore was considered stylish by the domesticated Indians. He wore a vest over his bare chest and a breechclout over a pair of black cloth trousers that had the seat cut out to make them into leggins. He wasn't armed except for a Spanish knife stuck in his belt.

I picked up all this at first glance. When I asked once again what he was up to, he told me he was going to the river to drown himself.

"How's come you're walking backwards?" I asked. "You might miss it!"

He told me that it'd be pretty hard to miss a river as big as the Missouri, which was a good point.

I had an itch to ask about why he wanted to do away with himself, but I didn't. Instead, I took a good hard look at him. I noticed the slant of his forehead, the spacing of his eyes, the line of his mouth, and the depth of those adjacent lines that join its edges to the outer wings of the nostrils. I was trying to figure out whether he was an imbecile or just a desperate man. It looked pretty much like it was the latter. Then I persisted and told him I could understand a thousand reasons why a man might want to drown himself, but what I wanted to know was why he had to do it by walking backwards into the river.

He considered my question for a minute and this time it looked like what I was asking might have sunk in, so he told me he'd been disgraced among his people, and now he figured he'd do the only honorable thing, which was drown himself.

But I stuck in there, and asked him once again *why he had to walk backwards* to do something like this. Then he finally seemed to catch on and answered that he'd been walking backwards to his death because all his life was now behind him and he wanted to take a good look at it right before it all came to an end.

This made me stop and think a minute. It was logical, in an odd sort of way, and it was also what you'd have to call poetic. It was right then that I figured I'd try to help out the poor critter, so I told him if he was going to go to the Happy Hunting Ground, he might as well go with a full stomach. I told him he was welcome to join me for supper, such as it was.

When he didn't answer, I decided to play my ace card. "I have firewater," I said. And sure enough, right then and there, his face came alive and he gave a little nod. I figured that nod was his first step back onto the land of the living.

But even if it wasn't, it seemed the Christian thing to do. It's part of the Redman's nature that when they get dead drunk, they think it's like they've died for a little while, maybe even getting a taste of the afterlife. So I figured that this Indian might settle for some whiskey as a kind of substitute for the real thing. Even though the substitute was temporary, the Redman's sense of time is not what you'd call very accurate. The fact that something is only temporary doesn't mean a whole lot to them. They live by clocks that are considerable different from ours, indicated by the slant in their foreheads below the frontal eminence, where the Bump of Time is located.

So I took him in and fed him and gave him whiskey until he was sitting there by the fire gasping and singing every now and then, and making sort of kissing noises at the air. He was good and drunk, and he told me his name was Henry Buck.

"Burke?" I asked, not getting it right.

"Nope. Buck," he said.

Then he told me a little about his life. He didn't say why he was ostracized from the tribe, however, and I didn't ask about it, because I figured it wasn't any of my business.

Henry Buck finally staggered over to the edge of the firelight and sat down on the ground and then crossed his arms and rolled over and went to sleep. It was a warm August night, and he'd be comfortable lying there. For half an hour after he retired, I sat by the campfire chewing a considerable cud of tobacco and thinking about what a coincidence it was for me to come on this critter like that, just in time to save his life. Then I thought about what a coincidence it had been that that fire had broken out just in time to save Stillingfleet and myself.

I figure it was right about then I began to suspect that I might be one of the gifted ones that coincidences happen to in this life.

Overhead, the stars looked uncommon bright, and all around us, the wild land was silent, except for a soft night wind.

The next day, Henry Buck was considerable hung over, but otherwise he seemed all right. He acted like nothing had happened the day before. There wasn't any sign he was still feeling inclined towards drowning himself or stepping out in front of the loaded cannons of self-slaughter, as the poet Shakespeare put the matter.

I made coffee, which Henry Buck wouldn't drink, but he did join me in a breakfast of biscuits and salt pork and ate hearty as a young dog. I washed the pans and thought about the Osage and wondered where he'd go now that I'd stepped in and saved his life and had turned him around to walk forwards.

He didn't seem to be in much of a hurry to leave, however. He sat and watched me while I cleaned the pans, and then he asked me what the white man's writing on the canvas of my wagon said. He pointed to my name that I'd had painted over Stillingfleet's shortly after I'd traded wagons with him.

I told him that the words signified my name, Thaddeus Burke, and my profession, which was Physiognomic and Cranial Analyst. He nodded like he understood, and then kept quiet a minute while I harnessed the mules.

But then he couldn't stand it any longer, and he asked if I was a Head Reader. I told him yep, that's what some people called me.

Then sure enough when I was about ready to get started, Henry Buck took off his top hat and asked me to read his head. I'd already figured he was stubborn, so I didn't argue, but grabbed his head with both hands and treated him to a brief analysis.

I told him that his head showed a prominent Boss of Firmness (*Fermeté*), median, on the sagittal suture from the bregma to the front of the obelion directly on the top of his skull, along with convolutions signifying qualities of considerable destructiveness and secretiveness predictable in a savage.

You could tell he was impressed, even though I'd toned down my observations a little, which is something I usually do only when it's a paying customer, because nobody wants to spend money to find out he is by nature a scoundrel, cheat, whoremonger, rogue, spitlicker, liar, fool, or buffoon.

When I finished and asked Henry Buck where he was going to head for now, he didn't answer, so I let the matter drop and told him good-bye and good luck. This critter was deficient in talk, you could tell, probably because he didn't know much English.

I set off with my mules, not bothering to look back, but feeling morally satisfied that I'd done something worthwhile in saving a man from suicide, even if he was only an Indian.

But a few minutes later, I turned around in my seat, and by God, there was Henry Buck sitting on the rear of the wagon. He was going backwards again, but this time sitting on the tailgate of my wagon.

I asked him just what in the hell he thought he was doing.

No answer.

Then I repeated the first words I'd ever spoken to him. "Would you tell me just what in the hell you are up to?" I asked.

Still no answer.

The mules kept on plodding along, and I kept on sitting there, twisted sideways on my seat, trying to figure out the shadowy son of a bitch at the rear as he bobbed along loose-jointed, with what I fancied was something of a relaxed and proprietary air, to the bounce and jolt of the wagon.

Right then I figured out why I'd turned around. A shift of wind had brought to my nostrils the bouquet of Henry Buck's presence, by which I mean a faint aroma of rancid buffalo grease.

"Where do you think you're going?" I asked.

Still no answer.

Then an uncomfortable idea came to me. It's well known that if you save an Indian's life, you're judged to have assumed a kind of responsibility for him from that time on.

It felt like a cold draft had crept inside my coat right then and touched my backbone. It looked like Henry Buck figured I'd saved his life. I suppose I had, if you viewed the matter a certain way.

So now it looked like the two of us were mated in some sort of superstitious bond that, at least according to the way Henry Buck figured it, was sacred and indissoluble.

All the rest of that day, and all the day after, he followed me as close and quiet as a shadow.

Yep, it looked like he had it in his mind to stick with me, wherever I was and wherever I went.

8

Since, however, truth emerges more readily from error than confusion, we consider it useful to leave the understanding at liberty to exert itself and attempt the interpretation of nature in the affirmative, after having constructed and weighed the three tables of preparation, such as we have laid them down, both from the instances there collected, and others occurring elsewhere. Which attempt we are wont to call the liberty of the understanding, or the commencement of interpretation, or the first vintage.

— Sir Francis Bacon,
Novum Organum

ONE OF THE things that I'd inherited along with Stillingfleet's wagon was his personal journal. When I first started leafing through it, I kept trying to figure out what Stillingfleet had ever done that made him think he should keep a journal.

But then I got to reading it, and in spite of myself, I got interested, even though the farther I read, the worse that poor son of a bitch appeared. I'm convinced that a more pathetic lunatic has seldom learned to write his name, let alone a journal. It might sound far-fetched, but the truth is I could have predicted the character of this journal from my first glance at Stillingfleet. His face and head were not much, believe me.

I won't waste time on Stillingfleet's adventures, or on his philosophical observations, if you could call them that. The pages were filled with mistakes, some of them howlers. For example, he called the Mound of Veneration the *Mons-Venerationis*. I near split when I read that. I wished I'd had somebody to share it with. I guess just about everybody but Stillingfleet knows that it wouldn't likely be called this, since it sounds too much like *mons veneris*, which is the little fatty protuberance anterior to a woman's most precious possession.

After I'd finished reading the journal, I put it away with some other junk in a box I kept in back of the wagon. Then I'll be damned if I didn't start thinking the whole business over, and before you could crack your knuckles, I made up my mind to start keeping a journal myself. I figured if Stillingfleet could do it, why then I could do it considerable better. I wouldn't hesitate to write down philosophical thoughts, either. If Stillingfleet figured he had a right to do that sort of thing, why I'd raise his bid and do him one better. Not only that, I even started in writing a poem, here and there, which I figured Stillingfleet had never even thought about doing.

When I'd first given Henry Buck's head a reading, I thought about Stillingfleet's journal and that *Mons-Venerationis* business. The fact was, Henry Buck had a head that was mighty interesting. The Mound of Destructiveness (*Instinct Carnassier*) was pronounced in Henry Buck, just as Stillingfleet had claimed he could detect in my own cranium. This region is right above the ears. You can look at a dog's head, or any flesh-eating animal, and you'll see how developed it is.

Henry Buck's bulges of Secretiveness, right above, were even more developed. The Mounds of Causality, Comparison, Continuity, and Benevolence were pretty weak specimens, you might say, or in a state of marasmus.

I took stock of old Henry Buck, and this is what I came up with and jotted down:

> Henry Buck's history: uncertain
> Future: problematical, but probably unfavorable.
> Age: somewhere beyond thirty, maybe forty years
>   (hard to tell with savages).
> Height: average or a little more.
> Gaze: treacherous and sinister.
> Physiognomy: hooded.
> Features: impassive.
> Cranial Prominence: the Mound of Veneration.

It was that Mound of Veneration that caught my attention. I thought about it. I turned it over and looked at it from every angle during the next few days, and then it finally sank in. What did Henry Buck venerate? Henry Buck venerated *me*.

I wrote this down in my journal and called it, "The Passionate

Adhesion of an Unsought Fidelity." Samuel Chadwick would have approved of that phrase. I also called him my Shadow, which is kind of obvious, I suppose, but accurate when you think of Henry Buck's dark skin and the quiet way he moved. Also, he didn't ever have much to say.

Henry Buck had fastened on me like a tick. No matter how I shook it and looked at it, there wasn't any doubt but what he really *did* figure he'd spend the rest of his life with me. According to the way he saw it, he didn't have any choice in the matter.

We traveled on back into Missouri, where I learned how to make pretty good use of Henry Buck. I used him for demonstrations in a variety of ways. Between him and Daniel Webster's bust, I had a good portion of humanity mapped out.

I wrote in my journal that Henry Buck's cranium and physiognomy epitomized that inscrutability of the Redman that so fascinates the civilized, or even the partly civilized, segment of the population. I liked to write this way in my journal, now and then. Those pages seemed to bring out this kind of language in me.

Henry Buck's manner and appearance were just right for my lectures. Also, he was somebody I could more or less talk to during those long hours on the road. The trouble was, our conversations tended to be one-sided.

One day when we'd circled back almost to the Kansas border again, I decided to go on across and travel out onto the plains a way, and see what the heads were like out there in those sparsely populated parts. So I sent out some handbills with a young preacher named Hardacre, got provisions together, and made all necessary preparations. On the next day, we took off with the idea of crossing the river before nightfall, if the ferry was working and wagons weren't backed up waiting.

All morning Henry was silent. I was getting used to his taciturnity, but now and then it bothered me. Today, for some reason, he just didn't by God want to say anything at all, not even answer direct questions, let alone respond to any casual sort of observation I happened to feel like making. I figured this was carrying taciturnity too far.

Into the early afternoon we traveled in silence. I talked to the mules and recited a few of Shakespeare's sonnets and other poems, including one or two of my own, which struck me as holding up pretty good. I even whistled a little bit. If I'd had only a dog for company, I told myself, it wouldn't talk, either. Or a cat. A lot of people carried a cat with them on the trail, tucked into some little cranny of their wagon. A cat was something for the children to pet and make over and talk to, and it didn't eat much.

But when we came to a familiar scene late that afternoon, I got to feeling kind of nostalgic and said, "Henry, I'll bet you recognize this place, don't you?"

He looked like he might have been sound asleep, even though he was slouched over there beside me with his arms crossed. But I figured he knew exactly where we were. All Indians know that, even when they're asleep. And Henry was no exception. His boss or Mound of Locality (*Sens de Localité*, situated on the forehead above the inside of the eyebrow) was pronounced, which is characteristic among all the tribes I've had experience with.

When I asked him this question, Henry Buck still didn't answer, but just kept on nodding along beside me with his arms comfortably folded and his eyes closed.

Finally, I lost my temper and yelled at him. I told him I knew damned well he wasn't asleep, so why in the hell didn't he answer me? I carried on with a spit and a holler.

Old Henry still didn't come around, and I got so wound up that I finally cocked my leg back and kicked him clear off the seat of the wagon. I yelled at him. I sang a few choruses in a loud voice, at the end of which, I asked him how he could have the audacity to travel with me and eat my food and drink my whiskey and still not give me a civil word back when I asked a question.

By the time I'd finished with this flourish, the mules had carried me far beyond the place on the ground where Henry Buck had landed, so that I had to turn around and yell at him through the back opening of the wagon canvas. He wasn't anywhere in sight, so I didn't know for sure that he was still there on the ground, but I figured he probably was. I could picture him lying there with his arms still crossed.

I was about ready to rein in the mules and take a better look, when I saw him walking along beside the wagon. He still didn't say anything, but damned if he didn't climb up on the seat and sit down beside me like nothing had happened. It came to me then that indignation and wrath were probably worthless tactics when it came to Henry, so I shook the reins and chucked the mules on ahead.

A couple of minutes later, I explained that I'd only wanted to point out that we were passing the exact place where our paths had first crossed. I told him I'd never forget that first sight of him walking backwards as long as I lived. I told him I'd figured it might be worth mentioning.

Henry nodded and said, "That the place where you save my life."

"Yep," I told him, "that's what I was trying to point out to you."

9

The flora seems also to undergo a change. The grass was everywhere starred with large crimson anemones, a variety of the
helianthus, with golden blossoms, a velvety flower of the richest
brown and orange tints, white larkspurs, and dark-blue spi-
derwort. For many a league the country was one vast natural
garden of splendid bloom. There were places where a single
flower had usurped possession of a quarter-acre of soil, and
made a dazzling bed of its own color. I have seen nothing like
it, save on the hills of Palestine, in May.
> — Bayard Taylor's *Colorado:*
> *A Summer Trip*

ALL THROUGH July and into August we traveled up and down,
hither and yon. A couple of times we poked our heads out of the
rolling and lightly wooded hills of eastern Kansas and took a look
at the open plains. But mostly we stayed among the farming settlements, where the population was thicker and more settled. Many
times we stopped in settlements so small that even a one-night
lecture was too much for their population to fill a schoolhouse.
Sometimes we'd draw only ten or fifteen people for the occasion.
It wasn't that folks weren't interested. Some of them would ride
twenty or thirty miles, if they knew far enough ahead of time that
I was going to lecture and demonstrate phrenological truths and
show them a genuine, accurate wax model of Daniel Webster's
head.

A lot of times they wanted to know how I stood on the issue of
slavery. There were other issues they asked about, but it was slavery, mostly. Other issues could wait. Slavery was a subject on
everybody's mind. At first, I tried to explain that as a natural
philosopher, I didn't care much one way or other about partisan
issues. My goal was truth, I told them, not advocacy. I told them

my politics was knowledge, not the manipulation of the crowd by means of political contracts. I said my adversary was ignorance, not a segment of humanity which had principles and judgments that when you stopped to think about them were pretty much beyond your power to criticize.

But this wouldn't always work, in which case I'd have to figure out what the lay of the land was. I had to weigh the temper of those around me, and act accordingly. I don't take pride in this fact; but I'm not ashamed of it, either, and it has to be recorded. I'd be for the Abolitionists in one place, and I'd be a Slave Stater in another. I learned to judge with considerable accuracy and anticipate what they wanted to hear. "Is the Negro a human being or not?" was a question they'd put to me, and my answers would vary 180 degrees of the compass, depending pretty much on where I was and which way the wind was blowing.

This is hypocrisy, sure enough. But it seemed like a small price for me to pay so I could tell the truth about human proclivities, as I saw it. I figure no black man was going to be helped if I was shouted down, tarred and feathered, or shot dead in my tracks. And what benefit would there be for a Slave Stater if I wasn't listened to by the Abolitionists? I figured if I went along with audiences on both sides, I could have a shot at expressing some abiding and general human truths. Later on, these could be used as a foundation for the discovery of whatever political truth might be needed at the time.

I'd usually begin my lectures with a brief history of phrenology and say something about the founders of the science. I would tell about Spurzheim and Gall, Buchanan and Combe. I made a claim for the ultimate compatibility of religion and phrenology. I told my audiences that phrenologic science carried a message of hope, too, because you can't have hope without truth. Without truth, you've just got illusion.

There was one time when a drunk in the audience began to argue with me the minute I opened my lecture. This was at a schoolhouse in Council Grove, where they made up the wagon trains for Santa Fe and points west. Only it was late summer when I was there, and nobody was going to start out in a wagon train now, because there wasn't enough grass for the oxen.

Sometimes I gave my lectures in the oratorical style of Samuel Chadwick, and this evening was one of those times. Only this drunk didn't like it. He wouldn't let me say over ten words but what he'd interrupt. If he didn't have an argument to start, why he'd mimic me, repeating what I'd said with grand gestures and considerable r-rolling, and then turning around to grin at the audience. I got mighty sick of it, and decided to do something. I figured I'd had to put up with numskulls and scoffers for too long, and this one was too much for anybody to tolerate.

He was a man whose face was not only what you'd have to call unpromising, it was downright hateful. I invited him to step up on the platform with me, and he came ahead, slouching up to the teacher's desk and grinning out at the audience. He didn't even look at me. I don't think he would have if somebody had paid him. He was guilty and shiftless, inside and out, you could tell.

"What's your name?" I asked him.

"Samson Gaines," he said.

"Are you what you'd call a *resident* hereabouts?"

"Yep, I'm one of those."

His answer got some laughs, and I just sort of nodded, and pretended not to notice. I told him to sit down, and he did. I reached under the desk and pulled out a filthy rag I'd seen lying there, and then I used it to wipe my hands before touching Samson Gaines' head. The crowd kind of enjoyed this, and right then I could feel the weight of their sympathy shift away from him. Just a little, but I could feel it.

I gave his head a couple of pokes and said, "Do you *really* figure you want to know the truth about your head?"

Samson Gaines shifted in his seat and said, "Sure I do. I ain't afraid."

"In front of all these people?"

"Yep."

"It might take a lot of courage to face up to it," I said.

"I don't give a dadblame," he grumbled uncomfortably, shifting in his seat.

The audience was kind of snickering along about here. They were simmering, and all I had to do was bring them to a boil.

I nodded and grasped his head. It really was what you'd have to call a flawed vessel. It was deficient in just about every promising form. It was swollen with destructiveness and combativeness and practically devoid of sympathy and hope.

I guess I could have stopped right here and thrown Samson Gaines back into the crowd, the way you throw an undersized fish back into the water. But I didn't. By God, I let him have it with both barrels. If he happened to lack some vicious or humiliating quality, I gave it to him free of charge. I even invented a couple.

Maybe I should be ashamed for taking advantage of such an ignorant and worthless victim. I don't take much pride in the fact. But nobody could say he hadn't asked for everything he got.

When it was all over, Henry Buck and I got out of there in a hurry. I didn't like the atmosphere. It had gotten murky, all of a sudden.

All I wanted was a drink of whiskey and solitude. What Henry Buck wanted, nobody in this world or the next could have figured out.

10

Men of fierce temper bear themselves erect, are broad about
the ribs and move with an easy gait; their bodies are of a reddish
hue, their shoulder blades set well apart, large and broad; their
extremities large and powerful; they are smooth about the
chest and groin; they have great beards, and the hair of the
head starts low down with a vigorous growth.
— Aristotle in *Physiognomica*

THE NEXT morning, Henry and I took off and headed west. I didn't
want to follow either the Santa Fe Trail that veers to the south or
the Smoky Hill Fork, which Captain Fremont had opened up a few
years before.

I'd heard of a little-used trail in between these two major routes,
that led meanderingly to a town with the name of Shoestring, which
was a corruption of "Shostenengo," an Indian name of some kind
or other, and then joined the southern trail to Fort Dodge, where
it went on to join the Santa Fe. Not a whole lot was known about
this trail, and I wondered why. It was called the Walnut Creek
Trail by some people, and just plain Middle Trail by others. But
mostly people didn't much talk about it, one way or other, and
had no occasion to call it anything. In fact, it was hard to figure
out what that trail was doing there in the first place. Not to mention
Shoestring.

However, I got the idea that it was kind of a renegade trail, and
if you traveled on it alone, you were not very smart. But I didn't
let this bother me. I was in low and bitter spirits, of late. Even if I'd
given a damn, I might have risked it, because I was a good shot with
a rifle, and figured I could defend myself against pretty tough odds.
Not only that, Henry Buck's senses were as quick as a coyote's.

Also, my sip of whiskey the night before had gotten to be considerable more than that, and I woke up with nausea and a headache.
My breath would have poisoned a ten-acre swamp. When you feel

like that, a dangerous trail is not much. Neither is Death, or the Four Last Things. I took a hair of the dog that bit me, explaining to Henry Buck how this was a tried and true homeopathic remedy. Henry Buck was as bad off as I was, and he seemed to like the idea just fine.

After a couple of turns at the whiskey jug, we ate a big breakfast of pork and johnny cake and coffee, which made me feel a whole lot better, but kind of light-headed and vague. I decided to harness the mules and get a good trot on. Henry Buck was pure, 100 percent drunk again, and ready to go straight to St. Louis, Fort Dodge, or hell, whichever came first.

Along about noon, we came on a sod dwelling, where I figured we might be invited to eat something. But the minute we stopped, a great big gray dog attacked us. He was 100 percent vicious, with the yellowest eyes I've ever seen this side of a rattlesnake. I laid the sting of my whip on him once, but the damned thing managed to skip out of range most of the time.

A couple of seconds later, a woman came out of the soddy, and just stood there and looked at us without saying a word. That look she gave was one of great suspicion and distrust, beyond any doubt. She was a thin and mean-looking woman, and her skin was burned about as dark as Henry Buck's.

Finally, she asked us what in the hell we wanted, and when she opened her mouth, I saw a snaggle of teeth stained brown from tobacco.

I told her I was Professor Burke and said that my friend and I were hungry.

"I recognize ye," the woman said, and then she spit at her feet and stared at me coldly. "You and the Red Nigger both." She jerked her thumb at Henry Buck.

I picked up my reins and told Henry I figured there wasn't much use in our staying around.

"Not with you having a damned Red Nigger with you!" the woman yelled. "Not at this house! Not with you using all them big words to shame them who has to work with their hands for a living and do a honest day's toil! Showing off and such in front of everybody! Not with all them insults you poured over Samson Gaines' head! Let me tell you, you're gonna *hear* from somebody about that!"

All the time this was happening, that damned dog just kept on snarling with his head close to the ground and his yellow eyes fixed on us. The mules didn't seem to mind, even though I do remember seeing one of their ears sort of twitch.

"You don't know *nothing*," the woman screamed. "You don't know nothing at all. Go on back East where you belong. We don't want you out here. Go on! Git!"

I asked her who'd given her the right to speak for such a big country. Then I motioned with my hand at the openness beyond, but the irony was lost on her. She had the character of a pick ax, you could tell.

"Don't make no difference!" she cried. "We don't want you. You had your fun with Samson! Now git! You don't know *nothing*, do you hear?"

"I sure would like to get that head in my hands!" I muttered to Henry.

"Git out with that Red Nigger!" she screamed. "Git! Git!"

But I couldn't keep from yelling at her one more time. "Samson Gaines will murder you in your bed some night! He has the head of a killer. The most criminal head I've ever touched! I've seen weasels with better heads than his!"

"What?"she cried.

"You heard me," I yelled. And then I shook the reins and our wagon moved off down the trail, such as it was. We left that lunatic still standing there yelling at us, but the dog followed the wagon and kept on barking at the mules.

I laid the whip on the damned critter then, and caught it a good one right on the muzzle, which cleared its head of other thoughts and sent it screeching back to the mad woman, right where it belonged.

We kept on going all day and didn't see another soddy or dwelling of any kind. We didn't see anybody else on the trail, either, and the terrain had gotten considerable rough and wild. When we made camp that night, I told Henry Buck it didn't look like anybody'd taken this route since Moses had been a boy.

But that was nothing compared to what we found the next day. The terrain itself wasn't a whole lot worse, but the trail got bad.

No wonder people didn't come this way. It was said they didn't even take this route to Shoestring, and it didn't seem likely there were very many people who wanted to go to a place like Shoestring, anyway. I'd never found anybody who could tell me what Shoestring was *doing* out there, in the middle of nowhere.

I was getting kind of sorry I'd picked such a destination, let alone this trail. The land all around was treeless, but it was covered thick with the pale shrubs that are about all that can grow in such an alkaline soil and semi-arid climate. The ground underfoot was so rocky in places that the trail was hard to find.

I wrote in my journal while we were riding. I wrote a poem, and then described how we'd come from a land of long swells covered with buffalo grass and dotted with clusters of red and blue flowers into this mean and infernal landscape. I told how we saw some buttes that loomed like ancient ships abandoned forever in smoky silence way out there on the horizon, and antelopes bounded like ghosts along the near ridges half a mile away. I described how the prairie dogs occasionally sat up and stared at our progress, as if astonished to find humans venturing this far into a lost world. I mentioned hearing the cooing of the prairie chickens at dawn, which sounded like nothing on earth, except maybe a gentle and distant waterfall.

Now, on the farthest ridge to the south, a herd of buffalo could be seen, extending in its enormity like the inlet of some vast clotted brown avalanche over the land. This is the way I put it, all in a poetic vein, and I got it all down. Samuel Chadwick would have smiled.

It had been a long time since we'd seen any sign of a human dwelling or even of recent passage. This thing we were on was hardly like a trail at all. I turned around to Henry and said, "I figure maybe we drew a bad hand when we decided to come this way. I guess there might be some hostile Indians around, wouldn't you?"

Henry Buck didn't give me an answer and I had half a notion to kick him out of the wagon again. But he was the only company I had, and I figured he was maybe about 2 or 3 percent better than nothing.

I got to thinking about that crazy woman again, and this got me to thinking about Samson Gaines. I asked Henry Buck if he figured

I'd been a little bit too hard on the poor mean critter, and Henry surprised me by claiming that some of the things I'd said had been awful strong medicine, and not just anybody could stand up under them.

His answer irritated me considerable, I don't mind admitting. It wasn't what I wanted to hear. But I kept my mouth shut, for a change, and then I thought about it and explained to Henry that I hadn't really wanted the poor son of a bitch to come to any *harm*, particularly. But he'd mocked my oratory and tried to make a fool out of me. He'd asked for it, hadn't he?

Henry sat there as wise and quiet as a judge and seemed to ponder the matter. But after a while it came to me that he wasn't going to answer at all. Maybe according to him that hadn't really been a question I'd asked.

This possibility occupied my attention for a while, and then I told Henry Buck the story of Lily de Wilde. I told him how infatuated with her I'd been, and what a solid-gold fool I'd made of myself. I said, "Women can do that to a man, you know."

But the minute I said it, I realized that Henry Buck probably *didn't* know, because it didn't look like Indian women had much of a chance to make a fool out of their men. Still, you could never tell for sure about something like that. There was always a chance, if you were a woman with a woman's power, and enough cunning, and could bide your time.

Along about four o'clock, when we were hot and half asleep from our slow, rocking progress behind the mules, there was a great crack — loud as a rifle shot — and our seat lurched, firing both of us out of the wagon like two cannon balls. One of the mules staggered and then scrambled forward, while the other started to wheel about in a dance of confusion. The wagon heaved like a stricken animal. I scrambled to my feet and managed to run to the lurching mule and grab its harness. I was dragged about thirty or forty feet up a slight incline before I could bring everything to a halt.

When I got both of the mules calmed down, I gave the reins to Henry Buck and got down under the wagon to see what the trouble was. It was just what I'd figured. The right front wheel had dropped into a gulley and broken the axle. That gulley was covered with grass, almost like a trap. I asked Henry Buck if maybe it *was* a trap, but he said no. If the axle had not been broken, the mules would have taken the wagon away so fast I wouldn't have had a chance of catching it.

After I'd looked things over, I told Henry it looked like we were stuck.

"Axle, him broken," Henry Buck said, nodding.

"Yep," I said, "that's the problem, all right."

11

Nature intended him for a savage state; every instinct, every impulse of his soul inclines him to it. The white race might fall into a barbarous state, and afterwards, subjected to the influence of civilization, be reclaimed and prosper. Not so the Indian. He cannot be himself and be civilized; he fades away and dies. Cultivation such as the white man would have given him deprives him of his identity. Education, strange as it may appear, seems to weaken rather than strengthen his intellect. Where do we find any specimens of educated Indian eloquence comparing with that of such native, untutored orators as Tecumseh, Osceola, Red Jacket, and Logan; or, to select from those of more recent fame, Red Cloud of the Sioux, or Satan-ta of the Kiowas?

— *Wild Life on the Plains and*
Horrors of Indian Warfare

I TRIED to get it all down in my journal.

I thought of Samuel Chadwick and what he'd called the requisites of style. Now was the time for such emergencies. I was inspired, in a cussed sort of way. I tried to create word pictures of us as the sweltering afternoon sun descended toward the horizon and we sat there, helpless as puppies, waiting beside the lame wagon. I considered the long stretches of pale green buffalo grass, veined with purple bunch grass; the rock bluffs looming silently to the distant reaches of the southwest. I had them rising in fantastic shapes, like feudal castles, obelisks, fallen gargoyles, palatial ruins, and spires erected by madmen. Nature's Xanadu and Tyre. And I pointed out that "over all this, indifferently passed the eternal wind," which kept blowing my pages over as I tried to express the truth about it.

Finally, I put my journal aside and got practical. I asked Henry what he thought we ought to do. I pointed out that we couldn't very well leave the wagon here, because it had everything I owned in it.

Henry didn't say anything so I cussed a couple of times and got up and went over to the wagon and took out two long Virginia stogies from a carved and painted tulipwood box and gave one to him. When Henry Buck lighted his with a fancy sulphur match, his face lit up like a devil's in the shadow of his big top hat.

But what's the point of giving way to wrath? I've fought this foolishness all my life. It's connected with sassafras, and a little bit goes a long way. Right now the voice of philosophy asked me this question, and I decided I'd forget the whole business. Marcus Aurelius had the right idea. So did Epictetus. And after all, Henry Buck was the nearest thing to a friend I had at the time. I don't make friends easy, which is something a number of folks have tried to advise me about. I know it's the truth. There's something that is either missing in my character or else something extra that doesn't belong there. I've thought about this fact and have even looked for signs of it in my head, but no luck.

Finally, I blew a peck of smoke from my lungs and said, "Well, at least we're lucky we've got the comfort of tobacco. And what the hell, our water keg's nearly full."

"You gottum whiskey, too," Henry Buck said.

I told him that was God's truth, but I reminded him that a man was a pedigreed fool if he drank whiskey before the evening fire was lighted. I pointed out that this should almost always be an iron-bound rule.

But I'd said all this before, and I was thinking that right now might be another good time to break the rule. The fact was, loneliness sat on us like the shadow of a buzzard. It was getting to me, and the moaning of the wind through the grass and stunted bushes made you think of sin and eternity.

So I dug out the jug, and Henry Buck and I took a couple of drinks. Then I stood up and took the jug with me about seventy yards up to the top of a low swell. I figured this was a good place to look all around, because you could see for miles in every direction.

After scanning the horizon for a few minutes, I turned and studied my outfit, which was just about all I owned in this world. The wagon wasn't too bad, except for the broken axle. It was full up with provisions, along with a lot of books, pamphlets, salves, ointments, display notions, food supplies, and considerable miscellaneous items, including Daniel Webster's bust. One of the mules was slightly lame, and they couldn't match Romulus and Remus when it came to mule quality, but they were both strong and dependable. I figured the whole outfit might be worth about five hundred dollars, when the wind was right.

There was enough water to get us back to Council Grove if we had to turn back. I didn't like this idea because it would mean the loss of a few days. It would be better to move forward into a region of fresh heads, to the town of Shoestring, or Shostenengo, even though I wasn't sure how far it was, exactly, or what would be waiting for us there. Nobody seemed to know much about it. It was something of a mystery what a town was *doing* there. You could look at the map and see it was odd. All there was was the river, even though that's considerable in a dry land.

I stood there thinking for a couple of minutes, while Henry smoked and occupied his mind in ways it would be hard for a civilized man to pin down.

Then I noticed a tear in the canvas top of the wagon. It was right near the fancy Gothic lettering in black and red paint, which I had had painted over Stillingfleet's name, that said:

PROF. THADDEUS BURKE
CRANIAL ANALYST

The memory of the audience at Council Grove, including Samson Gaines, hadn't left my mind for long, and now it all came back to bother me. There is no doubt a cussedness in our natures that causes us to kick at the truth with both hind legs. Mind, spirit, passion . . . all those qualities that make human life worthwhile have to come from some place that's as real and down-to-earth as pig iron and taters, or flesh and bone. The empiric base of phrenology proclaims this fact, which I've tried to explain many a time.

I thought about this for a while, and then looked up and was surprised to see a tiny cloud of dust far off in the distance, two or three miles away. Maybe four.

There was no doubt about it. *There* was an empiric fact. Something was out there, all right, and whatever it was, damn if it didn't look like it was headed this way.

12

My attention was next attracted by a sprightly lad ten or twelve years old, whose nationality could scarcely be detected under his Indian guise. But, though quite Indianized, he was exceedingly polite. I inquired of him in Spanish, "Are you not a Mexican?" "Yes, sir — I once was." "What is your name?" "Berbardino Saenz, sir, at your service." "When and where were you taken?" "About four years ago, at the hacienda de las Animas, near Parral." "Shan't we buy you and take you to your people? — we are going thither." At this he hesitated a little, and then answered in an affecting tone, "*No, senor; ya soy demasiado bruto para vivir entre los Cristianos*" (O, no, sir; I am now too much a brute to live among Christians); adding that his owner was not there, and that he knew the Indian in whose charge he came would not sell him.

— Josiah Gregg's
Commerce of the Prairies

I POINTED out to Henry Buck that there was a cloud of dust in the distance. I pointed out that this signified the approach of riders, or maybe even a wagon. Or two or three wagons, who could tell?

Sometimes it gave me a kick to explain the obvious to old Henry. It was a way of getting back at him for his ways. If he wanted to act stupid, why that's the way I'd treat him. I'd oblige him right down to the finish line.

"They been coming along about half hour now," Henry said, nodding past his segar. Even though he didn't have much temporal sense, and for him half an hour could mean any length of time from five minutes to all day, I didn't doubt but what he'd seen that distant feather of dust long before I had.

So I asked him why he hadn't told me about it, but all he said was, "Plenty time him get here."

I thought about this and just stood there and watched. And then

I noticed something odd: you would have thought that growing cloud of dust would prove encouraging and cheer me up, but for some reason it didn't. In fact, I was a little bit uneasy. It was a premonition, one of the few genuine premonitions I've ever had. I figure it might have had to do with where we were, because everybody said this was an odd trail, leading to an odd place.

So I armed Henry with the carbine and checked the loads in my pistols, even though I figured I'd keep them tucked inside my belt. It wouldn't be a good idea to show fear to these strangers, whoever they were.

They kept on coming closer. I was disappointed to see that there wasn't any wagon. It was just four horsemen plodding along, one after another, on the same trail Henry and I had traveled that morning.

Then, before long, I could see there was something mighty peculiar about them. When they got about two hundred yards away, I could see that one of them looked like he was about twice the size of the other three. In fact, he was a giant. The horse that carried him was a draft horse, but even so, it must have swayed and panted under so much weight. That giant's legs almost touched the ground. His features were brutal and the expression sorrowful underneath the long tangles of hair that blew in the wind. His supra orbital ridge was low and massive, like the brows of the higher simians. His eyes were almost invisible in the deep shadow of the eyebrows. His mouth was twisted in what looked like a permanent grimace of pain, bitterness, or melancholic dissatisfaction.

He was dressed in an enormous overcoat of military cut that you could tell had been specially made for him. And yet it was too long, even for him, except for the sleeves, which were too short, so that his wrists stuck out of the arms of that coat like two stained and varnished newel posts. And the dark, sunburned hands that held the bridle looked about the size of hayforks with tines like ax handles.

Henry Buck and I just stood there and stared as these critters rode up. I'm not sure about Henry Buck, but I couldn't take my eyes off the giant. He was far and away the most stupendous human production I ever laid eyes on.

But he hardly took notice of us. He didn't return the compliment. No doubt he was used to amazement and took it for granted.

It was the first man who saluted us, and when he did, I took a good look at him and was surprised to see that in his own way he was about as monstrous as the giant. He was average sized, though sturdy built with a head that looked permanently reared back on his neck, like he was about to yell whoa. He wore a deerskin jacket that was near black with age, filth, and sweat. A wide, loose-brimmed felt hat sort of flapped around and kept his face in shadow. But this shadow was not enough to hide the fact that he had the divided face of a harlequin. Half of it was bearded and normal, but the other half looked like the skin had been raked or clawed off. It was striated and eroded, maybe from some kind of burn or blast. This part was hairless and devoid of eyebrow as well as mustache and beard. And smack dab in the middle of that scarred and wrin-kled skin was set a pale, blind orb that had once been a living eye, but now looked more like a white grape stuck in a bleached and wrinkled patch of river mud.

This was the critter who spoke up and called out to the giant, "Well, what do you think, William Bone? What sort of outlaw's wagon do you reckon we have here before us?"

The giant answered in a bass voice that echoed like it was coming out of a canyon: "There is no telling."

I figured that Half Face was the leader of this little band. He talked like it and carried himself that way.

Since his head was pretty much covered with that big floppy hat, and there wasn't a whole lot left of his features, I couldn't get a good reading of his head and physiognomy, but in spite of that fact, right from the beginning, I had this critter figured for an utter misfortune. I muttered as much out of the corner of my mouth to Henry Buck. I told him to keep the carbine handy. It looked like the barrel might be heated up before long.

Half Face crawled off his horse like he was tired as sin. He wiped one hand over his blasted visage and with the other led his horse forward. Right then, the giant William Bone also dismounted. But when he was standing on his own two feet, he looked like more of a mountain than before.

"Quite a sight, wouldn't you say?" Half Face asked. "Gives me a kick ever time when people first sees him!"

The giant said nothing, but led his horse forward, blocking out the other two members of the band.

"Looks like you got trouble, Old Hoss," Half Face said to me, nodding at the wagon. "Looks like we come along just about the right time."

I was mighty wary, but I nodded and said, "Yep, you got it figured out."

The other two men dismounted and led their horses around William Bone, so that they were all right there before us, lined up and, if you weren't too close, looking like a man and three circus midgets. One of the other ones was a weak-looking critter wearing a top hat. The fourth was a young Comanche Indian, which fact struck two ways, dangerous and odd. What was the likes of him doing traveling unmolested and alone with three white men, up here considerable north and east of the Comanche land? The settlers hereabouts happened to be between Indian raids, but the memory of the last one was still as fresh and bloody as a new sausage, and the anticipation of the next was what you might well call vivid. This brave looked like he was only a boy of about thirteen or fourteen. Even though he wasn't given to talk much more than Henry Buck was, we later found out that his voice hadn't even changed yet. And the red cotton tunic he was wearing was two or three sizes too large, big enough for a man, but it sagged on his tiny little shoulders and flapped around his middle.

All four of them stood there in a line and kind of stared at us. And we just stood there and looked back at them. Nobody said a word, and later on I wrote it all down in my journal: how for a moment we must have looked in this unreal tableau there on the wild plains, with the wind blowing and whipping our clothes. I had a feeling that everything had all happened long ago, many times, and I could almost sense what would happen next.

But I couldn't quite manage it.

Pointing his finger at me, Half Face broke the spell and said, "Say, I know who you are! You're that damned Head Reader. I saw you perform that act of yours a year ago, way back in Missouri somewhere!"

I took a good long look at him, but I'll be damned if I could remember ever seeing him. I figured if he'd been in an audience of five hundred, I'd remember him. But I played along with his game.

"Whereabouts in Missouri?" I asked him.

"Blamed if I can remember," he said. "But I was there. You read a bunch of heads like they was so many newspapers. Man, woman, child, and in-between! Least I *think* it was you."

Right then I got a suspicion. "It wasn't some bastard named Stillingfleet, was it?"

Half Face frowned out of the living part of his phiz and shook his head. "I don't recollect that name. But I thought it was you. It was one of you Head Readers all right. Wore a top hat and used big words."

"Never mind," I said. Then I told him that we didn't have much in the way of food, but we had some whiskey, and I asked if they'd like to have a little.

"*Would* we!" Half Face exclaimed. "Now that is what I call a real question. How about you, William Bone? How about you, Crawford?"

The critter in the top hat nodded and grinned, and the giant simply nodded, while the Indian boy didn't move or show any more expression than the average pumpkin or grave mound. Half Face came up to me and said, "You just fetch us that whiskey and we'll sit right down and have us a cozy chat together."

I told him about the broken axle and said I sure hoped they could help us fix it.

Half Face said, "Oh, you ain't got nothing to worry about *there!* Ain't that right, William Bone? Ain't that right, Crawford?"

William Bone just heaved a great sigh and looked away without answering, but Crawford grinned and nodded with a couple of rapid darts of his head.

Right then, I snatched my two pistols out of my belt and yelled for Henry to cover them with the carbine. I figured we had the drop on them, but I was surprised to see that Half Face didn't jump or even quiver. He didn't react any more than if I'd said we needed rain. He didn't draw his Navy revolver and he didn't even look alarmed. Instead, he chuckled and said, "Why, you ain't got nobody to back you up, Old Hoss! Just take a look at your Injun friend. And then drop your pistol, forget the fandango, and go and get us some of that popskull whiskey."

I figured it was a trick, and at first I wasn't about to fall for it. But when I asked Henry if he had them covered and didn't get an answer, I began to suspect the worst. I figured this was one time when Henry would be sure to answer. I asked him again and still didn't hear anything, so I finally turned and took a quick look, and sure enough, that damned Henry Buck was just standing there staring at William Bone. It looked like it had taken considerable time for the giant's size to sink in, as far as Henry was concerned.

At some other time, I wouldn't have blamed him for acting this way. But right then I was sorry I had taken the trouble to save Henry Buck's miserable life.

Well, there was nothing to do but drop my pistols and go to the back of the wagon, where I crawled up inside and lifted out the jug I kept there beside Daniel Webster's bust. Crawford stood directly behind me, holding my own carbine pointed at my kidneys.

When I turned around, I saw Henry Buck talking to the Indian boy in a bastard Comanche, slapping out a little sign language in obbligato. William Bone had picked up my journal and was leafing through it, while Half Face was watching me with his two hands resting on the handles of his service revolvers. His bad eye glowed like a polished stove in the late afternoon sunlight.

"Hurry up with the whiskey," Half Face said. "I ain't been drunk in two and a half days, going on six!"

I tossed the jug to him, and then we all sat down in a circle and drank in turns. Before long, the four of them seemed to be considerable drunk, although I wasn't in much shape to judge.

William Bone kept on reading my journal as we drank, only half listening to the conversation of Half Face and Crawford, which was about what it was worth.

Finally, he tossed the notebook on the ground, and said, "I see you keep a journal."

"Yep," I told him.

He nodded. "Why?"

"For my descendants," I said.

"You're married, then? You have a family?"

"Nope, not yet. But I figure to get married at the right time. I'm waiting for the fit mate. I figure I'll know when I see her, and then I'll have the bonds tied quicker than spit."

"What good will this journal do your descendants?"

"It's for their edification," I said. "A body ought to know where he comes from, and I figure it's a good idea to get everything you can down on paper, since Man is a critter large in discourse, looking before and after. That's a quotation."

William Bone took a long look at me out of a solemn expression, but Half Face said, "You know, I kind of like the way this old hoss talks, William Bone!"

He shook his head admiringly and took another drink.

Then Crawford started singing some song about a Mexican maid, but no one bothered to listen. Crawford was born to be ignored, you could tell.

"The Professor is also something of a poet," William Bone said a minute or two later, with an expression on his face that I couldn't quite make out.

"How would *you* know?" Half Face asked suspiciously.

"There are poems included in this," the giant said, tapping my journal with his huge forefinger, like it was evidence in a trial, and he was the prosecuting attorney.

"Well, then, read us one of them damn poems," Half Face said. "I'm long overdue for having me a little fun!"

"I would prefer," William Bone said, "to hear them pronounced by their author."

"I don't always feel like reading them aloud," I said, "unless the conditions are right."

"Read 'em anyway, and forget the hoss piss," Half Face said. "Or maybe I'll shoot you in the gut. Now how does that sound? Don't that sound like a good idea, to read us a poem?"

"Yep," I said. "Sounds good enough. But I don't have to read it. I've got most of them by memory."

"Let us hear 'The Venerative Pod,' " William Bone said.

I nodded and stood up. Then I recited as follows:

THE VENERATIVE POD

The terrapin, the toad, the foolish loon,
The pig, the dog, the squirrel, the low baboon,
The elephant, with his prodigy of trunk,
The mule, the ox, the humble, fetid skunk,
The bison, copperhead, coyote, and all
Those creatures fixed inside a brutal skull . . .

Each is sentenced to perform his meager part
In a play devoid of genius, plot, and art,
And condemned to walk a meaningless terrain
Of pleasures doled by chance and random pain,
Deprived of even the questing guess of God
Because each lacks the venerative pod!

Crawford applauded and whistled, but everybody else managed to keep themselves pretty well under control. They didn't give any more response than Henry Buck.

Finally, William Bone got a faraway, judicious look on his face and said, " 'The questing guess of God' is not bad."

We were all quiet a couple of seconds, taking that in, and then Crawford started singing about the Mexican maid again, and once more, nobody bothered to listen.

A few minutes later, Half Face leveled his revolvers at me and commanded me to read his head. I didn't argue with him, and I gave him enough lies about hypertrophied zones of Benevolence, Constructiveness, etc., to choke a snake. But Half Face swallowed them all without any trouble, nodding thoughtfully at everything I said.

After that I read Crawford's head, tossing him another little bag of lies, and then I clasped the great head of William Bone in my hands. It was almost shoulder high, even though I was standing and he was sitting on the ground. I would have found it quite a study, if conditions had been a little better. As it was, I reported on it at some length, which was only appropriate, considering the subject.

But Half Face wanted more, so I finally gave in and had the Comanche boy come over and sit on the ground beside me. At the first touch, I felt there was something wrong. Something was not right, but I couldn't figure out what it was. No doubt part of my confusion came from the fact I was considerable fuddled from the whiskey.

But even though I was drunk, I could tell that this Comanche had just about the finest head I had ever clasped my two hands around. It wasn't like the heads of most Indians, which are flat in back from the papoose board. No sir, that head was near perfect. The feel of that head could have penetrated the whiskey in me if

I'd drunk a barrel. It was like the shock of a galvanic battery in its balance and symmetry. The primary regions as isolated by Gall were in perfect harmony.

My first thought was one of exasperated longing: why was a head like this wasted upon a boy? If those qualities had belonged to a girl, she would have become the kind of woman who shines in the dark.

And then I thought of one of those Shakespeare sonnets that Samuel Chadwick had challenged me to memorize. Right then and there, I recited that whole sonnet, out loud, even though I figured the Comanche boy didn't have any more idea of what I was saying than a magpie or coyote.

> A woman's face, with nature's own hand painted,
> Hast thou, the master-mistress of my passion;
> A woman's gentle heart, but not acquainted
> With shifting change, as is false woman's fashion;
> An eye more bright than theirs, less false in rolling,
> Gilding the object whereupon it gazeth;
> A man in hue, all hues in his controlling,
> Which steals men's eyes, and women's souls amazeth.
> And for a woman wert thou first created;
> Till nature, as she wrought thee fell a-doting,
> And by addition me of thee defeated,
> By adding one thing to my purpose nothing.
> But since she pricked thee out for woman's pleasure,
> Mine be thy love, and thy love's use their treasure.

13

Methinks I have outlived my self, and begin to be
weary of the Sun; I have shaken hands with delight;
in my warm blood and Canicular days, I perceive
I do anticipate the vices of age; the World to me is
but a dream or mock-show, and we all therein but
Pantalones and Anticks, to my severer contemplations.
— Sir Thomas Browne

HENRY BUCK was the first to pass out. He got to singing, and
then staggered over to a clump of weeds and pitched himself head-
long into them, still singing something that was unrecognizable.
It was part Osage, part English, and all drunk. Maybe it was his
death song. Who could tell? He kept on singing even after he was
capsized over there in the weeds, and then all of a sudden he just
stopped, and except for the constant whirr of the wind, everything
was quiet.

Crawford sort of laughed at the spectacle, although he was hardly
in any shape to laugh at anything. The Comanche just sat there
and watched.

I took a deep breath and said about as clear as I could, "I'll tell
you something: I would like to satisfy my curiosity regarding one
thing. I want information on one extraordinary phenomenon. I
want to be informed."

Half Face shook his head and said, "Professor, how's come you
don't speak American, since you are among American people."

I told him I was speaking American.

"That's right," Crawford said, nodding. "He's speaking American, all right."

"Shut up," Half Face said, without bothering to turn his head.
"Now, professor, you tell me what it is you want, and maybe I'll
see that you get it. Then again, maybe I'll see that you don't! Fair
enough?"

"Yep," I said. "I suppose that'll have to do."

Right then William Bone acted like he suspected something. He stood up and came near to blocking out the setting sun. His overcoat hung on the horizon like an open tent, and his hairy head loomed like the crown of a shaggy tree in the distance.

"Well, what is it?" Half Face said.

"What I would like to know is, exactly how tall is William Bone, and how much does he weigh?"

Half Face laughed and pounded the sod with his fist. "If that don't beat all *Rachel*! Here's this critter who has to figure he's just about ready to go the way of all flesh, and he spends his time wondering about William Bone!"

Crawford joined in the laughter, but William Bone himself was silent.

Finally, Half Face calmed down enough to say, "Well, I can't tell you within a inch, because to my knowledge they ain't nobody been able to climb high enough to find out for sure, figuring as how they'd get a nose bleed; but I reckon William Bone is somewheres around eight and one half feet tall, maybe taller by half a foot or so, and weighs somewheres between four hundred and six hundred pounds. Wouldn't you say that, William Bone?"

"I have no comment to make," the giant said.

"Come on," Crawford said. "Just how big *are* you, anyway?"

"That is between me and my Maker," William Bone said. Then he turned around and walked away.

"I'll tell you one thing," Half Face said, "they ain't much *else* between him and his Maker, being he is so dadblamed *tall*!"

He was considerable tickled by this numskull cleverness and damned near kicked over from laughing. But he survived, as bad luck would have it. Crawford kind of snickered along with him, but nobody else got much of a laugh from the joke.

William Bone was standing off by himself and gave no sign that he was even listening.

Along about dusk, Half Face staggered a couple of steps, pulled out his two revolvers, and said, "Let's stop all this fool talk and put them both out of their Goddam misery." That was a surprise because nobody had said anything for about ten minutes. Maybe Half Face had conversations going on inside his head that the rest of us couldn't hear.

"Aw, don't kill them now," Crawford said, "they's too blamed much fun for that. We ain't had much company of late."

I didn't like this much, so I delivered a brief lecture on the wages of sin and crime, especially the latter. Even though that lecture was brief, it had considerable eloquence, if I do say so myself. At least, as I remember it, which isn't very well.

After I came out of it, Half Face just sort of stared at me and blinked. Then he looked at William Bone, and seemed about ready to ask for a legal opinion of what I'd said, but he didn't follow through with it. He just shook his head back and forth several times and said, "You sure do talk a lot, Professor!"

"He's more fun than we have had in a long time," Crawford pointed out.

"Crawford," Half Face said, "you are right, for once in your miserable, no-account life. And I am one of those that likes a good time! Yessir, I always *have* been like that! All my life, I've liked to have a good time. I've always liked to kid and joke around. And why not, I tell people. I ask you: why not have yourself a good time?"

He went on and on like this, slowing down now and then, after which he'd wind up and start all over again. It turned out that Half Face really did like a good time. It was true, you could tell. He said so, in various ways. You would have thought this was an argument of considerable subtlety the way he went on and on, repeating himself.

For a while there I thought he might have outdone Samuel Chadwick, in the way of repeating himself, but that would have been laying it on pretty thick.

It was William Bone who finally interrupted him right when Half Face had stopped to take a breath.

"I think we should kill them now," William Bone said.

That took me by surprise, because there wasn't much doubt that William Bone was the most highly developed and the most intellectual of these four critters, and here he was casting a vote for our murder.

"No," Half Face said. "Crawford is right. We will tie up the two chickens until morning, and then we will see which way the sun shines. Then we'll cut a fresh deck of cards. There is still more to be milked from these here wayfellers."

"You are making a mistake, if you ask me," William Bone said.

"Well, that may be," Half Face said. "But Crawford and I agree that such is the best thing to do, under the circumstances. There's little enough entertainment in this barren, godforsaken country, not to mention fun."

I peered over in the direction of Henry Buck, but it looked like he hadn't moved an inch. All I could see in the firelight were the dark bottoms of his moccasins, the heels as smooth as two fire-blackened spoons sticking out of the brush. It was hard to tell if he was breathing or not, although I figured he probably was.

By now, the stars and moon were beginning to come out. I heaved a big sigh and tried to focus my thoughts. Right then, taking stock of the situation, I was damned near ready to give up and toss in my hand.

Then William Bone went over to Henry Buck, grabbed his ankles, and dragged him on his face back into the firelight, which got him to snoring. Crawford and Half Face proceeded to bind him hand and foot with leather straps.

Damned if old Henry didn't entertain them by mumbling a couple of times while they were tying him up! This was considerable eloquence from the son of a bitch, and I said so, but nobody paid attention.

Then they tied me up and laid me on my side, facing the low dancing flames of what in other circumstances might have been considered a cheery little fire made of buffalo chips.

14

There is said to be "Gnashing of teeth" in hell; and I have
plainly heard the grinding of the molar teeth of a cow which
was suffering acutely from inflammation of the bowels.
— Charles Darwin, *The Expression
of the Emotions in Man and Animals*

I COULD hear them talking somewhere on the far side of the fire
while I was lying there trying to think of a way to escape. Henry
Buck had taken up snoring in earnest, and if he'd been closer, I
would've given him a few kicks just to wake him up so he could
share in the suffering.

The Comanche had crept off somewhere into the darkness to
sleep, and eventually the three outlaws gave the impression they
were fixing to do the same.

But about an hour later, when I figured they were all sleeping
off their whiskey, a giant shadow loomed beside the fire, and I
twisted my head and raised my eyes to see William Bone standing
there with the jug in his hand. He looked like he might be about
ready to totter. He looked like a tree with the trunk almost chopped
through.

"I noticed you were surprised," he said, "when I recommended
that you and your companion be shot without further ado. If you
were to understand something of my history, though, you wouldn't
be surprised, nor would you blame me for casting my vote for the
death of any fellow human, since I myself don't place any value
on my life and, like Sophocles of old, consider that man happiest
who is about to shed all the follies of his miserable adventure on
earth."

In spite of the danger we were in, William Bone's way with the
English language gave me cause to wonder. I could tell that here
was no run-of-the-mill cutthroat, but a man of cultivation. His

speech was every bit as proper as Lily de Wilde's, and considerable more erudite. So I couldn't help wondering what might have brought him to his present state.

And it looked like he was about to tell me, because he started right in talking again. "Although I did indeed express my conviction that you and your companion should be shot," he said, "this should not be interpreted as insensitivity or cruelty, for it is neither more nor less than what I would wish for myself. But I have not yet renounced all moral bonds, and it must be clear to you that I owe allegiance of a sort to my two companions. The Indian boy is merely a guest on our journey. He has joined us for protection from such as ourselves, and it amused Half Face to bring him with us under that illusion, and — with the impetuousness and artlessness of such men (for Half Face has all the qualities, including innocence and limited intelligence, necessary for leadership) — he will undoubtedly keep his pledge, and release the boy at the end of our journey."

William Bone paused thoughtfully, and then tilted the jug once again, making it gurgle like a washtub. "When you were analyzing our characters an hour or so ago," he went on, "I was aware of something that the others were not aware of. Understandably, you flattered them, hoping to gain their favor, for it was evident that already you'd surmised that your life was in danger. I was aware of your motive, and I do not condemn you for it. You attributed almost every virtue, and scarcely a single vice, to the two men whom you really judge to be characterized by utter villainy. In the eyes of the civilization that fostered them, they are brutes; and you knew it, needing not the least help from the sciences of physiognomy and phrenology to ascertain this fact."

The giant paused and then sighed and eased himself to a sitting position beside me, next to the fire, in order to continue his speech. "And yet," he said, "I was aware of a different tone in your voice, a diction slightly altered in its nuances, when you analyzed *my* head! Men are everywhere, and without exception, vulnerable to flattery, so of course my two companions believed every possible virtue you managed to find in them. But when you discoursed so skillfully about the features you saw imprinted in *my* head, I was shocked to realize that now you did not have to resort to lying flattery, for you were speaking only the truth. How accurately you expressed my innermost sensations! How swiftly and unerringly you discovered my own most secret convictions! Here, I told myself, in contrast to what you had said about Crawford and Half Face, you felt no compulsion to speak any word other than what the evidence beneath your two hands commanded to be spoken."

Again the giant stopped and took thought. In the darkness, I could see him look up at the stars. It was like he figured he could make out the configuration of human truth up there in that ancient inhuman script of the heavens.

He sighed, shook his head and went on: "How great, then, considering this admission on my part must seem to you my betrayal in wanting you and your companion killed! Let me explain it as best I can, and trust in your own acumen to perceive the truth of my words.

"When I was a boy, I grew too fast, far too fast, and I was often aware of my parents looking at me in alarm at the excess of my growth. They were worried about me from the age of ten, when I had already attained the growth of a large man. I remember once that my crazed father, a good and simple man, went frenziedly through the family records, hoping to find that all my loved ones, including himself, were misled regarding the number of my years, and that I was really fifteen or sixteen years of age, instead of a mere child of ten. As if Time itself had tricked us all!

"Oh, it is laughable enough, in retrospect. But is not all terror, all tragedy, all human misery ridiculous when seen from afar? The vicious hawk swooping into a flock of doves seems, from the distance, merely to be drifting toward them, and they merely to be gliding away from their Nemesis in leisurely grace. But we know different! And as it is with remote distance and wild animals and birds, so is it with time and with men. My father's folly was merely an index of his despair; he was not otherwise a stupid or ignorant man. Already, I think, he was aware of what a monster Nature, in her blindness, had introduced into his household.

"For you see, by the age of twelve, I was stared at; by the age of fourteen, I was pointed at; and by the age of sixteen, I was regarded with either terror or fascination and sought out as one of Nature's most exuberant productions by people who often traveled as far as one hundred miles for the opportunity to witness my amazing bulk and lofty height.

"I ask you, then, to contrast this with the normal life of a sixteen-year-old youth, and ask yourself if the fate I had to endure was tolerable. For what I desired, in my most secret dreams, was a beautiful maid to love; but what girl or woman could tolerate such thoughts concerning a man so huge that his knees were almost level with her waist, and his waist with the top of her head?

"But this is the mere beginning of the catalogue of despair and misery I have to tell, for you see, the commonality of mankind in this regard — although they are contemptible and no doubt pusillanimous — are nevertheless right: Nature did *not* intend for men to stand over eight feet tall. My organs operate under a constant and unnatural strain. My bulk pulls at my skeletal structure constantly, so that I find no position — even the supine, which is of all the most relaxing — tolerable for long. You may smile, but I must tell you that I can feel the Earth calling me back, regretful already that She has committed an error of such magnitude as the creation of the miserable Creature who now confides in you.

"If you are wondering what all this has to do with you," the Giant continued, "be patient, for the connection will soon appear. Gaze upon me as best you can in this light. Perhaps you can see the lineaments of age and fatigue in my countenance, you who are uncommonly observant of such signs. Perhaps you will recall from seeing me in the light of day that my hair is turning silver, as if I were about to enter the sere of life, when most men have raised their families and look forward to the contentment and ease that come to the Fortunate as guerdons for a life well spent. Ah, but with me, it is different: for you see, I have just within the past week celebrated, if one may call it that, my twenty-eighth birthday! And yet my physique cries out to me continuously that it has had enough; it cries out that it is time to return to that bed of clay which is the common, ultimate bed we must all lie down in. Think of it! Think of how outrageously cheated I feel when my despair and moroseness give me leave to feel anything strongly enough!

"But I can sense your impatience at the length of my narrative, and I understand your attitude. Therefore I will forebear extending my autobiography any further, although you may be sure that I have given you only the briefest account of the adventures and disappointments that have been packed into my years. I will, for example, spare you an account of my days spent in a traveling circus, where I was advertised as 'Trombo, the Largest Man in the World.' Perhaps I was; perhaps I am. The thought only isolates me further — I who am already too terribly isolated; the thought only italicizes, as it were, the monstrous joke Nature, in her least indulgent mood, has written upon me in my very existence.

"But to return to my explanation: I have found out, spending most of my waking moments in reflection over the fate I am compelled to endure, *that most men are too large and are furthermore grotesque without knowing it.*

"Do not laugh. I, who go for days, nay months, without encountering another man whose head comes even near my shoulder . . . I, who walk among the commonality of mankind as an adult walks among little schoolchildren playing in the shadow of their schoolhouse . . . I, abysmally huge, tell you that you too partake in this hugeness. We are all of us monstrous to the squirrel, the fox, the little wren. Although you may cite the greater prodigies of Nature, such as the whale, the lion, and the elephant, nevertheless I will counter with the argument that they, too, are vaster beyond all measure. They, being carnivorous (excepting the elephant), feed upon the blood and meat of less fortunate creatures; and they shake the very earth when they walk, or — as in the case of the mighty whale — furrow the seas with their passing, causing waves, turbulence, tides, and swells. And in magnitude, danger dwells."

Here the giant paused again, and stretched out his mighty arm as he intoned: "Fling but a stone, the giant dies."

Speaking these words, he fell silent again; then, stood up and paced back and forth before me, with his head raised up like a rooster getting ready to crow.

"Yes, it is so. As both a human and a specimen in the circus, I have seen it. All life for a man of sensitivity must end in utter, abject misery. Do not pretend to me that this is not so! To be intelligent is merely to be more acutely aware of this harsh and terrible truth than the commonality of creatures who call themselves men. But you, sir, I must conclude after seeing the sentiments expressed in both your verse and your journal, and after listening to your disquisition upon the innermost secrets of my soul — you, I realized, are one of those few pathetic ones whose discovery of the enormity of evil and misfortune that are necessarily part of the human condition is imminent, if indeed it has not already occurred.

"Therefore, I vowed that I would exercise whatever influence I had in order to liberate you from the inevitable consequence of intelligence: namely, utter, astronomically lonely despair. You may wish at the moment to escape, but do not deceive yourself: Sophocles was right, and it were better that none of us or our kind had ever been born; but being born, it is better only to die. 'Do unto others as you would have them do unto you.' And I would die — it is that simple. I who have passed through that which you were about to enter tell you this. It is worth nothing, my friend. Nothing, but pain and foolishness and infinite despair!"

Having finished this long speech, William Bone dropped his face in his hands and sat there without moving. It looked like he was trying to hold back the tears that the recall of such a concerto of misery would release.

As for me, in spite of my surprise at his argument, and even though my arm had gone to sleep and was tingling considerable, I'll be damned if I wasn't affected, and I could almost imagine there was something to his ideas. All of a sudden it began to look to me like the lot of every critter born of woman was too miserable for words.

But William Bone didn't wait around for my recovery. He didn't wait for any comments. He took off, probably figuring he'd done his duty by explaining his motives. And now, like just about everything else, I was an object of indifference to him.

After a minute, though, my senses came back to me. If I'd had a chance, I would have taken up the cudgels. I would have joined the debate with fire and tongs. I'd have smashed his sophistries like so many idols, pointing out that nobody has the right to argue about what meaning life has for somebody else. Meaning lives inside the skull, as I can testify, knowing its outer bumps and signs as I do. And if the last turn in the road led all of us to some final glimpse of the Castle of Despair (this is the way I built my argument, while I was lying there thinking), then so be it: everybody was entitled to his own version of that experience. It is your right as a human critter.

But a speech on this topic would have been hard to yell out across the dying fire, hoping that William Bone could hear me from somewhere over there in the darkness, blotting out another patch of stars. This is not the way to conduct a philosophical discussion, so I made up my mind to keep my mouth shut and just lie there and chew on my misery. Or better yet, come up with some kind of plan to get Henry Buck and myself free.

The instant I thought of Henry Buck, he surprised me by whispering right in my ear. He'd crawled so close, it was a wonder I hadn't heard him. He told me he was going to turn over so we'd be back to back and could work on untying the thongs around our wrists. I could tell by the way he talked that he was still considerable drunk. He couldn't have had time to sober up, and I was impressed by how quiet he'd been in maneuvering up so close to me.

I heard a coyote bark nearby, but otherwise the night was as quiet as a widow's grave. I figured William Bone was asleep, considering the amount of whiskey he'd poured down his throat. The only thing that worried me was the Comanche, who hadn't touched a drop and was probably crouched like an owl someplace out there in the dark, taking in everything that was happening.

Henry was doing a pretty good job untying my thongs. I could feel the pressure loosen up a little, and right then somebody started in snoring, growling like a bulldog, on the other side of the fire. I guessed it was Half Face. His mutilated physiognomy was enough to cause stertorous breathing in sleep, not to mention other kinds of rhonchus.

Then, just as sudden, the snoring stopped, the way a man swallows it sometimes. I listened hard for a minute, but there wasn't any other sound.

I started making plans about how I'd steal over to the wagon, grab my carbine, and then we'd wake the bastards up and I'd have Henry tie them all together like a string of horses, the giant first in line. Then we'd trot them all the way to Shoestring, guarding them every inch of the way.

But such planning was considerable premature, because all of a sudden Half Face bent over me and gave me a kick in the stomach that took my mind off speculations of every sort.

"What in the hell are you doing, Professor?" he yelled.

Then I heard the hammers on his revolvers click and figured this was it. He was about to do us in. You could tell he was hung over, and cross as a turkey gobbler with measles, and I came near to dying of acute apprehension.

But Half Face changed his mind and settled on kicking me. Part of me was feeling better, because I figured he wouldn't be wasting his energy like this if he intended to dispatch us with his revolvers.

When he finally got tired, he dropped down on his knees and retied the knots on our wrists, lecturing us on various topics. He was breathing as hard as a pulling mule by the time he finished. Then I heard Crawford moaning and cussing somewhere out in the darkness, and a minute later I could hear him throwing up.

Half Face didn't pay any attention to him, and when he stood up, he told Henry and me that if we gave it another try, he'd blow our brains out like a bucket of bloody snot, even if it did disappoint Crawford when he sobered up and got his feet on the ground once again.

He also told us that at the moment he didn't think I was a whole lot of fun. He pointed out that I was not amusing, in spite of what Crawford thought. Then he asked me who cared what Crawford thought, anyway? It was William Bone who had sound opinions, and William Bone figured we'd be better off dead. Half Face said he might just think pretty hard about William Bone's idea.

Finally he ended his sermon and stumbled on back to the other side of the fire. Everything got quiet once more. After a few minutes, one of them started in snoring again, but it wasn't as loud as distant thunder or artillery. I figured it might have been William Bone, this time. It didn't sound like the Comanche or Crawford, for some reason.

Half Face was probably giving it a good try, anyway. He was sure as hell in a cussed mood, and as for myself, I wasn't only afraid, I was suddenly mighty tired, not to mention half sick from the whiskey.

15

THE PERICARP OF HOPE

Above sublimity's appointed mound
Before that subtle phrenotropic ground
Assigned to moral conscientiousness,
Behold the noble sanguinary boss!

Misfortune that rideth o'er the beleaguered heart,
Dragging depression's atrabilious cart,
Cannot abide upon that cranial sphere
That has a prominence above the ear,
High upon that mid-cephalic slope
In the region designated Mound of Hope.

Here's the seat of courage, glory, fame;
He who would earn a lasting, honoured name
To echo down the corridors of time
And be encapsuled in both song and rhyme,
Must be possessed of lofty goals,
A heart that carries passion hot as coals,
A patience slow and sure as growing grass,
Conjoined with humour, pluck, and sassafras,
A character spotless, as if cleansed by soap,
And a well-developed pericarp of Hope.
                              — Thaddeus Burke

IN SPITE of everything, I eventually fell asleep. I don't know how
I did it. I dreamed a kettle full of drunken and troubled dreams.
Just about everybody I'd ever known, popped into one dream or
another for a visit. There were both of my parents, along with
Samuel Chadwick, Stillingfleet, and Lily de Wilde. I don't remember
that Henry Buck or Half Face made an appearance, however.

In one dream, William Bone was dressed as a cardinal in a Eu-
ropean cathedral, touching my head with his two fingers. Those

fingers were as big as a couple of squirrel bodies. I guess this was some kind of ecclesiastical blessing. And then all of a sudden there were great big birds kind of stuck and thrashing around in the high windows of the cathedral. Then the cathedral was a mountain.

Near dawn, the dreams stopped and I slept hard and deep. Then I came awake to a hot bright morning sun shining right in my eyes. Half Face was shouting up a storm.

"Where is the son of a bitch?" he yelled, stamping through the ashes of the dead fire. "Just tell me one thing: where is he?"

"He done got away," Crawford said stupidly, scratching his head under his top hat.

Half Face was so mad, he shut his one good eye and fired a revolver straight up in the air. After the shot broke the silence, it was just swallowed up, instead of rocking away in the open air, because there wasn't any hill or mountainside to give back an echo.

"Son of a stinking ass bitch!" Half Face cried, scuffing his boots in the ashes, and sending up little white clouds of cinder dust.

"And that dadblamed Indian kid as well," Crawford said. "He took off too."

"Why *he* was the one that untied the *other'n!*" Half Face cried, still waving both revolvers. I figured he was about to shoot again, but he didn't.

At some other time I might have been pretty entertained by Half Face's dance of wrath. He was considerable drunk, not to mention hung over, as you could tell. But underneath all that, he was about as full of rage as a man can get.

What he was so mad about didn't sink into my brain right away. I was considerable disoriented myself, and I didn't even catch on when William Bone stood up in the distance and stretched himself against the sky and ran his fingers through his long hair.

I was awful frazzled and stale from the whiskey, and right before dawn I had slept so hard a goat could have stepped on my face and I wouldn't have woke up. Maybe that was part of the reason.

But then all of a sudden it came to me. And compared to what I felt right then, Half Face's loss of temper was no more than a prance and a flutter. It hadn't fully dawned on me until this minute that it was Henry Buck who had escaped, along with the Comanche, and that the damned scoundrel had not bothered to liberate me as well.

This was too much for me to swallow. I don't think I've ever been visited by such a charge of fury. No doubt it was partly the whiskey, because I was still not what you'd call 100 percent sober.

I managed to lurch to my feet with both of my wrists and ankles still tied, and then I lifted my face and let go. I started in yelling. It was more than just anger that set me off; it was fear and desperation, too, I don't doubt for a minute. Henry Buck had been my only ally, and now he'd taken off. How was I ever going to fight these three desperate buzzards when I was all tied up and trussed like a hog? The injustice of the whole business got to me, and I figured if you're going to be shot, you might as well die cussing. So I just about yelled my damned head off. A lot of men will act like that in the last extremity. I figure I was crazy for a while, and the memory of the whole business is still pretty dim to me.

When I finally stopped long enough to get my breath, I was surprised by how quiet everything had gotten. The silence came over me like a clap of thunder, and I sort of lost momentum for a second and looked around to get my bearings.

I had sure as hell captured the attention of Half Face. He looked at me with an expression of awe in his eye, and said, "What was all that you said?"

"Never mind what I said," I yelled back at him. I was fierce and didn't give a damn for anything. It was kind of like an ecstasy, because I'd faced up to it. It wasn't just the whiskey, even though that was a considerable part of it. "Go on an' get your bloodthirsty God damned work done with!" I told him. "Do you think I give a chipmunk's fart if I never see the red sun rise again, or touch a woman, or drink the health of a friend, or philosophize upon the moon, or read a head? Never mind, do your damnedest, you swinish platycephalic villain, and be double, triple, *quadruple* damned, for all I care. Go on and do your worst and to hell with you!"

Half Face had been holding both revolvers outward, as if to ward off an attack, but when I shot this barrage at him, damned if he didn't lower both firearms and turn his mutilated phiz toward William Bone, who stood crookedly, sort of tilted over, near the wagon watching us.

"Did you ever hear such talk, William Bone?" Half Face said. "Did you ever? Tell me truly, *did* you?"

"No," William Bone said in his deep voice, "I never did. It was remarkable. In its grotesque way, it was truly eloquent."

Half Face turned back to me and said in a hushed voice, "That's exactly what it was: *eloquent*. Why, with eloquence like that, you could rule a nation or command an army!"

Crawford finally found his voice and said, "Yessir! That's nothing but gospel!"

Half Face nodded and said, "I never *did* hear such eloquence. Why I have heard many a politician and many a lawyer, but blame my kidneys if you didn't just now orate *rings* around all of them! Bless my kneecaps, but you are *some* orator!"

"It's no damned wonder," I said, hopping up and down a couple of times to get my blood circulating, because my hands and feet were still tingling. Then I elaborated a little. "When a man falls into the hands of three of the greatest lunatics that ever put on shoes, it's no wonder he's driven to desperate words."

But Half Face was not about to settle for self-effacement. "*Never* in my born days!" he cried. "Never, never, *never* have I seen so much smoke come out of the mouth of mortal man."

"He cursed like a judge," William Bone said, and for the first time, I saw him smile. It was a piddly little smile. It was a sad, tentative, pensive, ironic little smile, like maybe a sweat bee had lit on one side of his upper lip and he had to twist his mouth a little to the side in order to dislodge it. But it was a smile, all right.

"Why he cussed *better* than a judge!" Half Face said, resting his hands on his revolvers and shaking his head.

William Bone just sort of raised his eyebrows and strolled away from us. When he was too far away to hear, Half Face said, "Now I always considered William Bone to be an orator of the first water, but son of a bitch, if you don't beat him all hog-tied."

"Thanks for the compliment," I said, but the sarcasm was lost on Half Face in his present mood.

Then he got an idea. He told Crawford to keep his eye on me while he took a walk and thought about it. He started out toward William Bone, but then changed his mind and kind of circled.

Finally, he came back and took a sip from the jug. Then he patted it, and said it was almost empty. He was considerable boozed already, and this last swig wouldn't make him any more sober. He stood there before me, licking his lips and blinking his eye real slow, like a man turning over his last card, the way you do when you're drunk. Then he said, "I'll tell you what I'll do. I'll make a deal with you, Professor. I will spare you your life if you write down some of them things you said just now, so as I can kind of memorize them, if you know what I mean, and use them when the . . . you know . . . when the time comes. God damn it, I always *did* look up to a man with the power of words!"

At first I had trouble believing I'd heard him right. This was hard to believe, even though I wasn't what you'd call awful sober myself. But when he repeated what he'd just said, I figured he was in earnest, and actually wanted me to teach him the arts of profanity, invective, obscenity, and vulgar speech.

There wasn't anything for me to do except agree. On second thought it didn't seem so peculiar. Everybody knows that soldiers and sailors will have one of their number write their love letters, if they're gifted in that direction and can write at all. And this wasn't altogether different.

So I told Half Face I'd go along with his plan, providing I could get another jug of whiskey from the wagon. He agreed, and then came close to shooting me for withholding information about the extra whiskey.

I'll never forget that scene as long as I live. The morning has gotten hot. Under the big sky, this little wagon sits inert, leaning to the side where its axle has been broken. Crawford lies there on his back, flat on the ground about fifty feet away, with his dusty top hat over his face and his hands folded behind his head. The mighty William Bone sits a hundred yards distant, on a little bitty rise . . . sits either on some rock or on the bare ground, looking off into space, his long wild hair blowing in the hot breeze.

At the edge of the late-morning shadow cast by the wagon sit Half Face and myself, about six feet apart. Half Face is sitting Indian fashion, his two loaded revolvers in his hands, pointed right at my brisket. I'm seated Indian fashion, too, studying the matter and writing down every blasphemy, curse, profanity, obscenity, and insult I can think of. I also include forensic tropes of just about all descriptions. I record all this with a badly chewed lead pencil on the backs of some cranial charts. The whiskey jug sits beside us.

We have been sitting like this for about half an hour, and in spite of nausea, headache, trepidation, and disgust . . . in spite of all that these Four Horsemen can do, I have filled four sheets with carefully written oratorial recipes for Half Face. But Half Face has the true collector's passion, and won't give up until he's gotten all the insults and curses in the world down on paper, *plus one!*

He squints his good eye and stares thoughtfully at a distant cloud. Somewhere, a coyote barks. Otherwise, everything is as quiet as the dreams of the deaf. Except for the sound of the wind, of course, which stays with you like the sound of your breath or heartbeat.

16

Deep in the man sits fast his fate
To mold his fortune mean or great.

— Emerson

WHAT YOU won't do to save your life! I have suffered humiliation
more than once, as who hasn't, but I consider that business out
there in the middle of nowhere, writing down blasphemies and
cusses and vulgarisms for Half Face, as pretty close to hitting bottom. It was worthy of Stillingfleet, which is about the worst you
can say about anything.

And yet, before long, I got interested. I couldn't help it. There's
nothing like having your mind occupied, no matter where you find
yourself.

I was drunk enough that I didn't much care what happened. And
the way I felt, I figured that writing down cusses wasn't the worst
way for a man to say good-bye to the world, especially if you've
got some sass in your spirit. This thought was a spur to my imag-
ination, so if I do say so myself, I managed to wax pretty eloquent.
The only thing is, I can't remember exactly what I wrote down,
so I have no way to prove that the words I put together were
anything more than drunken babble.

By the time I'd gotten through page six, my invention and recall
were beginning to stumble and stagger. They'd flagged considerable
by this time. Also I figured this one-eyed ruffian's word wasn't
worth two toots on a bugle. How did I know but what he'd lift
one of his revolvers and blow a hole through my head after I
finished?

I was like that captive in the fairy tale who was commanded by
a king to tell a story that never ended. I strained my thoughts to
the limit, and even tried to repeat one or two excoriations. But
Half Face always recognized them, so that I had to fancy up different
combinations, which he didn't seem to pick up on.

When I was starting on my seventh page, William Bone came up and sat down about twenty feet away. He sat there giving considerable study to what we were doing.

I didn't let on that I had noticed him; but I could tell he made Half Face nervous, because all of a sudden he turned around and said, "William Bone, just what in the hell are you doing over there?"

"I am sitting here thinking," William Bone replied.

"Thinking of what?" Half Face inquired.

"I am amusing myself," Bone said, "by contemplating the roles that each of us three seems to fill, and trying to fathom what role, what form of sensibility, might be the dominant one in creating this new land that our Nation has determined to settle and make its own."

"*What* new land?" Half Face asked, lowering his revolvers. "Kansas?"

William Bone waved his great hand slowly through the air, without taking his eyes from Half Face. "*This* one," he said, "the land that surrounds us. All of it, including Kansas. It is empty, and Nature everywhere abhors a vacuum. It is said that our manifest destiny is to fill it with our kind. If this is so, I am asking what will be the dominant and defining type of this region, as determined by the requirements of the land, as well as the tendency of our civilization."

"What in the hell kind of idea are you off on now, William Bone?" Half Face asked. There was a note of anxiety in his voice. Half Face wasn't comfortable being ignorant, the way most ignorant people are. In fact, knowing that he was ignorant made him downright uncomfortable. I figured this might be his most decent trait as well as his Achilles heel.

"We each have a part to play in the drama that unfolds about us," William Bone said calmly.

"What part do *I* play?" Half Face asked.

"You," William Bone said, "are the Anarchist, the pragmatic Visionary, the Innocent Banditto."

"Is that right!" Half Face said. You could tell he was impressed.

"Unquestionably," Bone answered.

"And how about the Professor here?" Half Face said.

"He is the Irrepressible Impresario. The Inevitable Manipulator who preys upon human gullibility. The Uncomprehending Enthusiast, spirited and impudently matter-of-fact, too energetic by far, and insensitive to the troubles of other people."

"Is that all?" I asked him. "Is that about it?"

But William Bone declined to answer.

Half Face nodded, however. Then he asked William Bone what role *he* fulfilled.

"I," the giant replied, "am the Idealist."

"Hogwash," I muttered. "If you figure you're an Idealist, how's come you follow Half Face, and call him your leader, since you say he's an Anarchist? Answer that, if you can!"

"It needs no answer," William Bone said, "for it is simply a fact."

With that, he rose up to his feet and walked away, not giving me any chance for rebuttal or question. He ambled back to that slight promontory where he liked to sit, and settled himself once again to face into the wind and gaze out upon the sky.

"Well, let's get on with it," Half Face said. "They's a lot to be gotten down on paper."

I started in again to rake my mind for expressions of vulgarity and insult. But the fact was, I had figured out a plan. The plan was plain and simple, and I knew it would take nerve to bring it off, so I helped myself to another sip of whiskey to prime my courage.

I started out by stalling. Half Face hadn't shown any signs of growing tired of his game. In fact he was getting annoyed because I was slow in coming up with new and more colorful material.

"What's the matter?" he asked me several times. "Have you come to the end of the trail? Have you reached the bottom of the barrel? Has the dadblamed well run dry?"

"Nope," I said. "I'm just considerable fatigued, not to mention half sick from too much whiskey. The memory, governed by the organs of Eventuality, doesn't respond for long periods of time to unrelieved stimulus."

He looked perplexed for a minute. If William Bone had been near, he would have asked for a translation. But since the giant was still morbidly fixed in his distant solitary post, Half Face just frowned and took a shot at my meaning: "That says you're getting tired, is that it?"

"Yep," I told him, "close enough."

Half Face stared at me an instant and then shook his head slowly back and forth. "I sure do like you a whole lot better when you just relax and cut loose, instead of talking all that stuffy shit, like you was performing for some God damned audience."

I told him I'd bust a blood vessel trying to keep his preference in mind.

"Well, have you got any more you can think of?" he said.

"You can read, can't you?"

"Of course I can read, you dadblamed fool! How come you think I want you to copy all them sayings down if I don't intend to put them to memory by way of reading?"

"All right, then: why don't you go over this list and see if I've duplicated any of them."

"What?" Half Face said.

"Look to see if I've got any of them down there twice."

"Hell, *you* can do that! I don't need to do it. I can do it later."

I leaned over toward him with a troubled expression on my face. I shoved the paper under his eye and said, "Yep, that's the truth, but lookee here: it seems to me some of these phrases aren't quite right. There's some overlap in what they signify."

"What do you mean, not quite right?" Half Face said. And right then he made the biggest mistake of his life. He made the mistake of looking down at the paper right where I was pointing. I dropped the paper and grabbed both his wrists so quick and hard, and lurched against him so violently, that the two of us rolled over into the dust, me on top.

One of the revolvers went off right next to my ear and made it ring like a bell, but I didn't feel anything like a jolt or burning pain, anywhere, so I figured I hadn't been hit.

I also knew that Half Face would have to be subdued fast, and I'd have to get one of the revolvers quick, before William Bone and Crawford could come to his assistance. With a surge of what you'd have to call desperate strength, I turned one of the guns back towards Half Face's head and, digging my knees against his other arm, let go of that one quick, and with the freed hand, pulled the trigger.

There was another roar, and for a second, Half Face's body

bucked like a wild horse underneath me, and then it started to quiet down.

I jerked the revolver from Half Face's hand and jumped around just in time to see Crawford walk around the wagon. He said, "Did you have to do away with him, Half Face?"

Before he could really take in what was happening, I shot him square in the chest, and he sat down on the ground with a whump, and then fell over backwards. His top hat rolled off his head in a semicircle.

I whirled about, figuring to face up to William Bone. But conceive of my surprise when I saw that damned coward lumbering as fast as he could go in the opposite direction, already out of pistol shot, his great coat flapping as he went.

At another time, I might have gotten a kick out of the spectacle that contemptible hypocrite made; but now I didn't, because of the excitement of the events just past.

I went back to Half Face's body lying in the dry grass and saw that his face was streaked with long tangles of blood. And that blood was coming out of a hole right smack dab in the middle of the bastard's well-developed Mound of Mirthfulness, which borders the hairline high on the forehead! It was what you'd have to call a ghastly sight, but there was something else that was even worse, namely Half Face's single eye, which was wide open and looking up at me.

I leaned over and said, "Can you hear me?"

The eye closed, then it opened again. It looked like there might be a faint light of intelligence in it, but that's always hard to tell at a time like this. I looked at his chest and saw it was still moving up and down.

I thought about shooting him again, administering the *coup de grace*, but somehow that didn't seem right. Then I thought about saying something edifying or religious to him, but I decided against that, too, since I couldn't think of anything appropriate.

I walked over to Crawford, who was already stone dead. His eyes were half open, but they were already beginning to glaze over, and his arm was outstretched with the fingers bent like they were about to clutch at something beyond human sight.

I stood there a minute, drinking up the nastiness of the scene.

All I could hear was the wind flapping the torn part of the canvas on my wagon and rustling the long grass alongside the trail, which is maybe the loneliest sound in the world.

Then I got the shakes. I shook like a dog that has just climbed out of a cold creek. I couldn't even keep my jaw still. If I'd tried to hum, I would have gobbled like a turkey, my jaw was moving so fast. I clapped my hand over my mouth, but that didn't help any, because my hand was shaking too. I don't suppose anybody on earth has ever looked more foolish than I would have looked right then, if anybody'd been there to see me.

I picked up the whiskey jug and gulped from it like it was filled with water. That was a mistake. Before long I was not only shaking, I was staggering. A voice came into my head, saying, "How far, oh Lord, has this thy servant strayed from the way of Quakers!"

I turned on that voice and told it I was quaking as much as any man *could* quake. And then I laughed out loud. Not only that, I yelled and whooped. I was alive, and nobody else was, wherever I looked and as far as I could see. It was an awful excitement that filled me then.

Finally I started in talking, explaining things. Then I asked questions. What was I supposed to do, let Half Face shoot me like a dog? Isn't self-preservation the first law of nature? Didn't I owe my life to my future children? What would society or religion ever get from animals like Half Face and Crawford? Granted, right at the moment I didn't look like a whole lot, myself, but at least I had it in me to change, and I figured I could bring the business off some day, especially if I could find the right woman to inspire me, by way of marriage.

Finally I got hold of myself and realized that I'd better move on out of that place soon, so I picked up Half Face's revolvers, and got my carbine from the wagon, and stood there for a minute trying to clear my head enough so I could figure out exactly what I had to do.

When I started to hiccup, I drank from the jug again. That was a fool thing to do, and I knew it right while I was doing it. But the fact was, I felt cold sober after a couple of swallows. It felt unearthly, like I was walking on top of a ground fog, but I didn't exactly feel bad and my head seemed so clear it was downright airy.

The first thing I did was to get out a cranial chart and make a sign. All I had was that lead pencil, but I went over the letters about twenty times so they stood out. Here is what I wrote:

THIS WAGON HAS NOT BEEN ABANDONED. I WILL RETURN FOR IT AND CONTENTS SOON. ALL IS PRIVATE PROPERTY AND SHD BE TREATED AC-CORDINGLY. HORSES TOO.

T. BURKE, PROP.

I took out a needle and thread and sewed the sign to the canvas with a double stitch, so that the wind would not blow it all the way to Mexico.

Then I went out and took a good look at Half Face's tough little Indian pony, which I figured would be the best one around when it came to endurance. I hobbled the other horses and let them go. They could drink from the stream, which had water in it now, and there was plenty of buffalo grass for them to crop. I figured they'd get along all right, if they weren't killed or stolen. I tied my mules together on a single rope so I could lead them. Then I went over to a clump of bushes and threw up, after which I figured I was ready.

A few minutes later I was riding toward the town of Shoestring, or Shostenengo, and damned if tears didn't start running down my face. They were tears of relief, as well as exhaustion and dismay. I tried to calm myself by reciting some poems, but it didn't do much good. I felt considerable unstable for the next couple of hours.

Later on I began to feel kind of sick and lonely, so I took off north where I finally came to the Smoky Hill Trail, and about an hour later caught up with a wagon train moving west. When I first saw them in the distance, I debated whether or not I should go up to them. I was lonely, but I was still feeling a little jumpy and distrustful. Finally I put aside my doubts and rode on up to see who they were and where they were headed.

It was a band of sixteen wagons, all pulled by oxen, and accompanied by ten or twelve men on horseback. The wagonmaster was named Gilchrist. He was short, squat, and friendly, with significant development in the region of Concentrativeness, which Spurzheim thought of as Inhabitiveness and found well-developed in cats.

When they asked where I was from, I told them about the breakdown of my wagon and the defection of Henry Buck, but I didn't mention Half Face and his gang.

It felt good to spend a night with these people, but I had a time trying to keep my eyes off their females, since I'd been without a woman's companionship for so long. As for the folks in the wagon train, they practically broke out the fiddle when they found out I was a phrenologist, so I analyzed a few skulls, but then complained of being tired and went off from the main campfire where I spent a night of tense and fitful sleep.

The next morning I left this jolly group, and went on ahead, turning back south on the trail to Shoestring, a place most wagon trains planned to miss. At noon I came across the fringes of a big buffalo herd, and rode pretty cautious, figuring that Indians might be near.

But there weren't any Indians, and I rode all that afternoon without coming upon any other human signs. And then, in the long slant light of early evening, I saw some buildings up ahead and finally rode into Shoestring.

The town was a cluster of clapboard houses, soddies, tents, and six unpainted buildings — the latter being a hotel, a livery stable, a store, and three saloons. All but the hotel faced the Smoky Hill River. Across the river stood a bluff dotted with scrawny red cedars.

The town's public dwelling house was called The Smoky Hill River Hotel, and its back end was supported in pilings over the edge of the river. The proprietor was a large, whiskered gent named Ulysses Morehouse, and he claimed that the spring floods never rose high enough to inconvenience his guests.

There wasn't any way to take a bath in the hotel, so I got a bar of yellow soap, about the size and weight of a brick, and went down to the river and waded in. The water was warm from the long summer sun, and the half-hour I spent that evening standing shoulder deep in the Smoky Hill River was an interval of what you might term unmitigated pleasure. I soaped myself all over until the grime and dirt flowed from my body, taking some of my fatigue with them. For the first minute or so, the water downstream was coffee-colored from the dirt I washed off. I figure I shed about as much filth in ten minutes as the average buffalo herd.

I soaped my hair, and when it was time to rinse, I swam out into the deeper part of the river and ducked under the water, letting the stream carry off all the mud that had thickened in my scalp.

When I finished, I looked around to see that no females were about, and then I waded to the bank and commenced drying myself with a rough gray towel. Then I got dressed and walked up to the hotel. But instead of going back up to my room, I stayed on the first floor, which was given over to the serving of food and liquor, and gambling with cards at the rear of the bar.

I drank a glass of rye whiskey and thought about the whiskey I'd left back in my wagon. I thought about the moon coming up, and in my mind pictured the slitted eyes of Crawford's corpse, with his top hat still lying undisturbed where it had rolled. He'd acted like he was mighty proud of that top hat. It was a shame, when you considered it. Then I thought about the lone eye of Half Face. I could almost see the prairie wind blowing the hair on the corpses. I got in a Samuel Chadwick mood and could almost see the lurking coyote as it approached in the moon shadow, and tentatively sniffed at that damned scene of what you might call crepuscular horror.

Right then was the first time I wondered about whether Half Face had really intended to kill me after he'd gotten his list. That was something I'd never know. Still, I figured I'd done the right thing. I wasn't in any position to guess. Half Face hadn't given me any choice. He hadn't given me much room to move around in. No reasonable critter could have blamed me for doing what I did, even though it was a considerable bloody business.

And yet, that question kept coming up. The sight of Half Face's dying eye would probably stick with me for about as long as I lived, a lesson of the extremes to which a body has to commit himself if he's going to stay alive in country like this.

It was good to be back among my kind again. In the hotel saloon there were about a dozen traders and mule drivers and such, and it felt downright homey to stand up there at the plank bar with them, drinking rye whiskey and talking about sudden fortunes and weather and trails and Indians and such.

As I sipped at my glass, I thought of the females I had seen on the wagon train, and right away got a longing for a woman. My bump of Amativeness is pronounced, which may have something to do with what they call sassafras, but living alone so much I'd learned that you've got to ignore the thought of female distractions. You've got to control those futile longings for their tender sex.

But now that I was in the presence of civilized dwellings, I could feel the awful power women have over us. It hit me hard. I started feeling poetic, and I began to think along the lines of: How tender their hearts! How noble their sensibilities! How steadfast their loyalties, once addressed to a man they love!

It was the comfort of a woman's presence I needed, if my meaning's clear. No doubt about it. I wanted to hold on to a woman's soft hand and look into her eyes. I wanted to calm my desire, like they say, in her warm and accepting presence. I wanted to understand her heart and spirit, and probe softly about the mysteries of her head, beneath soft, perfumed hair. I wanted her breath to mix with mine, and our hearts to beat together.

This powerful hankering was soon all mixed up with the phantasmagoria of memory, and I started to work at the whiskey like it was an obligation. Before I knew what hit me, I was on my third glass. My mind began to float a little, like a hat dropped in the water. All of a sudden, the fifth or sixth glass was in my hand, I couldn't tell which. Right about then I figured if I decided to spit, I'd have to take careful aim or I might miss the floor.

By now I was considerable fuddled, but I managed to eat a good dinner consisting of buffalo hump, beans, and biscuits, and keep my thumb out of the coffee.

I went to bed halfway afloat figuring that in another day or two, when I'd recovered my strength and a certain control over my emotions, I'd venture out once again upon that damned trail with a new axle and a man to help me set it, and then I'd bury Crawford and Half Face, if their corpses had not already been gobbled up by the critters God made for such duties. Then, I figured I'd drive my wagon back to Shoestring and pick up my life where I'd left off. Except that Henry Buck would not be part of it.

The smell out there would be getting worse by the hour, but I'd rather postpone the trip another day or two, and put up with more stink, than leave Shoestring right away. It felt awful comfortable here.

There was also the chance that somebody might come by and strip the wagon of everything I owned, but if such came about, it was beyond my control, and I'd be a damned fool to worry.

I settled myself down for sleep, with only one thought between what I've recorded and subsequent oblivion. This was the memory of the head of that Comanche, whose name I hadn't ever learned. Never even heard spoken, as a matter of fact.

Believe me when I say that Comanche's head was so different from the brutal skulls of Half Face, Crawford, and William Bone it could almost be said to belong to another species of critter.

The thought of that head haunted me and kept me awake. I could almost fancy the feel of it, and I kept thinking what a marvel it would be if I could only find me a girl with such cranial features!

In the midst of such speculations, I fell asleep, quick as a shot bird.

17

The African race as found in America, furnish another instance of the striking correspondence between their known character and their phrenological developments. They possess, in general, either large, or very large, adhesiveness, philo-progenitiveness, hope, language, and approbativeness *or* self-esteem, and sometimes *both*; large veneration, marvellousness, individuality, locality, and tune; with moderate causality, constructiveness, and mirthfulness. Combativeness, destructiveness, secretiveness, acquisitiveness, and, perhaps, conscientiousness, unlike these organs in the Indian head, vary in size, being sometimes very large, and in other instances, moderate or small. The size of their heads is generally moderate or small. Their extremely large hope, would make them very cheerful, and little anxious about the future; and, with their large approbativeness and small acquisitiveness, extravagant, and predisposed to lead a life of ease and idleness. Their very large hope and language, with small secretiveness and mirthfulness, would give them hilarity and garrulity, without much pure wit.

— Fowler's *Practical Phrenology*

THE NEXT morning I felt considerable better, so I changed my mind and decided to take off right away if I could find somebody to help me fix the axle. It was mighty hot, but I didn't want to wait any longer. Somebody said it was 100 degrees in the shade, but I'm not sure about that. People say a lot of things, only some of which are true.

I couldn't get my mind off that wagon, filled with everything I owned. If somebody came along, they'd no doubt take what they wanted, in spite of my sign. Some folks would do the right thing, but there'd be plenty who wouldn't.

When I told people the way I'd come, they acted surprised and asked me why I'd done a fool thing like taking *that* trail. They thought even less of it than they had back in Council Grove. So it didn't look like my outfit was in much danger, because from the way everybody talked, Half Face's gang and Henry Buck and I must have been just about the only people who'd taken that route since George Washington wore his first pair of britches.

Still, I wanted to get my wagon fixed. You could never tell, I told people, and they all agreed that you couldn't. I planned my departure so I'd arrive after dark. That way I figured I'd have a chance to surprise any human scavengers who might have taken up a position near the wagon, the sort of critters who might hide and get the jump on me if they saw me coming. It would be better to have the advantage night affords. They might even have a fire burning, in which case I'd see it flickering a mile away, and be able to take a good look at them before stepping up into the circle of firelight.

On the other hand, since the trail was a small and neglected one, I might miss the wagon altogether if there wasn't any fire, or no one had stopped there. But this was a chance I had to take, being the less of two evils. I could always backtrack the next day if I missed the spot. I was only a fair tracker, but I figured something like this shouldn't take too much in the way of skill.

I found a saddler named Elias Thompson who had a wagon about the same size as mine with the back axle broken, so I was able to buy the front axle for fourteen dollars. This was a stroke of good luck, because there was no wagoner in the town and there wasn't any place else where I had a chance of buying an axle or having one made.

Along with the axle, which we figured could be tied to the back of one of my mules, I managed to buy the services of an escaped slave by the name of Lionel Littlejohn. Elias Thompson swore up and down and sideways that this big black critter knew how to set an axle, and with my assistance would be able to get the wagon rolling in no time.

I didn't get a whole lot of cheer from my first glimpse of Lionel Littlejohn, however. He was naked to the waist, standing in the sunshine at the stable's entrance, having just helped Elias with some horses. It looked like he figured there was nobody around, and he stretched his beefy arms outwards like he was about to embrace the open sky. And then he flexed his biceps, first the left and then the right, sort of smiling at them in admiration. Then he blinked a couple of times, and started in massaging his genitals.

Lionel had an oxycephalous head, and a small goatee and mustache, the rest of his face being about as hairless as the belly of a bull frog. I was not what you'd call anxious to hire him, but Elias Thompson swore he was reasonable and capable of working once you got him started.

It sounded to me like maybe he was anxious to get rid of Lionel Littlejohn, but since there wasn't anybody else available, Lionel Littlejohn it had to be, and about an hour after lunch, the two of us took off. Lionel was riding one mule and leading the other with the axle strapped to its back, while I rode Half Face's Indian pony.

Shortly after we got started, I made a mistake. I told Lionel that the wagon and what was in it added up to everything I owned.

Lionel gave a long judicious look when I said that, pushing his lips out critically and frowning. "Whatchoo got *in* de wagon?" he asked.

I told him the wagon had a pretty good extra wool suit, along with boxes of charts, two jugs of whiskey, four boxes of Virginia stogies, several decks of playing cards, a wooden leg I'd once come upon lying beside a wild and lonely trail in Kentucky, a collection of about twenty women's garters, a small library of books on philosophy, poetry, and other subjects, a butter tub filled with beads for Indian trade (which I had won in a game of poker from an Irishman named Augustus Bidwell), a bottle of mineral oil for laxative use, several pounds of dried venison and jerky, a small barrel of flour, another of salt pork, a ten-pound tin half-filled with coffee, a sack of dried beans, and the usual five-gallon keg of sweet water, plus a wax bust of Daniel Webster. There was also a basket of potatoes that were withered in their skins like some little shrunken heads I saw from South America, once, along with several blankets of various description, and sundry other items that I couldn't think of at that particular moment.

"Dat dere is some crowded wagon," Lionel Littlejohn said.

"Yep. Pretty crowded."

"Aintchoo got no money?"

"Nope," I said. "Not enough to brag about. The fact is, I have suffered what you might call various considerable setbacks recently."

"What kind of *good* suit is dat suit you got in de wagon?"

I told him it was just the usual black wool suit. Along with a couple of white linen shirts, which I'd forgotten to mention.

"You got yohsef a hat?"

"Yep, but it's just a plain old slouch hat."

After this, Lionel got quiet.

I figured I'd talked too much, so for a while I rode with my hand on my revolver, ready to turn and shoot the black critter dead, if it looked like he needed it.

But it looked like he was more interested in assessment than acquisition. When I hired him, he'd called me "Gen'rel," but now you could tell he was disappointed in me, getting close to bored. He blew his lips like a horse when I worked myself up to expressing a philosophical idea, or started in reciting one of my poems. And then when he started calling me "Cap'n" I knew for a fact I'd been demoted. I wondered if maybe there were lower ranks waiting if I lost any more dignity in his eyes.

But that critter's contempt didn't give me any trouble. I had other things on my mind. The immediate problem was the wagon, and when I explained to Lionel over our evening campfire that we might run into some folks there and maybe we'd have to fight to get the wagon back, he looked thoughtful and a little bad-humored. I hadn't mentioned this part of the undertaking when I'd hired him, and I'll have to admit that old Lionel had some just cause for disappointment.

Early the next morning, Lionel was dilatory. He was full of hums and haws and moved like a man with a bad back and sore feet. Every move was what you'd call a minuet of pained reluctance. Four or five times I told him to get cracking because we had considerable traveling yet before we'd reach the wagon.

But he wouldn't listen. One time he broke his thumbnail, or claimed he did, and took out his bowie knife with a flourish, the way a magician pulls a scarf out of his sleeve, and began to pick at it. When I called out to him, he didn't even look up. And when I called out again, he just mumbled halfhearted answers.

Finally, I got exasperated and delivered a lecture. I braced myself so I wouldn't lose my temper and go into a cussing fit and make a fool of myself. But I told Lionel that he'd by God better learn to speak better. I told him he should learn how to talk like a civilized man, and not mumble like a God damned growling Pekingese dog. I told him that a man ought to be precise in what he said, because that was only right. I told him about Samuel Chadwick, only I edited things considerable. If we didn't express our thoughts clearly, we wouldn't be any better than hogs at a trough, I told him.

I thought about that a little bit, and then amplified on the theme. Before I finished, I had that trough meaning several things, including religion, society, and truth itself. It didn't do much for me, and I could tell it wasn't doing a whole lot for Lionel Littlejohn, so I took off in another direction. And by the time I returned to our base camp, I had gotten to the main point and issue, which was that the son of a bitch ought to give me a clear answer when I said something to him, but before he did that, he ought to look me in the eye and give some kind of evidence that he was listening to what I said.

This set Lionel Littlejohn off, and he said, "Whuffo I got to *look* to *listen* to you, Cap'n? Hell, a man can heah a man's words without a raisin' up of de damn *eyes!*"

I told him that wasn't the point. And then I told him what the point was, which had to do with you wanting to see how the words were sinking in when you talked to somebody.

But Lionel wasn't having any of that. He took the view that you didn't have to see to hear, which is all right, as far as it goes, but it doesn't go far enough. You could tell he wasn't going to agree to anything, so we argued back and forth, this and that, here and there, until I finally got it through to him that if he didn't do what I said, I wasn't going to pay him.

That was a new note in the music, and Lionel had to pause and go over it a time or two in his head to be sure he got the tune right. When he came out of it, he agreed to do what I said, since he was working for me, but only if it didn't go against his grain.

"Well, what about fixing the axle?" I said. "I don't suppose that goes against your grain, does it?"

Lionel thought a second, and then nodded, saying he thought that would be all right.

I figured the matter was settled at this point, but that wasn't exactly the case. Because later on, after we'd stopped to rest and eat some jerky, Lionel stretched and said, "Ah thinks mebbe ah takes me a little swim."

There was a branch of the Smoky Hill River nearby, which was filled near the brim, and I'd noticed a deep pool in it a few hundred yards back.

Lionel had noticed it too. "Right back deah," he said, turning and pointing. "Dat deah is de place ah is going to take me a swim in. Too *hot* to ride all day long! *Damn*, if it ain't!"

The idea wasn't too bad, and I admitted the fact. The only thing was, we had to get on and retrieve my wagon, because leaving it unguarded another day would be too much of a risk.

Lionel cocked his eye at something in the sky over my head and said, "Good, it settled, den. Ah's gone take me a little swim and cool off."

"Nope," I said, taking my revolver out and giving it a couple of hefts.

"You don't want me to go take myself a swim den, is dat right?" Lionel stood there with his brow furrowed, like this was hard for him to figure out. He was staring with a look of great concentration past my ear.

"Nope," I said. "It isn't that I don't *want* you to go take a swim. It's that I won't by God let you take a swim, because if you do, I won't pay you a God damn cent. I might blow your head off, too, just to help you grasp my meaning. *Now* do you get my drift?"

"Ah gits yo drift," Lionel said. And then he kicked at the ground in eloquent irritation. "Water sure do look damn cool and *nice*, though. Man, it sure *do*!"

"Yep, it sure does," I said. "But the water can wait. Hell, you can *always* take a swim."

"Not if'n I don't have no *water*, I can't," Lionel pointed out.

I agreed, but that didn't change my mind, and Lionel busied himself with his saddle, tightening it here and there, and grumbling to his mule.

Finally, the grumbling got louder, and I could hear it. He was repeating one word: "Hurry, hurry, hurry, *hurry*!"

"Work before play," I told him.

"Way I see it," he said, turning around and spreading his hands apart, "if'n a man has got de stars and de moon, why, hell, ain't no need to *hurry!* Nossah, if'n a man has got de stars and de moon, ain't no need to be one place instead of another! Hell, one place as good as another! Whatchoo gone do *theah* you cain't do *heah?*"

Then I played a bad card. I mentioned the grasshopper and the ant.

"Now what *dat* suppose to mean?" he cried out in a sort of ecstasy. "Don't go telling me nuffin' 'bout no *grasshopper* and no *ant!* All right, you say no *swimmin'!* Man say no swimmin', why da's dat. No *swimmin'*. But don't go telling me nuffin' about no grasshopper and no ant!"

"Forget it," I said, mounting my horse. "Forget I mentioned them."

As Lionel mounted his mule, he said, "Fohgit you mention *what?* See, I show you how quick ole Lionel can fohgit. Yessah, when it come to fohgittin', why ain' *nobody* gonna beat dis heah bird. Nossah!"

But this business was still not completely settled, and for about an hour, old Lionel kept dropping behind and wandering off the trail.

I yelled out at him one time, and he said, "Could I have me a *swim*, Cap'n, I mebbe could stay awake a little better and keep up witchoo."

This got to happening pretty often that afternoon, so when it was time to stop for dinner, I gave up and told him to go ahead and drown himself.

I built a fire and made coffee, while Lionel cooked the salt pork and then fried biscuits in the grease. When we'd finished, and I'd taken the pans to the stream to wash them, Lionel took off. I was hoping he'd get cramps if the water was deep enough.

"At least have the sense to go downstream a ways," I yelled out, "away from our drinking water."

He turned and looked at me for a second and said, "I'll tell you somepin: *dat was mah intention all along!*"

Now I figured I could enjoy a little peace. I kicked off my boots and sat down on the sod beside my hobbled horse. It had gotten late and was almost dusk, so I pulled out a long Virginia stogie and lighted it. I sat there reflecting upon the course that my career had taken and the various surprises that had always managed to pop up and keep me alert. I contemplated the odd coincidences in my life and thought about Lily de Wilde.

I wondered what in the hell had ever happened to her.

I sat and smoked a while, then stirred the fire and pulled out a brand to relight my stogie, which wasn't burning evenly. Somewhere a coyote barked, which struck me as a mite early, so I sat real still and smoked and listened. But things quieted down.

Right about then, there was the noise of a man running toward me. At least it sounded like a man, although I couldn't tell for certain. But it was sure as hell the sound of some big critter thrashing violently through the tangle of shrubs and grass nearby.

I dropped my stogie to the ground, took out my revolver, and rolled over into the sparse bushes, away from the fire.

But what popped out was only Lionel Littlejohn. He ran into the firelight and panted, "Listen heah, Cap'n! Listen heah!"

I stood up, put my revolver back, and asked what was wrong.

"Jes' de strangest damn sight I ever *done* see!" he panted. "I is drying off from dish heah swim I been talkin' about, and I was 'most dried off and had just put mah shirt and pants back on, and what do I see but dish heah Indian come a walking along towards me *backwards*! So help me, cross mah haht to die! Deh he was, a walkin' *backwards*, not even a looking round, but jas' a walkin' along and gittin' cotched ever now and then by some of dem briars, but not even a turnin' his *haid*."

"How far away was this Indian?"

"About a hundred yards. Mebbe two hundred. Jest a walking along *backwards* as big as you please! Most like he's done walk into de river by now."

"He was headed for the river?" I asked.

"Dat is exactly de way he was headed!"

I took off running in the direction Lionel Littlejohn had pointed. The terrain was rough, but there was already a three-quarters moon in the sky, and it was light enough for me to find my way to an opening in the brush, where I could get to the water and see if there was somebody in it.

And there sure as hell was. When I waded into the shallows and stopped, I could see the head of an Indian bob to the surface about forty feet away, and then go under again. A top hat floated nearby. I could feel small waves lapping against my knees and figured he'd just that minute stepped into the river. I could probably save him if I was lucky enough to see him in the water with the moonlight shining on the surface.

So I waded out until I was chest-deep. Right then I thought I could make out a darkness underwater, so I lunged for it and managed to grab Henry Buck by his hair and tow him out of the deep hole he'd stepped into, and up onto the bank.

After I'd pulled him ashore, I clutched him under the armpits and threw him over my shoulder. Then I carried him all the way back to the fire. Putting him down, I saw that the sleeve of his buckskin was all scabbed with blood.

Lionel Littlejohn was busy collecting buffalo chips for the fire and said he didn't want anything to do with Henry Buck.

"Dat man is crazy like I nevah *see* befoah!" Lionel said.

I didn't figure it was the time to argue the point. I took Henry Buck's deerskin tunic off, with about twice the trouble it takes to skin a catfish. He was soaking wet and a cool night wind had picked up.

When he was stripped to the waist, I saw that he'd been shot in the upper arm. It looked like the ball had passed through without clipping a bone or artery. I covered him up with my blanket and helped him up close to the fire.

"Ah *nevah* seen no man act like dat befoah," Lionel said, shaking his head.

Henry Buck just sat there without making a move. His head hung forward like his neck was half broken. I lifted his arm to look at the wound and saw that he'd lost considerable blood, but the wound had clotted and seemed to be healing all right.

"How come de blamed fool was walking backwards?" Lionel said, leaning over to look into Henry Buck's eyes.

"That'd be a long story," I said, "but I figure I know part of the reason for it."

Lionel gave me a scornful look, like I should know better than try to tell him such a lie.

Then I said that it was lucky the wound wasn't any worse, although it was hard to tell how much blood he'd lost.

"Wait jest a minute," Lionel said. "You act like you *know* dis heah Redskin!"

"Yep," I said. "We've traveled many a mile together."

"Well I be hog-tied and mule-switched!" Lionel said.

"We're old acquaintances."

"Out heah on de lonesome prairie, and who should de Cap'n run *into*, a walking *backwards*, mind you, but some old acquaintance! Could be he run into somebody else, but oh no! Cap'n heah, he got to run into some old acquaintance, jest a strolling along *backwards* and trying to *drown* his damn self!"

"It is considerable strange for a fact," I said. "A mighty odd coincidence, when you think about it."

"Craziest damn thing I ever *did* see! Coincidence don't *begin* to tell de tale!"

"Nope," I said. "It's almost too much to believe, the way things happen sometimes!"

"And dat Redskin out of his damn mind de way he act!"

"Maybe," I answered, "but you don't have any notion of what Henry Buck here has gone through, and how much blood he's lost. He's done me considerable wrong, Henry Buck has, and I admit that I was put out with him, but I've got an idea he's suffered more than anybody else could guess."

"You talk about dis heah *Indian* and de way *he's* suffahed," Lionel said, "doan you think *I* done suffah *my* share in dis heah vale of tears? Doan you?"

I nodded and admitted the possibility.

Henry Buck was sitting before the fire sound asleep, my blanket thrown over his shoulders. The locusts were still loud, even though the cold breeze meant they wouldn't live much longer. The fire was bright and warm, because Lionel had piled plenty of buffalo chips on it.

"Yep," I said, feeling philosophical, "I don't doubt you've suffered, Lionel, and I've probably not given you a fair shake, because I've been thinking about getting my wagon rolling and not much else."

"Someday, when you ain't in such a big damn *hurry*, I gone *tell* you about jest a *little* of what I done lived through, Cap'n."

"Well, some day I'd like to hear it," I said. "I always did like a good story."

"I thought mebbe you could hear it now. Lessen you wants to attack de wagon, like you said."

"Nope," I said. "Now that Henry Buck is with us, we'll wait a spell. We don't need any fire to guide us to the wagon. Henry Buck could find a thread in a wheatfield, and he's tough enough that he'll be able to help us out after a couple hours' rest. So it'll be best to wait. Not only that, after he recovers, he might be able to give us some news about whether the wagon's been taken over by somebody or gutted of its valuables."

"But you doan want me to tell mah story, is dat it?"

"Nope," I said, "I've got too much on my mind."

"Well, den, how about mebbe you touch mah haid and tell me is I a *good* man or a *bad* man or *what*. Tell me is I going to Heaven or to Hell. Tell me is I going to get rich and ever settle down and git married to a permanent woman, and all dat *othuh* shit a man jest naturally wants to know about."

"I can't unload all that on you," I said. Then I explained how phrenology is a science of analysis and not the art of divination. But I pointed out that the ancients figured a man's character is his fate, and if that's the case, then maybe phrenology can help out. Those old philosophers figured that we all have a hand in what happens to us, even if we don't know about it in detail, so they figured we should learn what we are to find out the future, or what we will *be*. "Yep," I told Lionel, "I've often figured we befall our accidents as much as they befall us, so that if you tell a man what he is, then you've come near to telling him what will happen to him."

"Dat's it," Lionel said. "*Dat's* what I want to heah!"

"Well, I'll give it a shot when I have time, but right now I've got too much on my mind."

"You mean I got to wait for dat, too?"

"That's about the size of it."

"If dat doan beat all hands! First you hurry a man like de world's coming to some end, and den you tell a man to wait."

"Yep," I said. "That's the way it goes, sometimes."

"More like de way it *doan* go," Lionel grumbled, taking off his coat so he could roll it up for a pillow.

18

So, whilst that man dothe saile theise worldlie seas,
His voyage shortes: althoughe he wake, or sleepe,
And if he keepe his course directe, he winnes
That wished porte, where lasting ioye beginnes.
— Geffrey Whitney's *A Choice of Emblemes*

AN INDIAN can fool you. It's a well-known fact. An Indian can
be wrung out like a wet towel, trampled on like a snake, jumped
on, thudded, and bruised, and even skinned and boiled, and all of
a sudden, you look up, and there he is, ready to steal a horse or
have a religious vision.

So it wasn't what you'd call a big surprise when I saw Henry
Buck sit up all of a sudden and stir the fire with a stick. And it
wasn't much of a surprise when he acted like nothing had happened.
If you judged by the way he acted, I might just have saved myself
the trouble of saving his damned miserable hide for the second
time. You'd think he'd know I would naturally be curious about
what sort of tricks he'd been up to since he'd escaped from Half
Face and his gang.

Finally I came out with it and said to him, "Henry, didn't I just
now save your worthless God damn life from drowning? Didn't
I? A *second* time?"

He agreed I had, which was considerable for Henry, so I said,
"Well, don't you figure I deserve an explanation of some sort? Like
how did you get that bullet hole in your arm? And do you think
we're too late to save the wagon?"

"Maybe," Henry said, nodding. "Me don't know, but could be
too late, Professor. Me go to him wagon yesterday to get food and
whiskey, and find everything just like we leave it. Nothing change,
except Crawford. Now he lie there in big lake of stink. Whew!
But last night, me leave wagon and scout around and see trail of

wagon and four horses coming that way. Who knows? They may
be scoundrels."

"Yep. Pretty damned likely!" I said.

"Me don't steal nothing out of him wagon," Henry Buck said.
And there was a little pride in the way he said it. "Me just get him
food and whiskey. Me ain't going stay around that place with body
of Crawford lying there in big lake of stink. Whew!"

Henry Buck held his nose to indicate the enormity of Crawford's
last message to the world.

"Hold on a minute," I said. "Do you mean to tell me that the
coyotes and magpies and such haven't already cleaned those bones
of flesh?"

Henry Buck shook his head no and then put his open hand over
his mouth, which signified he found it considerable odd, not to say
astonishing.

I asked him how that could be, and Henry answered that he
figured the cusses and obscenities and profanities I'd delivered were
probably so concentrated that the power of their medicine had made
the place too awful for wild beasts to come near.

I gave a shot at trying to talk Henry Buck out of believing this
superstitious hogwash, but I could tell he persisted, even though
he didn't really try to argue the point with me. And since I couldn't
otherwise explain how human flesh would lie there so long unmolested, in the midst of what had to be a pretty thick population of
scavenging beasts, I decided to let the argument rest.

But I got back to the matter at hand, and asked Henry if he had
any other ideas about my possessions.

"Me no know," he said. "Outlaws and scoundrels all around."

"I wouldn't be surprised but what we're too late," I muttered,
shaking my head.

"Like I say," Lionel said, "man got de sun and de moon, why
he got to be hurrying all around?"

The irrelevance of this observation interested me, but I managed
to let it go and return to something that had been bothering me
almost from the start of Henry Buck's story. "You talked about
seeing Crawford's body," I said, "but I didn't hear you say anything
about the corpse of Half Face."

"I don't say nothing," Henry Buck said with dignity, "because

Half Face ain't there. Only Crawford, him lying in big lake of stink. Whew!"

What in the hell had happened to Half Face's body? Who had bothered to take it or bury it? Or could there have been another explanation?

"Wait a minute," I said, "did you see any signs that somebody had buried a corpse around there? Was there a fresh grave?"

"No grave," he answered.

All of a sudden, right there in my mind, I saw Half Face's eye open up and stare at me, and damned if I didn't feel a chill come up my back like somebody had opened the door of a cold room behind me. Was it possible that Half Face was still alive? Had I maybe just dreamed I'd killed him? I'd been considerable drunk and fuddled, but Crawford had been killed, for sure: his corpse was proof of that. But what about Half Face? What had happened to him?

"I reckon we'll wait for daylight before we go to the wagon," I said. "And then we'll bury Crawford."

"When you going to tell mah haid?" Lionel asked.

"I'll do it," I told him, "but this isn't the time. I've got to figure out a way to get the wagon back and keep our skins filled up with blood, which maybe won't be so easy if that son of a bitch isn't dead."

Lionel thought about that a minute and then said, "But cain't you jest give it a touch, Cap'n? Hell, shouldn't take all *dat* long, jest to give a man's haid one of dem *touches!*"

I finally gave in, but I told Lionel I wouldn't do any more than take a brief trot over the territory. In fact, I told him that just glancing at his forehead told me something about him that I figured was characteristic of Africans: his Mound of Tune was prominent. It was right up there with the best.

"Does dat mean ah kin carry a tune, like dey say?"

"Yep, that's what it means."

"Hell, man doan need no *Cap'n* to come along and tell him *dat.* I knew *dat* in de *fust* place!"

"It's not always the case that the truth comes as a surprise, is it?"

"I tell you one thing: ain't no damn surprise in *dat!*"

I grabbed his head and gave it a vigorous twist or two, just to get Lionel's full attention, and then described some of the main features of the terrain, which included good development of Eventuality (*Mémoire des Choses*) or the median projection above the glabella. I explained what this meant, and Lionel accepted the news with considerable gravity and then withdrew into himself to reflect. Either that or he was getting sleepy.

Right then, the vision of Half Face's head drifted back into my own thoughts, like a head floating on water, and I started to shake and tremble. I kept telling myself not to think about it, but how can you call your attention off a subject, like a trained hound dog, when you have to bring the subject up in order to avoid it? You might as well tell a man to take off his boots and not think of Infant Damnation.

Still, you've got to do what you can, and the fact is, I figure that a measure of self-control is always possible to a rational critter, which most of us claim to be.

So I steeled my resolve, as they say, and blotted out the thought of Half Face. I kept telling myself that there had to be some kind of explanation for the fact his body was not rotting out there where I'd left it, and I'd soon learn what it was.

Then I turned to other matters, and asked Henry Buck why he hadn't tried to get me loose after the young Comanche had freed him.

"I suppose you had to figure you were leaving me to face certain death," I told him.

Henry Buck nodded and said that at one time that night, all three of the rogues and Henry Buck and myself fell asleep under the weight of the whiskey we'd drunk. The only one who stayed awake was the young Comanche.

This Comanche came over to Henry Buck and untied him. And when they were about to untie me — Half Face yelled out, like he was having a whiskey nightmare, and scared the two Indians away.

It was coming up dawn, and Half Face kept on groaning like he might have been about to wake up, so that the two of them didn't figure it was safe to come back and untie me.

Henry Buck said they didn't really mean to leave me in the lurch, though. He said they hid in the brush on a low ridge about a quarter of a mile away, hoping they'd have a chance to sneak back and untie me, and then we'd steal some horses and take off like a flight of ducks.

But it didn't turn out that way. Henry Buck said that right after daybreak, they could hear Half Face start in roaring and cussing about the two of them getting away. Then they heard my voice, even louder, and Henry thought he could even recognize some of the cuss words and epithets I had used on him before, although he said that some of the expressions sounded new to him.

When they later saw Half Face and me sit down together, and saw me begin to write on a piece of paper, Henry Buck and the Comanche were considerable puzzled. They figured that Half Face and I had suddenly become friends and were gossiping there with our heads together.

Right then, William Bone got up and started walking right in their direction and seated himself on the ground and looked all around like he was scanning the area, maybe looking for the two escaped Indians. Now they *really* figured that Half Face and I had come to some kind of understanding. So the two of them decided to take off.

I interrupted Henry Buck and asked him about the young Comanche. I asked what sort of critter he was. Henry didn't answer me right away, so I went ahead and talked, the way I do sometimes, just to fill up the silence, and began to tell Henry what a remarkable head that Comanche had. I told him it was one of the noblest heads I had ever held in my hands, which was only the truth. I even told him it was characterized by preternatural qualities of Sublimity, Ideality, and Firmness, and used those very words.

I asked Henry why I'd never been able to find me a young and marriageable Female with a head like that. I figured if he wouldn't answer sensible questions it wouldn't hurt to ask him some of the other kind. Then I told him that the Comanche was a credit to his race, and I hoped Henry had sped him on his journey or helped him in some way to show his gratitude.

When Henry Buck still didn't say anything, I said to him, "Damn it, how's come you haven't mentioned that boy?"

Henry looked thoughtful a minute, if you could call it that, and then said, "Professor, that boy, him no boy. That boy, him a girl."

When I remember Henry saying that to me, and I try to remember exactly how I took it, I kind of go blank. Then I think I can hear a voice saying to myself, "Oh, my prophetic soul!" as the Bard said one time, in the form of Hamlet.

All I can be sure of is that I was what you'd have to call stunned. And at the same time, all kinds of things kept tumbling through my mind, like "Of course, you blamed idiot! You knew it all along. You *had* to!"

But Henry Buck wasn't paying any attention to what was happening inside my head, as how could he? Instead, he kept on talking, now that the secret was out. He said, her name was Wuyoomi-Yaki, which is Comanche for "Frail Bird."

I asked him to give me that name again, so I would be sure to remember it for my journal, and Henry did. It was right about then that I heard Lionel Littlejohn snoring.

But you can bet that I was wide awake. And I told Henry to tell me Wuyoomi-Yaki's story, which he went right ahead and did.

19

The dead it is,
Rather than the living, who make the longest demands.
— *Antigone*

WUYOOMI-YAKI had an older brother who was a big warrior among the Comanches because of his bravery. His name was Naki-Napi, which means "Hears the Trail." One day Naki-Napi went on a war party against a troop of American soldiers who were leaning over some territory the Comanches decided was not only their own, but sacred, too.

They followed the troop of Cavalry for several days, way beyond their own range, but Naki-Napi kept on, figuring he was honor bound not to give up on a brag he'd made to count coups. Then early one morning they surprised the Cavalry, and in a short hot skirmish Naki-Napi was wounded and knocked unconscious by a half-spent musket ball glancing off his head.

When he came around, he found out he was a prisoner. The Cavalry troops figured he was a chief, or at least an important warrior, so they didn't kill him right then, but put him in shackles and took him all the way to Fort Riley, for the disposal of his case by someone higher in command.

There happened to be an Arapaho scout at the fort who saw Naki-Napi when he was brought in and thrown behind bars. He saw everything, in fact, including Naki-Napi's trial, when he was sentenced to death by hanging, which was carried out right away, without any fuss.

The Arapaho scout traveled around a bit and talked about Naki-Napi's fate, so that a few months later, the news got back to the Comanches. And when Wuyoomi-Yaki heard what had happened, she just about went crazy.

There was a reason for this, in addition to the grief she would naturally feel for a brother's death, because according to military law Naki-Napi wasn't only hanged, but he was buried outside the stockade. Not only that, he was buried in the White Man's manner, *in the ground*, and to the Comanche, this was an awful insult to the body of a dead warrior. There isn't anything in our own burial lore that comes near to equaling it. We just don't have insults like that, when it comes to a corpse.

And that isn't all, because most Indians figure there isn't any closer human relationship than that between a brother and sister, and Wuyoomi-Yaki was crazy about her brother and proud of him in a way that we can't hardly imagine. So after she heard the news about Naki-Napi, she couldn't sleep for four days and four nights, lying awake and thinking about her brother's dead body, unbundled, unscented, unpainted, unattended by his weapons, and just lying there somewhere in the dark earth with dirt in its face. There weren't any kinfolk around to set things right, because a party had just taken off for a raid to the east.

On the fifth evening, Wuyoomi-Yaki put a man's moccasins on, fixed her hair like a boy's, took her uncle's tunic, which was big enough to hide her bosom, and took off. She'd made up her mind to dig her brother's corpse up out of the earth, wrap it in funeral clothes, and put it in a kind of box made out of wood and skins, on top of the ground, the way the Comanches bury their dead.

She knew it'd be tough going, so she decided to steal a horse, and attach herself to the first band headed in the right direction. Stealing a little mare was easy, and so was joining up with the party of Half Face, Crawford, and William Bone.

So this was how she came to be traveling with that trio of brigands.

We were quiet a minute after Henry finished talking. I don't know what Henry was thinking, but I was wondering how far Wuyoomi-Yaki had gotten on her way to Fort Riley. I figured if I got the wagon fixed right away, I might be able to catch up with her the next day. In fact, I could ride ahead and try to catch her, while Henry Buck followed in the wagon. Except he'd be better at finding her than I was.

But what if he wasn't up to either task? It was hard to tell how much blood he'd lost. I pointed to his arm. "How'd you get that hole in your arm?" I asked him.

Henry picked up his story again, where he'd left off. He said that Wuyoomi-Yaki and he still hadn't completely written me off. In fact, after they'd gone a distance, they circled back and kind of hovered around the camp, wondering if maybe things weren't the way they looked and Half Face and I hadn't really gotten together, after all, and maybe I would need some help.

So they began to creep up to us, and all of a sudden they heard a shot in the distance. And then, after a couple of seconds, another shot. And after that, they were treated to the sight of a gigantic form rising up right before them, so close they'd practically stepped on him. It was William Bone, and his coat was flapping and his eyes were bugged out like a bullfrog's.

Well, they were so surprised at seeing him come galloping in their direction that it took them a couple of seconds to get a move on. They didn't trust William Bone any more than they did the other two, so their instincts were dead right. William Bone's instincts, on the other hand, were too slow, and it took him a minute to get his pistol out and shoot at Henry Buck, just winging him in the arm without crippling him or slowing him down very much. And the giant didn't take off after them. Instead, he took off in another direction.

"Yep, that sounds like the damned coward," I said, when Henry told this part of his story.

Henry didn't say anything, but he nodded, and then he told about how Wuyoomi-Yaki had nursed him through the night, and over the next couple of days. She got roots and berries for him to eat, and even brought fresh water from the stream.

Henry said he'd figured he'd drown himself because it looked like I'd been killed by one of those gunshots they'd heard, and my body taken away somewhere for burial. And ever since I'd saved his life that time long ago, he was convinced his life was tied to mine. In fact, he said that I was the only tribe he had left, and when he said this, I hardly knew what to tell him, because an idea like that is pretty hard to figure out. Hearing him say something like that made me feel kind of bad and even gave me a lump in the throat. I figure it had to do with friendship.

I just sat there for a while, thinking about Henry's story, and then I decided to come right out with it, so I asked him if he thought maybe we could catch Wuyoomi-Yaki before she got to Fort Riley.

Henry said, "You want see Wuyoomi-Yaki, me bring her here in half an hour."

Then he stood up, and cupping his hands about his mouth, gave some kind of bird call, and damned if she didn't just come walking out of the darkness.

It's a fact: Wuyoomi-Yaki, or Frail Bird, was standing right there at the edge of the firelight, looking down at the ground at a spot about twenty inches before the little toes of her moccasins!

20

It rageth with all sorts and conditions of men, yet is most
evident among such as are young and lusty, in the flower of
their years, nobly descended, high fed, such as live idly, and
at ease; and for that cause (which our divines call burning lust)
this *ferinus insanis amor*, this mad and beastly passion, as I have
said, is named by our physicians heroical love, and a more
honourable title put upon it, *amor nobilis*, as Savanarola styles
it, because noble men and women make a common practice
of it, and are so ordinarily affected by it.

— Robert Burton

SOMETIMES IF YOU hit a man over the head with a club, he'll
swallow his tongue and choke to death. I figure the way I felt when
I saw Wuyoomi-Yaki standing right there before me in the firelight
was somewhat like that. It wasn't exactly pleasant. In fact, it came
near to being a kind of misery. Only there was ecstasy in it, too.

I kept telling Henry Buck I wanted to tell her something and
wanted him to translate for me, but I never did get around to the
message. I just kept saying I wanted to say something, and Henry
Buck just kept on waiting there, and so did Wuyoomi-Yaki; but I
never did actually get anything said.

The fact was, my mind was filled up with things, like a stew,
and I couldn't sort them out. It was like a herd of wild ponies
galloping all around, raising up dust, and I couldn't make sense out
of the commotion.

Part of it was that damned Half Face. I couldn't get over the fact
that he'd crawled off somewhere, and might be alive and plotting
to get his revenge on me, right this minute. Thinking of that hole
in his forehead, I could hardly believe he'd survived; and yet, the
cartridge might have been undercharged, the way they are now
and then. That damned bullet might have just nestled in the skull.
Maybe it didn't even penetrate the periosteum. If the meninges had

been torn, he'd eventually die. But there might be time for him to work a lot of mischief before he did. There was something uncanny about the whole business.

When I couldn't figure out what to tell Henry Buck to translate for Wuyoomi-Yaki, I lost my temper and cussed a while, and then all of a sudden I was overcome with a powerful drowsiness, and damned if I didn't just drift off and fall asleep. I couldn't have lost consciousness faster if I'd been put under some kind of spell. I didn't wake up until the next morning.

The first thing I saw was Wuyoomi-Yaki building a fire. Henry Buck and Lionel Littlejohn were still asleep, so I got up and went over to her. I put my hand on her shoulder, and then touched her head, which made her eyes come up like I'd pressed a button on a doll. She was just plain beautiful, there's no other word for it. I touched her cheek with the palm of my hand, and she looked down at the ground again, and sort of smiled. I figure she knew all about me, somehow, even if she didn't know English.

When Henry Buck woke up, I told him to tell Wuyoomi-Yaki what I had to do, and that as soon as I could, I was bound and determined to help her rescue her brother's corpse. Henry spoke to her and slapped out a few ideas in sign language, and she looked thoughtful — which isn't saying much, because she *always* looked thoughtful. But anyway, I was glad I'd told her.

We collected our gear and got started, facing the morning sun.

Then Lionel said, "Hey, Cap'n, when you gone tell mah haid, like you say? De full treatment."

"When the time's right," I said.

"Sho hopes you doan fohgit!"

"Nope. I guess you wouldn't let that happen."

Lionel grunted and then said, "Ah figure you was gone creep up on that wagon under de covah of night. I figure dat was yo strategy."

"It was," I said, "until Henry Buck joined us. Henry won't need the cover of night." I don't know whether this made any sense or not. It was just something I said. I was confused and I also had a scratchy throat.

A minute later, Henry raised his arm and pointed.

"Are we about there?" I said.

Henry said we were, and then when I asked if there was anybody about, he shook his head and said he didn't think so, but he'd circle the wagon.

Lionel and Wuyoomi-Yaki and I waited while he rode on out, and about a minute after he'd left, the wind shifted a little, and sure enough, we could smell Crawford's decaying corpse.

When Henry returned, he said the horses were gone. I said I figured they'd broken their hobbles and taken off. Or were stolen. Whichever was the case, we wouldn't worry about it.

I gave Virginia stogies to Lionel and Henry, and lit one myself. Then we rode on out to the wagon, where we improvised a hitch and dragged it about a hundred yards upwind from the rotting corpse, so we could fix the axle without having to stop and gag every other breath.

I looked all around, but didn't see any sign of either William Bone or Half Face. I asked Henry, and he said there wasn't any sign they'd come back, so I rested easy for a minute, puffing on my stogie.

Then I looked inside the wagon and was surprised to see the wax bust of Daniel Webster staring back at me out of a physiognomy that was changed almost beyond description. All those pronounced convolutions signifying oratorical and intellectual genius had melted under the heat of the past two days. That brow which had been admired and exalted by just about every phrenologist in the land had softened and slipped loose, so that one eye glared out from under a surly, half-melted eyebrow; and the mouth sagged like an idiot's.

But there wasn't any time to waste sentiment or moralizing over something like this, so I pulled the whiskey jug out and we all had ourselves a snort, while Wuyoomi-Yaki kept a lookout on a nearby ridge. Then we went to work, and Lionel Littlejohn began to act like a different man, and got things organized so that in a couple of hours, we had the wagon standing up straight as a flagpole and ready to go.

I told Lionel I was impressed with the way he'd gone about things, and he said that people weren't always like they seemed, which struck me as true enough.

We passed the whiskey jug around again, and Lionel asked me to read his head, so I obliged. There were no surprises as big as his skill in fixing the axle waiting for me, but it wasn't a bad head. I was feeling pretty good from the whiskey, so I made it sound better.

When I finished with Lionel, Henry Buck asked me to read his skull again, which I had done about fifty times during our public demonstrations, but I obliged him for old times' sake. Then I turned around to Wuyoomi-Yaki, who lowered her eyes as I traced my fingers gently over the Mounds of Passion, Benevolence, and Hope, along with all those other configurations that separate us from the browless baboon and the pateless ape.

Then I got down to business again. I figured it would be a good idea to start for Shoestring as soon as possible, even though it was early evening. I don't know why. I just felt uneasy staying where we were. But before we took off, I decided that Lionel, Henry, and I would draw lots to see who'd have the job of taking the shovel I'd strapped to the side of the wagon and going back to bury the remains of Crawford.

I told them this was something that had to be done, because in spite of all appearances, Crawford had once had a mother. Even William Bone and Half Face had mothers at one time, I told them. They might have even been loved and fondled and chucked beneath the chin and had baby talk spoken in their direction. I also mentioned how surprising it was that the coyotes and wolves hadn't already distributed Crawford's remains; therefore, it was like a sign, and it was up to us to perform this act of piety.

"Even though I shot and killed him in self-defense," I went on, "because he took up his cards with those that wanted to murder me, nevertheless we ought to pause and acknowledge in our hearts that the poor son of a bitch might have turned out otherwise, if he hadn't fallen into their villainous hands. And not only that, we ourselves, if things had turned out a little different in ways only God could understand, might have ended up pretty much like Crawford did."

I don't know what had gotten into me to talk so much, but I did go on considerable in my Samuel Chadwick voice. However I was finally hauled in by Lionel, who said, "Hey, *Cap'n!* Why shit, man, why doan we just go ahead and draw the damn lots, 'cause if'n we wait much *longer*, we ain't gone have no light to *see* by so's we can *dig* dis heah grave!"

I took stock a minute, and had to admit that what he'd said made sense, so we got down to business and drew lots with blades of Buffalo grass, which I held. It turned out I was the loser, so it looked like my speech had been a considerable waste of breath.

I took another drink of whiskey, relighted my stogie, and started walking back along the trail to do my duty. I don't think I staggered a great deal. I found the body all right.

The hole I dug was right next to the corpse; in fact, a couple of times my shovel hit the boot, and one time the elbow, which was sort of puffy and gummy, like an upholstered chair that's been left out in the rain, the way it felt.

I dug down about four and a half to five feet, and took the shovel and pried the remains over into the hole. The corpse was considerable mushy and about a thousand flies that had been feasting on it rose up in a thick cloud and whirled all around my head. I went over and picked up the top hat and dropped it on top of the corpse at the bottom of the hole. Then I shoveled in the dirt, which after considerable stamping, left a mound about six inches high. I took part of the broken axle, which I'd dragged back with me, and dug a hole for it at the head of the grave, sticking it upright in the ground. I took my knife and carved Crawford's last name, which was the only name I knew, along with the date into the wood. The result wasn't very clear because the oak they'd made the axle out of was about as hard as iron. I figured it must have taken an awful jolt for it to break the way it did.

Then I said, "Well, Crawford, that's it." I figured this was about as elaborate a funeral sermon as he deserved.

When I got back to the wagon, both Lionel Littlejohn and Henry Buck were staggering drunk. Wuyoomi-Yaki kind of smiled when I looked at her, then lowered her eyes.

I picked up the jug and urged the two rascals to drink more, and in about half an hour they were laid out on the ground like hogs for scalding, snoring in harmony.

Then I picked up a blanket and motioned to Wuyoomi-Yaki, who glanced briefly at our two sleeping companions, and then sort of flicking her glance over my legs and waist once again, followed me away from the firelight. We walked about a hundred yards, maybe more, until we couldn't hear the snoring. Then I took her hand and pulled her down on the blanket with me, and right away she started in whispering to me in Comanche. What she was saying I'll never know, but I will say it sounded beautiful to my ears.

Wuyoomi-Yaki had such womanly strength and beauty that there are times when I figure I might have just dreamed about her. Once afterwards I tried to get that night down in a poem. I tried to capture what had happened to us. I talked about how under the ancient stars and the old moon we became one, Wuyoomi-Yaki and I, with her whispering the guttural words of her tongue in my ear almost up to the end, when her voice stopped uttering words at all, but instead spoke out in the oldest language of all — that mute cry we share with the antelope, the partridge, and the deer: I was talking about the language of Amativeness, the voice of mating, the prayer of the flesh to be remembered, crying out never ever to be forgotten.

21

All things are concealed in all.
— Paracelsus in *Coelum
Philosophorum*

WHEN DAWN came, Wuyoomi-Yaki built a fire beside my blanket.
This signified that wherever I was, there she'd build her fire, for
that was her home. Lionel and Henry snored away like two buffalos
in a wallow, right beside the wagon. Wuyoomi-Yaki woke them
up and told them to come on over and take breakfast by our fire.

When we'd eaten, we gathered together everything we needed
and started out on the trail to Shoestring, with the mules once more
in their rightful traces. Crawford's Indian pony was tied to our
wagon and trotted along behind as we jangled our way along the
trail. Lionel sat on the wagon seat and drove, Henry Buck rode
Half Face's horse, and Wuyoomi-Yaki and I sat together on the
tailgate of the wagon.

About an hour after starting out, we came on the corpse of
William Bone's draft horse. It had been shot in the head and had
swollen up like a balloon, although it hadn't reached the advanced
stage of decay Crawford had reached. Some critters had been feasting on its rump, but it was still pretty much intact, and it stank
like a city sewer.

The dust all around it was as soft and dry as a lady's talcum
powder, and there was one spot where Henry Buck saw the single
print of an enormous boot.

When Lionel Littlejohn saw the footprint, he reared back and
said, "What in de name of de Lawd does you call *dat*?"

"That," I told him, "is the footprint of William Bone, one of
the critters I've been trying to tell you about."

"You mean to tell me dat dere is a *footprint*?"

"Yep, that's what it is. It's a footprint sure enough. It was made
by William Bone."

"Good Lawd!" Lionel whispered. "Merciful Jesus!"

Right about here, Henry Buck, who'd been following William Bone's trail a short distance, came back and said, "Him walk like him plenty much drunk."

"Drunk?" I said.

Henry nodded and said, "Yep, him go all over, first this way and then that way, and don't stay in straight line when him walk."

"That's funny. I didn't figure there was any more whiskey missing from the wagon."

Henry shrugged and pointed up the trail. "Him go that way, though, when . . ." He frowned, trying to figure out how to say it in English. "When all the ways him go be put together."

I nodded. "What you mean is, he's headed in the general direction we're headed in. Toward Shoestring."

Henry Buck nodded and sat down on the ground.

"Then let's get ourselves set for a showdown, just in case," I said.

"You take some man with a foot *dat* big," Lionel said, "and if de rest of him measure up to de foot, Cap'n, you better get ready for *two* showdowns. Good Lawd didn't *mean* for no man to be *dat* big."

"Lionel," I said, "maybe you've got yourself a point, there. But for the moment, God damn it, stop quibbling: we're going to get ready in case those two sons of bitches from hell should try to bushwhack us and cut us down like jackrabbits."

I was trembling considerable, for some reason. I never could be sure when some rage would come to a galloping boil. It's part of having a volatile temperament, as they say. It's connected with sassafras.

Right then I felt it come on like a fit. I took off my hat and lifted my face and just let go for a while. I must have yelled and cussed for about a minute. There wasn't much direction to it, but there was considerable noise and commotion. My throat still felt scratchy, and my legs ached. I figured it was the fevernager coming back on me, only I vowed it wouldn't get me down.

"Cap'n," Lionel interrupted me when I stopped to take a breath, "wasn't you about to formulate some damn *plan*? Wasn't you about to figure out what we was gone do if'n we come up agin dis heah damn *giant?*"

I took a long look into Lionel Littlejohn's black, sweating face, and then nodded, figuring that nothing special was wrong, except that my damned temper had made a fool out of me one more time.

"Yep," I said, "damn if you're not one-hundred-percent right! So let's think of something."

And that's what we did. At least we tried to, but there wasn't a whole lot we could do except head for Shoestring by the shortest route, which was the trail we were already on.

That and keep our eyes and ears open, of course.

This was not much of a plan, if you think about it.

I figured Wuyoomi-Yaki ought to lag behind the wagon, and give us a warning if by some chance they came from behind. Lionel would sit up on the wagon seat and drive the two mules, while I figured I'd walk fifty or sixty feet to the left of the trail — which was the upper slope — and slightly ahead. Henry Buck was going to range back and forth up ahead. The chances were a hundred to one he'd keep us from being bushwacked.

We went along like this for about an hour. The air was as hot and thick as a bowl of soup. You could almost stir it with a spoon. It felt like a prodigious storm building up, and the sky showed it, too.

Then Henry Buck came on another sign of William Bone. There was another footprint, and right next to it, there was his greatcoat lying in a clump on the ground.

When Lionel Littlejohn saw the size of the coat, he held out his open hands, lifted his face, and asked the heavens, "What manner of man is *dis?* Does yoah expect me to believe dat one man and one man alone done put on dish heah coat and *wore* it?"

"You might as well believe it," I said, "because it's only the simple, unvarnished truth and nothing more."

"Maybe what we is following," he said, "is one of dem damn *circuses*, and dish heah man is de *giant*." He paused and thought a second. "And deah is de *tent!*"

But my mind was fixed on something else; and the minute I got it right in my head, I turned around and looked at the terrain behind. Then I motioned for Henry Buck to come with me, and we looked around for a couple of minutes and found four more of the giant footprints, but nothing else.

"Henry," I said, "where are the footprints of Half Face?"

Behind this question was that other one which had been making me awful uneasy, namely, how had Half Face stayed alive, when I'd seen clear as sin that I'd shot him right in the forehead, right in the Mound of Mirthfulness? I thought of that living eye gazing out of the bloody face. Picturing it in my mind, I fancied it had an expression of secret cunning as it looked at me.

Henry Buck didn't answer my question, which I hadn't figured he would, so all I could do was ponder upon it and cuss a little around the fringes of human ignorance.

We started in again, walking carefully, like we were in a village of rattlesnakes, still moving in the direction of Shoestring. For a while, I walked beside the wagon, where I could hear Lionel treating himself to a soliloquy. He said his past history would testify he was afraid of no man, but he didn't figure you should take on somebody else's troubles. Then he pointed out to himself that I'd only hired him to help me take the axle to the wagon and set it, and this business of trailing a giant wasn't any part of the bargain.

I interrupted him along about there. I said, "Well, there may be something to what you say, and generally speaking, I don't have any stomach to bring an innocent man into a private quarrel. But you're not taking into account the wickedness of these two renegades: why, they've got more murder, infamy, outrage, larceny, and wrath in their hearts than a regiment of devils. They proved that when they came up to Henry Buck and me in a state of pure helplessness and were all set to blow our brains out. I'm telling you these filthy, desperate bastards ought to be taken care of as soon as possible, *pro bono publico*, for the benefit of humanity in general, God damn it, before they strike again!"

"I ain't figuring on leavin' you," Lionel said, "I was jest making dish heah point. Old Lionel, he ain't *skeered*; he jest *curious*. Now what I say is, I ain't about to *leave* you, Cap'n, cause I want to *see* dish heah giant. If'n he got de rest of him as big as dose feet was meant to carry and dat coat was meant to cover, why he is somepin dish heah man has got to see!"

"Lionel . . ." I said, but right then I was interrupted by a sharp crack of lightning that came near to lifting me off the ground. I'd been so busy talking and watching the ground and the rims of the ridges, that I hadn't noticed how black the sky had gotten.

What I'd been about to point out was that we weren't really tracking the giant at all. It just so happened that we were on the same course. Not only that, there wasn't any evidence that William Bone knew we were anywhere near these parts. He might have thought I'd abandoned the wagon permanently.

But it looked like we were going to have a violent storm. The clouds drifting in our direction were as dark as night, and the wind was rising, blowing dust and tumbleweeds through the air.

"Get in the wagon," I yelled out to Wuyoomi-Yaki, who'd come alongside. "Lionel, try to keep the mules quiet. This looks like bad news coming on!"

There was another flash of lightning, followed by a long subsiding drumroll of thunder. The flash showed Henry Buck standing right before us on a little rise, facing our way. He was holding his hand up, palm forward.

I went up and asked him what he'd found.

"Him up there," Henry said, pointing behind him.

"You mean William Bone?"

"Yep, him up there two hundred paces."

"Did he see you?" I yelled, shouting into the rising wind.

"No, him no see me. Him up there going round . . ."

"Never mind!" I yelled out. I was excited by the wind and by the whiskey and the ague coming on. Not to mention the prospect of a showdown with that damned monster. "Protect my rear. Is he straight ahead?"

Henry Buck nodded, and I took out Half Face's revolver, saw that the cylinder was filled, and took off at a fast trot up a slight incline, and then down into a swale of sagebrush that covered a rolling terrain.

I had to clamber over so many rough rocky projections that I figured I'd done the right thing by leaving the horses and wagon behind.

By the time I'd gone about fifty yards, though, I got wary, figuring that Half Face might have circled behind me, ready to shoot me in the back as I approached William Bone.

But Henry Buck wouldn't be tricked. He would have warned me. I had faith in Henry, and kept on jogging ahead. I crouched close to the ground now and then, trying to take advantage of the flashes of lightning so I could scan the wild and brushy area all around and not make too much of a target.

Even though the clouds had gotten still darker, and the lightning flashed across the sky more violently every minute, right then the sound of thunder got quieter, for some reason, like somebody had shut a door somewhere up in the heavens. Now it had subsided and was just sort of rumbling along the horizon, like a bulldog growling.

I kept on and started up a stream bed of sorts — what they call arroyos, that fill with water after heavy rains, but stay dry most of the year. The gulley was lined with shaggy weeds, bushes, and dwarfed cottonwoods. It looked like a crooked little city alley when it pulsed from the periodical lightning. The firing of heavenly cannon, in the words of the poet.

It was just after one such flash, right before the sound of thunder could drum past, that I heard a hoarse mumbling ahead and to the right, and then the heavy breathing of a man laboring mightily.

While the thunder was growling sedately, I ran forward, turned the corner made by some scraggly bushes that edged the gulley, and in a sudden series of lightning flashes, came face to face with William Bone, carrying the corpse of Half Face in his arms. It was an awful looking thing — stone-pale, except where the dried blood was clotted like a mask over the face. The blood was near black and it was scabbed over the good eye, but that blind eye was untouched, and it still had that awful blind stare I remembered.

Once I tried to write a poem about this scene. I began by asking how much the mind can take in during those rare peaks of heightened excitement. How much do we pick up on that we don't understand until later? How vivid are the impressions that we sort of block out from our own understanding, because otherwise their full awesomeness might blight the mind, deaden the tongue, and make a man helpless to defend himself? The answer is, more than we could hardly believe.

It's a fact. In that first glimpse I saw everything: the giant William Bone standing with the corpse in his arms, staggering with the burden the poor damned wretch had carried for miles across this barren and heartless country; and then there he was, looking up to see his Nemesis, me, myself — Thaddeus Burke — suddenly before him, holding Half Face's revolver and ready to unload it in his direction.

"Go on!" he shouted. Right when he yelled this out, so help me, the wind died down, and the thunder stopped. I know this was just another coincidence, but it was like Nature wanted to be in on what William Bone had to say, too.

"Go on and kill me!" he cried. "For I consider my life nothing, for those very reasons I told you about. Yes, take my monstrous life, worthless as it is. I can hardly bear this heavy mortality any longer. Oh, Silenus was right: it would have been better if man had never come to exist! Go on and shoot, but spare the life of poor Half Face, I pray you!"

After he said this, he stumbled and half-dropped, half-placed, the grisly corpse on the ground. Rigor mortis had come and gone, and Half Face's body was as limp as a fresh corpse, only the stink was about four turns beyond considerable. His head was what you'd have to call the mutilation of a mutilation, because that's what it was, not to mention being pretty near the most godawful thing I have ever set eyes on.

William Bone dropped to his knees beside the corpse. He looked up at me again and yelled out: "Go ahead and shoot! Why do you hesitate, Professor Burke? Here, I'll bare my breast so you won't miss!"

And that's what he did, ripping his shirt aside and panting and staring at me out of the eyes of a real, by God, genuine, 24-karat lunatic.

"Go ahead!" he shouted. "But whatever you do, don't kill the kind and fun-loving Half Face, I beg and implore you! Don't think I didn't see you trick him when he was only trying to improve his vocabulary and increase his effectiveness among the vile Race of Men. I saw you take advantage of him and catch him offguard and shoot him in the head like a dog. It is only by the grace of God that he survives such a horrible wound! It is only because of his own stout spirit that his great, long-suffering heart is not broken by the thought of how you betrayed him!"

Up until then, I'd been what you'd have to call speechless at the scene before me. I wasn't able to say a word, let alone shoot the poor monster down, like I'd half intended right up to the time I ran into him.

But now, after listening to William Bone, I asked him how he could say such a thing. I told him that Half Face was sure as hell dead and you could tell he'd been dead for days. His corpse was puffed up and stank like a sick swamp. I told him to get control over himself, and take a good look at what he'd been carrying around. I told him that was a *corpse*, and if he couldn't tell by looking, he could sure as hell *smell* it, couldn't he?

William Bone gave a picky little smile and said, "Don't try to delude me. We know your clever tricks. We know your sophistries, don't we, Half Face!"

"You mean you won't admit that you tried to kill Henry Buck and myself," I cried, "and then steal all my belongings?"

"The only answer I can give should be sufficient," William Bone said, "even for one with such an impudent and twisted mind as yours: namely, we *did not* kill you, did we? And we had ample opportunity to *do* so, did we not? It is facts, Burke, facts we must look at, and nothing else!"

Right about then I started to tremble so hard, it's a wonder I didn't shake all the buttons off my clothes. I'll tell you, pure madness is a fearful thing. It got to me, I'll have to admit it. Even so, I managed to remind William Bone of the fact he'd recommended that we be killed, and I asked him how he could explain that away.

"Forget about me," he said. "It was Half Face you shot, wasn't it? And it was Half Face who insisted you be kept alive! It was he who promised your life in return for a few, paltry, vulgar words. This man you see resting here — this badly injured man, wounded by a shot from his very own revolver, which you yourself, schooled in the most infamous perfidy, shot full into his face . . . this innocent, playful, childlike man insisted on your living, and was content to let you live in exchange for the power of language, which he considered you to possess.

"And so far as your unmanly fear is concerned: surely you now realize that he was only playing a game! Surely you realize that he never once intended to kill you. I grant that his playfulness was crude and not always funny, but one doesn't kill a man because he disapproves of his sense of humor, does he? No, you had another reason, which I understand perfectly. *You killed him, Professor Burke, because you did not want him to speak!*"

"Oh, liar!" I cried, shaking so hard the earth itself seemed about to dance. "It was clear to anyone that he was just using me as long as I entertained him, and then intended to shoot me as quick as he'd shoot a limping rabbit!"

"Clear?" William Bone cried, mockingly. "Do you hear that, Half Face?"

"Yep," I shouted, "*clear!*"

"Clear to whom?" William Bone asked. "Don't you have any conscience, you vile mountebank? Don't you have any suspicion that the world may be something larger, greater, more complicated . . . yes, *grander* than you conceive of it and interpret it with your busy little hands? *The world has no head!* Do you understand? Few there are who can grasp this largeness, this greatness, the disorder, the random madness, the convulsive complication, the woeful deprivation of moral concinnity . . . but at least one should have the simple honesty to *wonder at its madness*."

Right then, I calmed down and got control of myself. I don't know how, but I did. I figured the best way to handle this critter was to be firm and businesslike.

So I pointed out to William Bone that he might accuse *me* of sophistry, but the fact was, he convicted himself with every word he spoke, every ridiculous argument he advanced.

"Listen to the staggering fool, Half Face!" the giant cried. He sort of whooped, which I guess was supposed to be a laugh of derision even though it would have been hard to identify. And then he said something else, but his words were obliterated by a detonation of thunder overhead.

"What?"

"You would not understand," William Bone muttered. "You would not understand simple gratitude and friendship. Or the antics of my benefactor's playful spirit."

"I'll be damned if I can figure out how that bastard could ever be anybody's benefactor."

"Your conception is sadly limited, then," William Bone said.

"For whatever little felicity I have experienced in this wretched life of mine derives from the compassionate heart and the innocent, carefree, fun-loving nature of the man you see lying there before me, resting from the hideous head wound you have given him. He is like a little father to me. It was *he* who rescued me from a traveling circus in Illinois, where I was put on constant display."

Right then, William Bone closed his eyes and moaned and chanted like a preacher. "Like the dancing bear, the wild tiger, the dwarf in armor, the elephant, the fat lady, and the simpering clowns, I was made a curiosity of; I was made a *thing* . . . I was made to sit upon a great bench at the center of a canvas ring. One of the dancing girls played the mandolin when people were admitted to view and gape at me, and a villain named Colonel Lysander Parks told the most outrageous lies regarding my size, my eating habits, my unfortunate history . . . and upon occasion he would even commit the insolence of tapping my shoulder with his toothpick cane, as I sat there facing the stares of the hundreds of gawking yokels who passed by to view my colossal and ineffable monsterhood!"

"I should put you out of your misery now," I said, "and do you the kind of favor you were ready to do for me, if you'd gotten your wish a couple of days ago. But leave that stinking body alone, so's we can bury it, and we'll get going to Shoestring, and when we get there, I promise I'll let you go your own way."

"Your terms are hateful to me," William Bone said.

"I'll be damned if you don't sing a different song now than you sang several nights ago by the campfire," I said. "You sure had plenty of contempt for *both* your comrades then, saying I'd obviously lied in analyzing *their* heads. But when it came to ascribing virtues to *yours*, why it was a different story. *Then* it was evident I was only telling the truth! That's vanity, William Bone! Vanity! The only head I didn't lie about that evening was the head of Wuyoomi-Yaki, the young Comanche girl you thought was a boy!"

"*Now* who's mad?" he asked, looking up at the sky.

"Come on," I said, "let's get the hell out of here."

"Come no closer," he said, "I'll defend Half Face with my life."

"You were of a different mind when I first shot him," I said. "I came after you and saw you flapping away like a big bird in your coat!"

"No man is what he would like to be. We *all* betray ourselves."

"Yep, I'll agree. Only we ought to hit a little closer to the mark than you've been doing lately. But enough of that: let's haul out of here. It's time to get going before we're blown away. I'll promise to see that Half Face is decently buried."

"Why do you persist in speaking of him as if he were dead?" William Bone asked. "If he were not so badly wounded from your perfidious shot, he would stand up right now and face you down like the cowardly villain you are!"

"Come on," I said. "It's starting to rain. We've wasted enough time."

"Step no farther!" he roared. And right then he pulled a revolver out of his clothing, and lifted it like a child's toy in his hand, ready to shoot. But I shot first — once, twice, and then three times, right up into the looming darkness of his chest.

He started to come down. He shook all over, and with his empty hand grabbed at the air, like there were cobwebs all around him. Then his whole body quivered, and his eyes glowed wildly. The hand holding the revolver convulsed, dropping it to the ground.

There was another flash of lightning and William Bone's body trembled rigid, and collapsed over the corpse of Half Face, right about the time a drumroll of thunder echoed out of the skies beyond.

But the great poor mad critter was not dead yet. William Bone got up on his knees and faced me once more, teetering this way and that, his arms hanging at his sides like they were both broken.

"Promise," he whispered out of his death agony. "Promise, promise!"

"Say it and you've got it," I told him. Then I took a couple of steps forward so I could hear better.

"Oh, Burke, promise that you'll write about William Bone in your journal and tell the truth about his suffering and his fidelity."

Damned if tears didn't spring to my eyes, then, because this was all of a sudden like the voice of somebody else. This sounded like a more reasonable person who'd somehow been imprisoned inside this dying ogre.

"Say it, and I'll do what I can," I told him. "What is it you want told?"

"That I was meant to be small and inconspicuous," William Bone whispered, "and it was my fate that this was not so. And say that Half Face was my friend and seldom laughed at me, and that I was often unreasonable through loneliness, and a preponderance of passion and suffering."

"I'll get it all down!" I said in a hoarse voice. "Just the way you said it, William Bone!"

"But there is more, and you must still give me your promise, Burke! *Will* you?"

"Yep," I said. "I'll do all I can."

Closing his eyes and nodding, William Bone then reached into his vest pocket and pulled out a fat envelope.

"Mail this for me," he gasped, as blood began to gush out of his mouth. "See that it's delivered!"

"I'll sure as hell do it," I told him. And hearing this, William Bone eased forward and collapsed into what they call the Final Sleep.

I stepped up and pried the letter loose from the heavy, limp fingers of the dead hand.

And then all of a sudden the rain came pouring down. It was a deluge of green and silver water. Right away, the two corpses before me were darkened with wetness, and before long small rivulets began to wriggle down the gulley between my feet. I've never seen it rain so hard. You could have stood there and filled a bucket in the time it took to name the books in the Old Testament.

In half an hour, this gulley would be a roaring torrent. I'd seen it happen before. That black sky had an awful lot of water in it, and it all had to go somewhere.

So I hurried back to the wagon, and we rode on up to the top of a nearby ridge, far enough away from the gulley. It was going to flood fast and deep, you could tell.

It rained hard and kept raining, well into the night. The four of us stayed as dry as we could in the wagon. Lionel Littlejohn told ghost stories, which Wuyoomi-Yaki couldn't understand and I didn't listen to, because half the time I was too depressed and the other half too excited by the presence of Wuyoomi-Yaki. There wasn't much in-between.

I don't know whether Henry Buck listened to Lionel's stories or not. If he did, it'd be hard to imagine what he made out of them.

The next morning, we couldn't cross the gulley, because there was a raging torrent of water where the day before there'd been only dust and grass and wind. It was just as I'd figured.

By midafternoon most of the flooded water had drained away, although the mud was such that we wouldn't be able to cross the stream that day, for we'd have sure as death gotten the wagon stuck. I walked upstream to the place where I'd last seen the earthly remains of William Bone and Half Face, but there was nothing there. Both corpses had been washed away to rot or be devoured far from the knowledge or care of anybody.

Maybe years from now some traveler will come across one of William Bone's boots, or maybe part of his skeleton, and I wonder what whoever it is will make of them.

While I was thinking of William Bone, something made me uneasy. In fact, if I could have reached into my mind and clawed it out, I'd have done it. Why hadn't I noticed it back then, when it happened?

I sat there and tried hard to remember. The revolver William Bone had held was not the specially made one, with the trigger guard removed. This was a regular forty-four, made to fit a normal hand.

I closed my eyes and thought about it. Yep, there was no doubt about it. William Bone had held that revolver the way a man holds a child's toy. He couldn't have fired it if he'd wanted to. And the fact is, *he hadn't wanted to*. He'd *wanted* me to kill him. It must have been his specially adapted hand piece, with the trigger guard removed, that he'd wounded Henry Buck with; but this revolver had a trigger guard on it, which I could remember seeing as clear as a wagon wheel — and it wouldn't have been possible for him to poke his index finger into the opening it provided.

There wasn't any denying the fact: William Bone had managed to commit suicide after all, and with his last gesture, he threw away the mask of hypocrite.

Why hadn't I picked up the gun? That's the first thing you do in a situation like that, if you have any sense. Everybody knows that. For one thing, a revolver is valuable and should be of some use to somebody, even if it has just killed somebody else. But I'd left it there on the ground, where it would wash away and rust under the ground somewhere miles downstream.

It almost looked like I'd just been waiting for William Bone to make a move like that, and he knew it from the start. It was almost like both of us had wanted me to kill him.

When this notion sank into my head, I began to shake like a man with palsy. I couldn't help myself. I didn't care who saw me or how much I looked like a fool or imbecile.

"Well, I might as well quake with the best of them!" I yelled out, and reached for the whiskey jug.

22

Just as the hangman brands his sons with degrading signs, so also bad parents mark their offspring with mischievous supernatural signs that people may be more cautious when they see the example of wicked men who carry the stigmata in their forehead or cheeks, or in defective ears, fingers, hands, eyes or tongues.

— Paracelsus in *Concerning the Nature of Things*

BY THE NEXT morning, the ground had dried considerable and we cleared out and headed for Shoestring, the town once called Shostenengo.

Wuyoomi-Yaki and I rode Half Face's old horse while Lionel Littlejohn drove the wagon. Henry Buck walked alongside. The horses and mules had all been spooked by the storm, and the mules didn't like the idea of being harnessed, but Lionel talked them into line, and soon we were jingling along like a Swiss circus.

The weather was cool and clear, and our trip was peaceful and without event, which I was in the mood to appreciate after all the violence and bloodshed of the past week. But I was feeling kind of spooky myself. I wasn't in the mood to trust good weather.

My throat wasn't exactly sore any longer, but it had a dry paper feel to it. I was still feeling a mite qualmish and donsy, like a man coming down with ague. I was getting tired of being all filled up with symptoms of various sorts, and not being either sick or well.

Part of my queasiness, I figure, was caused by the coincidences that had been happening to me, especially the way I'd found Henry Buck again. Such things are hard to understand. I couldn't get over it, and spent considerable time trying to explain how amazing the whole business was to my three companions, but it didn't seem to do much good. They all seemed to take it pretty much in stride, even Wuyoomi-Yaki, who heard the story from Henry Buck translating. As a matter of fact, I've talked this matter over to various other folks since then, but nobody seems to catch on. They don't take it as hard as I do. They just don't seem to get what it's all about. In a way, that makes it harder to take.

The town of Shoestring appeared on the horizon at noon. We'd come upon it faster than I'd calculated. We rode in, and I don't doubt but what we were a sight for all to see. Lionel Littlejohn, who hadn't laid eyes on William Bone, was still skeptical about his size, and shared his skepticism with just about any critter who'd listen.

When we got to the livery stable where he worked, I shut off his valves right quick by paying him every dollar I owed him. I told him I figured that I'd now be promoted back to the rank of General.

Lionel nodded and said, "Why Cap'n, you kin have jes any rank you want. Yessah, any rank at all!"

I thanked him for his generosity, shook the reins of my mules, and we took off at a brisk trot in the direction of the Smoky Hill River Hotel.

We camped nearby, and seeing that Wuyoomi-Yaki and Henry Buck were settled, I took off to look for a part-time preacher, named Henry Stokes. He lived in a little clapboard house that stood under some cottonwoods on the bank of the river. Everything looked kind of strange and milky when I was riding up to the house. The fact is, I didn't feel so chipper.

I knocked on the door, and Mrs. Stokes answered and told me that her husband had gone back to Fort Riley by the Smoky Hill Route. Then something odd came over me, and I started in talking at a gallop. I said things that were considerable strange, I'll have to admit.

"Mrs. Stokes," I said, "I have endured a whole lot lately, and I'm sure disappointed to find out your husband isn't at home. Not only that, I feel feverish, and the news you've just given me makes my head swim. Did I let you in on the fact that I'm what you call a Cranioscopist? I don't feel right at all. How's come I'm talking like this?"

The woman looked surprised and even alarmed. But I kept on talking. Part of me was feeling kind of sorry for her, as a matter of fact, and trying to put her at her ease. "But there's no reason you should know all that when nobody's told you, is there? The fact is, I've been on the trail a long time and finally came upon

William Bone. Now you won't believe this, but he was a man that stood about eight and one half feet in stature. Could you believe such a confounded prodigy?"

Mrs. Stokes was frowning and looking at me closely, like my face was lighting up. She kind of shook her head. She looked tentative, and considerable wary. I think she might have felt sorry for me. The poor woman didn't know how to take these frenetic disclosures, as you might call them, and who could blame her?

So I turned and stepped off her porch and shouted over my shoulder, "Tell him Professor Burke was here, and didn't mean any harm!"

The door slammed, and I walked unsteadily down the path to where my horse was tethered. I mounted it and rode away, cussing myself for being such a damned fool. That was another time, I said. I felt nervous as a rooster at a party of cats. There was no doubt about it, I was coming down with the grippe or some other kind of fever. My throat was raw and my vision was foggy.

I hadn't even thought to ask when the preacher might be coming back to Shoestring. What the hell, wasn't Wuyoomi-Yaki worth going to Fort Riley to fetch him?

I didn't come up with an answer to that question, so I went straight to the Smoky Hill River Hotel and walked into the saloon, where I ordered a glass of rye whiskey. I figured it might cauterize my throat.

I kept trying to tell myself that I'd gotten into one of those dangerous unsettled times, when I'm not lucid and controlled in the way I act. I figured it was more than the grippe that had gotten hold of me, though that was part of it. But it was more mysterious than that. An attack of acute sassafras, you might call it. Cure unknown.

After a few glasses of whiskey I decided to read some heads, which I by God did, and before long I'd made enough to pay for my food and drink that night.

It was about eleven o'clock when I cut out from the riotous room, now given over to gambling, singing, loud cussing, and other raucous activities that I figured might soon give way to drunken brawls with fist, dagger, or pistol. Drunk as I was, my sassafras had limits, so I was smart enough to know that further intercourse with these wild and contentious types wouldn't be safe.

The moon and stars were out, and when I'd gone about a hundred paces away from the lighted hotel into a fresh, breezy silence and peacefulness, I looked back upon the ravings I'd just left as muted, remote, and unreal.

My wagon was right there where I'd left it, and everything seemed to be in order when I walked up to Henry Buck who was lying in his blanket by the side.

I asked him if the horses and mules were all right.

He grunted assent, and then rolled over.

"Is Wuyoomi-Yaki asleep in the wagon?" I asked.

Henry Buck didn't answer so I went up to the wagon and looked in. I couldn't see her anywhere.

I turned around and asked Henry where she was sleeping.

"She gone long time," Henry said.

For a couple of seconds I couldn't say anything. Then I asked Henry what in the hell he meant.

"She gone long time," Henry Buck said. "Half-hour."

"A half-*hour?*"

"Right after you go, she go too."

"Early in the afternoon," I said. "And now it's damned near midnight."

"She gone long time."

"Damn you, why didn't you come and fetch me?"

"Me no fly around like chicken look in white man's village."

"Where'd she go?"

But Henry wouldn't answer my question, and I figured he'd likely be more loyal to her than to me. In fact, he'd never been exactly *loyal* to me, he was just what you might call *committed*.

I figured it was a pretty sure bet that Wuyoomi-Yaki had taken off in the direction of Fort Riley to dig up the corpse of her brother and bury it the way the Comanches believed the corpse of a brave warrior should be buried.

But I was too tired and sick to take off after her. I felt bilious and full of aches, so I crawled up into the wagon and tried to go to sleep. I had come down with the fevernager, sure as spit.

When dawn came, I woke up hot and nasty. I stayed there in the wagon groaning until Henry Buck showed up. I told him I was too sick to start out for Fort Riley. I said I'd felt it coming on yesterday, and that's why I'd acted so crazy with Mrs. Stokes. I told him I was thirsty and asked for the water bucket. Then I figured I might just roll over and die and get some relief that way.

When Henry got the water, I took a long drink and sank back into my bedroll, taking a dim view of the world, including ever getting Wuyoomi-Yaki back. I was pretty sure that after she'd taken care of her brother's body, she'd go straight home to her tribe.

I asked Henry Buck to go look for a doctor if there was one in Shoestring. If there wasn't, I told him to try to get some quinine or several grams of cinchona, if there was any around.

He came back about noon and reported bad luck on both counts. However, he did give me some herb tea he'd concocted, which I drank before sinking back into a heavy sleep.

I don't have any idea what it was Henry gave me, but by early evening I woke up sweating like a horse, and feeling a whole lot better. Henry was sitting on the wagon seat chewing tobacco when I came around and I said, "By God, I think I can sit up. The herb tea you gave me did the trick."

I shook hands with him, and right then and there he made another cup of herb tea for me to drink and I settled back to rest.

Along about evening, I got restless and had an urge to do something. It was then I remembered the letter William Bone had given to me, asking me to mail or deliver it. The envelope was blank, but the papers I pulled out of it were filled with writing in a small, meticulous hand, which I figured to be William Bone's handwriting, in spite of its small size. The letter read as follows:

Mine Own, My Dearest Phoebe:
Having cast my lot with one whose manner of life you would neither respect nor understand, I pause 'midst the current of affairs to write to you, hoping — in spite of the distance separating us — that you will understand and possibly even give a sigh in Memory of one who loved you.

No, Phoebe (for I can almost hear your protests), that is not too strong a word! It has ever been thus. Even from that time when we first lisped the Alphabet together, and then when we sat together, gazing upon our *First* and *Second Readers*, my heart beat with thine, yearning to join it in Life's deepest and most sacred Union! Even then, when I had begun to grow monstrous, and was, though a little boy in heart and experience, in size as a man sitting next to you, I yearned. My nights were divided equally between prayers to that God whose Judgment had condemned me to Monstrosity (already, too, too apparent, Phoebe!) and prayers to that sweetness of Honey that dwelt in the secret Chambers of your little girl's breast! Yes, it was so, even then; and it was my suffering that I would never be sufficiently bold to utter one word of the love that consumed me from within!

Oh, how I grew to hate that brow that the waxing years thrust forward over my eyes, and that increasingly brutal jaw, both endowing me with an undeserved Viciousness of Expression that all my inner tenderness could not contradict! How I dreaded those expressions on thine own Divine face, signifying your first realizations of what a gross metamorphosis your childhood friend was undergoing! My life was entering a path of incredible torture, anguish, and dismay, Phoebe, which one of your Divine Normality could scarce comprehend!

Do you remember, Phoebe, that I became devout at that time, and devoted my hours to the study of that Bible that has been the cornerstone of our Civilization? Yes, but even there, I was forced to gaze into that Mirror of Truth that was beginning to drive me mad, for soon I was reading only one passage from the Divine book: the story of Goliath and David.

By now, I was what the world calls a Giant, and since there was no possibility of my living a normal life in that community in which I was reared, I set forth — bearing only my Bible and a few extra articles of clothing — to find my way in this bewildering existence. The vicissitudes of my subsequent years, and the various humiliations, sufferings, and disappointment I was forced to endure, have no place in this letter, Phoebe. But I must tell of one thing, one abiding Fact, which has been always present in my Mind, throughout my life since that time.

It is this, Phoebe: in the countless references to that story of David and Goliath, throughout the long centuries since the time celebrated in the Hebrew Scriptures, *not one person has ever thought sympathetically of Goliath!* Often I brooded upon this fact, and often I terminated my reflections in Wonder at the limited Sympathies of Mankind!

Has no one ever considered what it is to be eight feet tall (nay, much *more*, Phoebe, in my case!)? Has no one ever wondered how it would be to lose one's Humanity in his awesome existence as a Phenomenon?

Oh, Phoebe, I often see it! I see the camp of the Philistines, those poor ignorant, superstitious people. (What did God have against them to deprive them of glory, understanding, and the Covenant?) I see the camp in early dawn. I see the Giant Goliath, lying in his great blankets, his beard matted with sweat and filth (for they must have kept him like an Animal). I see his great eyes open, brooding upon what must be the eventuality of his going forth every morning, for forty days, inviting the trickery of that vile Lilliputian race that surrounds him on all sides. (Yes, his own troops as well, for they understand nought!)

I see the guards awaken him on that terrible fortieth day, and he stands up, dazed by the dreams of too many nights, too long a suspense, too long a secret and foreboding Knowledge! He steps forth along the avenues between the tents of the Philistines, and even his own men (those who should have been his brothers!) stand back and stare in awe, resentment, secret envy, and even hatred at this man who shakes the earth as he walks, and leaves footprints upon the dry ground.

Yes Phoebe, I see it all, having worn those very sandals myself, and knowing that, either late or soon, some busy-minded David from that other world of successful pigmies will cast his stone at my only too vulnerable crown, bringing me back Lifeless to that Earth which should never have conceived me!

But why should I write all these things to you, my poor innocent, pretty Maid? You had no part in the creation of this man who loves you from afar!

Still, man must speak, be his message one of hope or despair. I write this to you in fidelity, my Dear One, and abiding love, no matter what madness and destruction the next months or years bring over my head.

I speak these silent words to you from afar, and say, "Remember that little child who sat beside you; it is he who is the real William Bone, held captive in a monster that he despises more than anyone else could conceive!"

And in spite of all, my Dearest Phoebe, be happy and content, no matter what letters come to you, and no matter who has written them! For it is evening of the thirty-ninth day, and oh, I can feel the terrible Dawn coming on!

William

When I finished reading this love letter, it was beginning to get dark, and in the dim interior of my wagon, I could barely make out the last words. I folded the sheets of paper up and stuffed them back into the envelope. Then I called out to Henry for another cup of his herb tea.

There wasn't any address on the letter, and not even a last name for the girl named Phoebe, whoever she was.

I put the envelope back in my pocket. "Damned if there aren't tears to things, like the poet said," I muttered when Henry crawled back into the wagon.

Henry Buck nodded and handed me the cup of herb tea he'd prepared. He sat down cross-legged on the wagon bed sort of tilted sideways, and even though it was dark in there, I could tell he was considerable drunk. A couple of hundred yards in the distance, the town of Shoestring started in on another convivial evening, as you might say. And after a while the whole damned place was lighted up like a bonfire, especially the Smoky Hill River Hotel, which was probably doing some bang-up business.

We didn't have any stomach to join in their frivolity. Henry Buck felt the same way, I could tell. We weren't in any more of a party mood than the half-melted, surly-visaged bust of Daniel Webster sitting there behind us in the gloom of the wagon. This was a different kind of celebration, not to mention a sadder and more sober one, that we'd found ourselves in, without having sought it out.

I settled down in my blanket, my mind filled with the sadness of William Bone's sorrowful existence and the mighty feeling of his letter. I figured that the giant had finally escaped his prison and now maybe he'd truly found that peace he seemed to be so hot after. Only what kind of peace is it if you aren't alive to savor it?

Never mind, I told myself, his sadness must be over, one way or the other, even if he lived on in some kind of afterlife. I thought about it and decided there's just one fear and that's uncertainty. What you can't stand is not knowing, and this goes for the uncertainty about what you are deep down underneath all the pretenses forced on you by whatever kind of existence you find yourself in.

Yep, I'd dedicated my life to this fact.

23

"I hope, that when I am dead they will not bury my skull. I wish it to be preserved as evidence of my natural dispositions. Posterity will judge by it whether I am a quack and a charlatan, as your Edinburgh Reviewer called me."

— Spurzheim in conversation with Combe

EVEN THOUGH I was still considerable weak the next morning, I decided to go and try to find Wuyoomi-Yaki. After a breakfast of salt pork, biscuits, and coffee Henry Buck and I harnessed the mules and started out in our wagon.

It was just light, but Henry could see well enough to follow the piddley little shortcut trail that led northeast to Fort Riley. About ten o'clock, my head ached considerable, so I turned my reins over to Henry and tried to take a nap in my bedroll. But the jarring of the wagon bed made it pretty hard for me to go to sleep so I gave up trying and abandoned my mind to a pretty wild phantasmagoria of feverish scenes.

These were interrupted now and then by the sudden appearance of Half Face's grisly head into my speculations. The hole in his Mound of Mirthfulness looked like it was getting bigger with each appearance. A couple of times the head came at me grinning, even though its eye wasn't open. Such tricks of the fancy were brought to an end along about two o'clock when the wagon suddenly jolted to a stop. I sat up and asked what the trouble was.

"Somebody up there on him trail," Henry said. "Him wagon stop, but nobody around."

I crawled up on the driver's seat beside Henry Buck and saw that there was sure as hell a wagon standing up there, just like he said. It was on a little rise of the trail about half a mile ahead. The wagon was faced in our direction, and it didn't show any signs of human life, except there was a team of mules or horses, I couldn't tell

which from this distance. It looked like the team was just standing
there in harness, maybe waiting for a driver to climb aboard.

"Watch out!" I said. "Something's sure as hell funny. They
haven't made camp. And yet it doesn't look like your everyday,
down-home sort of bushwhacking. Still, we better keep a sharp
lookout all along that brush beside the trail."

"Nobody in him wagon."

"Are those mules?" I asked.

Henry said, "Yep," and then I noticed that the way the haw
mule held its neck looked like it was tied. Henry said this was the
case.

"They're tied and yet they're just standing there in harness," I
mused.

I chucked our own mules forward along the trail, until we were
about two hundred yards from the other wagon, when I got a
considerable shock. I recognized it. Beyond any doubt. Every bit.
It was all familiar. There was a cranial chart painted in cracked and
faded brown on the side, with the name "Dr. Horace Stillingfleet"
set above the chart, and the name "Scheherazade, the Mind Reader"
printed underneath.

I once more chucked the mules forward, and right then I noticed
that Henry Buck slipped off his seat and just kind of evaporated
into the low scrub alongside the trail. Most likely he'd picked up
on something. But wasn't going to wait. I shook the reins and
yelled at the mules, and they broke into a trot, carrying my wagon,
rumbling and clattering like an artillery batallion up the trail toward
old Stillingfleet's outfit, which had once, years ago, been mine.

I figured the old lunatic might have accomplices, or the wagon
might be a decoy to lure me into a trap, so I picked up my carbine
and held it ready. I stopped about fifty feet away and looked all
around, real slow. Somebody had tied the mules to the trunk of a
cottonwood sapling that had taken root there.

For a minute I didn't breathe, hardly. I've tried to capture that
scene in a poem. I talked about how I could hear the eternal breath
of the wind slipping through the buffalo grass, and heard the sharp
call of two magpies that idled overhead, fluttering their wings lazily
as they drifted almost stationary against the current of air.

But all was as quiet as an Indian grave, and only the canvas of

Stillingfleet's wagon gave what you might call a simulacrum of life as it flapped in the prairie wind with the sound of bedsheets drying on a line.

I tied my own mules to another little sapling, and got down from my seat, gripping my carbine. I looked all around, slow and careful, and then began to ease up toward the wagon ahead.

When I was about twenty feet away, I stopped and called out Stillingfleet's name. There wasn't any answer, so I got nearer to the wagon and finally came up to the mules. They looked like they were reasonably fresh and well-fed and watered. Was the driver hiding somewhere in the brush? Had Henry Buck sighted him, so he could stop him if he tried to shoot me when I climbed up into Stillingfleet's wagon? Taking the bait, like they say?

I decided to chance it. When I took my first step up, my weight caused the wagon to lurch and right then I heard the longest, most miserable groan you are ever likely to hear.

I poked my head into the darkness back of the driver's seat and saw a man lying there in a buffalo robe. Even in the shadow I could recognize that face, creased down the cheek and around the mouth. I'd reflected upon the memory of it many times. I saw the familiar eyebrows, the big hooked nose, the crescent bulge over the ears, indicative of the Selfish Propensities he'd fancied *I* possessed. All of these told me that, sure as hell, this was Stillingfleet, himself.

"Who is it?" he moaned, trying to lift his head. "Is it you?"

"It's me," I told him, even though I could tell from his voice he'd thought I was somebody else.

A troubled look came over his face, and once again he tried to lift his head up to see. I helped him by cupping the occiput in my hand. You should have heard him wail when he clapped his eyes on me.

"Thaddeus Burke!" he whispered.

"Yep," I said, "it's me, you poor excuse for a son of a bitch."

Stillingfleet closed his eyes and sagged back, muttering, "Then it looks like I've died after all, and gone straight to hell!"

24

Thinking that probably he did not understand the words used on these topics, I tried to explain them; but found an obtuseness of comprehension that rendered the attempt unsuccessful. I found those intellectual powers to be of tolerable strength whose organs were fairly developed, and those to be deficient whose organs were small.

— Comment on a Flathead Indian
in George Combe's *Notes on the
United States of North America
During a Phrenological Visit in
1838–9–40*

STILLINGFLEET ACTED like he was drifting off, so I shook his shoulder and was about ready to say something to him, when I heard the sound of a horse blowing its lips. I crawled forward and stuck my head out over the wagon seat and came face-to-face with one of the dirtiest, ugliest types I've ever laid eyes on. He was wearing a dark slouch hat, sitting on a horse, and pointing what looked like a loaded revolver at me. Under that slouch hat you could see that his features hadn't been assembled properly: he had a big snub nose and big, pouched, oystery eyes that had sort of slid down his face on each side of the nose.

"Who in hell are you?" the man asked in a slow, stupid voice. He was covered with dust and had a week's growth of prickly red beard.

"*That's* the man you're looking for," Stillingfleet croaked weakly from inside the wagon. "He's the real Thaddeus Burke!"

"What are you talking about?" I said.

The stranger glanced at my wagon and then back at me. His eyes narrowed and he said, "Well, I'll be God damned! Two of you head-reading bastards right here together, out in the middle of nowhere! Like sitting ducks!"

"It's him, it's him!" Stillingfleet groaned. "I swear to God, I was never *near* the place. It was *this* man. *He's* Thaddeus Burke."

"What is it that's after you *this* time?" I asked, half-turning my head. "Weather? The Swedes? Constipation?"

Stillingfleet groped and clutched his way forward to the seat. He was a sight — skinny and pale, with his eyes bugging out of his head. He looked like it'd practically done him in to crawl up front. It's a shame such wasn't the case.

"Maybe I'll just kill the both of you," the snub-nosed stranger said, "and that way I'll be sure. Who needs your sort, anyway? Who on this here earth would ever miss either one of you head-reading bastards?"

"If you're going to apply that rule," I told him, "there isn't hardly anybody anywhere who should stay alive."

"I swear he's Burke," Stillingfleet croaked, leaning to the side and gasping with the effort. "Just look at his wagon and see!"

"Who the hell are you, anyway?" I asked the stranger.

"My name is Rutherford Gaines," the man said, "and I am after a head-reading son of a bitch named Thaddeus Burke, who has insulted my kin, namely my brother, by name of Samson. He said my brother had a criminal head, and made our name a cause for laughter throughout the land. In fact, the whole country. I followed the Middle Trail, but then heard of this here Head Reader that was headed west from Fort Riley, so I figured he must be the one, since I figured there wouldn't be *two* of you damn Head Readers in these parts at the same time. But damned if they wasn't. Who could believe a coincidence like this, out in the middle of nowhere! I'll tell you, I never *seen* such a coincidence! And here I was about to shoot this sick little bastard when I seen your wagon coming along, so I hid myself in that gulley over there."

"You can see by his wagon that he's the one," Stillingfleet whispered.

Rutherford Gaines nodded and pointed out that even though he couldn't read, he could tell that the word on Stillingfleet's wagon was too long for a name like Burke, so he said it looked like he'd almost shot the wrong Head Reader. He cocked one of his revolvers and pointed right in my face. Then he asked me formally if my name was Thaddeus Burke.

I was considerable shaken, but I said, "Nope, my name's something else." Right then I tried to think of another name, but for once my wit failed me, and I couldn't even think of Smith or Jones.

"Wait, don't bloody up my wagon!" Stillingfleet croaked. I thought he sounded a little stronger. "I'm a desperately ill man," he said, "and my assistant has left me, and I can't have this critter's blood splattered all over my good things."

"All right," Gaines said to me, "you heard him. Climb down off the God damned wagon."

"Nope," I said.

"What?" he roared.

"Nope."

"Get off!" Stillingfleet whispered, shoving weakly at my shoulder. "Go on and get off!"

Gaines made a face of disgust and said, "Are you or ain't you?"

"I am not," I said. "Why the hell should I?"

"Don't be such a damn coward," Gaines said irritably. "Climb down off that damn wagon and be shot like a man. Ever'body's got to go sometime."

Right then I saw a movement in the brush lining the gulley behind Gaines; then I saw it again. And all of a sudden Henry Buck appeared, creeping toward us. It was impressive how quick and silent he moved.

"Look out!" Stillingfleet cried, but before Rutherford Gaines could turn around, Henry Buck had shot up behind him and made a gesture that you'd have to admire, it was so subtle. His hand might have been doing nothing more than flicking away a piece of lint on Gaines' coat.

His horse danced sideways, fastidious like, and Gaines gave me a look that was about equally surprised and sleepy. His eyebrows went up as his eyelids half-closed. His head started to nod up and down like he was agreeing to something he should have known all along, and then he looked like he might be starting to climb down off his horse. But instead he just lost shape and dropped with a whump and two thuds on the hard ground.

His horse trotted off about fifty feet and stopped. Then it dipped its muzzle and began to crop some buffalo grass. Henry Buck wiped the blood from the blade of his knife, while Stillingfleet moaned like a man two seconds away from his last agony, which is what he probably figured he was.

I jumped down from the wagon seat and shook hands with Henry Buck and clapped my hand on his shoulder. I told him he was what you'd call one good friend. He was my partner, for sure. Then we had a drink of whiskey to celebrate. All this time Stillingfleet was lying there groaning in his wagon. I told Henry that groaning was like music to me. I said I'd prefer it to a string quartet or a Cavalry band.

Finally I went up to Stillingfleet and said, "If I had any sense, I'd either put a bullet through your damn head or leave you here to rot. But instead, I'm going to have mercy on you and ask Henry Buck to make an herb tea that will fix you up as good as new. God knows why I should do a thing like this, but I'll give you a break. Just stay away from me from here on out. That's all I want."

"It's all I want, too," Stillingfleet croaked. He was lying on his back with his head propped up against a blanket roll. His expression was doleful enough to make a Presbyterian laugh.

Henry Buck fixed some tea, and after Stillingfleet had drunk it and seemed comfortable, I told him good-bye and pointed out that there was a pretty good chance a band of Kiowas would come along and maybe lift his scalp before he could get to a settlement, but he couldn't hold me responsible for that.

Then we buried Gaines, and for a sermon, I said, "Your troubles are over, with luck."

Then I got up into my wagon and shook the reins of my mules, and Henry Buck and I took off, circling Stillingfleet's wagon, leaving it behind as ours nodded ahead over the trail.

When it was almost out of sight, I remember asking Henry Buck about "Scheherazade," whose name was on the wagon canvas with Stillingfleet's.

"Somebody him leave wagon on horseback about half-hour ago," Henry Buck said. "Maybe noontime on trail to Fort Riley. Him go ahead."

I told him I figured that must have been Scheherazade. Only it'd be a squaw, with a name like that.

To which surmise, Henry Buck didn't do anything other than nod his head.

25

We term sleep a death; and yet it is waking that kills us, and destroys those spirits that are the house of life.

— Sir Thomas Browne

WE KEPT on toward Fort Riley, and got there late in the evening, with the road all about us sunk in a thick fog.

We stopped our wagon down near the river, watered the mules, and then ate some supper. I was almost recovered from my fever, so I walked over to a two-story clapboard building, called the Lost Child Tavern, where I drank a glass of whiskey with a young captain by the name of Ferdinand Dupre. He was a tall stooped type with a long flat nose and a small puckered mouth. When he talked, he closed his eyes, which struck me as a pretty dangerous habit for anybody in this country.

After that first glass of rye whiskey, I began to feel elated. In fact, my spirits took off like a partridge. Right then, I was 100 percent sure that I would find Wuyoomi-Yaki and that everything would turn out just fine with us.

Why should anybody keep good spirits bottled up? I've never been able to answer that question, so I've never tried to hold back the fizz. There've been considerable numbers who've told me that's my chief trouble in life, but I've always said, if there's a price I have to pay, I'll just have to pay it.

Anyway, I got to talking there in the Lost Child Tavern, and pretty soon all the officers were as silent as a congregation in church. They were fascinated, you could tell. I committed various acts of oratory in the manner of Samuel Chadwick. I told them the story about how I'd analyzed a man's cranium one night in Chillicothe, Ohio, telling him his Bump of Constructiveness (*Sens de Mécanique*) was remarkable, and five years later I learned that he'd invented a new type of steamboat whistle.

Then I told them some of the amusing stories I like to tell to
loosen up audiences. I told them about the One-Armed Thief and
the Woman Who Hated Peaches. I told them about The Violinist
and His Pet Crow and then the Lawyer Who Left His Hat in the
Wrong Stagecoach.

There was considerable laughter from those present, only I noticed that some of it was aimed in my direction. And sometimes I
was left out of it altogether. It was a close-knit group, you could
tell, and they didn't necessarily like strangers who made themselves
at home right away.

I sensed this and decided to cut out the sassafras and get down
to business. I asked Captain Dupre if he could give me any information about Wuyoomi-Yaki. I told him I had reason to think
she'd come to dig up the corpse of her brother, who'd been hanged
and buried nearby. I told about how she wanted to give her brother
the proper rites of burial according to the custom of their tribe,
which was to wrap the body in appropriate garments and then lay
it on top of the ground and build a small enclosure of wood about
it to protect the body from animals.

When I got through, Captain Dupre closed his eyes and started
cussing in a rapid whisper.

"Damn and blast!" he said. "Damn and *double* blast! Damn and
triple blast!"

"Looks like you're having some trouble," I said when he finally
got stopped. "Have you seen her?"

"Nope," he said finally, opening his eyes and looking a little bit
surprised to see me sitting there on the other side of the table from
him.

"It sounds to me like you know *something* about her," I said.

"Yes," Captain Dupre said, nodding and closing his eyes again.
I thought this might trigger another cussing fit, but it didn't. "I
know *of* her, because I have seen her traces. Indeed I have. Yes sir,
I have smelled her spoor and seen her damned traces!"

I told him I didn't exactly like the way he referred to her.

Captain Dupre opened his eyes and looked at me thoughtfully
for a second after I said this.

Then he said, "Yes, you're probably right. Anger doesn't help
a thing. A breezy humor like yours is probably a better tactic, when

all's said and done." Then he barked sort of a laugh to show what he meant.

I told him I was 100 percent serious about Wuyoomi-Yaki and figured on marrying her, but Captain Dupre didn't seem to hear.

"The fact is," he said, "the girl you're looking for has been here and gone. The grave of that damned Comanche you mentioned was dug up two nights ago, and his body was dragged away and put on a horse and carried to God-knows-where. This is about all we know, for our scouts haven't been able to find any sign of the corpse, and we haven't found anything other than the traces of the grave robbery. Your explanation of the cause of your visit just now made me realize that the culprit we're looking for isn't a man, as we'd thought, but a female. Humiliated as I was at having a corpse stolen right out from under our noses and right out of the government ground it lay in, you can imagine how much *more* humiliated I now feel to learn that the one who did the trick was only a girl!"

When he'd relieved himself of this speech, Captain Dupre changed his tune and started acting real friendly to me. I couldn't figure out why. He made up his mind to drink a toast to Wuyoomi-Yaki, calling her "the Injun girl who outwitted Fort Riley."

I didn't like that much. I didn't like his tone. But I couldn't refuse to drink a toast to her.

Then Captain Dupre got it in his head to emphasize and underscore his remark, and he got what you'd have to call verbose. He talked about the Noble and Eloquent Redman, mixing it with comments about how amusing my own oratory was. It was hard to make a connection between the two subjects.

Then he stood up, swaying a little like a man at sea, and closed his eyes. Then he proceeded to deliver the following toast: "To the Injun Girl who outwitted Fort Riley and apparently had the Stuff to outwit Professor Thaddeus Burke here, who informs me that he is courting this Comanche rabbit . . ."

Here I broke in and told him to watch his language.

An officer with a fat, red face and flared nostrils grinned and punched my shoulder with his fist and said, "It's just in good fun, Professor. *You* should know that — a man of *your* wit. Good fun!"

Captain Dupre opened his eyes, nodded, and kind of smiled as he went on with his toast: ". . . is courting this Comanche *lady* . . ." (a roar of laughter from the officers) ". . . *Lady*, I say, for the purpose of holy matrimony, to be consummated, no doubt, under the smiling light of a Comanche moon, which . . ."

But his speech came to an end right along about there when I doubled up my fist and hit Captain Dupre a good one right in his puckered mouth. I didn't even wait for him to open his eyes so he could see what was coming. I knocked him back on the floor with so much force his two boots flew up in the air symmetrically. One of the soles had a hole in it, as a matter of fact.

I would have jumped him and finished him off, but I was right away grabbed by the other officers. A couple of others lifted Captain Dupre's head and patted his face, which was bleeding considerable from the mouth and nose. They worked pretty hard at trying to bring him around. Finally, when his eyes began to flutter, one of the other officers told me that this would require what he called the fullest satisfaction.

And so it did, because when he came to and found out where he was and what had happened, Captain Dupre demanded that I meet him on the field of Honor, under the cannon of the fort, at six o'clock the next morning.

I accepted and chose pistols, or revolvers with one shot in each chamber, as weapons. I told them I didn't care which. They asked me to name a Second, and I told them Henry Buck, who could be found in my wagon.

Pale as a preacher's corpse, Captain Dupre closed his eyes and nodded.

When I got back to my wagon, though, Henry Buck wasn't anywhere around.

I figured maybe he'd gotten drunk and gone off to visit with some of the Indians and half-breeds camped about the fort, of which there were a great plenty. I missed him, because I wanted to talk over the duel and maybe even figure out some kind of strategy, if you can do that with a duel. I hoped he wouldn't be too long.

I settled down and drank a swallow of whiskey, after which I tried to sleep, but ended up tossing and turning in my bedroll until the early morning hours, when I finally managed to drop off. However, what little sleep I got wasn't what you'd call restful, because I kept jerking awake like a man startled by a pistol shot.

The sun rose on a clear and beautiful day, but I had a headache and my stomach was tight. The morning chill would soon be burned off by the bright sun, but the question in my mind was would Thaddeus Burke still be around to appreciate it? But it's best not to dwell on such things.

Henry Buck was nowhere in sight. I asked a couple of German muleskinners from Missouri, but they didn't know anything about him, so I gave him a brief cuss, forgetting how he'd just saved my life only the day before.

I went out and tried to take some deep breaths, but that didn't work out too well because every breath had a lid on it. So I decided to go on over to the spot we'd agreed on.

When I saw Captain Dupre and a trio of officers standing there beside him, I told them that Henry Buck was nowhere around. I told them he'd taken off somewhere, so that it looked like I was without a Second. Maybe I could use a Third, I said, and Captain Dupre said he hoped my sense of humor would keep me happy in hell.

The fact was, they didn't seem disturbed by the news about Henry Buck and offered me the services of a lieutenant named Felix Barclay as my Second. They made it all sound polite and honorable, and I figured there wasn't any way I could refuse, because I didn't know much about proper behavior in a situation like this.

Lieutenant Barclay looked like a decent enough fellow, a trifle prognathous, but with an intelligent brow, so I didn't have any tangible reason for being suspicious. He was about average size, with what looked like pronounced ridges in the regions of Causality and Parental Love. Also, one glance told me he was good at history.

We marched out upon the field, which was still considerable foggy, and I was surprised to find myself thinking about the pleasure of reading heads — holding them between my two hands like a bishop blessing one of his flock, and exploring secrets of humanity and nature that are beyond the grasp of the common mind. It came to me all of a sudden that I might have read my last head, and never again would these delights of knowledge and understanding be mine, not to mention the jokes and stories I like to tell. I found all this a considerable dismal thought. But behind everything was the thought of Wuyoomi-Yaki, like a shadow waiting for me in some other sunlight.

Lieutenant Barclay and Captain Dupre's Second made all the final arrangements, and then the two of us were brought face to face, holding our pistols with the business end of the barrels pointed up. Captain Dupre looked like he was staring beyond my left ear. When I noticed this, I figured it was the thing to do, so I looked the same way past his.

The Referee was speaking, saying he'd give the command for About-Face, then we'd march ten paces, in step with his count, turn, and take aim and fire. If satisfaction to both parties was not received after this round, he explained, why we'd do it over again, but this time fire at five paces.

The buglar blew mess call somewhere inside the fort. It sounded faraway and unreal to me, not to mention peaceful. I got a brief feel of remote but simple pleasures, far removed from this deadly business we were in.

The Referee commanded us to turn about, and then he started counting out our paces. I made up my mind I wasn't going to take any longer steps than I usually did, because if I was going to be shot and killed, I didn't want my last move to be tainted by cowardice.

The Referee neared the end of his count. At nine, he paused a little.

And then, at ten, I turned and fired quick as a wink. But I'll be damned if Captain Dupre didn't wait a second, and then calmly and with a flourish that would have done credit to a drum major, fire his pistol straight up in the air!

Right away, I knew he'd got the better of me. Here he'd missed voluntarily, refusing to aim at me, while I'd obviously missed involuntarily, sending the ball whizzing past his head.

I figured this was humiliating to me, making me look like a coward in a hurry, while Captain Dupre had come off looking like a calm hero, generous at my expense. I'd read about duels like this, but I always figured there'd been signs beforehand that such behavior was called for.

Everybody remained silent and kept from looking at me. Nobody said a word. I could have been an extra horse, with nobody to ride. Captain Dupre frowned with his eyes closed and wiped the barrel of his pistol on the sleeve of his shirt.

After the Seconds had reloaded the pistols, the Referee stated that another round had to be fired, as the rules stated. Five paces.

This time I made up my mind that I wasn't going to be outdone in honor. I figured I'd learned my lesson. So at the count of five, I turned and held my piece barrel up, directly in front of my face, the way a swordsman salutes his opponent with his sword. I don't know why I held it like this in front of my nose, because in a way it seems unnatural.

But this detail is important, because the pistol saved my life, according to what I heard later.

At the time, I was snuffed out quick as a candle. By which I mean, Captain Dupre leveled his pistol right at my head and shot. And the ball hit my pistol and blew it up right in my face, knocking me senseless to the ground. The barrel of my pistol had halfway stopped the bullet, but the force of the bullet had slammed the fragments of the pistol itself into my forehead, almost square between the eyes, but up a little, over the frontal sinus in the middle line, or what is known as the region of Individuality.

26

Injuries of the brain furnish still more demonstrative proof. If
Phrenology is true, to inflame Tune, for example, would create
a singing disposition; Veneration, a praying desire; Cautious-
ness, groundless fears; and so of all the other organs.
— *Phrenology, Physiology:*
New Illustrated Self Instructory

I LOST ALL sense of everything, including time, so naturally I
didn't have any idea of what had happened. Later, I found out about
it in bits and pieces: how Captain Dupre's ball had smashed my
own pistol against my forehead, and how I had dropped like a dead
man right flat on my back, my face gushing blood.

Everybody naturally figured I was done for, and they carried my
body back to the Lost Child Tavern and laid me on a pallet in a
little storage shed in back, where they'd had occasion to put other
fresh corpses from past misfortunes. They figured somebody would
bury me in a day or two. But later that night, the proprietor came
back with a candle figuring on tapping a new keg of whiskey, and
he saw that my arm had fallen from the pallet so that my hand was
lying on the floor. Lifting it back up, it came to him that there wasn't
any sign of rigor mortis, which should have been the case with a
corpse twelve hours old, so he gave out a yell, and all the customers
crowded back into the backroom. They were all interested, not to
mention considerable drunk, with a lot of ideas about what they
should do with me.

The pistol ball hadn't finished me off, but it's a wonder the
meddling of this boozy crew didn't, because everybody got excited
and wanted to pitch in and help. Nobody wanted to be left out.
When it was over, they wanted to say they'd personally helped
carry the body of a critter that had practically come back to life.

So they set about to manhandle me up the narrow winding stair-
case. They told me later they all got in one another's way, and

halfway up one of them stumbled and they dropped me clear to the bottom of the stairwell, where I was all crumpled up with my head bent under my shoulder the way a heron sleeps.

They weren't what you'd call daunted, though, so they picked me up again, and this time made it all the way to the second story where they shuffled me into a low-ceilinged room, hardly bigger than a casket. There one of them felt my pulse and officially declared that I was sure-enough, by God, legally and practically alive.

When I finally came to, it was dark, and I felt an awful weight over my eyes and an awful numbness all over my face. It was like an ox was standing on my forehead and I couldn't get him to move. My hands and fingers tingled, like they'd been frostbitten, and my legs felt faraway and as heavy as if they'd had forty-pound clots of mud on them, so that they hardly moved an inch when I tried to shift them to a more comfortable position.

Everything was black as midnight, and I figured that curtains were pulled over the windows, because even the darkest night has a little light from the stars, a distant torch or candle, maybe, or a kind of phosphorous tint on roofs and wagons. But this was blacker than the jail where Stillingfleet and I had gotten to know each other.

Suddenly I heard a funny noise. It sounded exactly like some crickets tuning up on a late summer night, only in a minute I realized it was bed springs starting to squeak. And they began to squeak in rhythm. It was a sound I hadn't heard for a long time, but one I didn't have much trouble recognizing.

This squeaking increased in tempo, along with some heavy breathing and a duet of groans, one male and one female, and then it stopped all of a sudden, and silence reigned for a minute or two. Then I heard a man and woman talking. They sounded like two people discussing the corn crop or maybe the next election. I couldn't make out the actual words, but after a bit I figured they must have been transacting the sort of business that I could also recognize pretty well.

I heard a door open and shut, and after that the rustle of a woman's skirts come right up to the bed. I could smell her perfume. I groaned under the crushing weight on my face and groped numbly at what I discovered was a bandage around my head. Nope, there was no doubt about it: there was something wrong with my eyes.

I could smell a burning candle mixed with the perfume, but I still couldn't see anything.

I felt the bed beside me jiggle from somebody sitting down on it, and then a woman's voice said, "Oh, God, you're conscious! Can you hear me?"

"Yep," I muttered. And then I felt a sudden awful, aching thirst, so I asked for a glass of water.

"Of course," the woman's voice said, and a minute later my head was lifted forward, which felt like it was decapitating me, and a tin cup filled with cool water touched my lips.

"You're alive," she whispered as I tried to gulp the water.

"More," I groaned.

"Of course."

When she came back, I drank all of the second cup of water, even though she'd only let me have about a teaspoonful at a time. The woman began talking then, and kept it up for a considerable length of time. I don't know what she said, but it was a great deal. The way she talked was also very proper and educated, you could tell.

Finally, I interrupted her and said I couldn't see anything. I told her I hoped it wasn't daylight.

"It's no wonder," she said. "You were shot in the forehead. Your skull appeared to be smashed by the ball and other pieces of metal. It's a miracle you're alive."

I asked if I was blind, and she shushed me, the way a mother does when she's trying to calm down a scared child. She touched my cheeks with her cool hand.

I asked her again if I was blind, and she said, "Don't use such words."

"Well then, maybe I'm not blind, but just can't see anything."

"I'm sure your sight will return in time. Meanwhile, be thankful you're alive."

"Where's Henry Buck?" I asked after a couple of seconds.

"Who's that?"

"My Indian assistant," I answered. "He's an Osage. Hardly ever says a word."

"I don't know," she said. "No Indian has come to visit you."

"Then he's either skipped out on me," I said, "or he's in considerable trouble."

My voice sounded like somebody else's. It sounded like a gruff stranger. I got a brief glimpse of Henry Buck in my mind's eye and damned if he wasn't walking backwards.

"Good God!" I moaned and my thoughts began to wobble and get smaller like a coin that's dropped in muddy water and flips over and over while it sinks downward, until you can't see it any longer.

But before I passed out, it came to me that there was something else: I'd almost swear there was something familiar in that woman's voice. It made everything feel a whole lot stranger than it had a right to feel, which was considerable under the circumstances, when you think about it.

The next time I woke up, it was to the tune of bed springs again, squeaking away like a village of tree toads in the next room. I stayed there and tried to think, but it was pretty hard to do. I was dismayed and considerable nauseated.

When she was through with her business, my nurse came back and cooed and fussed like a mother over me. I don't know how she knew I was conscious, because I didn't say a word to her. Maybe my eyes were open and I didn't know it. I don't have any idea, because my upper face was numb, the way your hand gets when you've been lying on it and it goes to sleep. That numbness was widespread, and like a lot of numbness, it was probably a blessing in disguise.

She brought me the tin cup again, whoever she was, but now it was filled with hot broth. She spooned it out to me, talking all the time like she was gossiping at a tea party.

When I finished, I felt considerable stronger, and I asked who she was.

Right then, there was a long pause. Finally she said, "Don't you recognize my voice, Thad?"

Something stirred like a snake way down in the weeds of my memory, but I'll be damned if I could figure out who she was, so I said, "Nope, can't say that I do. Have we been introduced?"

"There was a time when you loved me," she said. "At least, you said you did. That was in Baltimore, many years ago."

Then it came over me like an avalanche, and I said, "Yep, I think I've got a pretty good idea."

"Yes," she said. "It's Lily de Wilde, Thad! After all these years, we meet again!"

Saying this, she leaned over and pressed her cool lips to mine and kissed me. Then I lifted my hand up to her head and touched that lovely sphere that had once inspired me and filled my heart with longing.

There was no doubt about it: this was the real article, Lily de Wilde herself.

27

Just as one Candle lights another, so we see also, that two, sympathetically minded, know, by the cleaving of their lips together, how to breathe into each other their burning hearts-desire, wherewith the one doth as it were kindle the other, and do every moment renew and blow on again their even just now extinguished delights.

— *The Confession of*
the New Married Couple

THE SURPRISE of running into Lily de Wilde was quite a jolt, but it wasn't enough to lift me out of my low spirits. It was pretty clear that my sight was not coming back with my strength, and I spent those days in considerable gloom. I was in despair and couldn't climb out. How would I ever find Wuyoomi-Yaki? What had happened to her? And where was Henry Buck? Everything was dark, like a swamp at midnight. I was miserable, which didn't do much to help my recovery.

There was one other idea I couldn't get out of my head. I thought about it for hours inside the darkness I was living in. I tried to convince myself that the whole notion was clodpated and no sensible man would believe it for a minute, and I didn't have any choice but to agree. It sure as hell was a damned fool idea.

And yet the minute I let up, there it was again. It was more like a notion that was just *there*, and not an idea at all. You can't argue with something like that. And yet it was kind of an idea, too: namely that I had been struck blind because I had killed another human being. Not just one, but three. I tried to joke myself out of it. I said to myself that if you judged by volume, I'd killed about *four* human beings, since William Bone was at least twice the size of the average man.

But this didn't evoke much laughter. People didn't seem to cotton to my jokes. They never had. People figured I was a smart alec or some kind of wily simpleton, and maybe they had the correct view. Right now, I was half tempted to agree with them.

Who was there to laugh, after all: And how funny was it, when you considered that I had been reared as a Quaker to believe that lifting your hand against another person is just about the greatest evil there is? I told myself that if my father's prayers had saved my mother's life, then things might have been different. I was a Doubting Thomas and always had been, when it came to spiritual realities. Pa had said as much, several times. He claimed that this was behind all my sass. It was a real weakness, and I'll admit it.

This was all bad enough, when you consider the poor shape I was in, but there was something that made it even worse. I began to think along the lines of William Bone's argument. And the more I thought about it, the more I figured there just might be something to it. There was a possibility, at least, which is all you need when the spirits are low.

Was it possible that Half Face *had* been just playing a trick on me? That was the question. That whole business about writing down cusses and profanity and smut had hit me as pretty extravagant nonsense right from the start. And yet, drunk as I was, I still wasn't too drunk not to *know* I was drunk. And I knew that Half Face was, too. And does anybody have to work at proving that when you're drunk you come up with pretty strange ideas? Or that your behavior is often fantastic? But this line of thinking didn't get me anywhere I wanted to go, because right then a voice inside my head said *Yes, and when you're drunk you also come up with some pretty strange ideas for playing tricks on people.*

All the time I was having these debates with myself, Lily kept on nursing me. At least when she wasn't busy serving her customers. She kept after me to tell her every detail about my life during all those long years we'd been apart, and I told her what I could remember and sent her to my journal for the rest. I figure she read the whole thing, because after a while she started in asking me a question about every half-hour. She unloaded her own story on me one day, and it was a strange one. At first, all snuggled up with my self-pity, I didn't much listen to her tale; but you can get used to just about anything, including blindness, and after a while I was listening, and even started to think about what she was saying.

The fate that had brought Lily de Wilde out here to Fort Riley was nothing other than a deep and romantic attachment to one man. That's what she claimed. And as hard as it might be for you to believe, that man was none other than me, myself: Thaddeus Burke.

She said that when I'd first analyzed her head, she knew I'd found out her secret. She said she could tell that I knew all, but was determined to conceal her weakness for the bodies of men. It was apparent to her that I'd understood everything the instant I touched the Bump of Amativeness at the base of her skull, but she figured I'd remained silent about my findings because I was a gentleman of honor, and had considerable decency, not to mention sympathy and delicacy of feeling.

This didn't have any more truth in it than a cow has religion, but I was so low in spirit at the time that I just kept quiet and let her blabber on and think whatever she wanted.

"And I knew what you must have suffered," she told me, "knowing about my weakness for the bodies of men. And yet, I tried to believe that you might have *some* passion and special respect for me! But when you stopped seeing me without any explanation, I realized that you must *not* have guessed the truth before, so I cried myself to sleep that night.

"Then after your departure, I abandoned myself even more desperately to the pleasures of the body; but oh, Thad, I was never able to forget you! You see, you were the only man who'd ever afforded me those little courtesies that a woman associates with romance. Thus it was that you had a particular claim to my feelings, because you were virtually the only man I knew who hadn't had conquest over my poor passionate body.

"Can't you see how this set you apart from all the rest? Don't you see how this fact added a certain grace, a certain wistful and noble sadness, a certain delicate mystery and haunting curiosity that no other memory could possibly have? It was true, Thad, and my reveries began to circle ever more and more closely in the orbit of your image."

Well, she went on like this at considerable length and in considerable detail. I wasn't up to listening very closely, but I could tell from the rise and fall of her voice that she was in a passion and figured I was picking up on everything. Her voice got soft and furry. She was almost whispering, and I wondered if maybe she'd heard a customer come into her room and didn't want him to hear what she had to say. But the way she kept on going convinced me otherwise.

She talked about how her life had progressed in spite of her morbid and futile preoccupation with her unrequited love. She talked about how she was even married for a while to a man named Alexander Chambers. I don't know how she managed to bring this about, but it looks like this Chambers critter finally woke up, because he left Lily after a while, and then right after that, died in a tavern fire.

But that didn't stop Lily. It doesn't look like much could have. And yet, she had her share of bad times, as she told it. She said she was treated as a common harlot by just about everybody, and she never seemed to be able to figure out why.

But the one thing that stayed with her, she said, was the thought of me. That's what she said. She said it three or four times, and likely meant it. She said the time came when she decided to throw everything to the winds and take off after me. She'd heard I'd gone west, so she went to St. Louis. There she heard that I'd gone on ahead, and eventually she found out I'd crossed the Big Missou and was out somewhere in Kansas Territory.

It's not too hard to figure out how Lily paid for her travels. She was vague about this part of it, because she liked to pretend at being shy and impractical, and I guess it didn't hurt anybody to pretend to believe her. I certainly didn't bring up the matter. I decided to let her be as vague and shy as she wanted. So far as I was concerned, she could even have the vapours and faint a couple of times, if that was the sort of thing to give her pleasure.

She went on and on, and her narrative got pretty airy. You would have thought she lived on honeydew and flowers, where the bee sucks, and so forth. But then, all of a sudden she dropped down to earth and got considerable practical. And it was right about then that she said something that near to brought me standing upright in my bed. She said she'd heard there was a phrenologist who'd recently lectured at a town in eastern Kansas, so she figured it had to be me and took off after him, but when she caught up with him, she found out he was a man named Stillingfleet.

Here, she got dramatic again. Her voice rose about half an octave, and she came damned near to singing. "By this time," she said, "I was little more than a poor starving wretch! My clothes were mere tatters, and I was filthy with all the grime of travel and penury. My hair was a tangle, and I had lost a front tooth upon my journey, rendering me old-looking and ugly."

Right then I interrupted because I couldn't hold back my astonishment any longer. I said, "That can't be true!"

What I was talking about was the coincidence of Lily coming on Stillingfleet, but she figured I was objecting to her statement that she was old-looking and ugly, so she patted my hand and said, "*Dear* Thad, for doubting that this can be! But it is true, though it breaks my heart to admit it!"

"Stillingfleet!" I muttered. I couldn't get over it. It looked like my Bump of Coincidence was about to fly out of control.

"What's wrong?" she asked me.

"Do you mean to say you became that son of a bitch's assistant!" I asked her. "Do you mean to say you were the one who left him sick and stranded there on the trail to Shoestring!"

"But how could you know that?" Lily cried. "Did you see him?"

"You bet I saw him!" I muttered. "And I guess you have to know that the two of us are bitter enemies!"

"Oh, but I *do* know that," Lily said. "It was the thing that made my life with him miserable almost beyond endurance. But how did you know about us?"

I told her how I'd come on Stillingfleet lying sick and stranded in his wagon. I told her how he'd tried to help me get killed by a ruffian by the name of Gaines. But then I said never mind all that: I wanted to hear the rest of her story.

She paused for a moment, as if she wasn't sure she should go on. But finally she did, speaking in a softer voice. She said that Stillingfleet had offered her a job as his assistant. And she'd accepted, since she didn't have any other honest way of earning a living at this time.

She said that not only had she kept from starving by working with Stillingfleet, but she'd taken hope that being in the same profession as I was, Stillingfleet would naturally be more likely to hear of my whereabouts than the average person. Especially since he was traveling pretty much where I traveled.

Soon after joining him, she told him about the object of her quest, and Stillingfleet was outraged and horrified. She said he almost burst a blood vessel. She said he figured she was a spy for me, seeking ways to do him in. She said he would have abandoned her right then and there, except for the fact that he'd already successfully stormed that chronically weak fortress of her virtue and felt somehow responsible for her.

"Do you mean to tell me that Stillingfleet has a *conscience*?" I asked her with considerable scorn in my voice. "You might as well try to tell me that cockroaches suffer from bad dreams or stray cats ponder metaphysics!"

"But it's true," Lily said. "And yet I'd like to think it's possible that it was not simply duty that kept him from throwing me aside but infatuation as well."

I told her that *there* she might have a point.

"Oh God, you're right!" she cried suddenly. "He *is* a despicable man, perhaps mad! I couldn't even mention my passion for you. I soon found that I couldn't even mention your name. However this only made my memories of you grow more secret, and deeper and stronger.

"But I had only one alternative, which you can guess; and this wouldn't have allowed me the range of movement that my association with Horace allowed, so I stayed with him.

"We traveled all over, and sometimes we heard of your whereabouts, but the report was always too old for me to risk coming in search of you. I knew that you were as elusive as we were, and many nights I cried myself to sleep."

"When you weren't otherwise occupied," I pointed out, but Lily didn't seem to pick up on it. She was too caught up in telling her love story.

"To help out," she went on, "I would sing Italian arias, while Horace accompanied me on the concertina."

"Now that's quite a picture!" I muttered.

"It seemed to please our audiences."

"You call him 'Horace.' "

"Of course. That's his name."

"I guess he must have a first name, at that! But damned if I'd ever thought about it!" I said this for effect only, because I knew his name well, the whole article, first and last.

"And then the two of us devised a means whereby I appeared capable of reading minds, and I was soon featured as 'Scheherazade, the Mind Reader.' "

"Yep," I said, "I saw that name on his wagon."

"There was news that you were traveling west of us," she continued, "and Horace was furious to hear of it, for he himself claimed to have planned to go westward, all the way to Santa Fe by wagon train, and he assumed you had somehow gotten wind of his plan and had deliberately set out to beat him there."

"I sure *would* like to beat him," I said, "but *any* damned where, not just in Santa Fe!"

Lily didn't pick up on this, which wasn't surprising, and she said, "That's not what I meant, Thad: I meant he thought you intended to be the first phrenologist to go to Santa Fe.

"Horace knew that other phrenologists had traveled to San Francisco, both by wagon train and by ship; but Santa Fe was 'virgin territory,' as Horace called it."

"That kind of sounds like the vile toad," I said. "Anyplace where he hasn't traveled is virginal in a way."

But Lily just kept on like I was mumbling in Choctaw. "So we started west from Fort Riley, hoping to overtake a party of wagons from Ohio that had left only the day previous. Since we were traveling light, and they were heavily burdened with manufactured goods for trade, we had good hope of overtaking them long before we reached a place where we would be in danger from Indians or thieves."

"You were already in a place like that," I told her.

"I know that now. But trouble came in another form. Horace fell ill. I was afraid it might be cholera and that soon his grave would be added to all those that lie alongside the trail. The onset of the illness was swift, and its effect on Horace was strange, for he began to rage at me, saying it was my fault that everything was going wrong, and that I was only staying with him until I came across your trail, and that I was your secret agent, not to mention an unwholesome, ungrateful bitch! Then he told me to take our spare pony and leave him. He said he couldn't stand the sight of me any longer, knowing that I was just biding my time until I could find you.

"There wasn't anything I could do to quiet his wrath, so eventually I did what he wanted and left him there in his wagon, stranded in that desolate waste, lying feverish in his bedroll, and came back to Fort Riley.

"Once more, I found myself in a place largely populated by men of a rough and unrestrained disposition, and possessing neither money nor means of livelihood, I again resorted to that old profession of desperate Womankind."

"One which seems to suit your own disposition considerable well," I pointed out.

By way of answer, she reached over and patted my head.

"I notice you don't deny it," I said.

"It wasn't easy for me, Thad," she said in a gentle voice, which surprised me a little. "There's a small hotel nearby, and the back rooms are occupied by Madame Vale and three girls from St. Louis. One of these girls is a German who speaks no English. She is younger than I, and if the truth be told, quite lovely. Madame Vale has authority and influence in this little community, and I wouldn't have the least hope of earning a livelihood if I hadn't gained a friend in Cyrus Morehouse, who owns the Lost Child Tavern. He took pity on me and has allowed me to live in one of the upstairs rooms so I can try to eke out a living. I talked to him just this morning, and he's agreed to let you rent the front room you're in right now, for only two dollars a day, which I've agreed to pay. Although, with your permission, I'll sell your mules."

I gave her my permission right then and there, because what good is a team of mules to a blind man? Then I asked, "Is this Cyrus Morehouse related to the Ulysses Morehouse who owns a hotel in Shoestring?"

"I think so. He's supposed to have a brother who owns a hotel somewhere."

I'd asked that question just so I could stall for a little time and think about Lily's offer to pay for my room. It was generous of her, I guess you'd have to say, and I had the good sense to tell her that.

"But you see, the fact is, I love you," she said in a quiet voice. "And Cyrus has been most kind. He has been my benefactor, and now he's yours as well."

"There's another word for him beside benefactor," I said, "which is pimp. I don't suppose you've ever heard the word, but it exists. People have used it. In some circles, it's considerable common."

Lily patted my arm. "You're still weak and sick from your wound. I know you don't really mean what you say."

I didn't contradict her, because there wouldn't have been much point to it.

"There's only one other thing," Lily said. "Sleeping space is hard to find in a place like this, as you know, so you'll have to share your room with other men whenever there's a wagon train coming through. It shouldn't be too much of a problem. People will do almost anything these days for a bed."

"Yep, it sure looks like it," I said, half under my breath.

But Lily didn't seem to hear me, and a minute later she left the room.

All the time she'd been saying these things, I kept expecting to hear the sound of a page being turned. She wouldn't have been running any risk by reading the speech she was giving, because she knew I was blind.

On the other hand, maybe she had memorized the speech. It had the sound of something spoken from the stage, maybe, omitting a few details, declaimed at a girl's finishing school. But in spite of my suspicious mood and general misery, there were parts I sort of enjoyed. Not only that, I listened to her, because Lily was a beauty, no matter how much nonsense came out of her mouth, and this fact made the nonsense a little more important than your average, everyday variety of nonsense.

These additional thoughts of mine sort of rode along on her words, even though I was trying not to miss anything she was telling me. And of course she just kept on talking, because she couldn't have seen any expression on my face, since I don't suppose there was any, by the way it felt. Not only that, she was a relentless talker, and always had been.

She had enjoyed every word of it, you could tell. There was something delicious in all that pain and suffering, now that it was over and she had a blind man in her clutches who had to listen and couldn't escape if he'd wanted to.

As for me, I couldn't keep my mind on her adventures for long, because behind all that fandango I kept getting a glimpse of Wuyoomi-Yaki, just standing there waiting for me.

The only thing was, I didn't have any idea *where* she was waiting, because if I had, I swear I would have taken off in a minute, blind or not.

28

Few persons, without some practice, can voluntarily act on their grief-muscles; but after repeated trials a considerable number succeed, whilst others never can.
— Charles Darwin, *The Expression of the Emotions in Man and Animals*

"YOU SHOULD know," Lily de Wilde said late that evening, "that I've just learned the whereabouts of your Indian assistant."

"Henry Buck!" I said. "Good God, where is he? I'll bet he didn't betray me after all, did he? I'm sure he couldn't help being off somewhere when I needed him!"

"No," Lily said. "He was innocent, just as you wish. He was in the guard house, and he's still there. He was jailed for drunkenness the night Captain Dupre challenged you to a duel."

"Jailed for *drunkenness*?" I said. "Why, how could that be, when two thirds of the white population, and all the Indians, are drunk every damned night and most of the day! I wouldn't be surprised if the troops aren't drunk as well! How could anybody be jailed for *drunkenness*?"

"It certainly is strange," Lily said. "But the story is that Captain Dupre himself saw to it that Henry Buck was arrested. Military law forbids unlawful behavior of any sort in the civilian population surrounding the fort, but this is usually considered a mere technicality, especially as applied to Indians and drunkenness."

For about twenty seconds I couldn't get it straight. Then it all came to me. It all fell into line, like an infantry platoon. I said, "Then it was Captain Dupre who had him arrested so that he could supply me with a Second from among his personal friends, and . . ."

"Oh, Thad, you are right!" Lily cried. "Your Second, Lieutenant Barclay, didn't even put a *ball* in your pistol! You could have shot accurately at Captain Dupre a hundred times without hurting him, so long as Lieutenant Barclay loaded the charge! You were cheated. And that farce they enacted was just to mock you . . . why, Captain Dupre could have shot you just as easily the first time you fired, but in the event you'd only been wounded, they wanted to implant in your mind the idea that you'd shot *with the intent to kill him*, in contrast to his seeming magnanimity in shooting up in the air. Oh, Thad, they say that particular group of officers have always clung together and have always loved to trick people and benefit themselves! They love to cook up practical jokes and have a good time at the expense of others!"

"That's quite a joke," I said. Then I asked where she'd heard all this.

"From a sergeant named Ogilvy. He nurses a secret hatred for Captain Dupre and all his circle. Sergeant Ogilvy told me everything."

"Yep, it sure as hell fits," I said.

"Sergeant Ogilvy hates that clique of officers because they side with one another against everyone, and they're convinced they're hated in return."

"Was this Sergeant Ogilvy one of your customers?" I asked.

"Well, as a matter of fact he was," Lily said, "but that's no reason he would lie to me."

"Nope, I guess not."

Lily didn't say anything further at the moment, and a minute later she left the room. When I heard the door close, I leaned over and felt a couple of spasms go through me. It was almost like crying. But I couldn't feel any tears, since my upper face was still about twice as stiff as a turtle shell and without any feeling. After a couple of minutes, the fit went away.

But I couldn't forget what Lily had told me, and I spent the whole afternoon trying to think of ways that a blind man, with practically no help or money, might kill a captain of the United States Cavalry and get away with it. I had already killed three men, and I figured I might as well make it four.

There was considerable pleasure in the fantasies I entertained, but there didn't seem to be a whole lot of practical use.

The next morning I figured I'd go back to my wagon and get a bottle of whiskey to take to Henry Buck, and when I handed over this little gift, I'd try to find out how he fared and what opportunities there might be to get him out of jail.

I held onto Lily's arm with one hand, and poked with a cane held in my other, and went outside for the first time since I'd been shot. The cool autumn wind felt good blowing on my face, which was getting some feeling back. I could smell the warm sunlight and feel it on my skin at first. I was all concentrated on these two things, along with the jolt of my feet on the ground, and everything seemed peculiar, as black and featureless as a midnight without a single star. But then I began to listen, and the result was remarkable. There are a lot of sounds you usually hear around a fort but don't pay much attention to. I'm talking about the barking of the Indian dogs and the horses blowing their lips and the cries and gossip and gab of men, along with the occasional sound of a gunshot, or an Indian drum, or a guitar, or harmonica riding on the wind. All of these sounds came to me with a strange and kind of sad beauty, because they seemed so close by, and yet reminded me of things that were lost forever, and for that reason, far away. Everything seemed like it was coming to me out of Past Times, when I'd first heard these sounds.

There was something else, too: the odors were stronger than I'd ever remembered: the smell of horse manure, ox dung, Indians smeared with their animal grease, a sudden whiff of burning buffalo chips or tobacco, the smell of dead and drying grass on the wind. These odors were so eloquent, I could hardly stand it, and for a second I almost felt sorry for critters whose minds are locked inside the prison of sight, as you might call it. But these ideas soon drifted away, and I plodded on ahead, putting my feet out into the blackness with only half a faith that the ground would be waiting somewhere down there when they landed.

I was curious about my wagon, which was being kept for me behind a livery stable. I told Lily I wanted to go out to it and put my hands on my things, including my jug of whiskey, so I was led around to the back where the wagon stood, and Lily said, "Let me help you up into the wagon. It is directly before you. Unless you would like me to ask the stable boy to climb up inside and get the whiskey."

"Nope," I said, "I want to put my hands on my possessions."

But right away when I climbed up into the wagon, there was something in the feel of it that was both strange and familiar. At first, I figured this had to do with being blind, where everything you touch is known in one way, but unknown in another.

I groped around for a while, and then sat back without saying anything.

"Are you all right?" Lily asked from the front of the wagon.

"To tell you the truth," I said, "I'm not sure."

"What's wrong?"

"Where's Daniel Webster?"

"I'm afraid the bust has been stolen, Thad," she murmured. "I didn't want you to know, but the stable boy says you were robbed of several things."

"Yep, it kind of looks that way."

"But you shouldn't worry."

I sat there thinking a minute. I thought hard, letting my mind drift, and didn't like the scene that was coming round the bend.

"And how about all my clothes, not to mention the books, charts, and other equipment?"

"Yes," Lily said in a low voice. "A lot of things were stolen, the boy says."

For about a minute I didn't move or open my mouth; then I crawled to the front and sat down on the wagon seat and let the cool wind blow over my face. An Indian was singing somewhere nearby, and I could hear the bells on his leg bracelets jangling as he danced in time with his song. It sounded like he was off someplace in his own world as sure as I was over here in mine.

"Lily," I said, after a few minutes, "this isn't my wagon. What I mean is, it used to be my wagon one time years ago, but I traded it for Stillingfleet's."

Lily didn't say anything, so I swallowed and went on. "Now it looks like Stillingfleet has come here and traded it again, that son of a bitch!"

Right then Lily started in weeping. It was loud and hysterical. She really let go. She used the whole orchestra, and then some. I lifted my blind face and pointed it into the wind, letting her get it all out of her system. Finally, she stopped and sniffed a little, and then cried, "Oh, God, you're so right, Thad! But you've got to believe me when I tell you that I tried to stop him! But he wouldn't listen to me, so he went ahead and took your wagon, along with everything else he wanted, claiming that they had always been his, legally, and he was only getting what was rightfully his own. And he left *his* wagon in its place."

"You saw him then?" I asked.

"Yes, he came to me," Lily said. "He found me."

"I see."

"But you mustn't get the wrong idea."

"Nope. It doesn't make any difference."

"Oh, it does! I love you, Thad!"

"Yep, and about four thousand two hundred and forty-eight others, including that bastard Stillingfleet."

Everything got quiet, and then Lily said, "I know I'm poor and weak, and Horace has always exercised a strange hypnotic effect upon me. But that's a far different thing from love. Believe me when I say that the fact I'm vulnerable to the conquests of Cupid helps me make distinctions that are subtler than most people care to think about, let alone understand."

Then she tuned up and let go with what I figure has to be one of the strangest arguments ever let loose in the Christian world, as follows: "Who gains my body, gains trash, for it's just the hot animal I have to live inside. But deep inside, there dwells a maiden of pale and soft beauty, unseen by the common eye. This maiden is my soul, and she will always love you and you alone, Thad!"

After she finished with this business, I used considerable strong language and climbed out of the wagon, giving her a final, good-bye cuss and asking the stable boy to lead me to the fort.

He came up and we took off together. I didn't care what happened to her.

When we arrived at the fort, the stable boy took me to the corporal of the guard, who told me that I couldn't come in to visit Henry Buck.

"Why not?" I asked. "Do you mean to tell me I can't bring him whiskey?"

"That has nothing to do with it," the corporal said. "And if I was you, I would haul your carcass out of here, Professor!"

"How's come?" I asked.

"Because your Injun friend escaped from jail last night, stole a gun, and shot Captain Dupre in the stomach. The bullet's lodged right near the spine, and if the Captain don't die, why he just might be crippled the rest of his life."

"Henry Buck's escaped?"

"Yes, but right this minute they got a hundred men scouring the countryside for him. I wouldn't give you a plugged nickel for his damned hide."

"And you say he shot Captain Dupre!"

"Yes, he did. And I ain't saying, just between you and me, that they wasn't a few of the men who wasn't glad to see the Captain have his damn flag lowered, but you quote me as saying that, and I'll make you deef as well as blind. Do you get my meaning?"

"Yep, I won't quote you," I told him. But I was thinking that they'd never lay hands on Henry Buck, who could run like a coyote and hide like a snake.

The corporal took my whiskey jug out of my hand, without even asking, and I could hear a couple of glugs as he drank. He smacked his lips and said, "You better be hauling on out of here, Professor, before one of the officers sees you and throws you in jail."

"On what pretext?" I asked.

"Why just *any* damned pretext! Don't you know you can make up a pretext as easy as spit?"

I nodded and walked back toward my wagon, still led by the stable boy. I was shaking my head about every other step. There was a lot to shake your head over.

Lily de Wilde was waiting for me at the wagon. She spoke my name, and I didn't say anything, but that didn't seem to matter, because she took my arm and guided me back to the room above the Lost Child Tavern, which when you come to think of it was the only place I had to go to. I was sort of sorry I'd talked to her that way, even though I still resented Stillingfleet's latest coups and what I figured was her complicity in it.

When we got back to our rooms, I was told by Cyrus Morehouse that two drovers were asleep in mine. Cyrus had rented them a part of the floor and roof for the night. Sleeping room was in scarce supply, here as elsewhere, and this sort of thing often happened, so I didn't pay any attention to it.

When I climbed up the stairs, I could hear the two of them snoring like the growling of beasts, but the way they smelled would have made your average hog or mule blush.

Lily came into my room and said, "Come and sleep with me. There won't be any customers this late. There's something I have to tell you: I've heard something I think you should know."

I agreed and sat down on that well-traveled bed of hers.

"I hardly know how to tell you," she said, touching the back of my hand. "Especially considering all you've suffered of late."

"I don't think you have anything to fear on that score," I said. "I've been tried pretty damned sorely in my life, and yet I've been able to ride out most of the storms of destiny, like they say. And after being blinded by that son of a bitch, Dupre, do you think there's anything you could tell me that would cause distraction?"

For a minute she didn't say anything, and then I felt the bed tremble a little and I figure she was shaking her head from side to side. "No," she said, "I suppose you really have achieved the dispassionate self-control of the philosopher, knowing the human condition as you do through your Science. I confess that this all seems to me incomprehensible and even a little mad at times; but never mind what I feel; the important thing is that you have achieved self-control, so I will tell you. The news is abroad that your Comanche girl is dead. An Irish soldier, named Alphonsus Murray, was brandishing her scalp at the Lost Child today. Cyrus himself told me, and I promised I'd tell you."

Lily stopped speaking then and I felt my heart lurch and beat four, five, six times, each time like a hammer blow. I cleared my throat and tried to speak her name, but all that eventuated was a heartbroken groan, like the croak of a dying man.

"What is it?" Lily cried, shaking my arm.

"Was it really Wuyoomi-Yaki?" I asked. I couldn't hardly speak above a whisper, because it felt like I was choking.

"The Comanche girl who dug up the corpse of her brother," Lily said. "If that was her name."

"Yep," I whispered and nodded. "I guess that had to be Wuyoomi-Yaki!"

"I'm afraid she has to be the one," Lily said, patting my hand once again.

"But the scalp alone isn't enough proof!"

"Listen," Lily said gently, "they found her guarding a recently built grave, enclosed in a small hut made of twigs and mud. Inside was the corpse that had been exhumed. When she saw the soldiers coming, the poor girl didn't hesitate a minute, but just cut her own throat with a knife, and bled to death before their eyes. This savage Irish trooper took her scalp in case there should be some sort of bounty, or at least a demand for proof. Thad, what other girl do you think it could have been, this far from Comanche territory?"

I nodded and tried to clear my throat a couple of times. I hadn't really figured on anything like this. I should have, but I didn't, and it hit me hard. I didn't know whether I could handle it or not. I felt sick all over and couldn't make it out. Nothing was coming clear, but then I felt her tug at my sleeve.

I asked her what she wanted, and she said she wanted me to forgive her for being the one to tell me. What sort of fool business was that, I said. But she kept on at me, wanting me to forgive her, until I said there wasn't anything to forgive. Telling me hadn't killed Wuyoomi-Yaki, and I would have been a damned fool to think otherwise. But I forgave her anyway, which seemed to make her feel easier.

However, I was so fuddled with grief and sadness that I couldn't quite make out what was happening. I can't remember whether Lily was still in the room or not. About all I can recall is getting my cane and groping my way down the stairwell and bumping along until I got outside.

The night air blew against my face and it smelled fresh and pure, only it didn't help anything. I turned in the general direction of the fort and lifted my face and before I knew what was happening I was talking out loud, like there had been a whole congregation of saints out there in front of me. It's a wonder I could make any noise at all, because I was still considerable choked up and staggered.

Where I went and what I did are mysteries to me until this day. A couple of times I cussed and roared and whipped my cane like a sword, but I didn't connect with anybody, and even if I had, I doubt if I would have broken many bones, because I didn't have my heart in it. If Wuyoomi-Yaki was dead, everything would have turned dark before me, even if I'd had my eyes to see.

As it was, I wanted to snuff it all out, every bit of it. Those little trickles of memory that remained, the way things had looked, the whole business. Without Wuyoomi-Yaki, it was just about too much for me.

Finally I went back to the Lost Child Tavern and tried to go to sleep in a world that had gotten darker than ever, since now I realized that it would be without Wuyoomi-Yaki, from that time on, forever and ever, and there was nothing anywhere that could ever bring her back.

29

But the greatest error of all is, mistaking the ultimate end of knowledge; for some men covet knowledge out of a natural curiosity and inquisitive temper; some for ornament and reputation; some for victory and contention; many for lucre and a livelihood; and but few for employing the Divine gift of reason to the use and benefit of mankind.

— Sir Francis Bacon,
The Advancement of Learning

I FIGURED I might write a poem about the way it was at this time. I tried to picture how I was seated deep inside my darkness — sort of an exiled King — tormented by fugitive storms of headache, while I brooded about life. I tried to express my feelings about how the world looked as it drifted off, because every minute the memory of things I'd seen got farther away. But the poem never got anywhere, even though I kept hearing Samuel Chadwick's voice encouraging me toward eloquence.

But the thoughts stuck with me. There is a lot to think about when you are blind. I kept trying to remember exactly how it had been to see, so I guess it was natural that the memories I would call back most often were the sunny ones, such as fishing for catfish on Raccoon Creek, or on the Little Miami River when I was staying with Uncle Henry, and cutting corn in the dry hot fields under a late August sun.

There was one more recent scene, however, that surprised me and came back with a fierce brightness. This was the time when Half Face and I had sat there by my broken wagon while I tried to write down cusses and smut and excoriations for him. In my memory, the sunlight that day heated up considerable, so that everything shone like silver. And there the two of us were, sitting across from each other, and I was writing down everything I could think of, just to stay alive.

I also thought about my head injury. Here was a solid-gold example of coincidence at work, when it happens to a phrenologist, you might say. And did this injury change my thinking about such things? Was the critter who recovered the same as the one who'd been wounded? I gave a lot of thought to such questions. I brooded by day and by night; I tossed and turned. With the tips of my fingers I traced and palpated. I went over the convolutions in my forehead to see exactly how they had been changed.

You might think these parts would have been smashed flat by the blow they received, but this wasn't the case, because even though my forehead had been cracked by the blow, it then swelled from a blood clot over the bregma, pushing out and enlarging the regions of Individuality, Eventuality, and Comparison. My supra-orbital ridge has stuck out ever since, which I guess you could say makes me look a little like William Bone, or maybe it would even remind you of the melted brow of Daniel Webster's bust.

The army surgeon at the fort took care of me. His name was Major Spingarn, and he said it was a wonder I'd ever managed to survive a wound like that. He pulled one of my third molars, that had been acting up, and took an interest in my case. Several times the two of us talked about the brain, and one time he said he was surprised at how much anatomy I understood, which struck me as an ambiguous compliment.

He also studied his books for references to wounds like mine, and later told me he figured I'd probably be blind from then on unless by some wild chance a similar traumatic blow to the head readjusted the bones of my skull in such a way that the pressure on the optic nerves would be relieved. But he said that would be a tricky business because another trauma might just as easily kill me as cure me, so it was hardly what he'd recommend for treatment.

I told Major Spingarn about the power of coincidence at work in my life. I mentioned that now my own head was a little bit mutilated, as if it was kind of a mockery of my faith in phrenological science. I told him about Dr. Carstairs and Half Face, and how we had all had our heads and features changed by violent means. Not to mention Daniel Webster's bust. Our skulls had been rearranged as surely as if Nature was sending us a message. Major Spingarn agreed that these were deep matters to ponder, but usually he just listened to what I had to say, asking a question now and then.

Mostly, though, I wrestled with these ideas by myself. How had all these things happened the way they did? Why had they picked on me, of all people? If such hadn't been calculated behind the scenes by Fate, then they were just accidental, which is to say coincidences. And the power of this faculty, if you can talk about it that way, is such that those around me are affected, too.

The mind won't leave questions like that alone. Even after you come to a conclusion that you're one of the people marked out for such things, you are still left with the one that won't ever leave you alone: and that is, what does it all signify?

So there it was. I spent hours sitting in darkness, running the tips of my fingers up and down my forehead, trying to arrive at some kind of self-knowledge and figure out what sort of man would have such a skull. But I came out of all this still pretty much a mystery.

This wasn't the case with other people, though. As soon as I'd begun to walk with a cane and feel my way about a room, I took up cranial analysis where I'd left off. It was the only way I could make money, so Lily de Wilde advertised and promoted me like I was a famous man.

And then something odd began to happen: my touch and insight began to get more sensitive and more accurate than they'd ever been. It's a well-known fact that blindness will make you sharper in your other faculties, so that you begin to hear, taste, touch, and smell better than you ever could when you had eyes to see. It's as if you have a quantum of perception, and if one of the openings is blocked, the others open up more and keep pretty much the same amount of information coming in.

These were broody times, and I didn't joke and tell stories at the same rate I used to. It looked like most of my sassafras had gone down the drain. I had considerable trouble getting over Wuyoomi-Yaki's death. Weeks after the news hit me, I'd still think about her. Being blind, I felt nearer to her in a way I can't explain, only it was like it was easier to recall her image now that there weren't any distractions from the world of sight.

Lily had her share of difficulties, too, like all human critters. Her moods ran all up and down the scale. She touched all 88 keys. Her feelings scrambled all over the place, like a herd of wild mice. It was obvious that not all the time she spent in the next room was devoted to entertaining her customers, even though I couldn't always tell exactly what she *was* doing. She would be singing her favorite arias one minute, and then weeping the next, trying to muffle her sobs in that pillow she used as part of her workshop.

When she was feeling spirited, she'd make up little rhymes to tease me. These were considerable foolish, but you couldn't shake her loose from them. Her favorite went like this:

> Oh, Thad,
> Thou art mad;
> And that is why
> Thy Lily loves Thee!

Sometimes she'd recite this and sometimes she'd sing it to some tune by Mozart or Haydn. Her ingenuity in fitting it to unlikely melodies was considerable. There was something of the artist in Lily, I'll have to admit.

One day when I finally asked her what she meant by this confounded drollery, she gave the following explanation: "Dearest, I long ago discovered that all men are without exception mad. Utterly, unmistakably, raving mad. But it's a woman's covenant to love men; so I pick the most manly — which is to say, the maddest — to love most. And that's you, beyond any doubt, my sweet Maniac."

I told her I wasn't exactly what you'd call amused by her explanation, much less edified, and she thought that was funny, too.

"But I'm not just teasing you," she cried. "I'm bored with the predictable behavior of others, which contradicts the truth of their raving inner selves, and seems to me to come from fear, and nothing else. I detest the hypocrisy born of fear! I like a man who is manly enough to be as mad as his mind and heart direct him."

She came over and sat beside me on the bed, and I gave her skull a few touches and said, "Yep, it's all there, plain as a potato cooked in peas. You're compelled to be whimsical and irrational, I can see it all."

She laughed and stuck her tongue in my ear. But I held her off, the way I'd done all these weeks. At first, this was because of weakness from my wound, but later it was because I figured she might be venereal, considering how good business was.

But that night, which was professionally kind of slow, brought her back into my room. And when she sat down beside me on the bed to chat, I smelled her perfume and was troubled by considerable tumescence and longing, so that I figured to hell with it. Right then, I had to have her. I threw her back on the bed in a thick rustle of petticoats and, after some cooperative skirmishing, took possession of her a couple of times in quick and passionate succession, like they say.

The days passed into weeks, and by the time winter came, Lily de Wilde and I had cooled off considerable, for reasons unknown. In fact, we sometimes went all day without hardly saying a word to each other. We didn't hit it off right. We lived together in what you'd have to call bitter comfort. I was reminded of a disillusioned old husband and wife who have come to half hate each other, but need each other just the same.

There wasn't any real news about Henry Buck, but the rumor was that he'd escaped for good. Captain Dupre had been sent back east to recover from his stomach wound, where he seemed to be doing all right.

At this time my skill in phrenology grew faster than you could hardly believe possible. The only textbook I had now was the human head; but I worked at it and studied it the way I figure few people in this world have ever studied anything. Sealed off inside myself the way a blind man is, I poured all my mind into my fingers, and they reached out and learned things that I wouldn't ever have understood if I hadn't been blind and a phrenologist both. A fiddler would understand what I'm saying.

But you pay a price for every thing in this life, and I paid for this. Not only was I blind, but all the time my analyses were getting better and sharper, people were beginning to take the whole business of phrenology as a joke. They didn't really listen when I explained things. The more I was able to tell them, the less they were ready to believe. Phrenology was getting to be nothing more than a parlor game, which I had seen beginning to happen before, in fact, even as far back as those days with Dr. Carstairs. Combe had mentioned the same thing, when he visited this country. There were too many Stillingfleets in the business.

It was getting so I was having trouble selling my services, so I reduced my fee to a price common soldiers could afford. Their salaries weren't much, and I didn't want to keep them away from whatever self-knowledge I could give them. I had posters put up saying that for twenty-five cents I would give a quick reading to anyone: soldier, Indian, or Dutchman. Everybody, one and all.

This helped a little, and it made me less dependent on Lily. A man has to have money. But the situation kept getting worse. I talked to Lily about my problems, and she said I wasn't solemn enough. She said I was too airy, especially for a blind man. I told her I didn't want to be another Stillingfleet, and she said maybe I was too proud to think I could ever learn anything from somebody else.

This made me mad, and I cussed some and told her she didn't have to keep paying my room and board, if that's the way she felt, and this made her mad in turn, so she said something I couldn't make out and left the room in a storm of perfume. I could tell how upset she was by how much aroma her body had pumped out in her departure.

I groped my way to a table by the window. I fancied I could feel the light on my hands, like a thin muslin cloth. I picked up the water glass and the whiskey bottle that Lily had bought for me, and I poured a splash and then sipped at it between a few meditative cusses.

When I finished, I picked up my cane and bumped and staggered my way down the narrow little stairwell and into the saloon on the first floor and on outside, where I cussed Cyrus Morehouse, and then Captain Dupre and all his fellow officers. For all I knew, some of them could have been standing around listening. I cussed the land we were living in and the world at large. I cussed man's Fate and the Light of Day.

Then I trundled down the plank sidewalks, and kept on talking even though I didn't have any way of knowing whether anybody was around to listen. But this didn't last long, because I tripped and stumbled down some steps and fell right on my face. For all the feeling I had, I might as well have been wearing a birdcage over my head. I heard somebody laugh, and I got to my knees and whipped my cane sideways with the idea I might pop a kneecap, but the cane didn't hit anything.

I got to my feet, sort of panting and sniffling, and then I moved slowly back to the steps I'd just fallen down and sat there and thought about Wuyoomi-Yaki. For a while, I could feel the cold wind blowing on my face, and then something surprising happened: for the first time since I'd been shot I could feel tears in my eyes. A little of the numbness had gone away and my forehead even hurt a little bit.

Right then I felt a hand tug at my shirt.

"Who's that?" I whispered, raising my cane.

"Is dat you, Cap'n?"

"Who's that?" I asked, not sure I'd heard right.

"Why, it's de Cap'n, sho nuff. But whatevah done happen to yoah *face!*"

"Lionel Littlejohn," I muttered.

"It's old Lionel hisself." The hand let go of my shirt and then I heard a rustling as he stood up. It looked like I'd sat right down beside him there on the steps, because I sure hadn't heard him come up.

"What are you doing here?" I asked him.

"Dat," Lionel Littlejohn said in a low voice, "is one of dem stories dat will take a little time to tell, like dat *othuh* story you didn't have time to listen to, and I ain't about to tell it so peoples can overhear."

"Do you figure you can take me back to the Lost Child Tavern?" I asked. "And tell me on the way?"

"Dat is jes what I aims to do, Cap'n," Lionel said. So the two of us started out, which I figured meant that Lionel knew his way around, because he didn't have to ask where the Lost Child Tavern was.

30

Motion is a necessary, an integral part or parcel of life itself.
What could man do, what be, without it? How walk, work,
or move? How even breathe, digest, or circulate blood? — for
what are these, indeed all the physical functions, but *action* in
its various phases?

— Fowler's *Phrenology*

THE STORY that Lionel told wasn't what you'd call a complete
surprise, because everybody was getting so agitated over the issue
of slavery, particularly in eastern Kansas. Things were touchy there,
not to say confused and considerable violent. Reports about the
burning of buildings, lynchings, shootings, and even armed conflicts
between small armies of men had filtered down to us on the frontier.
Some of these were exaggerated but others were underplayed. Now
and then, Lily would read a newspaper to me, but they usually had
more to say about their own convictions than about the actual
events.

Shoestring had felt the tremors shortly after I'd left town. Lionel
said that the town had declared itself pro-slavery, which surprised
a lot of people, Lionel included. The biggest Abolitionist in Shoestring, a man named Thomas Creely, had to flee at night with his
family, and he got away just in time to avoid seeing his house go
up in flames.

Lionel Littlejohn was the only man of African descent in town,
so he figured he could read the writing on the wall and he lit out
early the next morning in hope of attaching himself to Thomas
Creely's party as it traveled northeast.

About an hour after dawn, Lionel saw some horsemen coming,
so he got off the trail and hid while a mounted troop rode by,
headed in the same direction. He recognized several of the riders
as pro-slavery men, and assumed they were after Creely, in which
case it would be smart for Lionel to go in the opposite direction.

So he decided to come to Fort Riley, knowing I'd come here, and figuring I was a friend he could trust. This gave me a peculiar feeling, and I told him he could stay with me in my room until he had a chance to escape.

"No, ain't gonna do none of *dat*, Cap'n," he said. "Too many soldiers dat drink in dat Tavern, and dey's too many men from South Carolina in de army for old Lionel to take a chance like dat. You jes go ahead. Old Lionel, he be all right. Old Lionel, he got hisself some colored friends nearby. He gonna make out all right, old Lionel is! But if'n you gits yohsef a chance to leave dish heah place, or gits de word dat dey's somebody goin north or west who won't mind havin colored folks along, let me know. And I'll tell you somepin', old Lionel won't fohgit it foh a damn second. Nossah! When de time comes, you kin have de shut off'n ole Lionel's back!"

He took me almost to the door of the Lost Child Tavern, but wouldn't cross the threshold. So I told him good-bye and went inside and climbed the stairs to my room.

Lily wasn't busy. In fact, she was asleep, and I could hear her snoring in a genteel manner.

Since I'd lost my sight, I'd learned to move quiet and undress and crawl in bed without waking her.

But in spite of how careful I was in the way I moved my body, inside I was a cauldron of memories and images, and when sleep finally dropped like a curtain over my teeming mind, as some poet said, it was a blessing as absolute as death.

The next morning I woke up to the sound of Lily singing a sad aria. It was one by Mozart, she'd told me once. I didn't appreciate it a whole lot this morning, because I was in bad shape. An old molar was acting up, and I was feeling donsy.

I called out for Lily to come and fill the water pitcher. Her sad trills came to a halt, and a couple minutes later, she entered the room slow and solemn. By the cadence of her step, along with what had been a pensive quality in her singing, I figured she might have some bad news for me. It was just a feeling, but there it was. I'm not often what you'd call prophetic.

She fetched the water and poured a glass full and handed it to me. I thanked her, and while I was drinking the water down, I felt her sit down on the bed beside me.

"Damned if I don't feel wretched!" I groaned, and put the glass beside the pitcher on the table. I didn't want her to tell me any bad news, and that's the truth. I wasn't up to it.

"As well you should," Lily said in a quiet voice.

I asked her what she meant.

"Only this," she said. She paused, and I heard her swallow. "I'm afraid for your life, Thad. You've talked too much. You've been far too outspoken. You're too active and unpredictable and . . . *irreverent*. People don't know how to take you. They're upset by what you've been saying about the troops. Especially the officers. Your wrath and outspokenness have become proverbial here. And when you haven't been insulting them, you've been breezy. That's exactly the word they use: *breezy*. You've made them into enemies, and no blind man has the power to do a thing like that!"

"Well, I've said so many things, they probably cancel out. And I don't figure anybody's going to single out a few remarks from the whole!"

"I'm afraid you have no understanding of politics, or you wouldn't be so reckless. I'd think a blind man would learn prudence above all others. Do you know how helpless you are?"

I said, "Nope, I'm too breezy."

But then I thought about what she'd said and told her not to waste her time giving me lessons on the subject of helplessness.

"All right," she said, "but let me give you another kind of lesson: I have heard that Captain Dupre has recovered from the wound your assistant, Henry Buck, gave him. He's expected to return any day to Fort Riley. He has influence and a lot of friends among certain of the officers. And Captain Dupre is your sworn and deadly enemy, and his friends have been here all this time and have heard about your outspoken comments, if they haven't actually heard them directly . . . for being blind, how could you know who has been listening when you've given way to those outbursts?"

"I don't suppose even a coward would shoot a blind man, would he?"

"No," Lily said, "but there are more ways than shooting to destroy somebody."

I laughed at that and said, "Yep, there sure are! But the blind prophet hasn't been wasting his time while he's been wandering around. *I* know a thing or two, so I'm not exactly helpless." This might have sounded brave and wise, but the fact is it was ninety percent bluff and fluff. In fact, I wasn't sure what I meant by it, which means I probably didn't mean much of anything.

But Lily was willing to be convinced and said, "I only hope you are right. Still, you mustn't forget: prophets and fools are near allied, as are madness and insights of genius which you've often displayed. I love you for your carefree madness, it's true; but it is precisely this which places you in danger. Don't you understand what I'm trying to tell you?"

"Nope, can't say I do."

I could hear Lily take a deep breath, like she was getting ready to heft a big load to her shoulders. In view of past complaints from various people, I don't doubt but what my problem would be considerable difficult to get into words. And this is the way it turned out.

"It's puzzling how you affect certain temperaments," Lily said. "At least it's puzzling to me. But of course I love you, Thad, and accept your faults as if they were virtues."

"Never mind the applesauce," I said. "Go on and pull the trigger."

"Have you no self-knowledge?"

"Nope, I guess maybe I don't."

"See?" Lily cried. "Even now, when I'm trying to express my concern for you, your words smart . . . they are casual, irreverent, insensitive! I'm afraid it's this quality that gets you into trouble so often. People don't know how to take so much sauciness."

I thought about this for a minute, and then told her I figured that sass was a pretty thin charge to level against anybody.

But Lily said it was more serious than I realized. She told me that nothing was more exasperating to a serious temperament than a breezy manner. She pointed out that we *do* have to live in the world, and I said that was pretty hard to do sometimes, even if you wanted to.

Then she took off in another direction. She told me that people didn't know what I was talking about when I started in on the subject of coincidences. She said I was always bringing it up, so that people got tired of hearing about it. "Don't you know that everybody has coincidences in their lives?" she said.

"Not like mine," I told her.

"But you make so much out of them, Thad! Except that some of the things you talk about, like the two times you found Henry Buck walking backwards in order to drown himself, are simply *too* preposterous. I'm afraid nobody would ever believe a thing like that."

She went on in a similar vein. What she couldn't seem to get over was how my stories were either uninteresting because they were obvious or unbelievable. And what I kept trying to get through to her was that it was those unbelievable things that had really happened, and the fact they were unbelievable was what gave them so much authority as coincidences.

But all this was too much for Lily's head, and she didn't spend much time on it. She finally did a little pirouette in her sermon and found herself back somewhere near where she'd started. "I'm afraid nobody could ever believe such stories," she concluded in a sorrowful voice.

"I don't tell them so they'll be believed," I said. "I tell them because they're true and have to be told. They won't stay down. They won't keep quiet. They won't stay bottled up. You don't have to tell me they're hard to swallow, because I'm aware of the fact. But I can't help it, they're true just the same."

"Indeed, they are hard to swallow," Lily said, which was her way of saying that she didn't believe any of them, either.

I felt her stand up and move away from the bed a couple of steps, and then a minute later I said, "And how about that coincidence of you being here to nurse me back to health, after all those years? Don't tell me that isn't considerable hard to swallow, too!"

"Ah," she said, "but that was the result of a woman's determination, Thad. And love!"

"Nope," I said, "that won't do it. It's no wonder I keep buttonholing folks and telling them my story. I'll tell you something, the Ancient Mariner didn't have anything on me!"

Which may have been the truth, but Lily didn't give an answer.

Then it came to me that the reason she hadn't answered was that she'd left the room, and I hadn't even heard her go, which is a pretty strange thing for a blind man, when you stop to think about it.

31

Antigone, from that distant Dark
Lift thy atavistic Head
And See thy Sister, darker yet,
Come to Death through her own Dead.

Yet that double Darkness fades
Into Brightness from such Deeds;
Wuyoomi-Yaki's light will raise
The shades of Death beyond Life's creeds.

Arrogant Kings and Generals lie,
Finely dressed in earthen gold;
But Girls, thy Sacrificial Hands
Have for an instant cracked the Mold!
                        — Thaddeus Burke

THE NEXT DAY I moseyed about the town for a couple of hours, and even circled the fort once, sort of testing Lily's fears. Nothing particular happened. I could feel sunlight on my face, and there was a fresh breeze, but I couldn't make out any change in the way people said hello or passed the time of day.

I was trying to figure what to do next. I didn't like the idea of living off the charity of a warbling whore. I figured it was time for me to give up the life I'd been living. I also knew it was time to give up thoughts of revenge against that hateful bastard Dupre. I had wasted too many hours devising complicated plots for doing him in.

I figured it would be best for me to leave Fort Riley right away. But how could I manage? Maybe I could sell the wagon Stillingfleet had traded for mine, and with the profits buy passage back to Council Grove or other points east. Or maybe I could borrow money and buy a team of mules and then hire somebody to drive me around, so that I could continue my phrenological career.

Whatever I decided, it was time to get away from Lily. Her way of life was too much for me. Not only that, it wasn't a comfortable life, living cooped up in a room not much bigger than a coffin.

It looked like a good bet that Lily herself would soon have to leave town. Considerable conflict had grown between Lily and Madame Vale. Everybody knew it. Lily herself was getting worried about the outcome, because Madame Vale had the strength of numbers and the security of being a permanent resident in the West Wind Hotel. Madame Vale was said to resent competition from an independent whore, since she claimed to be running a clean and attractive establishment big enough to take care of the needs of all the officers, soldiers, civilians, and transients in the region. She couldn't see why this situation should be troubled by a free lancer like Lily de Wilde, whose activities were beyond the control of anyone, even Cyrus Morehouse.

When Lily first brought up the subject, I said, "Well, if you're so intent on pursuing this way of life, why don't you go join Madame Vale and her girls."

Lily said it wasn't that simple. She said I didn't understand.

"Understand what?" I asked.

"Well, first of all, there's pride. I'm not just a common whore, in spite of what others might think. And I resent the idea that I should have to give up my freedom and live like an animal in a stable with other girls and submit to just any dirty beast who that precious Madame Vale wants to send me to bed with! It's not that simple."

"Nope, I can see it isn't. On the other hand, how many critters do you refuse the way it is?"

"That's a cruel question to ask and you know it! It's not so much the actual *numbers* I reject as it is the simple freedom I have to exercise my own judgment. Don't you see? Surely you do, for I remember how often you used to remark upon the Bump of Firmness at the top of my head. You talked about how singularly well-developed it was, and how impressed you were with its size and configuration!"

This was hogwash, because I had never made such a statement.

For one thing, it wasn't true. She didn't *have* any Bump of Firmness to speak of. The only possible sign of less firmness in her make-up would have been a concavity behind the area of Veneration.

That woman was a marvel, and I knew it right then. She sighed and toyed with the collar of my shirt. "Oh, why is it we cannot be happy?" she asked in her small intimate voice. "Why cannot we live here together and pursue our destinies without rancor and jealousy and envy obtruding into our lives?"

"Just you and me," I said, nodding.

"Yes," Lily said.

"And Cyrus Morehouse."

"Don't be bitter."

But I was just getting wound up. "And any number of drovers and sergeants and scouts and teamsters and gamblers and . . ."

"Hush," Lily said, putting her finger over my lips.

And strange to tell, that's exactly what I did. I'd been getting my wrath wound up, but all of a sudden it went away, and I just shut my mouth and for once had the sense to keep it shut.

It looked like Lily de Wilde didn't have any place in my future. She didn't seem to be in the cards, even though I would always owe her something in the way of gratitude for taking care of me all this time.

But telling her about my decision might be a sad and tricky business. I made up my mind the next day on my morning walk. I decided to let her know about it as soon as I returned to my room in the Lost Child Tavern. But the minute I walked in, Lily practically jumped on me and told me in her excited voice that she had news. She said a messenger had come from the fort with an invitation for me to attend the Reception Banquet the next evening.

"What Reception Banquet?" I asked.

"Why, everyone knows that a new Cavalry regiment is due to arrive tomorrow! They're on their way west to patrol the main trails against Indian marauders. And the banquet is to be a festive one. It's practically the social event of the season. Your invitation suggests that you will be honored in your role as phrenologist! Oh, isn't it wonderful, my sweet Maniac?"

Well, this was news, all right, and it made me forget all about my plan to tell Lily I was about to take off for parts unknown. "How about reading the invitation to me," I asked her; and Lily cleared her throat and read as follows:

> "The presence of Professor Thaddeus Burke is cordially requested at the Reception Banquet for Colonel Lester and his Officers of the U.S. 8th Cavalry tomorrow night at 8 P.M. where it is hoped he will entertain and edify those present with a demonstration of his famed abilities as phrenologist and physiognomic analyst."

"There," Lily said, when she had finished. I could hear her fold the note and put it back in the envelope.

"There, sure enough!" I said. Then I pointed out to her that considering the invitation I must not after all be a whole lot what you'd call *persona non grata*.

"Yes, you were right," she cried. "Oh, my mad one, you've won!"

"How about it if you stop calling me that," I said. "Some people might not think it's a compliment."

"Not if you don't want me to, Thad!"

"You know, this may mean a change of luck," I said. "Once I'm officially recognized like this, there's no telling how much success will follow!"

"Oh, you were right!" she cried. "How could I have been so cynical and mistrusting?"

"But I'll be damned if I'll flatter their heads with lies," I said. "They'd better not expect that sort of obsequiousness from me."

"No, my sweet mad one!" Lily cried. She was in what you'd have to call an ecstasy of excitement.

She rushed into my hands, and I caressed her head, soon letting my fingers find their way southward into what they call Warmer Climes, so that before long we found ourselves on my bed, where she performed her professional services for me free of charge, and with a considerable gallop of passion.

That evening she sang just about nonstop, dancing all around and touching me with her fingers. At one point, she sang the familiar "Thad, thou art mad" song, complete with glissandos and vibratos and even a kind of recitative, and she ended up whispering in my ear, "And that is why thy Lily loves thee!"

After a while her evening trade started, and with a kiss on my cheek, she left the room and went to work. I sat there and tried to figure out how I could dominate the assembly at tomorrow's banquet.

I sort of wished that Lily could come with me, because I understood what such an event might mean to her. But of course, that would be pretty hard to manage.

I smoked a segar standing there at the window. I lifted my face so I could feel the evening breeze on it and hear the voices of people passing by on the street below.

There was no doubt about it. Things were looking up.

32

Hollow eyes mean villainy, as in the ape; protruding eyes, imbecility, by congruity and as in the ass. The eyes, therefore, must neither recede nor protrude: an intermediate position is best.

— Aristotle's *Physiognomica*

EVERY MORNING Lily washed my eyes in saltwater, and the morning of the next day was no exception. I'd felt tears for the first time a few days previous, and now I could feel the warm wetness of the saltwater while Lily sponged my face.

This morning she gossiped while she sponged. She talked about who might be there and wondered how many of her customers would be among them. And I started remembering a time shortly after we'd first gotten in bed together.

She'd broken out the whiskey bottle that evening, which was uncommon with her, because she claimed a whore couldn't afford to drink liquor, and her conversation turned to our peculiar relationship. I can't remember her exact words, because I was drinking two glasses to her one, and my analytic faculties were a little dulled and staggered. But I distinctly remember the gist of what she'd said. What she said was that now that I had possessed her body, like so many other men had, it might turn out that I'd be less of a mystery to her. She claimed that in the carnal act itself, all men were pretty much alike.

But after saying this, she right away contradicted herself and claimed that she couldn't actually believe she'd ever love me less. The mystery I had for her was permanent, she said, like a vaccination that had taken. I told her if that was true, she ought to start thinking about changing her way of life.

Lily didn't answer right away, but I could hear her breathe a little harder, like she was laboring at some kind of decision. Finally she said, "But we don't have any other way to earn our living!"

"We could paint my name over Stillingfleet's," I told her, "and start out once again."

"Scheherazade, the Mind Reader!" Lily cried.

"Yep," I said, "that sounds pretty good."

"Scheherazade, Maid from another Realm, with Mystic Powers!"

"Why not?"

"But since you can't see, there wouldn't be any way for us to use a visual code. How would we be able to operate?"

"Is that the way Stillingfleet and you worked?"

"Yes. We had a code that fooled crowds everywhere."

This would be a problem, no doubt. I gave it some thought. Finally, I said, "Well, we could figure out a code between us. Like, if I mention I'm interested in the subject's benevolence, you could say something like 'dignified lady' which I'd take to mean she had combs in her hair. We could have a whole list of codes. Or you could just figure things out from my analyses, which don't need anything in the way of chicanery for their effect. And you could be my assistant and nothing more. There's nothing that says you would have to be a mind reader."

"Oh," she cried, "that would be lovely, wouldn't it? You could lecture and analyze, and perhaps I could play on the mandolin and sing to the crowd."

"Yep. That's not a bad idea! And it would be honest."

"I'm so excited I don't know how I can work today! I won't be able to stop thinking about it."

"By the way," I said, "can you really play a mandolin?"

Lily paused a moment and then admitted she couldn't, but she figured she could learn. I think the question surprised her.

"Do you *have* a mandolin?" I asked her.

"No, as a matter of fact, I don't."

"Well, then how do you figure to play one?"

She thought about that a minute, seeing it might be a problem, and then said, "Well, I guess we'll have to buy one. I am truly quite musical, and I could learn."

"I imagine they're pretty expensive."

"We'll save our money," Lily said practically.

"Traders from Santa Fe might have some in their wagons," I mused.

"Oh, dearest," she cried, "is it not all splendidly, gloriously mad?"

"I don't consider it what you'd call *mad*," I told her. "It's perfectly logical."

"That's what I meant," Lily said, hugging me.

A private soldier was sent to fetch me. For some reason, I was nervous, so I'd had a couple of drinks of whiskey. I gave the soldier a brief reading, right there in my room. It turned out I'd done it once before, for a quarter.

By the time I arrived at the fort, there was already considerable revelry. When I walked into what felt and sounded like a big room, a man came up and took my hand and shook it, introducing himself as none other than Lieutenant Barclay, the perfidious Second who had attended me during the duel with that damned scorpion, Dupre.

I was surprised and wary, but didn't have much time to collect my thoughts before Lieutenant Barclay was rattling a teaspoon in a glass to get the attention of everybody present. They all got quiet and Lieutenant Barclay said, "Gentlemen, I have the honor to present to you Professor Thaddeus Burke." There was some clapping, and then silence for a minute during which time I swear I could hear somebody whispering.

But before I could brood over the matter, a glass of champagne was stuck in my hand, and before you could say Tippecanoe and Tyler too, we'd drunk half a dozen toasts.

Then they asked me to give cranioscopic analyses of several volunteers, so I agreed and set to work. The whole room was quiet while I commented on my findings. Just about all I was aware of, beyond the particular head I held between my hands, was the smell of segars and the faint sound of an occasional champagne glass being placed on a table. Never have I felt more suspense or more interest in what I had to say about the human head.

Finally, Lieutenant Barclay took me by the arm and led me to another part of the room. I could hear people stepping back as we passed among them. Lieutenant Barclay said, "Now we are all *particularly* interested, Professor Burke, in hearing what you have to say concerning our *next* subject!"

I was led to a chair and my hands were put upon the head of a man sitting in this chair, facing away from me.

"Now, tell us exactly what you find," Lieutenant Barclay told me.

After tracing the configurations of this head, I had an uneasy feeling of something familiar. This was somebody I ought to know, and I told them as much.

"Tell us what features you find in it," Lieutenant Barclay said, ignoring my comment.

"Well, this figures to indicate a highly developed power of memory," I said. "An uncommon propensity towards Combativeness, or *Instinct de la Défense*, which you can tell by the enlarged mound in this area, behind the ear. Then there are adjacent tendencies toward Friendship or Adhesiveness, and Conjugality. I guess I'd predict that this subject is a considerable friend and a formidable antagonist. I figure he'd prove to be less mirthful and constructive, as shown by these areas above and at the edge of the eyes, than he is orderly and calculating, which are indicated by the protuberances directly underneath those areas I just mentioned."

I went on this way for a while, talking about what I found. It was an interesting head, all right, partly because of the contradictions in it. All the time I talked, the silence grew and the segar smoke thickened, and I began to feel a little bit uneasy.

When I finished, I said, "Now, maybe you'll introduce me to the subject, and then tell me how accurate you think I've been."

"I think that is only just," Lieutenant Barclay said. "Therefore, let me take pleasure, Professor Burke, in introducing you to Major Dupre."

I don't think I showed any emotion right then. I didn't say anything. Somebody grabbed my hand and started pumping it up and down. I guessed this must have been the major himself, who'd been only a captain the last and only time I'd seen him.

But I didn't say a word. As he shook my hand slowly up and down, Major Dupre said, "It is a distinct honor, being introduced to such a celebrity, Professor Burke." I could picture him closing his eyes while he said it.

This mockery hardly had time to sink in before Lieutenant Barclay was leading me in another direction. I swear, the room got even quieter. I could hear the quiet. It was the kind of quiet produced by fifty or maybe a hundred men breathing. I could feel the heat from their bodies. Lieutenant Barclay said, "Ah, but the analysis we are all *most* anxious to hear from your lips is that of the head *now* awaiting you. You see, we've brought a still more interesting specimen for you to examine!"

By now I was getting near to being what you'd call spooked, and I began to hold back a little. I was suspicious. I couldn't guess what might be waiting for me. I began to drag my feet a little, because it was clear that a surprise had been prepared for me, and there was no way I could back out.

I was brought up to a sort of table, and in spite of the champagne and segar smoke, I could all of a sudden smell wood alcohol. Two men on each side of me clutched my arms with one hand above the elbow and the other gripping my wrist. Then my hands were pulled forward until the palms were placed above the ears of a cold, damp head. I was only half holding back, or they'd have never moved me. The dampness was that of the wood alcohol I had just smelled. The smell rose up in my nostrils and burned all the way up to the brain. One of my hands slipped down as I staggered, bracing myself with it, against the table.

Somebody kind of laughed, but he bit it off. I couldn't even tell which direction the sound had come from. But that didn't matter, because the first touch had damned near paralyzed me. There wasn't any doubt. This was the head of a decapitated corpse, and it had been preserved in alcohol.

For a second I felt my body kind of weave under me, like it was something unconnected and about to drift away. Then the hands on my wrists jerked my own hands back to that loathsome head, so that I couldn't keep from touching it, especially in view of the fact I was considerable stunned by the whole business.

A shout of laughter exploded all around me. I cried out and damned near lost all sense of where I was or what I was doing. But there was no mistaking it. The identity of that head had registered itself on my brain. There wasn't any doubt about it at all. Not a whisper of doubt. It was the head of my old partner and friend, Henry Buck.

33

It is by virtue, that wee enjoy
   Deservedly the stile of beautifull,
Which neither time nor fortune can destroy;
   And the deformed body a faire soule
From dust to glory everlasting carries,
While vicious soules in handsome bodies perish.
                 — Sir Thomas Urchard

I'LL NEVER know how I got out of that place. The roar of laughter sounded like it was following me, echoing all around my head. I staggered first this way and then that, poking wildly with my cane as I groped my way toward the main gate. I must have acted like a crippled spider trying to get out from under a man's boot.

By the time I did get out, I was considerable hysterical and lifted my face trying to breathe, until I tripped over some loose harness leather lying there on the ground and stumbled and fell forward, slamming my face into the edge of a wagon so hard it was like somebody had hit me with a ballpeen hammer right in the Bump of Eventuality, which is the median projection above the glabella.

I'd forgotten to keep my cane in front of me, and I hit that wagon awful hard, so that I was stunned for a few seconds, and then when I sort of came around, the sensation was almost enough to make me forget Henry Buck's head. I finally turned over and vomited, and then felt a pain like scalding water running behind my eyes and brow. That pain went clear down the back of my neck into one shoulder. Then I could taste warm blood seeping past my nose into my mouth. I must have fallen against a piece of metal sticking out from the wagon and cut myself.

But I didn't really give much of a damn. I turned over in the dust and moaned and spit blood and coughed and gagged and then moaned again. I called out to my old friend Henry Buck. In addition to the damage to my forehead, there was all that whiskey and champagne I'd drunk, and it all came up one more time and gushed out of my nose and mouth, which put a stop to my wailing for a while.

Right then, I heard a man say, "What in tarnation is going on out there?"

Another voice answered, "Oh, it's that damned blind drunkard of a Head Reader. We just let him out, and he was so drunk he couldn't have found the gate even if he *hadn't* been blind!"

I crouched forward on my hands and knees and once again vomited blood and whiskey and champagne all together, until I thought maybe I could see stars shooting up and down inside my own head.

I groped around until I found my cane, which was sticky and wet to my touch, but I couldn't help that, and I stood up and staggered off in what I thought might be the direction of the Lost Child Tavern.

After I'd walked awhile, I felt a hand on my shoulder, and heard a familiar voice say, "Lookee here, Cap'n, yo sho is some damn *mess!*"

"Lionel," I said, starting to gag again, "Henry Buck's dead."

"Say what?"

"Henry Buck! He's dead."

For a second or two, Lionel was silent, and then he said, "Did he finally walk hisself backwards into some damn *river?*"

"I figure he was executed," I told him. "Or shot down like a dog." I hiccupped two or three times before I could go on. "He was decapitated. His head was cut off and pickled in alcohol like some animal trophy."

"You looks like you been havin' yourself a taste of de same treatment, Cap'n. Come on and we'll go somewhere and wash off yo face."

He led me away and after a few minutes he managed to get a bucket of fresh water. He said, "Lookee heah!" and whistled a couple of times while he helped me off with my shirt and suitcoat, which I could tell were smeared with blood and filth.

"Look like somebody done hit you in de face with a damn *brick,*" Lionel said. "You sure you feel all right, Cap'n?"

The truth was, my head was hurting considerable, but I told Lionel I was all right. In the mood I was in, I didn't care enough about anything else to care about how bad I was hurt. The self is a mirror as well as a lamp, they say. So be it. Maybe a blood vessel had been punctured and my brain was this minute filling up with venous blood. I didn't much care, one way or the other. Right then, life seemed too black and ugly for any sensible critter to regret leaving it. It looked like William Bone might have been right, after all. Never in my life have I had less sass than I had right then.

When he'd cleaned me off, Lionel led me back to the Lost Child Tavern and I went on in. Judging by the noise, it was getting on toward midnight. There was laughing and bragging and singing and the scraping of chairs and the slap of cards.

For the second time, Lionel had decided not to come with me to my room, so I figured he was sleeping with those colored friends he'd mentioned, or maybe under a wagon, somewhere. I figured he'd probably be all right, no matter where he slept, because even though the weather was cool, it was clear. There probably wouldn't be any bad weather for another month.

Lying down in my bed, I clutched my throbbing head in my hands, and told myself to hang on. After all, I'd gone through bad times before, and I'd probably come out of this sad business somehow, one way or another.

Right before I went to sleep, I could hear Lily in the next room, talking in a low voice to a customer.

Down below, there was the same old noise of drunken talk and laughing.

But then it got quiet all of a sudden, and I'll be damned if I didn't hear somebody start playing "The Spanish Cavalier" on a mandolin.

34

In like manner, the investigation and discovery of the latent conformation in bodies is no less new, than the discovery of the latent process and form. For we as yet are doubtless only admitted to the antechamber of nature, and do not prepare an entrance into her presence-room. But nobody can endue a given body with a new nature, or transform it successfully and appropriately into a new body, without possessing a complete knowledge of the body so to be changed or transformed.
— Sir Francis Bacon,
Novum Organum

BEING BLIND never bothered me more than in the mornings when I woke up. When I was asleep, I figured I wasn't any more blind than I'd always been when I slept. But when it was time to wake up and I opened my eyes and nothing happened, then I'd remember. It didn't make any difference if you tried to open your eyes. It was still the same old black. Part of you might just as well have stayed asleep.

That night I didn't sleep much, and yet I wasn't really awake, either. I was sick from liquor and a throbbing in my temples and the shock of having my hands placed on Henry Buck's cold wet head. It's no wonder I didn't sleep very well, and yet toward dawn, I did go off into a considerable deep sleep. It reminds me of one time years before, when I was a boy, washing in the murky water of Raccoon Creek and I stepped in a deep hole and sank way down under.

But it was when I came awake the next morning that it happened. When I opened my eyes I could see something all streaked with gray. It was like somebody had tied up a dirty white sheet before my eyes and they were shaking it so that it trembled there before me.

My stomach turned over and I groaned. I was considerable bilious, and my head hurt like somebody had hit me with a shovel. I moaned again and then yelled out.

It must have been an awful sound, because two dusty, stinking drovers that had been sleeping on the floor of the room jumped up like a couple of spooked horses and asked me what was the matter. Then Lily came rushing into my room, asking the same thing.

When I told them I thought I could see light, one of the drovers said that called for a celebration, so the two of them tramped downstairs with the idea of waking up Cyrus Morehouse so he could serve them some liquor.

Lily grabbed my hand and wept. It was true, I could see a little bit. I kept telling her that, and she kept saying "Yes, yes!" as if she could see that I was seeing.

I couldn't see very much, just vague shapes. I could see the window, which was gray, and the doorway leading downstairs, which was a darker gray, and Lily in her white nightgown, which was about the same gray as the window.

The drovers never did come back, so I figured they either got sidetracked or forgot what they were supposed to celebrate or maybe weren't able to get Cyrus Morehouse awake and just departed for regions unknown.

But Lily clucked like a hen who's just laid the biggest egg in Christendom. She tried to dance with me, turning me around in a circle until I was so sick I almost had to throw up, and I yelled for her to let me go. Then she started to trill one of her arias, but using different words, some of which were, "Oh, Thad, thou art glad!" and a few other things that were just about as silly.

I finally got her calmed down and explained how last night I'd tripped and hit my forehead on the edge of a wagon and how that blow had probably dislodged an embolus of scar tissue that had been blocking and paralyzing the optic nerve.

I told her I figured this meant that I was probably going to get my sight back, maybe even close to 100 percent in one of the eyes. I told her I couldn't figure out how that one obstruction could have put pressure on both optic nerves, making me blind in both eyes. Major Spingarn had talked about the same thing, which made him curious, too. That's one reason why he was interested in my case.

But Lily wasn't listening. She'd started in on her damned trilling again, and I had to shut her up so I could tell her how funny the whole business was. I told her it was just downright mystical and homeopathic the way a blow could bring back my sight, when you thought about the original injury.

"Oh, Thad, is it true you can see a little light?" Lily asked.

"Isn't that what I've just been telling you?"

"Yes, but isn't it wonderful, my sweet Maniac?"

"Yep. It's kind of a miracle."

"Ours not to question the gifts of Providence, Thad!"

"No, but I sure would like to understand them a little better." I guess she'd talked long enough, however, because she started in once again, trilling like a mockingbird, going from one aria to another. I settled back in my cot and got sick at my stomach again, and my head hurt so much I thought maybe I was going to throw up and pass out at the same time.

I tried to take deep breaths, but that didn't help much. Lily stopped singing and brought out the slop jar and held it out in front of me.

"Do you want me to hold your head?" she asked.

"Nope," I told her, "I figure I can ride out the storm."

Lily acted like she was now about as alarmed as she had been happy. She went to fetch some cool damp cloths and pressed them against my forehead.

Everything seemed to be jumping up and down, and having sort of tasted what it was like to see again, I got scared and hardly knew what to do. I grabbed Lily around the hips and hugged the side of my head to her stomach. She patted the top of my head and for once managed to keep her mouth shut.

Everything was whirling around. My head felt like it was attached to a wagon wheel with a long rope, and the wagon was bouncing down a hill, out of control, hitting rocks and stones and kicking up dust in every direction.

I didn't have any idea when it was going to stop or even if that damned hill would ever come to an end in some sweet valley.

There's no telling how long I slept, but when I woke up I felt a whole lot better, and could actually make out objects. I could see the wash basin and the mirror. I could see the window and the door and the roof, which was slanted above the window. You had to duck your head a little if you were going to look out. But I'd known all this before, because that room had come to fit me like a suit of clothes.

I didn't go over to the window. I didn't figure I could take it right away, looking out there and seeing people walking around. The sound of the bugle came drifting over the breeze. It was a lonely sound, for some reason, even though it was mess call and I was considerable hungry.

There wasn't any sound in Lily's room, which probably meant she was out someplace, the way she liked to go around during the day and visit and gossip with folks. She certainly was a sociable creature. In many ways.

I sat there for about half an hour, thinking of Henry Buck's head and started to shudder all over. Then I thought about Wuyoomi-Yaki and wept a tear for her. I figured if I ever got my sight back all the way, I might kill every soldier in the fort, beginning with Dupre and Barclay, and then working my way down. Only I knew better than that. Most of them were decent enough critters. I'd heard about Indian massacres, and I wasn't about to get all woozy and palpitating about the fate of the Redman, the way folks back East tended to get. No, it was pretty much that damned pair of Dupre and Barclay that ought to be dug up and extirpated like a couple of bull thistles.

My thoughts were interrupted by the sound of Lily's steps on the stairwell. I heard her go into her room and open a drawer. I could hear her rummage around in it, looking for hairpins, maybe, or a ribbon to tie in her hair. Right then I got a whiff of her perfume, which she doused on pretty heavy, the way whores have a way of doing. And then I heard her come to the door of my room and take the knob in her hand.

Even though I'd run my fingers over her face a number of times during the past months, I wasn't ready to see her right there in the flesh, life-sized and real. And it was quite a shock. Her face had gotten sort of bloated and lopsided, with a slight leer built into her left eye. In fact, that eye looked like it was half caught in a wink. Her lips and nose had swollen beyond their youthful dimensions, and her skin had changed color. Maybe Stillingfleet or somebody had hit her. It was pretty bad. Whatever the case, I hadn't realized she'd gotten so old-looking, and it took me a minute to adjust to it.

She caught me looking at her and there was a quick sort of puzzled expression that came over her face. It was like she wasn't all that pleased that I could see, even though she didn't know right then how much I could take in. But it was obvious she was shaken up a little.

So I lied in order to buy a little time. I told her I was afraid I couldn't see anything but blurs. I told her my sight hadn't improved at all since the last time.

She actually looked kind of relieved and got a tender expression on her face and came up and stroked my head. "Never mind," she said. "It will come back to you, Thad. I know it will!"

I just nodded and put my face in my hands. My forehead was still mighty sore, so I didn't put much pressure on it.

Lily excused herself for a minute, after she'd asked if I'd be all right and I'd told her yes. She went into the other room, and I sat there and tried to think the whole business out. I didn't want to hurt her, and it looked like the best way I could keep from doing that was to pretend I was still blind. But that was going to be considerable hard to do.

And then a plan came to me. It didn't have to do with Lily, exactly, but with everybody, the whole set up. I figured I'd been given an opportunity, and I'd be a damned fool not to take advantage of it. Everybody knew me for a blind man, and if I could keep it that way, I could see things without anybody knowing I *was* seeing them. I could operate and nobody would know it. It was almost as good as being invisible, which was the thing that gave the Greek and Roman gods so much power. The thing was, I could cook up some real vengeance for that damned devil Dupre.

When Lily came back after a few minutes, I asked her if she'd mentioned to anybody that I could see a little bit.

"Why, no one," she said, "except for those two drovers who heard you cry out."

I nodded. "And they were just staying here for the night, weren't they?"

"I'm sure they're part of that train that's headed for Santa Fe. They left about an hour ago."

"So now that they've left, you and I are the only two people who know I got a flicker of light when I opened my eyes this morning."

"Why, I guess so. But what difference does it make?"

"It doesn't really make much difference," I said carefully, "except I'd sort of like you to keep the whole business quiet, if you don't mind."

"But why would you . . ." She stopped and frowned for a minute, and then she smiled. "Oh, I see! Thad, you are truly clever. During our act you want to pretend that you're still blind even after your sight returns — because it *will* return, you know! And then you can pretend that you know things by divination or sorcery which you've actually seen physically! Oh, that *is* a clever idea! I can see how it would help us once we take to the road!"

I told her this was pretty much the way it was, and when I looked at her, I was careful not to look like I was really seeing her, which is not hard to do if you think about it.

But when she left my room again, the whole idea seemed almost too big for me to want to wrap my mind around it. I thought of that damned infernal banquet and it made my mind start whirling again. I got sick and groaned and fell back on my cot. I started shaking and sweating. I was afraid I was going to throw up again, but I didn't. Henry Buck's head seemed to be looking at me from a shelf in the room.

I slept for a while, and I felt a small hand rubbing my back. Lily had come into my room and I hadn't even heard her.

"Poor Thad," she said. "It has been almost too much for you, hasn't it?"

I couldn't take that. I wasn't ready for it. Right away I started bawling like the damnedest baby who ever lived, and Lily de Wilde stroked me and soothed me like she was my own mother, who had died so tragically all those years before.

35

The face is a weak surety; yet it deserves some consideration. And if I had the punishment of the wicked I would more severely lash those who belie and betray the promises that Nature has implanted on their brows; I would more harshly chastise knavery under a meek and mild aspect.

— Montaigne

I WAS CONSIDERABLE sick all that day and late into the night, but I was careful not to let on how my eyesight was improving.

Along near midnight, I fell into as deep a slumber as I can ever remember, deep as any sleep I'd had when I was blind. The next morning, I woke up feeling like maybe I'd survived another disaster, and I could see close to 100 percent in my right eye, and maybe half that in the left. I stayed there for a few minutes with my head on the pillow, staring up at the low ceiling that I'd slept under for almost a year, without ever seeing it. I got up and went over to the window and looked out upon the narrow dusty road and the shacks and tents that bordered it. About two hundred yards away, right next to the fort, stood the West Wind Hotel, a little box-shaped building, where Madame Vale kept her girls.

I listened for sounds in Lily's room, but I didn't hear anything, so I decided to go open the door and step in. It all looked mighty strange. There was a small blue-painted rocker, a bed, a fancy lacquered dresser and a marble-top washstand crowded all together. There was one window looking out upon the edge of the stockade. Every piece of furniture was familiar to me, and yet it all looked different. I thought about this and told myself that all these things had been looking this way all that time and I hadn't known a thing about this part of their existence. I figured there was a lesson in this, because philosophy tells us our view of everything is only partial.

The biggest piece of furniture, next to the bed, was the dresser, which had a big mirror attached. I'd known about the mirror, of course, because Lily liked to stand before it and comb her hair while we talked.

I went over to this mirror. I approached it the way a man walks up to a thicket with a bear in it. I figured that mirror might have more truth in it than I could swallow. But I took the dive and looked into it.

The face that looked back at me had a huge beard. No surprise in that. But the scarred and battered brow was all scabbed over with a velvety crescent. It gave the features a pretty wild and withdrawn look. The eyes were wrinkled and sagged a good deal. Here was a map of human suffering, all right.

I didn't tarry long before the spectacle. I went back into my room and stood there and took a few deep breaths and sort of got control of myself. Then I picked up my cane and started down the stairs, but found out I was getting kind of spooked for some reason. I couldn't figure it out, but finally I closed my eyes and this seemed to work. It calmed me down a bit. I kept my eyes closed and went downstairs, not opening them until I reached the bottom floor. A big shaggy man was in front of the tavern, straddling a rum keg. A young colored man was standing at his side, smoking a pipe.

This large man greeted me, and I could tell by his voice that it was Cyrus Morehouse.

"There's a message for you," Cyrus said. "This here soldier brought it."

I didn't turn my head, because that would have betrayed the fact I could see, so I just nodded and sort of shook my cane. A young private came in front of me and held out an envelope.

Cyrus Morehouse stepped up and said, "Can't you see he's blind, soldier? Here, give me that note; I'll read it to him."

Cyrus shook the paper out and read a message from Colonel Blaine himself, the commanding officer of the fort, requesting that I visit him at my earliest convenience.

"If it was me," Cyrus Morehouse said, "I'll be damned if I'd go. Not after what I heard they done to you yesterday. No sir, I'd tell that Colonel to go belch in a cave."

"Nope," I said, "I don't figure there's anything they can do to hurt me now. Not only that . . ."

But all of a sudden there wasn't anything in my mind. I closed my eyes, which was kind of hard, because there was stiffness in them. Then I kind of staggered, and started to cuss and rave a little. I whipped my cane around hard enough to crack a kneecap if anybody had gotten near me.

When I got through, I kind of stumbled half blind over to a bench and sat down, still breathing hard. I wiped some tears from my cheeks. I hardly knew where they'd come from.

A minute later, I saw Cyrus Morehouse standing by the unopened rum keg, looking at me pretty hard.

I let on I couldn't see him and tried to look blind.

But Cyrus Morehouse had gotten suspicious. He walked up to me and slowly moved his big hand back and forth in front of my face. I didn't blink and I didn't change the direction of my gaze.

"That is the first time," Cyrus Morehouse said to the young black man standing next to him, "that I ever saw his eyes close up like that!"

"He sho do cuss hisself up a damn *storm!*" the young black man said, taking his pipe from his mouth and shaking his head.

To get Cyrus Morehouse's mind off me, I asked the young black man if he happened to know Lionel Littlejohn.

He laughed and said, "Sho do. He sleep down at de livery stable."

"I thought he had some friends he was staying with," I said.

The black man laughed again and said, "He allus talking about how he got all dese here friends. Man, *he* ain't got no friends, less'n yo call de hosses and mules friends. But he ain't got no *people* friends. Not dat *I* know of. Old Lionel, what he got hisself is chiefly a lot of mouf."

"I didn't even know he could close his eyes," Cyrus Morehouse mumbled, giving me one last look. And then the two of them went back to the rum keg and started rolling it up to the tavern door, where Cyrus Morehouse himself gave it a mighty heave with both hands and placed it on the floor inside.

"Are you going to come with me to Colonel Blaine?" the young soldier asked.

I'd been working so hard at acting blind I'd almost forgotten he was standing there. But I told him I would, and the two of us started out for the fort, where the Colonel was waiting for me in his office. Major Spingarn was there, too, and made himself known. He was a tall, thin type, considerable older than I'd thought, close to fifty. He had graying sandy hair and pronounced outer epicanthus folds around little bitty pale eyes that gave him sort of a sad, owlish look. His uniform was mussed and soiled, and the tips of some Spanish cigaritos were sticking out of his breast pocket.

Colonel Blaine cleared his throat and said, "Professor Burke, I've asked you to come so that I could apologize officially for that disgraceful episode at our banquet. I have given the severest reprimand to Major Dupre and those other officers who were part of the fun made at your expense. I found that so-called humor tasteless and sadly inappropriate, Professor Burke, and lament the fact that you should have suffered so at the hands of officers of the U.S. Army. It is perhaps understandable, given the sort of life my men are forced to live, dealing as we must constantly do with the savagery and duplicity of certain hostiles that we should eventually come to consider all of them little more than beasts to be disposed of as quickly and conveniently as possible. But even this fact cannot excuse Major Dupre and his friends — only three officers, out of eleven presently under my charge, I should point out — for their ungentlemanly and unmilitary behavior. Most of us there were as surprised, if not as shocked, as you yourself."

The Colonel's words triggered a spasm of grief. I'd been unstable lately, unsettled by events, and by the time he'd ended his comment, tears were streaming down my face.

Major Spingarn jumped to his feet and came over to my chair. He put his hand on my shoulder and said, "Come, come, Professor Burke! It was a terrible ordeal for you, I'm sure, but the trail of human existence is full of ambushes for all of us, not to mention bushwhacks, especially out in these regions where a man's life doesn't always have a great deal of value. Brace up, man, for we've all lost friends and brothers, and we've got to reconcile ourselves to a world in which such sadnesses are part of the contract we signed by being born."

"Old Henry was both to me," I said. "Both friend and brother!"

"Then you are doubly fortunate in having once experienced such friendship and such brotherhood," Spingarn said gently. Colonel Blaine nodded his head in tune with these words, and the obvious decency of these two critters — especially in view of the fact they wore the same uniform as Dupre — moved me considerable, and before long I was nodding along with them.

"Yes, we understand," Major Spingarn said, patting my shoulder once again.

Then he did something I found pretty odd: he leaned over in front of me, struck a match and lighted a cigarito, so close I could feel the heat from the match.

Naturally, I didn't blink. I made a point of it.

36

My next preliminary shall be to recommend the use of Comparative Anatomy, as well in the same as in different species of animals; for belief it, as one man may be known from another by his face, or by his Voice, or by his tread, so one man may be known from another by every part and bowell of his body. For the bowells of every man do differ from another in bignes, shape, and substance, and the various proportion which one varieth to the other.

— Sir William Petty (from an
uncompleted lecture on Anatomy)

COMING BACK from the visit with Colonel Blaine and Major Spingarn, I shook off the helping hand of the soldier who'd fetched me, saying I'd managed with a cane too long for him to trouble himself over me.

He drifted off, but right then two other soldiers came up and asked to have their heads analyzed.

"I hear tell," one of them said, winking at the other, "that you are one hell of a Head Reader, Professor."

"Well, that might be the case," I told them.

"That's what they claim," he said. "Ain't that right, Fred? Yeah, Fred here agrees that you have one hell of a reputation."

And I believed him, because Fred was standing there kind of grinning and nodding like a toy duck.

"Here's a quarter for your pains," the soldier said, putting a nickel in my hand. I could tell the difference without having to take a look at it. It was a pretty sad business, but I took it and pretended to think it was a quarter, so I held my hands out for him to step forward.

By this time, a couple of other soldiers had gathered around, watching us. Their presence made me a little uncomfortable. I asked myself how often I'd analyzed heads blind, surrounded by clowns and mockers.

Damned if I *hadn't* been blind!

But I held on to my temper and gave the soldier a true reading, which was close to being the most eloquent thing I could do against him under the circumstances.

I finished with this man and made my way to the Lost Child Tavern, where a considerable shock was waiting for me. Cyrus Morehouse stopped me just inside the door, and told me that Lily de Wilde had gone. He told me she had left. "Departed," he said.

"Where'd she go?" I asked.

"Well, I don't rightly know," Cyrus answered. "But there was this fellow come and got her. He acted like he knew her from way back. She left you a note."

I got sort of weak in the knees and cussed a little, then I asked where the note was.

"It's right here in my hand," Cyrus said. "I suppose you want me to open it up and read it for you, don't you?"

I shook my head and swallowed. "Nope," I said finally, "just give it to me and I'll get somebody to read it after a while. The fact is, I don't feel so good. I'm under the weather. I've got to go and lie down in my bed and take me a little rest."

"Have you been hitting the bottle again?" Cyrus asked.

I said I hadn't and saw him return to the counter in back, where two Germans were busy arguing with each other in thick accents about slavery.

Upstairs, I opened the envelope and with considerable strain and trouble read Lily's note to me, as follows:

Dearest Thad:

You must know that I leave you with a broken heart, but not without Reason, my Darling. I will try to make you understand. My decision originated the other morning when you first began to see light, and I realized that you were improving so much that soon you might be able to see fully as well as before, and then our dark little Paradise would be shattered. At first when you exclaimed over those streaks of gray you could see, I was ecstatic with joy over your recovery. But then when you became ill from the shock of returning sight, and lay down to sleep, I returned to my room and sat for a few minutes, reflecting as I gazed into my mirror, taking in all that you might soon be able to look upon and trying to see me as you must. In a moment, I was weeping quietly (so as not to disturb you) . . . for oh, Thad, the years have been harsh to your poor Lily! You would hardly recognize me now, after all the suffering I have gone through! I have lost four teeth through various hardships, and also my face has begun to look so swollen and coarse from age and hardship that my features are no longer those you remember from so many years ago in Baltimore! I am only thankful that my voice has not been lost, so that I could still sing for you, and speak to you at tender moments! No, Thad, I could not bear the thought that you should soon awaken to gaze upon the terrible changes that time and suffering have wrought!

And since I was already sensible of your disapproval of my way of life, and had sensed increasingly your impatience with me, and your desire to leave me forever, I knew there was only one course for me to follow. (Oh, the thought of this breaks my heart, and I must lay down my pen to let tears have their way for a moment!) So you see, there was no other choice for me. Soon, you will be fully sighted again (I know!) and fully recovered. You will remember only as a dream those dark days when your dark Lily de Wilde nursed you back to health, and loved you without thought of burdening you with her old and useless presence!

You must also realize that my life here at Fort Riley would be impossible were it not for Cyrus Morehouse, my original protector; but there have been increasing signs that even with his help, I could not hope to remain here much longer, for there has been an outbreak of clap in the fort, and Madame Vale is up in arms, claiming that I have infected the soldiers and that they are in turn infecting her girls. You'll be interested to know that she is aided and abetted in this vile slander by that terrible Major Dupre! He is the natural instinctive enemy of all who would protect you.

I could not under the best of circumstances hope to remain here much longer; I could not hope to let you see me ravaged as I have been by the years and lascivious deportment. Thus it is that I cannot neglect the opportunity that presents itself this very morning, for one whom we both know from the Past has come to take me away with him. I have heard that Colonel Blaine has called you in today for the purpose of apologizing to you, so I know that temporarily, at least, you are once again not in ill-favor with the Military (although I beseech you to be more prudent in the future, you sweet Mad Man!) . . . So I know that you are out of immediate danger; and therefore, since Horace Stillingfleet has come to me this morning, begging me to accompany him back to Santa Fe, where he has been living and thriving in his business . . . since he has asked me to accompany him once again, to become my old Scheherazade, I cannot resist, but have made up my mind quickly and definitely to accept.

So now I am gone, Dearest Thad. I give you my Angel's blessings . . . blessings from that pure and maidenly girl that still lives on, somewhere deep inside thy Lily's ageing, beaten, and withering Breast!

Adieu, my sweet Mad Prince! Adieu!

Thy Eternal Love,
Lily

When I finished reading this note, I tossed myself on my cot and let my brain fill with thoughts of Lily, which after a while gave way to the sorrow of Wuyoomi-Yaki's death. Then my mind wandered all over the place, including thoughts of Henry Buck, William Bone, and Anastasia Cunningham — a critter I hadn't thought of for years, but there she was, looking at me, as spry and perky as ever.

Then I thought of the considerable coincidences in my life, enough to occupy a wise man for years. Which I am not, nor have ever claimed to be.

37

Floute me, Ile floute thee: it is my profession,
To jest at a Jester, in his transgression.
— *Quips upon Questions, 1600*

THE NEXT morning I pretty well made up my mind to kill Major
Dupre. Just up and do it. I didn't like the idea of murder much, but
I figured that I could hardly continue to breathe the air while that
vile serpent lived. Several times in my room even the thought of
him made me choke and cough and roar incoherently. Once, I broke
out in a cussing fit. Cyrus Morehouse obviously thought I was
drunk and came to the stairwell down below to ask about my health.
His tone of voice was not as sympathetic as the words he spoke.

After a while, I realized I couldn't think inside, so I bit off a plug
of tobacco and went out. I was careful to take my cane with me
so that I could keep up my pretense of blindness. I still figured that
the appearance of being blind would help me in my plan to get
even with Dupre.

But I noticed something curious. Now that I could see, I couldn't
walk as well as before, when I'd depended on my cane and other
senses. Part of this was the way I was trying to act like I was still
blind, but part of it had to do with the fact that I hadn't yet adjusted
to being able to see, and seeing things just added a kind of confusion
to the touch and hearing I'd depended on for so long. It was what
you'd call distracting.

I was thinking about this while I was walking down the street,
moving my cane back and forth, when I was surprised to see old
Lionel Littlejohn coming toward me. I almost called out his name,
but caught myself in time and waited until he came up in front of
me and introduced himself.

"I thought maybe you'd hauled your carcass off for parts unknown," I said.

"Dat is jest exactly where ah's headed!" Lionel exclaimed.

"Where?" I said.

"To pahts unknown, Cap'n. Old Lionel, he's had enough of dis here place. He's gonna venture forth into one of dem regions unknown!"

"Did I hear you say you were staying with friends?"

"Yeah, I got me a lot of friends all over. I been gittin along all right. But now I has had *enough*! What I mean is, old Lionel ain't never yet seen de Elephant, and he means to take hisself a gander at it. Yes suh, he's going to see de damn *Elephant*!"

"Where do you figure you'll go?" I asked him again.

"Never mind about where old Lionel *figures*, Cap'n. You jest remember he's gonna git hisself outa dis place and to one of dem regions unknown."

I thought about this a minute and finally said, "If I were you, I'll be damned if I'd put my chips on some faraway place being any better than where you are."

"Yeah, but I is headed out yondah. Maybe I'll jest take de next wagon train dat comes through dis here place. Den again, maybe I *won't*. Being free means you is *ignorant* and don't know *what* you gonna do right up to when you do it."

"That might not be a bad idea, going farther west," I told him. "The news from back East isn't too good. Any day now there's going to be war over slavery. Nobody doubts it."

"Dat don't concern old Lionel, cause old Lionel, he ain't no damn slave."

"Well," I said, putting my hand out, "here's luck to you."

Lionel closed his eyes and thought. "You know," he said, "ah never *did* get a chance to tell you mah story."

"Nope, you never did."

"But it ain't time now, and ah ain't gone start unless ah kin give it its due."

"That sounds like good sense to me."

Lionel nodded. "Yeah, I wish you luck, too, Cap'n. What I mean to say is, you is quite a man, even if you is blind. Old Lionel's bin hearing about da way you talk shit back to ever'body. I tell em: old Cap'n he ain't about to knuckle down to *nobody*, don't make no difference whether he blind or *not*!"

I told him that was considerable decent of him to say so, and then we said good-bye, shook hands, and Lionel took off.

I felt better after Lionel's conversation, and stood there for a couple of minutes thinking about his spirit, which you'd have to say was on the strong side.

Then I started walking again. I had to figure out some things. I didn't have much money, and I couldn't stay on at the Lost Child Tavern now that Lily de Wilde had left. She'd been turning over a good part of her earnings to Cyrus Morehouse to cover the cost of room and board for both of us.

I wondered if she'd suspected that my sight had already come back and now I wasn't helpless any longer. I thought about this, and all of a sudden realized I'd walked up to the military corral, where a few of the troops were breaking horses. I stood and watched them for about half an hour. They didn't waste time or patience on the horses. They just plain beat them into submission with clubs and controlled them with choke-ropes. Not only that, I knew that the horses had been starved and kept from water before breaking, so they didn't have much strength to resist. But I also knew that those animals were about as wild and mean as snakes and they needed to be broken this way.

I was so wrapped up in watching this business that I forgot to act like I couldn't see, and when I turned around to spit some tobacco, who should I find standing right there beside me but Major Spingarn. I almost spit on his foot. He was standing about four feet away and smoking a Spanish cigarito while he looked at me. He must have been pretty quiet when he'd moved up.

"Hello," he said.

For a second I didn't know whether to answer or not. But then I nodded and spoke. Major Spingarn said, "I have been thinking about you, Professor Burke. I wonder if you would like to join me in a game of chess."

I paused, wondering how to answer, but Major Spingarn took me off the hook. "Oh, never mind about your eyes," he said. "I know you are again sighted. I knew it before seeing you just now watching them break the horses. I knew it yesterday in Colonel Blaine's office, because when I struck a match to light my cigarito,

I saw your pupils contract. Your gestures when you first entered the office were not exactly those of a blind man. So I knew you'd regained your sight. But never mind. Whatever your reason for pretending, I'm not interested in betraying you. Your secret's safe with me, Professor Burke."

We moved a short distance away from the corral, so we could talk a little better. Since I couldn't very well argue with what he'd said, I just admitted it.

"And furthermore," Major Spingarn said, tapping his cigarito so that the ash fell down the front of his coat, "I think I can guess the reason for your deception."

"Well," I said, "what's your guess?"

"My guess is Dupre. You want him to go on thinking you're still blind so you can trick him the way he so infamously tricked you . . . not just once, but twice. Yes, Professor Burke. I know your story well."

I didn't say anything but just sort of studied Major Spingarn's little pale eyes. "The fact is," he said, "I have thought a great deal about you, Professor Burke."

I nodded and spat. "Yep," I told him, "I'd say from the evidence you have."

"But there's more I have to say. Why don't you come to my office. Sick call is over for today, and the infirmary is virtually empty. The cholera scare turned out to be nothing, thank God. Nothing!"

"I'll have to admit I'm a little surprised at your guess about Dupre," I said.

"Oh, there's more to surprise you," Major Spingarn said, nodding. "Come, come. I want to talk to you. I *must* talk to you. I have a fresh bottle of whiskey in my desk. I also have intelligence that you enjoy a glass of whiskey upon occasion."

He gave a loud short laugh, sort of a bark, and the two of us walked on over to his office in the fort, where we made ourselves at home. The fort hospital had just been built, and still smelled of fresh lumber after the smell of Major Spingarn's cigarito had cleared away.

Major Spingarn took out a bottle of whiskey and filled two little water glasses a third full, then handed me one.

"My comment about your drinking," he said, "was not lightly

made. I've seen you a number of times, wandering drunk and blind about the fort. It's an extraordinary sight, Professor Burke: have you ever seen *a drunk blind man?*"

"Nope, can't say I have," I told him, taking a drink. It was good whiskey. "What's it like?"

Major Spingarn barked his laugh again, but ignored the question. "This stuff," he said, shaking his glass and looking at it, "is an abomination. I've seen more good men wrecked by whiskey than by all the wars and Indians put together." He paused and thought about what he'd said. Then he shook his head sadly and drank from his glass.

"But I haven't gotten you here to deliver a temperance lecture to you. Although that might not be a bad idea. Still, if I were to lecture all those who were in need of it, I would have to call an assembly of most of the men, women, children, and dogs within fifty miles of here. So, what's the use? No, that's not my intent, Professor Burke. Nor is it to play chess."

"Well, then," I said, "just what is it you've got on your mind?"

Major Spingarn pondered a minute and then said, "I have asked you to come share a drink with me so that I might tell you the story of my life. Providing, that is, you will condescend to listen."

"Of course," I told him. "I'm always curious about the lives of others. What man isn't? And I'm even more curious about the life of a man like yourself. Your observations back there at the corral hit the nail on the head."

"Speaking of heads, would you say from a glance at mine that I am perceptive?" he asked. His eyes got sort of narrow when he asked this, like he was suddenly getting sleepy.

"I'd have to take a closer look and palpate your skull before answering that."

"Palpate my skull," Major Spingarn repeated in a low voice. "Yes, why don't you do that for me? As a physician, I'm interested in your methods, Professor Burke. As I have told you in the past."

"Sure, I'll analyze your skull," I said. "But I don't make all the crazy claims some phrenologists make. I figure I know something about the complexity of the brain, so I don't generalize any more than necessary."

"Yes, yes, I am aware of that, Professor Burke. Don't forget our conversations."

"That time is already as murky as a dream to me," I said, standing up and going over to him. I went behind his chair and clasped his head between my two hands, and then began to trace the convolutions in his skull.

"Perhaps your findings will suggest to you whether the account I give you of my life will be an honest one or not."

"I'm ready to believe your word," I said. "The Mound of Conscientiousness is well-developed, for example. But the fact is, I would have known you were conscientious from our acquaintance."

"Please continue," Major Spingarn said. "And comment as you wish. I'll keep still."

And he did keep still, while I traced the topography of his skull and passed along my findings of great analytical power, good memory (as shown by the Mound of Eventuality), strong Conscientiousness and Firmness, and Giftedness in Language, Calculation, and Sense of Order (as manifest in the enlargements outside the eyes, that helped hold up those protruding outer epicanthus folds that I'd already noticed as part of Major Spingarn's physiognomy).

When I finished, I was perspiring. It wasn't just the heat, even though it was warm; and it wasn't just the whiskey, even though we'd both drained our glasses by this time. It was also because I figured Major Spingarn was probably listening to me harder than just about anyone I'd ever analyzed. Also he was *after* something. You could tell.

He stood up and splashed a little more whiskey in our glasses. Then he asked me who had taught me Phrenology.

I told him Dr. Felix Carstairs.

Major Spingarn nodded and said, "Yes, I've heard of him. Briefly, if I'm not mistaken, he was associated with Combe when he was a young man."

"Yes," I said.

"A man of some reputation," Major Spingarn said, holding his glass of whiskey up to the light. "And of course I knew that you would perform competently, Professor Burke. I've learned to respect you during our conversations. I have admiration for your mind, if I may say so. That is why it has distressed me to see you so often drunk and idle, wandering about the fort. You were throwing your brain away, if you don't mind my saying so."

"Well, I'll tell you something," I said. "I was a desperate man. I didn't have any way of knowing my sight would ever come back to me!"

Spingarn nodded and said, "Just so. Just so. But still, it was a terrible waste. And this on top of the other . . ." His voice trailed off, and he sipped at his whiskey.

"What other?" I asked.

Major Spingarn just sat there. It looked like he was turning over the question of whether he ought to speak or not. He frowned and turned his right hand up and studied his own palm like he'd never seen it before. Finally, after considerable deliberation, he decided to tell me. In a voice almost as low as a whisper, he said: "The terrible delusion that has absorbed you for so many years."

"What delusion?" I said. And right then I felt a kind of sickness rise up in my throat.

"Phrenology," Major Spingarn said in a whisper. "The whole mad scheme. It's nothing but a lie and a delusion, Professor Burke! You must know it is! *Surely you know!*"

I sat there considerable stunned for a minute, while Major Spingarn sadly shook his head back and forth, not even looking at me.

"A terrible, terrible lie," he said. "For it confuses the brain with the skull, and their testimonies do not necessarily coincide!"

"I've answered that argument many a time," I said. "What you say is true, but the skull and brain do grow together in their development. Doesn't the glove take the shape of the hand?"

"Does the shoe take the shape of the foot?" Spingarn asked.

"After you wear it long enough it begins to," I muttered. But I'm damned if my heart was in it, and I sort of lapsed into a morose silence. Both of us had gotten a good start on our second glass of whiskey by now, and we were beginning to show the effects of it.

Spingarn pointed this out. "You drink fast, my friend. And I've picked up your tempo from you. The beat. If we associate very much together, I'm afraid you'll be a bad influence. Fact is, you *are* a dangerous man, you know."

"What do you mean by that?"

"Your gift for believing is infectious," he said, pouring some more whiskey into our glasses. "Your gusto for life. Your gift for hoping. Even your irreverence! We're all helpless before a truly sanguine man. He shows us what we all might be. And we instinctively yearn to emulate him!"

He offered me a cigarito, then, which I took, and for a minute the two of us sat there smoking, thinking our private thoughts, which were considerable.

"But I didn't bring you here for the purpose of attacking your profession," Major Spingarn said, tapping his cigarito ash on his pants and the floor. "No, you are still a young man, and I think the time would have come, independent of any opinion from me, when you would have given up following the phrenological path. Because, you see, it isn't simply that phrenological theories are based upon what are clearly false premises . . . no, it's not this alone, but the fact that the *Zeitgeist* will not allow you to believe it for long. The winds of custom have changed course, and you must eventually be blown in another direction.

"No, Professor Burke, we are not free. Twenty years ago, even ten — as your history shows — it was possible to pursue phrenology, but now the tide of opinion has changed, except in a few backwaters. A man can never believe something that runs against the current of his time, no matter how hard he tries!"

"Damned if I like that!" I said. "We aren't *that* hemmed-in!"

He looked directly at me and smiled sadly. "It is even part of our time that we must believe we are not compelled to be part of our time!"

"That's damned foolish double-talk!" I said. "You can't believe that!"

"Oh, but I can and do," he answered slowly. "Rather, I should say, I *must*. Q.E.D., Professor Burke."

"You don't have any idea," I said, "how long I've had to stand up for my principles in the face of cynicism! You don't know how many insults and snickers I've heard from the audiences I've faced through the years!"

"Oh, but I can guess. And that's why I say that you yourself, deep inside your mind, have already secretly decided to abandon the commitment you made as a youth to a theory that has neither scientific nor philosophical validity. All that I've been saying to you is simply what you've been waiting to tell yourself. Isn't it thus with all our deepest recognitions?"

I didn't say anything to this. I refused to recognize it. The two of us just sat there smoking our cigaritos. And then Major Spingarn once more poured whiskey into our glasses, repeating what he'd said about liquor being such a vile thing.

And then, as he'd promised, he started in to tell me his life story.

38

Men with small ears have
the disposition of monkeys.
— Aristotle's *Physiognomica*

"When I first heard your name," the Major said, "I was interested, because I was born and reared a Quaker, in Indiana, and there was a Quaker family named Burke that used to attend the Annual Conferences when I was a young man. Henry, I think his name was."

Right away I interrupted him, saying that must have been my uncle, Henry Burke.

"Just so," Major Spingarn said, nodding. "I was sure there must be a family connection."

"Yep, it's an old English name," I said. "Although sometimes it's Irish. Sometimes Irish, sometimes English."

"Yes, yes," Major Spingarn said, nodding again and then pausing to sip from his whiskey. "I had expected as much. Although, I didn't really *know* your uncle. I simply remember his name. I possess, if I may say so without boasting, a very tenacious memory. And this you will see demonstrated in a moment, and you'll further understand my particular interest in your sudden appearance at Fort Riley.

"You see, Professor Burke, I have long been interested in our sect of Quakers. I am still a Quaker in spirit, even though I wear the uniform of a United States officer."

"But you're a medical doctor," I pointed out, "and that makes a difference."

"Just so. This is my argument, at least. But before enlisting, I was connected for a number of years with a Quaker Mission for the Osage Indians in eastern Kansas — a very small Mission at a place called Blooming Grove. I had just graduated from medical college, where I had had the opportunity to study under several distinguished men. I was recently married before taking the post at Blooming Grove, and during our years there, three things of great personal significance happened: two children were born to my wife and me, and then I lost my wife to cholera the last year I was there. My sister and her husband in St. Louis are now raising my children. After my wife's death, I enlisted in the Army. A career as Missionary was no longer possible to me in my restless and agitated mood; nor was the idea of settling down to a private medical practice tolerable. So I enlisted, and thus you see me here."

Major Spingarn paused and with a faraway look in his eye, sipped from his glass.

However, he soon got back to his story. "But what will prove of particular interest to you, Professor Burke, is an episode that occurred at the Mission shortly after our arrival there. It was sufficiently extraordinary for anyone to remember, but as I've mentioned I seemed to be blessed or cursed (sometimes I scarcely know which) with a particularly retentive memory.

"There was a young Osage there who seemed to have a remarkable calling for grace and piety. He was an exceedingly quiet and contemplative man of about twenty-five, and he had remarkable dreams. One such dream inspired him to go forth and dwell for a time with another branch of the tribe who were living at that time on the Neosho River. These Neosho Indians had not been civilized to any great degree; certainly, they were not Christian. As you undoubtedly know, the Roman Catholics maintained a great number of Missions in eastern Kansas at that time — their priests were called "the Black Robes" by the Indians — and still do. The Quakers were not nearly so active, being a far smaller sect. But we tried to do what we could.

"Anyway, this young man — whose Indian name was Two Fires — went forth as his dreams inspired him to do, and lived with the Neosho group for a while, and apparently was somewhat successful in Christianizing a few of them . . . although, the fact was, he was by nature so taciturn and so reticent that it appeared to be very discomforting, even painful, for him to impose his conversation on others.

"Therefore it was perhaps not surprising that we soon began to get reports that Two Fires was becoming somewhat tribalized after a few months. Living day and night among people who are mad and persist in their madness will eventually contaminate the thoughts of even the healthiest man, Professor Burke — which is what I was essentially, allowing for inversion, arguing only a short while ago, with regard to your not being able to maintain a vital belief in phrenology against the sweep of public opinion.

"Still, Two Fires did not completely give in to their ways, as the following tragic occurrence will make clear. There was a young warrior in the Neosho group named Crippled Hawk. One night while he was drunk, his horse was stolen. It so happened that Two Fires had been seen by Crippled Hawk (or so he claimed) admiring the horse earlier that evening, even feeding it some sweet grass from his hand.

"Therefore, while he was still badly hungover, Crippled Hawk stood up in front of other warriors and accused Two Fires of stealing the horse. When Two Fires did not respond, Crippled Hawk challenged him to the Indian version of a duel of honor. Still not responding, because of his Quaker renunciation of violence, Two Fires was soon laughed at and taunted by all the other warriors present. Crippled Hawk laughed loudest of all, and began to walk in a mincing manner, calling the accused 'Squaw Pants,' and other insulting names.

"No longer able to bear up under such a burden of insult and humiliation, Two Fires jumped to his feet and left camp. He did not return all that day. The next morning, however, Crippled Hawk's body was found lying face up outside his lodge, with his throat cut. Two Fires was never seen again, but one of the old women of the tribe claimed to have dreamed hearing him sing his Death Song that very night."

Here Major Spingarn stopped speaking and let his words sink in. After several puffs on his cigarito, he said, "There is one correction I have to make."

"Yep," I said.

"You *do* know, don't you?" Major Spingarn said gently.

"Yep," I said. I closed my eyes and took a long, deep breath.

"Just so," Major Spingarn said. "*Now* I know that Two Fires *was* seen again. When Major Dupre invited us all to his banquet, giving us a promise that we would be mightily surprised and entertained (the first, at least, proved true), most of us went, having no idea of what Dupre had in mind. But when they took your Indian companion's severed head out of the bucket of alcohol they had preserved it in, I knew immediately, in spite of my revulsion at the sight, that this was the head of that young man I had known so many years before as Two Fires."

"Henry Buck!" I whispered.

"Yes. I referred to him as Two Fires because I tended always to forget his Christian name. I always *thought* of him as Two Fires. The reason for this is perhaps interesting. While I was at the Mission, I got curious about the names of the Indians — partly because of the symbolic nature of naming, generally, but also because of the additional significance of a people who attach great importance to names being challenged to choose new ones with the advent of their new faith.

"Two Fires had gotten his Indian name because of something that happened during his initiation as a warrior. There was a great prairie fire at this time, and one night the people of the village were awakened by the barking of their dogs and the whinnying of their horses. When they came out of their lodges, they saw nothing in the way of danger from an enemy, but they did notice in the far distance the faint glow of the smoldering fires, which had been burning slowly away from them all day, so that they could go to sleep in safety. But in the sky above this glow, there was another repeated as if reflected by celestial mirrors, so that the whole western expanse seemed to be a dense blackness crossed horizontally by two glowing bands of fire.

"This signified great power, or medicine, to the people, and Henry Buck, or Two Fires, was thought to have a great and unnatural destiny."

"It sure is hard to figure how he could have kept all that hidden inside his breast!" I said. "He never once gave me a sign that he had all that hidden inside!"

"Folks do have their mysteries," Major Spingarn said, nodding.

"That expression hardly does the trick," I said.

But Major Spingarn didn't hear me. He had more to say and was intent on saying it. "As for his Christian name, it is no wonder I should have let that pass, because there is a story in that, too, which you'll find particularly interesting. At one time there was a saintly old man at Blooming Grove, who was majestic not only in his piety and humility, but in his high spirits. He was so jovial and carefree, his more sober brethren tended to think him a trifle deranged. He seemed to lack the gravity that we equate with wisdom and worldly importance.

"This good man died before I came, but there was no doubt that he'd been a man of great influence, because Indian children everywhere had been given his name; and even some of the older people, too. There was a Jacob Buck, a Thomas Buck, and an Isaac Buck. Yes, to be named Buck at Blooming Grove was almost to be anonymous. But a name like Two Fires . . . ah, that was something, was it not?"

"Yep," I said. "That's quite a name."

Major Spingarn drank meditatively and shook his head. There was something else eating at him, you could tell. "Only thing is," he went on after a minute's reflection, "that wasn't the real name of that old Quaker saint. His real name was not Buck at all. Do you know what it was, Professor Burke?"

I nodded.

"Just so. It was Burke. Thaddeus Burke, the same as yours. Only the Indians didn't figure that could be quite right, so they changed his last name to 'Buck,' which the old man accepted cheerfully as he did all things, and kept until the day he died."

For a long time I just sat there and thought about Major Spingarn's story. Then I finally nodded and said, "That was my great-uncle, sure as shoe polish."

"I figured he must have been a relative," Major Spingarn said.

"Yep, I was named for him."

We got quiet, then, the two of us, and just sat there wrapped up in our own individual speculations. I don't know what Major Spingarn's were, but as for me, I kept thinking of how little you can ever get to know another human being. Even if you spent most of your waking hours studying somebody, and talking with him or her, think of how little you'd ever get to see.

Then I got to wondering if I'd ever told Henry about my own Quaker background, and for the life of me, I couldn't remember ever doing so, even though nothing would have been more likely at some time or other while we were spending a long evening by the campfire.

But in all that time, think of all that silence existing inside Henry Buck's head! How could he have kept his story a secret through all those hardships and throughout our long acquaintance?

After a while I told Major Spingarn the story about how I'd first run into Henry Buck. I told him that when I came across him it must have been the morning after he'd killed Crippled Hawk. Because he was sure as hell bent on self-destruction when I got to him, even though he didn't ever get around to telling me the reason. But after hearing it now, I figured he'd decided to kill himself because of his Quaker upbringing, which also encouraged him to keep his mouth shut! And this upbringing had also taught him to hate violence, so that he couldn't go on living with the knowledge he'd done in a fellow human being, even if he was only a drunk Indian who was just asking for it and didn't have any more sense than a pit terrier with a sore tail.

"Just so," Major Spingarn said, nodding.

"Not only that," I went on, "the part of him that was still Indian had been shamed by not accepting Crippled Hawk's challenge to a duel. So *both* of the truths he'd lived by convicted him. I wonder why he didn't ever tell me and ease his burden a little!"

"His name of Two Fires seems appropriate," Major Spingarn said in a low voice.

"But do you know something?" I said. "Henry Buck also killed a man for my sake. This son of a bitch was the brother of a man I'd bested in a phrenological argument some time back, and he was sure as hell about to shoot me, when old Henry came up behind him and sank his knife up to the hilt in his right kidney. I wonder how bad his conscience got to him over that."

"Just so," Major Spingarn said, taking another sip from his glass. Then he said, "Just so, just so, just so . . ." on and on, about twenty times, until I realized that he'd gotten pretty badly fuddled, which is no wonder, considering the whiskey he'd put away.

But the inference was sort of mute. In fact, the idea came to me like I was clear down at the bottom of a deep well.

I finished my glass in a gulp, and don't remember a whole lot that happened the rest of that evening. But I doubt that much took place, because I have the impression that I couldn't hardly talk, but was moved by sadness. And Major Spingarn was hardly in any better shape, because I seem to remember he was asleep in his chair when I left.

I do halfway remember going on for a considerable time about the role of coincidence in my life. This business about Henry Buck having been named after my great uncle was part of it; but there was also a lot about all those other coincidences in my life, which this account has featured.

It's a shame I can't be more lucid about how it went. Or that Major Spingarn wasn't more lucid when I told him about my theory that there are some people who draw coincidence to themselves the way a magnet attracts iron filings. It's an empirical axiom, is the way I figure it.

I'm sure I covered the territory with considerable thoroughness, but then I probably didn't make a whole lot of sense out of the matter, which is pretty hard to do even at the best of times. It's a shame I wasn't more lucid then, too, even though my audience was busy snoring.

39

And yet doth nature loudly laugh them to scorn, with all their conjectures . . .

— Erasmus

Now, it's late autumn, and everybody is getting ready for what looks like a hard winter.

Lionel Littlejohn has disappeared. Nobody knows where he went, but I figure he took up with one of the recent wagon trains to Santa Fe. This might have been the same one that Major Dupre and a small contingent of his men escorted. There have been rumors of Indian trouble out on the Staked Plains, but the winter weather will calm them down. Not to mention the dead grass.

I didn't see Major Spingarn for several days after our conversation together that night. I've stayed on at the Lost Child Tavern, in spite of the grumbling of Cyrus Morehouse. The problem isn't that I haven't paid my way, because I have. But Cyrus Morehouse is convinced I'm not a sound bet. He makes his living off drink and gambling and renting a place to sleep under a roof, but he doesn't like to get too close to the first two, and the truth is, I have done my share of both. I've made a little money from reading the heads of itinerants. And as for gambling, I haven't won more than enough to pay for the liquor I've drunk.

Last Saturday it snowed, and I sat in my room and laid my money out on the little table in neat rows. This didn't take long. I had $38.22.

I need a new coat, because when I stepped outside this morning, the wind just about cut me in half. But after nosing about in various places, I found out that the prices are considerable steep so I've decided to wait. I don't have to buy one just yet. Maybe I can get a squaw to make me one out of buffalo hide.

Let me back up a little bit. Fifteen days ago I bought three thick packages of paper, three sturdy quill pens, and a bottle of India ink. Since then, we've had that snow I mentioned, and after that, we had what you'd practically call a blizzard. The military and civilian population, not to mention the Indians, have just about hibernated.

But not Major Spingarn. Two days ago, he set out all the way for Council Grove, where there's supposed to be a cholera outbreak. Here at Fort Riley, there's only the customary fevernager that comes to people just about any time it feels like it, regardless of the weather. I heard that Major Spingarn was real drunk the night before he had to go, and I wished I'd had a chance to talk with him, because I figure there are a few things between us that are still unsettled.

I've pretty much escaped the fevernager. What I mean to say is, I haven't been bedridden, even though I've had my share of aches and pains, including some headaches that come considerable often, which I figure are echoes of all those beatings my head has taken over the past year or two.

Poor health doesn't bother me much, because I have been working hard on getting all this down about my life. It's a lot of work, but you'd be surprised at how many things you can remember that you figure you'd forgotten forever. Little things that probably don't mean much, and yet there they are, part of your time on earth, and just asking to be put down on paper, the place they've been headed for all the time.

Don't think I haven't been thinking about Major Spingarn's talk that evening. Even though he was drunk, there was a lot of wisdom and scientific learning in what he said. Even if a wise man is drunk, he's still a drunk wise man and not a fool, although I'm willing to admit that sometimes it's hard to tell the difference.

But what about the things he said? What about phrenology, which I have dedicated my life and talents to (supposing I have any talent, which a man can never know for sure, if he's got any sense)? I don't know. One thing I'm sure of, it isn't as simple as Major Spingarn says it is. What I mean is, maybe he's partly right, but I figure this isn't in the way he thinks, exactly. Most of what he believes as scientific gospel might come apart some day when people know considerable more about the human head. In fact, this is pretty much what his argument adds up to, even though he didn't add it up that way when we were talking.

So I won't just drop what I've been doing. What I figure you have to do is adapt. There's enough truth in phrenology for any man, if he can just keep his eyes open and not stop thinking about what he's doing. And the fact is, there was something I learned back when I was blind that is pretty hard for me to ignore. I mean, there were times when I would hold somebody's head in my two hands and what I'd suddenly *understand* about that person would stagger your ability to speak. There's a lot we know — and some of this is the deepest there is — that can't be translated into anything else, even though we've got to give it a try. How can an Indian tell you that he figures there's somebody coming, even though they're out of sight and out of hearing? Or how can a shrewd old woman tell you how she picks up on things about people at a tea party, when everybody's talking about everything *but* what she's found out?

Nobody understands how these things work, and that is what I learned back in those days when I was as blind as a bat in a cave and laughed at by just about everybody except maybe Cyrus Morehouse, Lionel Littlejohn, and Lily de Wilde.

One other thing I haven't mentioned is that I had my twenty-eighth birthday several months ago. Now I am the age William Bone had attained right before he departed his miserable and mis-spent life. As for me, I figure it is a good time to take on a journey, and maybe even new ways of thinking.

You've got to watch out for your opportunities, and there's a good one waiting for me right now. This morning we were sur-prised to get a report of an outfit that arrived last night. The wagon master is said to be kind of a mad man, named Benjamin Creeley. They say he has only three fingers on his right hand, and claims that he talks with God every night. They say his crew must be just about as mad as he is, because they've all agreed to strike out for the Chisholm Trail tomorrow morning, even though there are reports of eight-foot drifts of snow in the gulleys along the trail, and there's a prediction of heavy snow within the next day or two.

There's nothing but talk of Benjamin Creeley's madness, but the talk itself shows a kind of secret admiration. *Here is a man who has someplace to go!* Never mind his reason for going there. It could be to feed peanuts to a Mexican whore or play the banjo before buz-zards. But this man by God has an eye on the horizon. Lionel Littlejohn would understand.

I figure I'll go join him today, right after I finish writing this entry down. I feel the start of an ache creaking in my bones, like they're part of a ship that wants to set out from port. Tonight, I'll join their party. In a few weeks, if we get there, I might see Stillingfleet in Santa Fe, and maybe have a reunion with Lily de Wilde.

I'll leave this account with Cyrus Morehouse, in case we don't make it across the rest of Kansas and the Staked Plains.

I haven't lost any confidence in myself, which I developed so early in life. My Mound of Hope is well-developed, as Major Spingarn noticed in his way. Also, my Mound of Vitativeness, seated at the base of the skull, is about as big as it can get on the human skull. It's been part of my problem. Herophilus figured this had to do with the intellectual powers, and not just what they usually think of as enthusiasm and love of life, or what some call sassafras.

I figure these traits are all connected in some way. Not to mention other features hard to detect.

For a while I'll read heads after I get there, and I'll do my best at it. I haven't given up on this business, as I just now said. I figure there are many different ways to approach truth, not to mention Santa Fe, with many side-tracks and detours and false moves and delays.

But all of it, every step forward, has what I figure is a certain justification and what you might even call a certain claim to glory.